Praise for

An Enchanting Case of Spirits

"Part rom-com, part ghost story, part love story, and all heart. This is a fun novel with a little bit of everything for everyone."

—Red Carpet Crash

"A perfect weekend read for fans of Emily Henry and Sarah Adler."

—San Francisco Book Review

"*An Enchanting Case of Spirits* is a book I would typically classify as a cozy mystery, but this book definitely has more teeth than your average book in that genre. Still, it has all the right ingredients including romance, mystery, murder, and even a collection of opinionated ghosts."

—Game Vortex

"*An Enchanting Case of Spirits* by Melissa Holtz is a must-read. Its blend of cozy mystery and paranormal abilities is a recipe for a captivating read that will keep you turning the pages long into the night."

—Tessa Talks Books

"A laugh-out-loud mystery that blends the supernatural with the murder mystery in a way that's irresistibly charming."

—Words & Books & Things

"I adored this cleverly penned tale of realistic woo-woo."

—Books and Bindings

Also by Melissa Holtz

An Enchanting Case of Spirits

A Charming Touch *of* Tarot

Melissa Holtz

Berkley
New York

BERKLEY
An imprint of Penguin Random House LLC
1745 Broadway, New York, NY 10019
penguinrandomhouse.com

Book design by Alison Cnockaert
Interior art: Tarot cards © Bigmouse 108 / Shutterstock

Library of Congress Cataloging-in-Publication Data

Names: Holtz, Melissa, author.
Title: A charming touch of tarot / Melissa Holtz.
Description: First edition. | New York : Berkley, 2025.
Identifiers: LCCN 2024037566 (print) | LCCN 2024037567 (ebook) |
ISBN 9780593640067 (trade paperback) | ISBN 9780593640074 (ebook)
Subjects: LCGFT: Magic realist fiction. | Novels.
Classification: LCC PS3608.O49443447 C47 2025 (print) |
LCC PS3608.O49443447 (ebook) | DDC 813/.6—dc23/eng/20240816
LC record available at https://lccn.loc.gov/2024037566
LC ebook record available at https://lccn.loc.gov/2024037567

First Edition: May 2025

Printed in the United States of America
1st Printing

The authorized representative in the EU for product safety and compliance is Penguin Random House Ireland, Morrison Chambers, 32 Nassau Street, Dublin D02 YH68, Ireland, https://eu-contact.penguin.ie.

For my mother,
who taught me that kindness is the foundation of a meaningful life and that stepping on others will never lead to true fulfillment. You ignited my love for all things spooky and inspired a deep appreciation for the traditions that add a touch of magic to the everyday. Your unwavering love and support have shaped me into the person I am today.
This is for you, with all my love.

A Charming Touch *of* Tarot

The Moon

I WATCH FROM the doorframe of my great room, savoring the moment. My favorite people are all here, under one roof, celebrating Christmas Eve together, and it's a sight that warms my heart.

Lanie, Nina, and Ava are huddled together in their matching red-and-white plaid reindeer jammies, alternating between shoving holiday goodies into their mouths and sipping from piping-hot mugs of Baileys hot chocolate, minus the Baileys for Ava.

The largest charcuterie board I've ever made sits on the coffee table, overflowing with an assortment of cheeses, crackers, popcorn, and various cookies and candies I purchased from a bakery in downtown Knox Harbor.

I've been running back and forth from the kitchen playing the part of hostess, a role I've always enjoyed but haven't been up to for some time.

In the past few years, the merriness of the season was tempered by sorrow and self-pity. Tonight, it's been all laughter and no tears.

The way Christmas Eve should be.

Those who matter most are in this room, singing along to the song playing on the television. Lanie belts out "Deck the Halls," punching at the air; Nina pulls in her upper lip, grimacing into the side of Lanie's head; and Ava sings the song without a care in the world, just happy to have her two aunts here with us.

We're bonded by more than blood and DNA. These are sacred friendships that we've chosen. They weren't thrust upon us out of duty and an age-old tale that blood somehow trumps all. While my parents are hundreds of miles away, likely playing cards with friends, my made family is here, choosing me, and that's not something I take lightly.

Since the accident that took Garrett from me, Lanie has made Christmas Eve our thing. It was her attempt to pull me out of my despair long enough to ensure that Ava had the Christmas she deserved. This time, we have the bonus of Nina being here.

Before this year, she has always been required to attend Knox Harbor's Christmas Eve ball, a charity event that her slimy ex had nothing to do with organizing but took all the credit for. Due to the shocking events that unfolded earlier this year, the event was cancelled.

I take a second to relish how this year, Richard Dunbar is celebrating Christmas in prison, while Nina gets to curl up on my oversize couch, comfortable and cozy. Not only did Richard cover up his son's drunk driving homicide, but he was also behind two murders and the car accident that took Garrett from me and Ava.

Pure evil.

He's eating crappy food while Nina gorges on treats that she typically didn't allow herself, because he would throw a fit over any weight gain. He's sitting in a cell, staring at concrete walls, and she gets to binge-watch every sappy Hallmark movie she can fit into one night. Movies he never allowed her to watch in her own home.

Oh, how sweet karma can be.

"Are you done stalking?" Lanie calls over her shoulder, not bothering to take her eyes off the television.

"I wasn't stalking anything. If you haven't noticed, the platters of food don't magically fill themselves."

Ava turns toward me, smiling like a loon. "You should really get on that. A magic house that cooks and cleans sounds like a game changer."

I smirk. "I'll make sure to add that to my Santa list next year."

Ava half rolls her eyes, grinning wide and twisting back toward the television.

"I just figured you were keeping an eye on the house next door for any signs of movement," Lanie says, shoving popcorn into her mouth.

"We just started dating. I'm hardly inspecting his house for proof of life. It's not like I haven't talked to him."

Lanie peaks one perfectly microbladed eyebrow. "Have you? Talked to him? Because I've seen you check your phone no less than ten times in the last hour . . ."

"Why do you always make me sound so pathetic? I've been having too much fun with all of you. I haven't thought about him once."

A slight lie, but Lanie Anderson doesn't need to be proven right.

"How about you come sit and finish the movie with us," Ava suggests, patting the couch cushion. "Ignore Aunt Lanie. If you were thinking about Mr. West, that's perfectly normal."

"I agree with Ava. Ignore Aunt Lanie." Nina purses her lips when she turns toward Lanie, who isn't at all bothered. "Come join us. We have plenty of food. Enjoy your time with Aves."

I should absolutely be soaking in every moment I have with her. The two-week break she gets is never long enough. Soon she'll be returning to school, and I'll be in this empty house all alone.

I make my way to the couch, taking the seat next to Ava. She smiles at me, squeezing my hand as she scooches in closer, offering to share her blanket.

"What have I missed?" I ask, eyes trained on the big screen.

"She just got whisked back in time by that sand thingy."

I lift an eyebrow at Ava's explanation.

"I think you mean *hourglass,*" Nina says.

"Whatever it is. She's about to see the hot actor," Lanie says, grabbing a handful of Cheez-It crackers. "It's about to get swoony."

"Are you hungry, Lanie?" I ask, completely mystified by the sheer amount of junk she's consumed in the past ten minutes. While she has never shied away from food, she typically grabs healthier options. I feel bad that I didn't opt to serve a meal.

She purses her lips. "Is that a fat quip?"

"I'm offering to make you actual food if you're hungry." I motion to the large platter. "I really didn't think this through."

She wipes her hand on her pajamas. "I'm simply using the holiday as an excuse to indulge. Nothing wrong with that."

"I didn't say there was. I was only attempting to be a proper host."

"You failed," she singsongs.

"Can you two just get along so we can watch the meet-cute?" Nina reprimands, a hint of humor in her tone.

Ava squeals, clapping her hands and shimmying in her seat, clearly ready for what's to come. "Meet-cutes are the best part."

My head shakes and my chest bounces, barely containing the laughter that bubbles within at Ava's reaction. My little girl is sixteen. She's a young adult, interested in love and romance, something that wasn't the case a year ago.

"Here, this is yours," Nina says, passing over a mug. "It might be a tad cold by now, but it's good."

"Thank you." I take a sip and sigh.

The temperature is perfect. Not too hot and not too cold. The hint of Baileys just enough to make the cocoa even better.

We all settle in to watch the movie, oohing and ahhing at every twist that arises. It's cute. Your typical Christmas love story, complete with magic and humor. The type of movies we all enjoy this time of year.

Over an hour goes by, and we're moments from the movie's conclusion when the doorbell rings.

Ava looks over her shoulder, grinning from ear to ear. When she turns toward me, she lifts one brow. "Who could that be?"

My eyes are narrowed as I run through the short list of possibilities.

I quickly eliminate Nick West. I've peeked at the house next door for any signs of him a few times tonight, only to find it dark. He's likely working late at the station.

That's been his excuse for the three dates he's cancelled in the past two weeks. Ever since the night Nina showed up on my doorstep, looking as though she'd been run through the mud, he's been distant.

I did send him away without an explanation, but he can't be angry with me about that. Nina's practically family, and she was distraught. I needed to be there for her and didn't think she'd be open to spilling her guts with Nick hanging around.

"Well . . . are you going to answer it or let them freeze out there?" Ava asks, cutting off all thoughts of Nick.

I jump up from the couch and rush toward the door because she's right—it's a chilly night, and nobody should be left to freeze on Christmas Eve.

Pressing my eye to the little round hole, I check to see who it is, but there's nobody out there. At least, not that I can see. A strange feeling washes over me, and I decide not to open the door. Instead,

I make my way to the white-trimmed picture window, staring down the road both ways.

The soft glow of twinkling lights glistens off the freshly fallen snow all the way down my street. It's a stunning sight that distracts me from my initial reason for peering out my window into the dark night.

There's nothing and no one to be seen. Not even taillights in the distance proving that someone had been on my doorstep.

Bizarre.

I'm about to turn around when a figure pops up from the bushes, two horns protruding from a demonic face. Its hands reach out to tap an eerie cadence against the window. I screech, stumbling backward, grabbing at air. With a quick twist, I crouch low, instinctively assuming a defensive stance. Thankfully, I manage to avoid the embarrassment of falling on my ass. I swiftly right myself in time to see the creature remove its head to unmask Corinne, bent over, laughing hysterically.

"What the hell's going on?" Lanie says, rushing into the room with Nina and Ava right on her heels.

I motion toward the window, working to calm my racing heart.

"That asshole," Lanie says, throwing her head back and laughing. "I love her."

Leave it to Lanie to find this funny. I about had a coronary, but who cares about that minor detail?

Nina throws open the front door, standing to the side, giving Corinne enough room to enter. "Get in here, you menace."

I take a step forward, hands planted on my hips. "What were you trying to do? Give me a heart attack?"

She shrugs out of her coat, throwing it over the chair. "Playing Krampus. Have you been naughty?"

"It's not Krampusnacht, idiot. You're a few weeks off," Lanie says, half rolling her eyes.

"*Idiot* is too kind a term." I grab her coat and head toward the office, where the others have been stashed.

"What are you doing here? I thought you were tied up with Moradi Madness," Lanie says, but I miss Corinne's reply as I step away from the group.

I deposit the black bomber jacket into the pitch-black room and give myself a moment to laugh at the absurdity that just occurred. I almost went down, and if it had been Lanie, I would be rolling on the ground laughing.

That's the thing about the friendships I have with these girls. They all bring something unique to the group. Corinne's happens to be youth and the reminder that no matter our age, laughter and silliness is the best medicine.

I chuckle to myself before rejoining my friends who are all gathered in the front room, chatting away about Corinne's brother, Darian. From what I've pieced together, he was ordered to bring her here to ensure something goes down.

"What exactly is going down?" I ask, glancing around the room for someone to explain.

"Not you," Lanie says, chuckling at herself.

My nose scrunches, and I glare daggers at Lanie, looking out of the corner of my eye at Ava, who clearly got the joke, if her giggling is any indicator.

Nina sighs heavily. "Do you always have to be so crass, Lane?"

Lanie doesn't answer, and Ava has inquired about the lore surrounding Krampus. Corinne is far too eager to give all the horrific details. I zone out, knowing the story behind the Christmas devil.

My head turns toward the window, and I watch as large flakes continue to fall from the sky, blanketing the ground. It's a winter wonderland out there, the perfect scenery for the holiday.

Movement to the left has my eyes narrowing as I lean forward.

"What the . . ." My words trail off as I stand to get closer to the glass. "Is that Mrs. Fields?"

Standing on the sidewalk, out in the dark, cold, winter night, a barely dressed Mrs. Fields appears to be talking to thin air. She's in her pale pink nightgown, hair secured under a white shower cap, finger lifted as if she's in the middle of a lecture.

The others get to their feet, joining me at the window.

"Is that a nightgown?" Nina asks, and I nod.

"She's not wearing shoes?" Ava says, nose practically pressed against the window.

"Looks like she's wearing slippers," Nina replies to Ava.

The frail woman has her fist raised into the air, moving it around like she's moments away from crashing it against someone's head. Something isn't right with her.

"She's going to freeze out there," I say, heading toward the door.

With my hand on the knob, I look down, recognizing that I'm not exactly dressed appropriately either.

"Let me grab our coats," Lanie says, rushing off before I can agree or protest.

"Nina, throw me that blanket." I motion to the unused fleece throw hanging off the back of the couch.

Within a minute, Lanie is back and practically hurling my coat at me as she slings hers on. She makes her way out into the freezing night with me close behind.

"Mrs. Fields, what on earth are you doing out here? You're gonna freeze," I say, jogging across the street, hitting a piece of ice that nearly takes me out. A patch of snow saves me from my second almost-fall of the night. I'm holding the blanket up to put it around her shoulders, but she stares right through me. It's like this for several moments until her eyelashes flutter and her mouth drops open. She pops a closed fist on her hip and begins a tirade.

"Well, I came out here to see what she was doing out in the

cold." She shakes her head, tsking. "Dressed like that. I've never," she grumbles. "Last time I saw a woman dressed that scandalously . . . well . . . it was you," she says, pursing her lips and looking up at Lanie. "Ladies don't dress like that."

"It was Halloween, Mrs. Fields. I was a nurse."

Mrs. Fields makes a noise that sounds an awful lot like clearing phlegm from her throat.

"What woman?" I ask, looking around the area only to find it absent of anyone aside from Mrs. Fields and us.

"That one," she says, gesturing behind me.

We all turn to find nothing but cold air and darkness.

"That's odd." Mrs. Fields rubs at her forehead.

Lanie and I share a glance, both of us knowing there isn't a woman aside from us out here.

"Where did she run off to? She was just here."

It's clear that Mrs. Fields is confused.

I admittedly know very little about Charmaine Fields, aside from the fact that she's lived in this neighborhood since well before we bought our home. The only other information I have about her is that she's widowed and lives alone. Her daughter and son both reside in other states and come to visit on alternating months, except for holidays when they're all here.

"Mrs. Fields, are your children in town?"

"I'm telling you she was out here," Mrs. Fields says, completely ignoring my question. "I saw her through my window. She was wearing a skimpy dress. No coat."

"Much like you," I say, trying to contain the scolding tone. "We really must get you back inside."

She stands up tall, pursing her lips at me.

"I didn't have much time now, did I?" She levels me with a scowl before continuing in a clipped tone. "Far too cold for anyone to survive long out here. She would've gotten hypothermia." She turns to Nina. "The girl was clearly drunk, dear. Her appearance gave it away. She was disheveled and just stood there, staring at the Manns' house." She looks over at me again. "I think she took a swim tonight. What kind of person swims in this cold?"

Chills rush over my body, and it isn't due to the cold. The fact that she's described someone in detail and says they were staring at my house has me a bit on edge.

"Let's get you back home," I say, placing my hands on her shoulders and steering her toward her house.

"I don't need an escort, Alyssa. I am perfectly capable of walking home."

I sigh. "Humor me. There's black ice, and I would feel awful if you slipped."

She sucks her teeth, glancing at the ground skeptically. "Never a good idea to break a hip at my age." She taps her chin. "I have been fortunate enough to live by myself all these years. Wouldn't want to put myself in danger of being shipped off to some moldy old center for the elderly." She huffs. "You shall escort me."

I vaguely hear Corinne whisper under her breath, "It's happening."

I'm about to question her, but a car pulls down the street, headlights beaming over us. I squint, raising my hand to shield my eyes as it passes, pulling into Nick's driveway.

It's him.

He makes quick work of parking, jumping from his cruiser, and heading toward us.

Lanie grins at me, but I ignore her.

"Hi, ladies. Can I help you with anything?" He addresses the group, but his eyes are locked on Mrs. Fields, a look of concern etched into his stare.

My teeth are chattering, and my entire body is shaking. I hesitate too long, so Nina jumps in and explains what's occurred. He says something to Lanie and then turns his attention back to Mrs. Fields.

"Char, where's Tom and Sandy? Why are you out here all alone?"

The way he talks to her gives the impression that they're well acquainted. They do live next door, but this seems more familiar than that.

"They're . . ." Her words trail off, and her hand comes up to her head. "Well, I don't know."

Nick bends down so we're eye to eye. "Alyssa, why don't you allow me to help get her back inside. I'll stop by after she's home safe. It's awfully cold out here, and you have guests."

I want to wave off his concern, but I know he's only being chivalrous. Old habits die hard, and Nick West doesn't know anything other than helping people.

"All right," I acquiesce, more than happy to get out of the cold.

He nods, taking over and steering Mrs. Fields toward her house, which is situated right next to his.

"You heard the man. Let's go," Lanie barks, and we all rush back across the street into the warmth.

Nina takes the coats this time, while Ava and Lanie join Corinne in the great room, huddling under the warm blankets they'd left to venture outside.

I start to make a fresh batch of hot cocoa, knowing we could all use it. I take a moment to run down what just occurred.

Mrs. Fields was adamant that a woman, dressed inappropriately for the weather, was staring at my house.

What are the odds that she actually saw someone?

There are too many places that someone could've run off to hide, the protection of the dark keeping them out of sight. Then there's the obvious question . . . *why* would anyone be looking at my house? Let alone a girl not dressed for the weather.

I shake off the chilling thought. Mrs. Fields is in her eighties, and it's very likely she imagined the whole thing. Right?

High Priestess

THE COCOA IS done and distributed, and I'm about to take a seat when there's a knock on my door.

My heart beats erratically, and my fingers tap the side of my leg. I know without a doubt that it's Nick, but I'm unsettled. Between Corinne and her Krampus stunt, and then the talk of a woman being outside in the dark, it feels more like Halloween than Christmas.

I take one quick second to compose myself before swinging the door open to a scene that instantly relaxes me while simultaneously stealing my breath.

Nick West stands under the dim front porch light, hands in his pockets, as the snow falls around him. One side of his mouth lifts when he sees me. Cold air rushes through the opening, but I barely register the chill, because I'm warm all over.

"Can I come in?"

I purse my lips and narrow my eyes. "I suppose."

He grins, knowing I'm only kidding. My heart races with the realization that he's happy to see me. It's evident in his smile. The way his eyes are fixed on me.

As he brushes past me, he places a chaste kiss on my cheek. His icy lips instantly cool my flushed skin, and a heavy sigh escapes me. He chuckles as his fingers ghost across my own, causing me to quiver.

I close the door and turn in time to see the six-foot-four man cross his arms and shiver. "It's a cold one tonight," he remarks, and I have to smother a smile.

Small talk is not Nick's thing, and right now he looks all sorts of nervous.

"Can I take your coat?" I ask, hand extended.

He bobs his head, removing the black, fleece-lined jacket, white logo on the breast of the coat upright. As soon as it's draped over my arm, his shoulders shake as his hands rub together.

"Come away from the door and get warm," I suggest, pulling him toward the center of the house with my free hand. I drop his coat on the kitchen table before ushering him to the great room.

"Hey, Mr. West," Ava calls, hanging over the back of the couch, waving a single hand through the air.

He waves back. "Hi, Ava." He smiles warmly. "You know, you *can* call me Nick."

Her teeth press together in a smile that would look deranged on anyone but her.

"Would you like something to eat? Drink?" Ava asks, and I make a face that suggests she can be quiet now and allow me to take the reins. "I'm just going to watch this," she says, motioning over her shoulder and smirking before turning back toward the TV. They're on to yet another Christmas-inspired romance.

Nick turns to me, grinning. "Is this what you ladies have been up to all night?"

I shrug. "More or less." I glance at the screen in time to see a woman stranded in a snowstorm, and it's not hard to deduce that the hero is about to arrive.

"Would you like something to eat?" I ask, and he shakes his head.

"Thank you, but no. I ate at the station. Captain had food delivered."

"That was nice of him," I say, feeling the awkwardness of small talk in front of my friends and Ava.

They may be facing forward, but I know without a doubt their ears are homed in on everything happening behind them.

"Do you wanna go somewhere private? To discuss Mrs. Fields?" I quickly add, not wanting Ava to think I'm suggesting something else entirely.

She's old enough to know my relationship with Nick isn't simply platonic. We had a conversation when she got home for break about the status of my feelings for Nick. I explained that it was new, and might not amount to anything, but we were attempting to go on a date at some point.

To my relief, she was supportive. She even seemed a bit giddy about it.

"Sure," he says, and we make our way to the front room. "I like the new furniture."

I glance around the room that's recently received a major upgrade. Gone are the gaudy hand-me-down floral couch and outdated chairs. With fresh paint and new curtains, the room is quickly becoming a favorite morning spot for me. It's where I like to sit and enjoy my coffee.

"Thank you. Me too," I say.

He takes a seat, with a groan.

"Long day?" I chuckle.

He grunts. "Long month." He sighs and then continues, "I knew this case was going to be a bi—" He stops mid-sentence, face flushing. "Tough."

"It's been a real bitch, hasn't it?" I chuckle, knowing that's what he wanted to say. "I'm not easily offended by language."

His chin dips, and a smile curves his lips up on both sides. "It has. A real bitch." He shakes his head, chest shuddering. "Anyway, I knew it would be rough with all the moving pieces and players, but it's turned into a nightmare."

"Is it something you can talk about or . . ."

I leave my words hanging, looking for him to steer where this conversation goes. I don't want to pry, because I know he can't share everything. Considering my relationship to the suspect's near-ex-wife, he likely feels the need to watch what he says. He can trust me, but this is still new.

"It's boring stuff. Just a lot of red tape. Richard is an idiot, but his attorney is not. They're going to do whatever they can to have his plea deal reversed."

I sit up straight. "Can they do that?"

He inhales deeply. "Unfortunately, in this case, yes. Due to the timing of everything happening over the holidays, the judge hasn't sentenced him." Nick shifts, appearing uncomfortable. "Between you and me, I think Judge McKnight is dirty. He's purposely stalled sentencing. He's had more than enough time, and his reasons for not doing it are all bullshit."

My eyes bulge, surprised Nick would admit that. To openly criticize the judge could be really bad for Nick. This is a small town, and accusations like that are often met with harsh reprimands. If not worse.

He trusts me.

Nick leans forward. "Alyssa, please keep everything I just said between me and you. I don't want it getting out to . . ."

"Anyone," I say, and he nods.

"And . . . well . . . It's the holidays. I don't think we need to ruin Nina's."

He's right. Knowing there is any chance that Richard could get off would devastate her.

"I won't say a word." I blow out a breath. "What happened with Mrs. Fields?"

He huffs a laugh. "She gave me an earful the entire way. I'm expected to investigate. Pronto."

I chuckle. "She was convinced a woman was out there."

"Oh . . . she told me all about the woman. She was scandalized by her choice in dress." He grins and I roll my eyes.

"It's Christmas. Lots of people dress up for the occasion," I say, picking at lint on my pajama pants. "Not me, but some do." I laugh.

"Personally, I like this look better." He grins, and my stomach dips.

I rush on with questions about Mrs. Fields to fill the silence. "Was anyone at her house?"

"Tom met us at the door."

"Her son?"

"Yeah." He rubs at his chin. "He's in town for the holiday. Her daughter, Sandy, is too, but she was asleep."

"How the heck did she manage to sneak outside? She was out there for at least five minutes," I say, worried that it could happen again.

"Tom was taking a shower. When he got out and realized she was gone, he was about to come searching for her." He shakes his head. "He said she's been hypervigilant because of the recent thefts in the area."

There has been some recent activity in the neighborhood. Mostly little things. Missing Christmas décor and yard ornaments. Nothing as scary as break-ins. Not that I like the thought of someone nosing around my house in the dark, taking my things.

"What did she plan to do in her nightgown?" I ask, lifting my brows skyward.

His shoulders shake when he laughs. "That's a great question, one that you'll have to ask her come tomorrow."

I peer toward the picture window, out into the dark night. "Do you think she saw someone?" I ask, looking at Nick once more.

He runs a hand back through his hair. "Doubtful. She wasn't wearing her glasses, and the woman's eyes are terrible." He shakes his head. "Thankfully, I don't have to be the bad guy who reprimands her about how unsafe it is to take matters into her own hands. That'll be Thomas's job tomorrow."

I whistle. "Yeah, not a good idea for her to be chasing after suspected criminals."

He nods, rubbing at his scruffy chin.

"You seem to know them all pretty well," I say, curious.

He clears his throat, looking away. "Char is—was—my fiancé's aunt. It's how I ended up with my house."

My mouth opens and then shuts. I'm not sure what to say.

"Well, I'd better get going," Nick says, standing up and stretching. "I just wanted to stop back by because I told you I would."

Instantly, my mood sours. He's been here for a whole ten minutes. I know he's had a long day, but I was hoping for a bit more time with him. It sounds selfish even to my own ears, but we've yet to have our first date, and I'm already insecure where he's concerned.

"Is everything okay, Nick?" The words are out of my mouth before I can think twice about them. "It's just . . . since the night I cancelled our date, you've been a bit MIA." His features harden, and I rush on. "I know you've been busy. I'm not trying to push or sound needy. I only want to ensure you're . . . good." I blow a piece of hair out of my eyes. "I've been nervous that you're angry with me about sending you away that night. When Nina showed up."

Nick stands, making his way toward me, hand extended to help me out of the chair. When I'm on my two feet, he pulls me in so we're chest to chest, our breaths mingling in the small space. "I'm not angry. I get your reasoning." He looks down at me, eyes roaming over my face. "I promise I'm not avoiding you or our date. This has everything to do with work and nothing to do with you and me."

He places his fingertips under my chin, lifting my head so that we're staring into each other's eyes. My entire body is alive. My chest rises and falls, my heart beating out of my chest.

"We will have that date. I can promise you that."

His lips descend on mine, and I sigh into the kiss, feeling equal parts exhilaration and relief. I didn't realize how badly I needed this moment with Nick. Craved it. *Him.*

My mouth parts, allowing his tongue to sweep across mine in a dance that feels familiar. Perfect.

It ends far too quickly. When he pulls away, I sway on my feet, lightheaded and gooey. Air rushes from my chest, a lightness I haven't felt in a week washing over me with that kiss.

I didn't think it would feel like this at forty. Like that first kiss as a teen, on a hot summer night, in the back of a pickup truck, down by the river.

It's a silly scene I concocted in my head due to the many hours of reading inappropriate books in my youth. Definitely not based on experience. Not that it matters.

This is so much better than I could've imagined.

There's nothing awkward about us like this. At our age, we're both confident and more than skilled in the art of kissing. My mind wanders down a path that's not exactly PG, and my face warms to inferno levels.

Nick smirks. "Everything okay?"

I blink several times, the images I had playing on a loop disappearing, leaving me a bit off-kilter. "All good," I croak.

"After the holiday, we'll have that date. Okay?" He doesn't break eye contact with me. "I want more time with you."

I can't get words out; I'm too caught up in the moment. I do manage a slight head nod, all while blinking uncontrollably.

He grins. "I need to get some sleep," he says, barely containing a yawn.

I hand his jacket over, and he slips it on, making his way toward the door before he even has both arms in.

"If you're not doing anything tomorrow night, you're welcome to join Ava and I for dinner," I say. "It won't be anything too fancy, but I am cooking."

He turns back around, smiling down at me, placing a hand on my cheek. "I wish I could. My mom might skin me alive if I'm not at family dinner."

I'm disappointed, but completely understand. This is new. We're not at the point of family introductions or forgoing our usual holiday plans to be together. That day will hopefully come, but I get that we're not there yet.

I open the door, and Nick steps out onto the porch step. "Merry Christmas, Lyss."

I lift onto my tiptoes, placing a kiss on his lips, out in the open for anyone looking to see. "Merry Christmas, Nick."

Movement just over his shoulder catches my attention, and my breath hitches. I blink a few times, but the figure doesn't disappear. A young woman, wearing a sparkly red dress with no coat, stands perfectly still, directly across the road from my house. Her long dark hair blows in the breeze, but otherwise, she doesn't move an inch.

Mrs. Fields was right.

The specter flashes in and out, signaling she's not just any ghost, but a poltergeist.

The woman is dead, and whatever happened to her was terrible.

Nick's eyes narrow in on me, and he looks over his shoulder. "Everything okay?"

I inhale and look away from the woman, back to Nick, forcing a smile.

"Yeah. Fine."

One eyebrow lifts minutely, alerting me to the fact that Nick isn't buying my lie, but what am I going to say? There's a dead woman you can't see standing behind you? She was likely murdered and wants me to solve her case?

Yes, Alyssa. You actually can say that to him.

I can, but I won't. Not tonight. Not on Christmas Eve, when he's tired and so am I. There will be plenty of time for me to open myself to whoever this angry spirit is.

"Good night, Nick."

He offers one last smile before heading off toward his house. I watch him until he's out of sight. When I glance back across the road, the woman is gone, and I can't shake the creepy feeling crawling over my body from her presence.

Mrs. Fields can see ghosts too. *Interesting.*

Except she didn't seem to recognize that the woman is dead.

I've learned that these sightings don't occur for everyone. Not unless the gift is nurtured. For me, the ability sprung up out of nowhere, unwanted. Thankfully, I discovered rather quickly that they just need my help.

I only hope this particular ghost doesn't decide to wake me in the middle of the night. Poltergeists are something else entirely. She'll haunt me until I solve her murder. She wouldn't be simply slinging insults and driving me up the wall—something I've learned I can handle.

The thought of Billy surprisingly calms me, and I smile. In the end, the pesky ghost wasn't so bad. He grew on me like a fungus. One that was easily removed once the issues were clear.

Merry Christmas, Billy. Wherever you are.

I sigh, closing the door on this night and ghosts.

Ace of Swords

I WAKE THE next morning to a quiet house, tiptoeing my way downstairs so as not to wake the others.

Once Nick left, the girls and I stayed up late, laughing until our bellies hurt and tears streamed down our faces. It was just what we all needed after the heaviness of the last month.

Especially Nina.

She seemed to be back to her old self, before the days of Richard. Carefree. Hilarious. I can only hope that over the coming weeks, while the snake attempts to slither his way out of charges, she doesn't lose that light in her eyes that I saw briefly last night.

I'm finally able to put to rest my worries surrounding Nick. Everything is fine. He's simply busy trying to wrap up a case that was always going to be troublesome. The villain has too much money to not go down without a fight.

I lift my arms over my head and stretch with a yawn.

The smell of freshly brewed coffee washes over me as my feet hit the wood floor. I'm grateful I had the forethought to prepare it the night before, considering the late hour.

I grab my favorite mug from the cabinet, one Ava made me several Christmases ago. *World's Best Mom* is scrawled across the bottom of a picture of the two of us. Ava's smile is extended from ear to ear, her cherub cheeks rosy. She'd just hopped off the swing set, where I'd pushed her into the air for well over an hour as she giggled and squirmed, relishing the way her belly dipped every time she swooped through the air.

It's a day I begged god to burn into my memory. A time I never wanted to forget. Days when Ava was carefree and small, wanting nothing but to spend hours swinging in the backyard, with her mommy and daddy close by.

I smile, filling the cup with scalding-hot coffee, splashing just a bit of peppermint creamer to turn the dark liquid a shade lighter. Bringing the mug to my lips, I inhale, sighing in contentment. All is right in the world on this perfect Christmas morning.

Curling up on my new gray corduroy chair, under my creamy cloud blanket, a Christmas gift from Lanie, I enjoy the peaceful moment, running through the events from last night, smiling all the while.

So much has changed in these last couple of months, and heading into the new year, I recognize that I have a giant list of things to be grateful for. At the top is Ava, and the fact that she received all A's on her report card, yet again.

Despite everything she's endured with losing her father, her tenacity and work ethic has only gotten stronger. The girl is destined for greatness, and I'm loving the front-row seat I have, watching her shine.

I'm not sure how much time has gone by, but my cup is nearly empty, and the sound of feet pattering on the wood floor tells me that someone else is up, and my moment of quiet is over.

"Merry Christmas, Ally." Nina takes a seat across from me with her own cup of coffee. I smile, raising my mug to her.

"Merry Christmas, Nina." I take a sip, smacking my lips upon swallowing. "How did you sleep?"

"Like the dead. I haven't slept that well in ages." Nina groans as she rolls her shoulders.

"Maybe it's time you get out of that mausoleum," I suggest, and she bobs her head in agreement.

"Not that I have much of a choice."

I tilt my head to the side.

"It's the mayor's mansion, and with the current one behind bars, the town council has appointed an interim mayor until an official election can take place," she explains.

"They're forcing you to move? Now? With everything you're going through?" My voice pitches, indignation rising at the reminder that Richard's actions continue to affect my best friend.

"No. Not immediately. They're allowing me to stay until after the election. I'll have a few months." She takes another sip of her coffee, blowing out a harsh breath after swallowing. "If I'm being honest, the sooner I get out of there, the better. I don't want to be in that hellhole anymore."

I huff. "You *never* wanted to be there."

She dips her chin, shrugging her shoulders. "That might be true, but now I *really* don't want to be. There's something off about the mansion. Strange noises, and I swear I hear voices." She shrugs. "Maybe I should have you come over and search for spirits."

I crinkle my nose. "Pass. They're likely to be worse than the likes of Billy."

Nina's leg bounces, her typically calm and collected façade slipping yet again. I'd hoped after last night that things might be turning around, but that doesn't appear to be the case. Could her talk about the mansion being haunted have her rattled?

"How are you doing?" I ask, recognizing how loaded a question that is.

"About as good as to be expected. I'm the wife of a murderer." She shakes her head, chuckling darkly. "In this small town, that's grounds for exile."

"Nobody is exiling you," I scoff. "You aren't the bad guy."

She makes a strangled sound. "Come on, Ally. You and I both know that I'm the local pariah."

The unfairness of the situation only manages to anger me more. Since Richard's incarceration, the town has acted cold toward Nina. You'd think she was behind it all too. That she helped plot and execute everything.

"What he did has nothing to do with you," I say, trying to keep the bite from my tone but failing miserably.

"I know that *you* know that, but the town will believe what they want, no matter the evidence that says otherwise. The police won't find a single shred of proof that points to my knowing what Richard was up to, but that won't matter. I'll still be labeled the wife that kept the villain's secrets." Her voice cracks. "And it's all my fault."

My lips turn down, sadness for Nina sweeping over me. "It isn't."

She sniffs. "No . . . it is. I played the part and fooled the entire town into thinking our marriage was strong. That we were a unit." Her head falls back. "Nobody knew what my life under that roof was truly like. That we were less than roommates." She huffs a humorless laugh. "I fueled their current distrust, and now I can't go back to the school."

"Why? You love your job. You're good at it." My voice rises, and my fingers curl into fists.

"There will be parents who won't find me an acceptable counselor. They'll petition the school board, and I'll be removed, if I don't resign first."

She rambles this off as though someone has already pointed out the likelihood of that scenario playing out. It wouldn't surprise me if Landis Jones, the school superintendent, did just that. He's an arrogant asshole who might be a bigger gossip than Nan Jenkins and the Red Hatters. The man has no tact, yet we continue to allow him to lead our youth.

"Are you going to? Resign?" I say, to clarify my previous question.

She clicks her tongue. "What choice do I have? It's what's best for the kids."

As much as I wish she were wrong, I know she's not. Small towns can be amazing places to grow roots, but they're also unforgiving and incredibly unfair at times. The circus that will rain down will only hurt the kids in the end.

"What can I do?" I ask, feeling helpless.

"Nothing." Nina's sternness catches me off guard. "I want you to do absolutely nothing. If something is said, you remain quiet."

I blink several times, completely baffled by this Nina. It's unlike her to take that tone with me, which only tells me how serious she is.

"I don't want you fighting my battles. It will only put a target on your back too, Alyssa." Her voice is softer with this delivery, but there's still an edge of warning.

"I don't care about any of that," I say, eyes pinned to Nina's hands as they twist around each other.

"You should," she snaps. "You're finally getting your life back, and I won't be the reason things go south for you."

"I don't care about that," I repeat, voice rising. "I care about you." I want to get it through her head that I won't abandon her.

"I know, and that's the problem. You care too much about everyone else when you should be selfish. This is your time. Your second chance. And you're going to take it." She puts her cup down and leans forward. "I'll be fine. I just need to keep my head down and hope that Richard goes away for a long time." She closes her eyes, inhales deeply, and exhales harshly.

"I have to hope that he's too preoccupied with his own situation to feel the need to drag me down with him."

Here's my chance to pry. She's opened the door for me to press about her secrets, and I have to take it. She needs someone to shoulder the burden. There's a massive secret needing to be unearthed, and once it's out, she'll have to feel a little better.

"What does he have on you, Nina? I know you don't want to talk about it. But you need to tell me. Whatever it is, it's eating you alive."

She looks away, and I follow her movement, staring out the window at the picturesque scene beyond.

Massive flakes of snow gracefully pirouette from the sky, resembling shimmery feathers as they make their way to the ground. They capture the few rays of sun peeking through the cloud-filled sky, glimmering like diamonds against the muted backdrop, creating an enchanting winter scene. The perfect Christmas day, if not for the heavy conversation currently occurring.

"The summer before my freshman year, I lost my virginity to a boy named Ian Whalen."

"I'm . . . What?" I say, unable to keep the humor from my voice. "I mean . . . that is pretty early, but you were from the city. Maturity tends to move a bit quicker there than in the country."

"There were a lot of issues with it, age being one factor for sure," she says. "But it didn't matter. Ian and I were best friends."

"Wait . . . is this the neighbor boy you've told me about before?"

She nods. "That's him."

I don't miss the way Nina's voice goes soft when she says that, the way her lips tip up at the corners as if she's recalling a fond memory.

"When my mother and Gary found out, they shipped me off to

St. Mary's." My eyebrow lifts, and she rushes on to explain. "It's a convent in Rhode Island."

I scrunch my nose, one eye squinting. It seems like a severe punishment, even for them. But my confusion is less about that and more about the fact that I'm only just hearing this. She never mentioned being at St. Mary's before moving to Indiana.

"I was pregnant."

My head jerks forward.

"Nina." Her name slips from my lips, a mere whisper. I'm shocked, but more than that, I'm terrified at what that means, considering she doesn't have a child.

"If it got out, it would ruin Gary's reputation." She sucks her teeth, seeming far too calm, when my palms are sweating and my heart is beating out of my chest.

"Couldn't have that," she continues rather flippantly. "Not during an election year."

Gary was Nina's mother's third husband—a wealthy politician, whom her mother was determined to wed as soon as she realized how many dollars he had to his name.

Belinda Rothchild married for love the first time, which only led to broken bones, black eyes, and bills piled to the ceiling. Nina was the only good thing that came of that relationship. Unfortunately, she had to bear witness to the atrocities.

Their escape came when Nina's father suffered a massive heart attack at a young age, leaving them both alone and better off. Until Belinda met her next abuser.

Husband number two wasn't physical, but he slung words like daggers, holding Nina's mother in a perpetual state of insecurity. He made it so she felt she couldn't live without him. Then one day he filed for divorce, choosing his mistress over Belinda, leaving her in a financial and mental pile of rubble.

After that was Gary, and while not perfect, he was a far cry better than the first two. Or so I thought.

Belinda's currently on husband number four, Patrick Rothchild, heir to an oil dynasty, and he seems to be just slightly better than the last four.

Nina was never modeled a healthy relationship. It's no wonder she ended up with Richard, a man so much like her mother's husbands.

But none of that currently matters, because Nina just said she'd been pregnant.

Where is her baby?

"What happened, Nina?"

She swallows, lips trembling. "Gone."

A tear slips from the corner of her eye, descending slowly down her cheek, but she doesn't remove it. She takes a deep breath, closing her eyes on an inhale.

My breath hitches, and my chest tightens, but I remain quiet. This is her story. One I have no doubt she's needed to tell for a very long time.

"I gave birth to a healthy baby boy, and then I was forced to hand him over to a family I didn't even get to meet."

My hands fly to my mouth, the shock pressing down on my lungs. "He's alive?" My question is barely audible through my labored breathing.

Nina is like a sister to me. We tell each other everything, and yet, she's kept this secret all these years. It's not only shocking but also heartbreaking. Having carried a child for nine months, I can't imagine the devastation that would come from being separated from my baby.

"I couldn't tell you, Alyssa. Not because I didn't want to, but I couldn't." Her crisp blue eyes hold mine, and I see the desperation that hovers over her.

"I understand, Nina."

I don't actually understand, but I won't make this harder for her. Nina must have her reasons for keeping silent on the matter, and I will respect that.

"Is that how you ended up in Fort Wayne?"

"Yes. When Gary was elected to the Senate, it allowed him the ability to move out of Indianapolis. Mom thought a fresh start might be best for us."

Bullshit. Belinda and Gary chose a small town far removed from the city, hoping to keep the gossip at bay and Nina in line.

Regardless, I can't hate them for the move. It's what brought Nina into my life. She was bubbly and warm. Not a girl who showed signs of the trauma I know she experienced.

A seasoned actress, forced to perform.

Nina licks her lips. "I think Gary chose Fort Wayne because he would have an excuse to be overnight in Indianapolis every week. Made it easy for him to continue his affair with our former neighbor."

I bite my lower lip, shaking my head. Nina's grandparents tried to get her out of there on multiple occasions. I remember her grandma showing up, telling Nina to pack a bag and that she was going to live with them.

Belinda had thrown a fit, and Gary had ordered her grandma away. That was the last time I ever saw the woman around. At the time, I'd been grateful for Gary. I didn't want to lose my best friend.

I didn't realize that going with her grandparents was best for Nina. I was just a kid, unwilling to part with the one person who understood me.

"Before we moved, I was warned to never speak of the baby. I knew the ramifications of talking."

My eyebrows tilt inward as I try to unearth the meaning of those words.

"They had already run the Whalen family out of town, Alyssa, and if Gary's reputation was spoiled due to the scandal, they wouldn't stop there. They'd have ruined them. Ian wouldn't have had a future."

Nina kneads her chest as tears continue to stream down her face.

It's clear that her feelings for Ian ran deep.

"What does any of this have to do with Richard? What did you see when you touched him?"

She sighs heavily. "I'll get to that, but first, you need to understand why I married him in the first place."

I sit back, because this is something I've often wondered about through the years.

When Nina met Richard, it was not love at first sight. He went out of his way to woo her, and eventually she caved and went on a date with him. But it always baffled me how he'd made her fall in love with him.

"I married Richard because he made it clear he was digging around, trying to find dirt on me. He was determined to trap me."

My stomach drops, and bile rises up my throat.

How had I missed the signs?

At Nina's wedding, she wasn't the blushing bride, excited to rush down the aisle. I'd assumed all the champagne she attempted to guzzle was to calm her nerves, but if I'd paid closer attention . . . I'd have known.

"That's why things shifted so soon after the wedding. He'd officially trapped you."

She nods.

"Stop looking like you're to blame, Ally. I made you believe I was happy. I knew what I was doing."

I groan, looking to the ceiling. "Why you? Why not all those women who threw themselves at him?"

Her head falls forward and shakes back and forth. "It wasn't me Richard wanted. It had everything to do with who my stepfather was. He wanted access to Gary and his contacts."

My heart shatters into a million pieces for my best friend. To know that all these years she's worked to help others, while she needed saving just as badly.

No matter what she says, I let her down.

We all did.

"He threatened to expose my secrets." She huffs a humorless laugh. "I didn't realize it at that time, but he didn't know anything. It was all a ruse. Smoke and mirrors."

Richard Dunbar is a predator. One I hope Nick can put away for a very long time.

I bite my bottom lip, wading through all the information she's shared.

"Why didn't you ensure he actually knew something?" I ask, knowing Nina is smarter than that.

"Because it didn't matter. He had the resources to make good on the threat. I feared what lengths he'd go to." She clears her throat, swiping away a tear. "I didn't know he was capable of murder, but I did know he'd do unspeakable things to get what he wanted."

"You agreed to marry him to protect your son and to keep Ian's identity a secret." It's not a question. I know Nina, and it's the sort of thing that she'd do.

She'll sacrifice herself for those she loves every time.

"I told him I'd play the doting wife as long as he promised to stop digging around."

My fingers flex as I try to tamp down the rising anger, but it's no use. "I hate him."

Nina sighs. "I know. Me too."

Her eyes close, and I watch as her chin trembles and hands shake.

I take a deep breath and sink to my knees, making my way toward Nina. Grabbing her hands in mine, I squeeze.

"What I'm about to say, I say with all the love in my heart . . ."

She opens her eyes and pulls her mouth to one side of her face.

"You need to seek a very good therapist."

To my horror, she bursts out laughing. Her chest shakes with the force of the manic outburst, and I'm not sure what to do.

Right now, she appears on the verge of a major crisis, and I'm ill-equipped to help her. I do the only thing I can think to do, pulling her into my chest and holding her close. Her cachinnation turns to sobs, and I clutch her tighter, allowing her whatever time she needs to grieve.

Minutes go by as she weeps in my arms. When she stops shaking and pulls away, I grab a tissue from the table next to me and hand it over. She blows her nose in the most unladylike fashion, entirely unlike Nina, but that's good. Based on everything she's said, who is the real Nina? Maybe her façade is slipping, and we'll get to see a glimpse of the girl that's remained hidden all these years.

It appears her family and then Richard dictated what the world got to see of her. Yet one more truth that's utterly tragic.

When she's composed, I broach the subject again. "I know you might not want to hear this, but after everything you've been through, talking to a professional is necessary. You know this, considering your profession."

She nods. "Even therapists need the reminder," she says, offering a small smile. "There's just so much trauma to dig through."

"And that's exactly why you're going to find the best of the best. This runs so much deeper than Richard, Nins. Surely, when you think on it, you see the parallels between the life you've lived and the life that was modeled to you by your mother."

She gulps, face paling. I can practically see Nina slipping into her role as therapist, paddling through her past, dredging up the damage that needs healing.

"Men have dictated both of our lives. We've both stayed in unhealthy situations despite having all the means to get out." She inhales, chewing on her bottom lip. "We've allowed ourselves to be controlled by cruel men, and we're still doing it to this day."

I offer a sad smile. "That's the first step. Now, allow someone to help you heal."

"I'll look for someone. I know you're right. I've just been too lost in self-pity to take the steps."

I know all about self-pity. It's hard to pull ourselves from it. We all need a hand. Nina was part of helping me out of mine, and I will be here to help her.

"You are smart and caring. You'll find your new normal and you'll escape his hold, Nina. I know it."

She taps my hand. "Thank you for not being mad at me."

"Why on earth would I be mad?"

"All the secrets. All the lies." Her lip quivers.

"You had your reasons. I'm just glad you decided to allow me to shoulder some of this burden."

"Want to shoulder more?" she says, voice catching. "Turns out, Richard went digging anyway. He found Ian."

Oh shit.

"Is that what you saw when you touched him?" I lean forward, recognizing a little too late that I probably appear far too eager to hear a very painful story. Despite the seriousness of the situation, I probably look ready to bust out the popcorn and soda.

Cringe.

"I'm sorry, Nins. I don't want you to think I'm getting any joy out of your pain. I'm invested. That's all."

She smiles. "I know that, silly. I would never think that about you." She sits back in her seat, appearing a bit more relaxed. "Apparently, Richard tracked Ian down at a university."

"Where? Close by?"

"Providence University. As soon as I left the prison, I started to research Ian and found that he was a TA there. English Literature." Her voice has a swoony quality to it, but her face falls into a mask of stone, and I begin to worry.

"What did Richard do?"

"I . . . don't know. I didn't see anything but Richard stalking him through campus." She leans in toward me. "Ian vanished."

My head jerks back. "Vanished how?"

"Your guess is as good as mine."

My eyes widen as all the possibilities surface. "He killed him?"

"I don't know," Nina says, voice rising. "Based on the timeline of information I found on the internet, the end of Ian's digital footprint coincides with Richard's visit to the university."

Oh god. That's not good news, considering Richard's track record of violence.

"Richard did something," I say, chewing on my fingertip.

A pained expression crosses over Nina's tear-stained face. "I don't know, but I need to find out."

I pull my top lip into my mouth. "I'll help. Whatever that entails," I promise, and she frowns.

"What did I say about focusing on you?"

I shrug one shoulder. "Consider this my first non-ghost PI assignment. It's good practice."

She rolls her eyes, trying to contain a smile, but it falls away quickly, replaced by something resembling horror.

"What if . . ." Her words trail off. "Could you . . ."

My head tilts to the side, waiting for her to continue, but then it hits me.

I gasp. "What if he's a ghost? And I can summon him."

We gulp simultaneously.

Things could get very grim very quickly, and I'm not sure I'm prepared to be the one to uncover something so dark. Not when Nina's attached.

"If it's any consolation, I haven't seen any deceased men hanging around. A woman? Yes, but no man."

Her eyebrows lift skyward. "You saw a dead woman? When?"

I chuckle darkly. "You know how Mrs. Fields claimed to see someone in the snow?"

Nina's shoulders shiver before I've even managed to finish my story.

"Turns out, she did see a woman. A poltergeist."

Nina's puffy, bloodshot eyes widen, making her look like a cartoon character.

"Did she reach out to you? The ghost."

I shrug a shoulder. "I mean . . . I saw her. She was staring at my house, just as Mrs. Fields described, but I haven't seen her since Nick left last night."

She whistles. "Thank god. Ghosts are scary enough, but poltergeists . . ."

"Are frightening," I say.

"What do we do?" Nina chews on her bottom lip, a habit she's recently formed.

I stand, moving beside her. "Let's get through Christmas, and then we'll discuss what to do. Okay?"

She bobs her head, taking a sip of coffee and spluttering.

"Eck. It's cold."

I pat her shoulder. "Time for a refill."

"I'll take mine with liquor," Nina calls.

Me too, girlfriend. Me too.

Page of Pentacles

THE PAST FEW days have been nothing short of pure laziness. I haven't left my house since before Christmas Eve, and I have no regrets.

"Mom," Ava calls up the stairs.

"Just a sec," I yell back, running a brush through my hair one more time to work out a stubborn knot.

Ava and I have spent as much time together as possible, lounging around and continuing our movie binge. She'll be heading back to school in just a couple days, and I'm soaking in all the time I can.

I practically jog down the stairs to find Ava at the door, bundled up and ready to go.

I lift a brow. "Going somewhere?"

She gnashes her teeth together, scrunching her nose at the same time. "Yes?"

"Is that a question?" I chuckle, placing my hands on my hips and tilting my head to the side.

"Carly, Simone, and Tarrin are all home and hanging out at Carly's."

"It looks like you're joining them." I motion toward the purple paisley overnight bag sitting by the door.

She winces. "Are you angry?"

I move down the final steps and pull her into my arms. "Of course not, baby girl. Go have fun."

She squeezes me a little tighter. "I'll come home tonight if you want."

While I appreciate her attempt to make me feel better, it's not necessary. I'm more than capable of being alone. In fact, after all the hoopla of the holidays, I could use a few solo hours.

"Stay. Have a great time." She levels me with a look, but I won't back down. "I don't want you driving on the snowy roads in the dark. I'll probably fall asleep early anyway. I'm exhausted."

She grins. "From what exactly? Lounging?"

"Hardy har har. Get out of here, sassy." I turn her to face the door, but she shifts back around and rises to her tiptoes to place a kiss on my cheek. "See you in the morning."

I smile. "Maybe we can do some shopping tomorrow. Catch the sales."

She grins. "It's a deal."

I watch her until she's pulling down the road and out of view. It never gets easier watching her leave. The worry is there, and I suppose it always will be for me.

Having lost someone I love in a car accident, I'm likely to always feel a bit uncomfortable every time she gets behind the wheel. There are so many things out of our control, and I learned that firsthand in the worst way.

I blow out a breath, taking a look around the house. There's not much that needs to be done, but I can't sit any longer. I have to do something productive. Making my way to my office, I pull out my business plan and run down my to-do list.

Schedule a meeting with Nick's former colleague.

Schedule Firearm Safety course (just to be safe).

Look into Watch Guard Patrol license instead.

What does that include?

Can I operate from my home?

I start at the top and work my way down the list. Over an hour later, I've managed to get a date on the books with Greg Eitz, Nick's contact. We're meeting April second at Milly's. I've scheduled my safety course for the beginning of March, and I'm prepared to move forward with the Watch, Guard, Patrol unless Greg has some other suggestion that's a better fit.

It's three p.m., and I'm restless. Done working on my business plan for today, I make my way into the kitchen in search of a snack, only to discover my house is bare. There aren't any leftovers, and I'm almost out of milk. I start putting together a list of all the things I need and sigh, knowing I'm not going to avoid leaving the house today.

I close the refrigerator door and stop breathing when my eyes connect with the spirit I saw on Christmas Eve. The same one Mrs. Fields had been giving a lecture to.

Except this time, she's in my space, staring right through me with her sunken eyes. Her form blinks in and out, much like Jenna Cruz did.

I take in everything I can about the woman before she disappears for good, hoping it will help me to identify her.

Her stringy brown hair is matted to her head in places, and her dress appears as though it was run through a rinse cycle and never fully dried. Her hands are withered like a prune.

My best guess is that this spirit drowned. *Or was dumped in water.*

Based on the similarities to Jenna, this is another poltergeist situation, and according to Corinne's mom, that indicates a horrible ending.

"How can I help you?" I whisper, knowing she can't communicate with me.

She doesn't respond, as expected. She doesn't even move, aside from flashing in and out of existence.

I take a deep breath, but she's already gone, leaving me a bit rattled.

I've gotten over the worst of my fears surrounding ghosts. Having them in and out of my life these past couple of months has helped prepare me for life as a medium. However, there's a different energy that comes with poltergeists. It's unsettling, to say the least.

While I'm not scared that she'll harm me, I'm not exactly jumping at the thought of being here alone. Might as well push up my visit to town.

I grab my purse, phone, and keys and haul ass to the door. I'm much more composed than I was the first couple times Billy presented, but there's still room for growth.

I'll master it one day. Today is not that day.

My phone dings, and with shaky hands, I pull it from my black crossbody to find Nick's name lighting up the screen. He's sent a text.

NICK

SOS . . . are you around?

ME

Yes. Everything okay?

NICK

My sister Jackie needed a huge favor and dropped my niece off.

I'm about to ask him how I can help, but another text comes in.

NICK

She's crying hysterically. I don't know what to do.

Will you come over here?

ME

On my way . . .

I don't bother with a coat because I could tell from his messages that the typically calm and collected Nick West is panicking. I slip on my boots and run next door. I don't even have a chance to knock before Nick's door swings open and the wailing sounds of a very upset infant sound somewhere toward the back of his house. A harried-looking Nick runs his hand back through his hair.

"Thank you so much, Alyssa." He's standing in the door, not moving.

I smirk. "Mind if I come in?"

He blinks, shaking his head and standing aside. "Shit. I'm sorry. Come in."

I've never seen Nick so rattled. Not by my insistence that ghosts were feeding me information. Not from watching a séance unfold.

His niece, Zoey, is sitting on the floor, screaming at the top of her lungs. She's holding her belly as tears pour down her face in a flood.

"What happened?" I say, looking back to Nick.

"I have no idea. One minute she was fine, and the next . . . this." He motions toward the dark-haired baby, who's the cutest thing I've seen despite the blotchy face.

"She's holding her belly," I comment. "Did something happen?"

"No. Well . . . not that I know of." He rubs at his forehead, clearly out of his element here. "I mean she's been a little off tonight. She typically likes to be a terror getting into everything, and she's just sat here all night."

"That's not normal," I say, falling to my knees next to his adorable little niece.

"Hi, Zoey," I coo, knowing she's not going to give two shits about anything I have to say. She's clearly in pain. "Do you happen to have any Mylicon?"

Nick peers at me like a deer in headlights. "I don't even know what that is."

I lick my lips, trying to contain the smile. This is all new to him, and I can tell he's flustered. He might be a brave and calm detective, but when it comes to children, all bets are off, apparently.

"If you do, it would likely be in a diaper bag. I'm assuming your sister left one with you?"

He nods several times, rushing toward the kitchen. He comes back moments later with a black-and-white checkered bag. I rifle through it, coming across her stash of children's Tylenol, but there's no Mylicon.

"Could I get you to go to the store? I have a feeling she has an upset stomach. I'll give her some Tylenol, but she could really use the Mylicon drops."

He looks at me like I have three heads. "Where . . . what aisle?"

"I'll find what I need online and send you a picture of it. If you ask someone at the store, they'll be able to tell you where to get it."

"Okay. Yeah . . . sure. I can definitely do that." He starts to leave, but stops, coming back to me, and holding his hand out.

I take it, and he pulls me to my feet, crushing me against his chest.

"I owe you big time," he says into my ear, giving me the chills.

He steps back, but not before placing a kiss on my lips. "Big time," he repeats, emphasizing *big*.

I smirk. "Go get the drops, and I'll take care of her."

He rushes off, leaving me with a bellowing infant. I make quick work of giving Zoey the infant Tylenol, allowing her to cry it out while I sing lullabies to her in the most soothing voice manageable.

It's been several years since I've had a child this young, and while some things you never forget, others you do. And for good reason. Watching this tiny person clearly in pain, crying, wiggling, and squirming all over the floor is heartbreaking, and she's not even mine.

Eventually, the medicine kicks in, and her crying calms a bit.

"Do you want to watch a movie, Zoey?" I ask, making quick work of finding a station appropriate for her age.

Some blue dog with pointed ears sings and dances, and Zoey seems to like it. While she doesn't dance along, she does manage to stop crying. I glance at my watch, recognizing that Nick has been gone for quite a while already.

ME

Please tell me you aren't wandering around aimlessly . . .

NICK
Okay . . .

ME
Okay?

NICK
You said not to tell you.

ME
That's . . . not a good sign.

NICK
I just got someone to help.

ME
Just?

NICK
. . .

My chest shakes with laughter as I picture Nick's furrowed brow, searching the aisles for Mylicon drops. If I had to guess, he's looking in the pharmacy, and the drops are likely in the infant aisle. We're going to have to work on his ability to ask for help.

Although he did manage to text me tonight. So that's a good sign.

I look down to see that Zoey's eyelashes are fluttering. She's fighting the urge to fall asleep, which is a good sign. Poor thing has to be exhausted from all the crying. I give it a few more minutes, and finally she dozes off.

Waiting to be sure, I watch two more minutes of the cartoon

before I've had enough. I grab the remote and scan the channels until I land on Hallmark. A Christmas show I've already seen is playing, which is perfect. I don't want to get sucked into anything new, because Nick will be back soon.

I've been watching the prince fall for the nanny, remembering how much I enjoyed this one, when the picture freezes before the cable box resets itself. When the screen comes back on, the movie resumes a minute before the part where it last cut off. I'm listening to the same words as before, and again, the television malfunctions.

"Strange."

The front door closes, alerting me to the fact that Nick has returned.

"I've got the Mylicon drops." His footsteps falter, and he stops right inside the room. "She's asleep?"

I glance down at Zoey, still asleep in my arms, and nod, not wanting to wake her.

"Thank god." He throws the grocery bag on the couch, taking a seat next to me. "You're the best."

I smile, bringing one finger to my lips.

Nick winces, mouthing *sorry*.

I place her on the floor, creating a barricade around her. It won't keep an awake one-year-old contained, but at the very least, it'll keep her from rolling around in her sleep.

When I'm satisfied with my makeshift crib, I walk to the kitchen, which is still in the same room, but a little farther from the sleeping baby.

"Do you have her overnight?" I ask, as Nick pours himself a glass of water.

He takes a long drink, sighing after he's drained the glass. "I don't know. My brother-in-law is working overnight, and my sister had to take herself to the hospital."

My eyes widen. "What happened to her?"

"She has a bad stomach bug and is likely dehydrated. So, there's a good chance Zoey will be here overnight."

"Oh crap," I say, glancing toward Zoey. "I bet you she has the same stomach bug that your sister has."

His mouth drops open, and his head snaps toward Zoey. "Do you think?"

"Yes, and if I were you, I would get some towels and a bowl because it might be a long night."

He closes his eyes, taking a deep breath. "I don't know if I can watch her be sick."

I attempt to cover my smirk. "Do you have a weak stomach?"

Nick narrows his eyes at me, lifting one eyebrow. "Nothing weak about it. I just mean, it will be horrible to watch her like that."

My heart melts. He's such a good uncle, and it makes me wonder if he ever wanted kids.

At forty, my baby-making days are over. Not that I physically can't do it, but I have no interest in starting over with an infant. I can't imagine at forty-five he's gunning for babies, but you never know. One day I'll ask, but there's no sense in bringing it up now. I'd like to enjoy whatever is happening between us for as long as I can. No need to scare him away with talk of babies and the lack of them where I'm concerned.

"Why don't you go take a shower," I suggest, seeing that he's still in his uniform. "I'll stay here with her until you're done."

"Are you sure?"

I smile. "Positive."

He returns my smile, shaking his head while looking at the ground. "I'm gonna take you up on that." He motions down at his pants. "I'd barely made it in the door when Jackie called."

"I noticed. Go ahead. I'll be all right."

He nods before jumping to it. I watch him until he's all the way down the dark hallway, out of sight. A smile is plastered across my face. Nick West makes me feel things I haven't felt in years. The beginning butterflies that tickle and make you feel lightheaded.

I'm lost in thought when the television begins to play that same tired cartoon, at least two volumes higher. I practically jump out of my skin, head darting to the floor where, thankfully, Zoey still sleeps soundly.

What the hell?

It wasn't even on that channel. I changed it. I snatch up the remote, stopping on the first thing that isn't full of dancing characters. It's a true-crime channel discussing a missing-person case in California. The girl is young and beautiful. She was last seen leaving a club two years ago.

There's something about the girl that feels . . . familiar. I lean forward, getting a closer look at the image of the young woman that's locked on the screen. That's when it hits me. She looks similar to the girl in red. They're not the same woman, but they do have a striking resemblance.

I sit back, wanting to know more about this missing girl. The scene changes to a shot of a bay, the camera sweeping out at the dark water, the sun long gone. The narrator is discussing how the club had been close to the water, and they'd feared she'd stumbled off, drunk, and possibly drowned.

The television freezes again.

"Why? What gives?" I whisper into the silence.

"What do you mean?" Nick's husky voice startles me, and I yelp, grabbing the front of my sweater.

"Sorry. Didn't mean to frighten you." He chuckles.

I take a deep breath and let it out slowly. "I was talking to myself," I explain. "Something seems to be wrong with your TV."

I turn to look at him, and my mouth dries. He's wearing a pair of black sweatpants, no shirt, one hand drying his hair with a white towel. I gulp as I take in every inch of him.

I have never seen a sexier sight in my life. The man is drool-worthy.

"I feel so much better," he says, throwing the towel over a chair in the kitchen. "Has she stirred?"

"Not at all. She's out cold."

"Joe just sent me a text. Apparently, he found someone to cover for him and met Jackie at the hospital. They gave her an IV and discharged her about ten minutes ago. He's gonna get Jack home and settled, and then he'll be stopping by to get Zoey."

"That's good news about Jackie," I say, and he nods.

"And that they're coming for Sleeping Beauty over there," he says, smiling down at his niece. "Not that I don't want her to stay here," he quickly amends.

"I'm sure she'll get better sleep in her own bed." I yawn, stretching my hands over my head. "I should probably head back home."

"I'm sorry. I didn't mean to keep you here for so long."

I lift a hand. "You didn't. I'm glad you texted."

I stand, and he follows me to the door. He reaches out and grabs my hand, twisting me into his chest.

Leather and sandalwood wash over me, and I inhale deeply. He's intoxicating.

Droolworthy? Intoxicating? Ava would call me cringe for using such adjectives to describe a man. And maybe I am, but both are true.

"Thank you, Lyss. I mean it. You saved me."

My head wobbles around as I struggle to take the compliment, something I intend to work on and soon.

"I'm always happy to help."

He pulls me in and places a lingering kiss on my lips.

His forehead leans against mine. "Do you have plans for New Year's Eve?"

"No," I say, breathlessly.

He steps back, putting some space between us. "You do now. I have tickets to a party in Silverton. Malone gave them to me because he decided to work the night shift." He searches my face. "Will you? Come with me?"

A smile spreads across my face. "I'd love to."

He rocks back on his heels, head dipping slightly. "It's overnight. We'd be . . . sharing a room."

I swallow, the thought of sharing a bed with Nick both exhilarating and terrifying. I was ready to take things to the next level a few weeks ago, but the distance as of late has tempered my nerve.

"If you aren't comfortable, we can—"

"No," I rush out, shaking my head. "I don't mind. I want to . . ." My words trail off, cheeks burning as the image of Nick lying beside me plays on a loop in my head.

"It's a date," he says, and his voice is gravelly.

Could he possibly be thinking about what I'm thinking about?

I guess we'll find out soon enough.

The Magician

IT'S THURSDAY NIGHT and the first meeting of the Gin and Tarot Club since before the holidays. Lanie barrels into the kitchen with her arms full of poster boards, her oversize knockoff purse hanging off her shoulder, brimming with additional supplies from the looks of it.

She drops the boards haphazardly over the dining room table, and I lift an eyebrow, staring at the blank white cardboard inquiringly.

"What's with those?" I ask, curious about what Lanie has planned for this evening.

We haven't discussed the specifics for tonight. The only instructions I got were that it would be held here at eight o'clock, and that it was my job to ensure there were plenty of snacks and booze.

Which is not typical for our traditional girls' night. Lanie and Nina both are sticklers for having something on the books. Whether it be a reservation or an organized night in, there's usually more planning involved. Things have changed since my abilities presented.

The Gin and Tarot Club was briefly explained as a way for our group to work together, using our unique skills to solve crimes. However, it isn't a true club, in Lanie's opinion, if we aren't sipping—or guzzling—our official club alcohol, gin. A liquor that I only drink on Thursday nights.

"It's our craft for tonight," she explains, not bothering to look at me. She goes about sifting through her bag while simultaneously attempting to move her sweater back into position on her shoulder.

I snort because Lanie is not the arts-and-crafts kind of girl.

"So now we're doing crafts? This is an interesting development."

She bobs her head. "A very important craft, considering the new year is upon us."

Good grief. Lanie is slipping right into her woo-woo tone, which means things are about to get interesting tonight.

"What is this craft that's so important?" I ask, leaning back against the kitchen island. "I mean . . . more important than solving crimes and saving lives?"

Lanie huffs, rolling her eyes into the back of her head. "Vision boards, Alyssa. We're manifesting our best year."

I suck on my teeth, thinking through all that I know about that sort of thing. Many people do vision boards, and I've never understood the craze behind them. What's the point in taking time to glue pictures of things you want but don't have onto a board that you'll throw into a closet and never look at?

"Vision boards are an essential practice for manifestation," Lanie says, looking up at me. "Now that you have an awakened ability, you should be able to manifest easily."

"That sounds like . . . fun?"

"It is, and it's also an extremely important practice," she says, searching through a pouch of markers for who knows what. "One that I want to share with my best friends."

I smile at her because it's rare that she's even remotely sentimental. Whether I believe or understand the purpose of vision boards, I'll happily partake in this activity to humor my best friend. Based on the copious amount of supplies she's carrying around, she's put some thought into this.

"Okay, so aside from the boards, what else do we need?"

She waves her hand in the air. "All taken care of. Corinne's bringing the expired magazines from the spa over, and I have markers and glue guns in my bag." She rifles through her large tote, presumably searching for the supplies. "You just concentrate on the snacks and keeping the booze flowing."

"So it's gonna be one of those nights?"

"It's Thursday," she deadpans. "Girls' night is always one of *those* nights."

She would not be wrong. The whole point of Thursday is to get together and put our shit week behind us. Which almost always includes a few drinks.

For the next twenty minutes, I gather the food and set it up in the great room as she creates workstations for each of us. A board, thick black marker, and pair of scissors is placed at each spot on the floor. The glue guns are set up in the kitchen.

"I'm very impressed, Lanie. You've really gone all out with this," I say, looking around at her setup.

She shrugs. "This practice is important to me. Believe it or not, this will be my fifth board, and every year I receive more of the things I've added."

I'm about to pry into the things she's received when Corinne saunters into the room carrying a stack of magazines.

"Can you put those in there?" Lanie says, pointing to the great room where the boards and supplies have been set up.

"Hello to you too, Lanie," Corinne grates, moving right past us, heading straight for the great room.

We watch from the kitchen as she tosses the magazines into the center of the makeshift circle of stations. They scatter everywhere, but she doesn't bother to straighten them. She's too busy checking out the setup.

"You're looking fancy today, Cori," Lanie says, eyeing her up and down.

Corinne has clearly come straight from the spa. She's wearing her signature black slacks and white blouse with trumpet sleeves.

"I'm changing," she says, heading straight toward the bathroom, still not bothering with greetings.

Not that we were any better.

Nina is the last to arrive, fashionably late, which is not her MO. She's carrying a tray of cookies in the shape of clocks. I lift an eyebrow, and she shakes her head, looking exasperated.

"Lanie," she explains, tilting her head down at the cookie platter. "I was tasked with bringing New Year–inspired cookies."

I chuckle, looking between the plate and Nina. "Clocks?"

She shrugs. "They represent the countdown. What else signifies New Year's?"

"You've got me there." I tap my chin. "The only thing that comes to mind for me is champagne."

Her mouth drops open. "Good one. I should've done that."

I wave a hand in the air. "I think your clocks are cute."

"And very thoughtful," Lanie says, making her way toward Nina.

I grab the tray of cookies and place it on the counter as Lanie envelops Nina in a hug that has me questioning if something has happened and I missed the memo.

"I'm so glad to see you," Lanie says, taking a step back to give Nina her personal space.

Nina takes a cleansing breath. "I can't tell you how badly I needed this night."

Lanie claps her hands together. "Should we get started?"

Lanie, Nina, Corinne, and I make our way to our stations, sitting in a circle on my great room floor.

"I call to order this meeting of the Gin and Tarot Club," Lanie calls out, in a tone that sounds a lot like Madame Corinne.

I have to refrain from making a face at Lanie, not that she'd see it. She's too focused on her notepad, which brings a host of questions.

"Tonight, we will be working on our New Year vision boards, but before we dive into that, I want to make it clear that there's a process to this." Lanie looks up, meeting each of our eyes.

I bite my top lip, glancing at Nina, who appears more than a little amused.

"The art of vision boards is not simply picking out a bunch of lavish things and throwing them on a board with no thought. That's not how you manifest."

"Isn't it?" Corinne says, and Lanie glowers at her.

"Corinne, you should know better," she chastises, earning an eye roll. "I can assure you, if you follow my method, by next year, you'll be married and well on your way to children."

Corinne practically chokes, face twisted up in horror, while Lanie tries very hard to refrain from bursting into laughter.

"You . . . are evil," Corinne snaps. "I don't want to be married, and I most definitely never want children." She points a finger at Lanie. "Don't you dare put that kind of juju on me."

Lanie tosses her dark hair back over her shoulder, wholly ignoring Corinne.

"Whatever you ladies want, you'll have," she says to Nina and me.

"How exactly do we do it? The manifesting," Nina asks, getting us back on target, and currently seeming rather into the notion.

Lanie cracks her neck and then her fingers. "I want you to think about four categories that really speak to you. They can be anything from wealth, health, career, family, friends, etcetera, but narrow it down to four." She lifts a hand with four fingers raised as if she's teaching a bunch of kindergartners.

Next, she holds up her board to display that she's already gotten started. There's a large eye drawn in the middle, separating the top of a tree from the trunk and roots. The roots extending from the trunk and branches full of leaves extend from every side at the top. Lines protrude from the symbol in the center to create four separate sections to the board.

She has one labeled *health*, another labeled *prosperity*, one labeled *career*, and the last section is *love*.

"This is how you will set up your board. In order to determine your four keystones, I want you to each take a different room of the house. Find a quiet spot. Get comfortable and meditate on it. The first four that come to mind are the four you're going to concentrate on."

"What were those categories again?" Nina asks, and Lanie purses her lips.

"There aren't particular categories. You just choose areas of your life you'd like to grow." She turns back to the whole group. "While you're in your quiet spot, set your board up as I have, and then we will all return back here. You have ten minutes to complete this first task," she says, effectively dismissing us.

I look around at the room to find Corinne already on her feet, grabbing a marker from the middle and carrying her board underneath her arms, heading out of the family room.

I shrug my shoulders at Nina. "I guess we have ten minutes."

She grins and grabs her supplies.

"You can come with me. I don't need a quiet space. I already know my four," I say, making my way toward my office.

"Me too," Nina echoes, following on my heels.

We sit cross-legged on the floor, putting our boards in front of us, getting to work. We divide our boards into four sections, but leave space in the middle for a symbol. I choose career, self-care, love, and prosperity as my pillars, already compiling a list in my head of the things I want out of each of the four.

"Good ones," Nina says, and that's when I notice she's just staring at a mostly blank board. She's created her sections but hasn't put a single pillar down.

"I thought you said you knew what you wanted to do."

She lowers her head, hands twisting around each other. "If I'm being honest, I was just going to copy Lanie's." She shakes her head. "Then I realized she chose love as one of hers, and I don't want love. That's not in the cards for me."

I grab Nina's hand, holding it on my lap.

"I'm not going to say that you'll be ready for love this year. Not after everything you've been through, but don't close yourself off, Nins. You deserve happiness. Whatever that looks like for you." She offers a tight-lipped smile. "Don't think about this so hard. Just listen to your gut. Whatever it tells you to do, just do it." I'm regurgitating Lanie's instructions, but it appears to work.

Nina swallows and nods her head before picking up her marker. I watch as she labels her own board. She writes *personal development*, *travel*, *spirituality*, and then she glances over at me.

"Do you mind if I steal one of yours?"

I shake my head. "Go for it."

She finishes her board with self-care.

I smile wide at my friend. "Those are great, Nina. Lanie is going to be so proud."

She smirks. "I'm doing this for me."

I lift my hand in the air as if I'm holding a cup. "Cheers, my friend."

"I think we should go get the real thing. What about you?"

While I'm not a huge fan of gin, I think I'm going to appreciate it tonight.

"One hundred percent."

We make our way to the kitchen to find that Lanie and Corinne are in there, grabbing themselves a snack and a drink.

"Looks like you guys had the same idea as us," I say, motioning toward their glasses.

Lanie takes a bite of a carrot, but it doesn't stop her from talking as she chews. Which is not unlike her at all.

"I find that having a drink while meditating works really well for me."

"Last I checked, having a drink while doing anything works really well for you," Corinne teases.

Lanie shrugs. "That too. I'm in my salty dog era."

"Oh? What's that?" Nina asks.

Lanie walks her through the gin-inspired drink, which admittedly sounds delicious.

"I brought all the garnishes." She points toward the grapefruit juice and salt. "Use the dry gin," she says, as if either of us knows the damn difference.

I bought a few variations, but I put no thought into why I chose the bottles I did.

Lanie ends up making Nina's while I stick to what's familiar. Tanqueray and tonic to start, and perhaps I'll try the salty dog next. We head back toward the family room, all eager to get to work on our boards.

I have to admit, I'm more excited than I first thought I'd be. The whole idea was a perfect way to get our minds off all the negative and onto more hopeful things.

"Don't get too comfortable in there. We have to break out again," Lanie calls to my back.

When she comes into the room, she hands us each a small journal that she pulled from her oversize bag.

"The next step for you is to sit with these four pillars and journal what each means to you. If you chose career, what does that perfect career look like? Think about how you'll feel when you have that career."

I think about what she's saying, envisioning a room set up with whiteboards filled with suspect profiles. Something akin to what I've seen on television. It fills me with excitement and an edge of danger. A different form of butterflies fills my stomach. A rush of adrenaline that makes me excited for the future.

"Write down what feeling is attached to each of the pillars." Her hands rise and curl into balls as she gets into her role. "Really dive deep into why it's important to you. Why will it bring you joy this year?"

So far, this assignment is easy. No journaling required. I feel like I've been mapping out my next twelve months for weeks.

"When you feel really connected to what you've written for all four categories, then you'll be ready to come back and start searching for images that correlate with each of the pillars."

I try imagining what sort of image I can find within the pages of the magazines that would represent my career, but Lanie cuts off that thought, adding more.

"Find images that speak to that feeling that you've associated with every one of the pillars. When you find it, cut it out, and tack it to your board."

"I thought you brought glue guns," I say.

Lanie's eyes cross. "I did, and you will eventually glue them all on. This is the process. You're creating your board and ensuring you have it set up in the way that makes you most happy." She stares at me. "*Before* you make it permanent."

Not too long ago, Lanie's condescending attitude would've thrown me. These days, I find it funny. It's just who she is. Dramatic and over the top. She doesn't mean anything by it. She's sarcastic and dry, the complete opposite of me, and it brings a flair to our friendship.

"If there's a word in the magazine that fits your themes, cut that out too, and tack it on the board."

"Can you give us an example?" Nina asks, grinning over at me.

Lanie is so into playing teacher that she doesn't realize Nina is only messing with her. She dives right in with examples.

"One of the things that I find to be very important with all manifestation is gratefulness. Make sure that you either write or place the words *thank you* or *gratitude* or whatever word or phrase represents your gratefulness to the universe. It will make a huge difference for your manifestation."

"Why?" I ask not to be combative, but because I'm truly curious as to Lanie's practice. She's shown in a matter of an hour that this is serious for her.

"I think it's important for the universe to know that you're already grateful for these things, even though they haven't occurred yet. For your manifestation to work, you have to have an abundant mindset. Don't go into this board thinking, *Oh, how great would my life be if I had these*; go into it saying, *My life is amazing because I have these things.*"

"But I don't have these things." The words fly out, and I can't take them back, which is a shame because it's clear within a fraction of a second that Lanie is about to throttle me.

Lanie sucks on her teeth, glaring straight at me. "What's the deal, Ally? Are you trying to ruin your manifestation before you've even begun?"

I splutter. "I don't have a deal. I'm just truly trying to understand. I want to do this right."

She sighs. "It's just my practice. I find that when you're grateful, and when you live your life like those things are already yours, the universe provides."

"No matter what, you have to believe you deserve them," Corinne jumps in. "Believe, and they will be yours."

Lanie bobs her head. "The universe feeds on positivity. When you go into things with a lack mentality, they feed off that too. Believe it, receive it. Doubt it . . ." She scrunches her nose. "I can't come up with anything that rhymes with doubt, but you hear what I'm saying. It will not be yours if you doubt."

I nod my head, following her. "Got it. Believe and achieve. Doubt and drought."

"Yes," Lanie praises, clapping. "That's the spirit."

"Take as much time as you guys need with this. It's the most important step," Lanie sings.

I turn to Nina. "Go ahead and take my office. I'm gonna head upstairs and do this in my room."

She tilts her head. "Are you sure?"

"Yes. I'm more comfortable there, and it sounds like that'll be important for journaling." I smirk, and she smiles, shaking her head.

"Good luck," she says, making her way to my office.

I head up to my bedroom, taking a seat on my new chaise longue chair I have positioned by the window. I open the journal, writing my first pillar at the top.

Career.

I take a deep breath and begin journaling whatever comes to me as I consider what I want out of my career. Then I concentrate on how that would make me feel. I continue with each pillar: self-care, love, and ending with prosperity. By the time I'm finished, I feel lighter. Motivated.

Glancing at the clock, I see that over an hour and a half has gone by. I flip through the pages of my journal and my breath hitches. I swipe through page after page to find paragraphs that have one phrase repeated.

Stop him.

The Star

STOP WHO?

Better yet . . . why?

I was truly lost in thought, reimagining my life, and basking in the joy the changes brought. I clearly remember jotting down the feelings connected to each pillar, but I have absolutely no memory of writing *stop him* repeatedly.

The words are haphazardly scribbled between my vision board thoughts, and if it weren't so clearly my own handwriting, I'd question if someone else had written them.

Could I have been possessed? I mean . . . stranger things have occurred in the past couple months. And if that is the case, something needs to be done about it.

Possession is where I draw the line.

Corinne and Natalia, her mother, have both made it clear that poltergeists are not entities I want around, and it's becoming clear why.

Unfortunately, our night of vision boards might have to be cut short so that we can begin to investigate this ghost and help her on her way.

When I make it back into the family room, the girls are already well into gluing their visions on their boards. Lanie and Corinne are finishing up the last of theirs, and Nina isn't far behind them.

"Looks like I'll be completing mine another night," I say to the group. "I got a little . . . bewitched."

Lanie looks up. "What does that mean?" Her eyes are narrowed in on me. "What have you been doing?"

"Journaling. And let's just say it went a little sideways."

She smiles. "That's a good thing, Alyssa. Take your time with this. It's not the new year yet. You have time."

"It's not all good, but we'll discuss that in a moment. Right now, I need a stiff drink," I say, heading toward the gin.

I pour a double and slam it before pouring another.

"Whoa there," Nina says, coming up beside me. "What's with the gin guzzling? That position within our friend group is firmly reserved for Lanie."

I offer a half smile, trying hard not to allow my hands to continue shaking.

"Are you going to start clipping pictures?" Nina asks, and I shake my head. "I think I'm going to sit with my journal for a couple days. I'm not sure what words are mine in that thing."

Her eyes squint, and she's about to say something when Lanie addresses the group.

"Corinne is done with her board. How about you, Nina?"

She nods. "Mine is done."

Lanie claps. "Good. Will you share yours with us?"

Nina scoots closer to me. "What's wrong, Ally? Your hands are shaking."

I plan to tell all of them, but I need a minute to collect myself. I'm not even sure what to say. I'm seeing a ghost, and I think she's able to use me like a marionette?

"I'll go first," Corinne says.

We follow Corinne into the room, taking our seats as she walks to the front, facing the couch.

"My main objective this year is to hone my spirituality and build my career around it." She points to a section that says *Third Eye.*

"My goal is to understand the gifts I have and how they work," she says.

As she walks us all through, I'm surprised by how thoughtful her vision is. We're getting to see a different side of the typically sarcastic, moody woman Corinne presents to the world. She's radiating excitement as she explains how she'd like to utilize her gifts to help others.

It makes me think about my plans for my business and how I could really use another medium or someone who has gifts of their own. I stuff that away for another day. The time will come when I'm ready to involve others in my dream, but not now.

"Eventually, I want to open an entirely different type of spa. A place that focuses on healing."

"That's amazing, Cori," Lanie says. "Are you getting Reiki certified?"

Corinne's nose wrinkles. "Hell no. I'm not touching strangers. I'm hiring a Reiki expert."

"That's . . . great," I offer, not having a clue what that means exactly.

I'm still very new to this whole spiritual world, and that's yet another thing I tuck away—the need to research and learn more.

"What's with the stretch limo and seventeen handbags?" I ask, since nobody else does.

Corinne stands up taller, looking haughty when she says, "I want a driver. I absolutely loathe driving, and Darian said he's done being my chauffeur." She huffs. "And the bags are a necessity to my happiness."

"The driver seems far-fetched, and you could manage happiness with half those bags, but I digress," Lanie says. Corinne looks prepared to fight for her dream, but Lanie speaks up. "Nina's next."

When Nina doesn't move, Lanie repeats, "Nina, you're up."

Nina turns her board around, and my eyes widen. The others' eyes are narrowed in, trying to make out what they're seeing. Apparently, Nina came here tonight prepared to spill her guts to the collective.

She points to *personal development*. "After the last year, it's become painfully clear that I don't know who I am. That my identity has revolved around Richard and what he expected of me." She straightens her back. "This year, I want to find myself. To truly know me." She points toward the board and an image she's duplicated multiple times. "The mirrors represent that. When I look into the mirror, I want to know the woman looking back at me. I'm a multifaceted person, and I don't expect to be one-dimensional. I want to have layers."

For a moment, we all sit here, staring at Nina's board, speechless.

Of course, Nina is the insightful friend. She's the one with fancy terms to explain all our quirks, but it's rare that Nina has the spotlight on her issues. She's a private woman. She grew up that way, taught to not show the world her hand. Tonight, we're getting Nina uncut.

"That's . . . very deep, Nina. I'm proud of you," Lanie says, with a hint of awe.

Nina bows her head slightly and continues.

"The woman who looks like she's teaching represents my interest in expanding my coaching services. I'd like to mentor and coach women who are in similar circumstances as me. I want to help them rebuild all areas of their lives." She glances at me and smiles. "Help them with their second chance."

I suck in a breath. I had no idea that Nina was interested in leaving the school behind forever. The way she talks about this dream doesn't make me think it's a backup or second choice plan. She's excited about it.

My eyes scan her board, words jumping off the white background in bold colors. Red, yellow, and vivid shades of blue letters pop, and I'm not sure where to look first. I read the words several times.

Service.

I am more.

Find myself.

I belong.

My stomach twists with each phrase I read. Knowing just how lost Nina has felt is like a knife in my gut. How could I have missed her pain all these years? It was plain as day that she wasn't happy with Richard, but this goes so much deeper.

She wasn't happy with herself.

"The last image is a therapist. I want to seek help for the damage that has been done to me over the course of my life. From Richard, yes, but from my mom and her husbands as well."

Lanie's eyes snap to me—clearly about to speak—but I shake my head. I know what's to come. The secrets that Nina is about to share will clear up Lanie's confusion.

Nina moves to the next pillar.

"This year I want to focus on all areas of me, and one of the most neglected parts has been self-care. You can easily see on the board that my goal is to feel better about myself. To work out, get a new hairstyle, have someone teach me makeup tricks and tips, and lastly, to pamper myself at the spa, something I haven't enjoyed in quite some time."

"I'm in," Lanie says, raising her hand. "Let's do all the pampering."

"Me too," I say, raising my own hand.

Nina smiles. "I figured I could count on you two."

She peeks over at Corinne, who's looking down at her black-painted nails. "What the hell . . . I'm in too."

This pillar is a much-needed break in seriousness before Nina shocks Lanie with the secrets she's been keeping.

She moves on to the next. "I'm sure you two are looking at this part more than a little baffled."

"You could say that," Lanie drawls, eyes narrowed in on Nina's board. "Does that say *spirituality*?"

Nina nods. "I have a secret to share with you," she says, baring her teeth. "The night that Billy showed up, well . . ." She glances toward me, and I nod. "Alyssa wasn't the only one impacted."

Corinne's head snaps to Nina, eyes wide and mouth agape.

"After that night . . . I began experiencing a phenomenon. One I haven't enjoyed at all," Nina says, sighing heavily.

"When you touch someone, you see things about them," Corinne says, and now all eyes snap to her. Mine included.

"How do you know that?" Nina asks, eyes narrowed in on the brunette.

"I've been experiencing that same thing. The night we went to see my mother, I touched you and . . ."

"That's why you were odd with me," Nina says, mostly to herself.

Corinne nods, pulling her hair into a high ponytail and securing it with a black rubber band that she's had around her wrist.

"I saw you curled up on your bed, weeping like a baby. You were cradling a raggedy teddy bear." Corinne shrugs. "I didn't know why you were upset, but I saw it plain as day."

Nina swallows, bobbing her head.

"I'm so confused," Lanie says, exasperated.

Nina turns toward her to explain further. "When I touch people, I see private things about their lives. For instance, I touched a woman in the grocery store this week and saw her having an affair with a married man. Yesterday, the postal woman touched me when handing me my mail, and I saw that she's been battling cancer." Nina takes a deep breath, collecting herself. "I touch people and see things I shouldn't, and apparently, Corinne siphoned that ability too."

"I didn't siphon anything. It transferred to me," she bites out. "And for the record, you won't be touching me," Corinne says, pursing her lips and crossing her arms over her chest.

I make a face at Corinne, but Lanie just continues to stare at Nina in wonder.

"Wow, Nina. That's . . ."

"Sucky?" We all turn toward Nina with varying looks of surprise.

Sucky is not a word that Nina Dunbar uses.

"I was going to say *awkward*, but *sucky* works too," Lanie says.

"Sure is." Nina chuckles darkly. "And that's not all," she confesses. "I realized this was happening because I touched Richard and learned of the secret he had on me."

Lanie gasps. "Wait . . . are you saying you truly didn't know?"

"I had my suspicions, but I didn't realize he had uncovered something that I wanted to remain unknown. Something my mother went to great lengths to keep hidden."

Lanie's head tilts, and her eyes turn to mere slits. "What secret, Nina?"

She takes a deep breath and spills.

"I had a baby."

She tells the whole story, and nobody says a word through the whole thing. Even Corinne is quiet and melancholy. Lanie is clearly equal parts speechless and shocked. Her mouth has hung open the entire time, and the creases at the corners of her eyes tell that she's struggling to rein in her emotions.

"Which brings me to my travel pillar. I need to go to Providence. To search for Ian," Nina says, leaning forward. "To ensure he's alive. I'm ready to find out what happened to him."

"What about your son?" Lanie asks, practically choking on the word. "Have you searched for him?"

"I haven't, but now, I'm ready. I want to know that his parents were there for him in ways I couldn't have been."

Lanie nods, and Corinne bobs her head too.

"I don't want to interrupt his life," she continues. A tear slides down Nina's cheek, and she doesn't bother swiping it away. "I only want to know that he's okay."

"I'll be right beside you," I promise.

"Ditto. You had to know we were gonna help, right?" Lanie asks, sounding skeptical.

Nina's quiet for several moments, chewing on her bottom lip, but eventually she looks up and nods.

"I'm ready for all the help you're offering." Another tear slips down her cheek, and Lanie and I rush her, throwing our arms around her.

Every time I hear the story, it just gets sadder. It's clear that Nina never wanted to part with her son, or Ian for that matter. But she's the first to admit that at that time of her life, she wasn't responsible enough to care for another human being.

None of us would've been.

"You know, we don't have to wait to ensure Ian's alive." We all look to Corinne, who's picking at her nails, attempting to appear unaffected and failing miserably.

"We could do a séance right now," she says, and my breath hitches.

It only takes one glance at Nina to know that's exactly what's about to go down. She's wearing the same expression I must've worn the night of my birthday when the mention of a psychic came up. Determination. Hope.

This could go terribly wrong.

"Let's do it," Nina says, looking to me as if she can sense my unease. "Please."

Lanie catches my eye, and I know she's thinking what I'm thinking. Nina isn't in a great place currently. She's yet to find a therapist, which means whatever happens, the onus will fall on us to care for Nina.

I can only hope that Ian doesn't show up, because if he does, it might just break Nina completely, and I'm ill-equipped to handle that.

Within a half hour, Corinne has my kitchen transformed and ready to go for our impromptu séance.

Three tall candles flicker in the middle of the table. Their light dances around the dark room in a mesmerizing show.

Corinne has removed a leaf from the oval table, making it round and easier for the four of us to join hands. I found a dark tablecloth to cover the light wood, recreating the night at Cori's Nail Spa as close as possible.

The last time we did a séance here, Charlie Dunbar appeared before being thrust back into his body, ultimately surviving his wounds. He possessed Corinne in order to speak with us, and with my latest issue with the poltergeist, I'm not so sure I want to open any of us up to a hostile takeover.

Positive thinking. No ghost shall enter my body.

"Leave it to Alyssa to assure her backside is protected," Lanie quips, and I crease my nose.

"What the heck is that supposed to mean?" I fire back curtly.

Nina chortles but doesn't agree or disagree with whatever Lanie is implying.

"It means you've conveniently chosen the only seat that backs up to a wall, leaving the rest of us exposed. And might I add that you're the only one who can actually see spirits."

"So . . ." I drawl, not getting her point.

"*So* it would've been grand of you to give one of us the safe seat," Lanie explains.

I make a face. "Don't be an idiot. I'm actually saving you."

I've come a long way, but I haven't completely left the ranks of chickenshit, and knowing a spirit could manifest itself, I likely did subconsciously position myself in this seat. But I am sure as hell not going to admit that to these girls. I'll never live it down.

One of Lanie's eyebrows lifts skyward.

"Think of it this way," I start, determined to make it sound like I thought this through. "I'll see them coming . . . you won't. I make the most sense to have a clear view of the open spaces."

Nina grins, Lanie rolls her eyes, and Corinne shakes her head, clearly not buying what I'm selling.

"Are you ready? I don't have all night," Corinne barks, getting into position, placing both hands on the table with her palms facing the sky. "Besides, it's nearing midnight, and that's when we're most likely to attract wayward spirits that we don't want to encounter."

"Cranky Corinne has come out to play," Lanie jests, but Corinne doesn't open her eyes or make a face. She ignores Lanie completely, getting prepared.

"I'm with Corinne," I say, placing one hand on top of hers and the other on top of Nina's. "No wayward spirits tonight, ladies."

They all murmur their agreement and get into place.

We are all connected in a circle, and I know what's coming. Another show worthy of Broadway, by Madame Corinne. Except it isn't a show. The combined energy in this room is more than capable of truly summoning spirits.

Corinne takes a deep breath, and then blows it out before launching into her over-the-top monologue, calling to gods, goddesses,

Mother Earth, and about ten additional deities, before finally finishing her outreach to the spirit world and going silent.

All I can hear is our intermingled breathing and Nina's foot incessantly tapping against the wood, a sign of how nervous she is.

"I call upon Ian Whalen. If your spirit can hear me, follow my voice. Join us. I have a friend here who's been looking for you," Corinne calls out, eyes remaining closed.

She's quiet for several moments, and we wait, but nothing happens. She peeks one eye open, looking around before closing it again and falling back into her deep breathing.

"I call upon Ian Whalen. Ian, come to me." Corinne shouts this last request, and I jump but manage to keep my hand in hers.

Again, a few quiet moments roll by, and no spirits or noises are to be heard.

I'm about to call this a bust and celebrate with Nina that he must be alive when the television in the great room turns on.

"Guys," I say. "Something is here."

All heads snap to me, and I tip my head toward the family room.

Nina's breath hitches, and Corinne groans. "Great. Another poltergeist. Alyssa, why, pray tell, do you always seem to attract the angry ones?"

"We're working with a feisty spirit?" Nina attempts to appear calm and casual, but her voice shakes, giving away her fear.

"Yes . . . and let me tell you . . . it's not what I wanted to deal with tonight," Corinne grumbles, obviously missing the anxiety pouring off Nina.

The television stops on the Lifetime channel. A body is being dragged out of the water and placed into a bag.

"That's morbid," Lanie says, and I shiver. "Should we be worried, Cori?"

I'm shaking, not from the image on the television, but from the woman who flashes into existence right next to the mantel. The dark-haired girl that I've been seeing turns her head, which is the first time I've seen her move any part of her body. She's angled toward the television as if to point out something that's important to her case.

"What are you trying to tell me?" I ask, leaning toward her.

"Who are you talking to?" Corinne whispers, but I ignore her, focusing on the woman.

The TV channel switches again, stopping on the ID channel. There's a girl that looks a lot like the spirit, closing out a tab at a bar and saying goodbye to her friends. She walks out to a dark parking lot, where her car is parked in a far corner away from the lights of the bar. A man comes up from behind and grabs her.

I run through all the things that I've been shown since her first appearance to me. It seems plausible that the ghost is using the images to detail how she died. I begin to spit out guesses, hoping that she can convey when I've said something accurate.

"You were murdered by a strange man." She blinks out of sight and then returns.

I'm not sure if that's confirmation or not, since she's played the disappearing act every time I've seen her.

"It happened while leaving a bar?" Again, she flashes away.

"Your body was tossed in the bay?"

She doesn't return, and I wonder if she's departed when the volume flicks off mute and the word *dead* blares through the speaker. Everyone but me shrieks, ducking their heads.

"No shit," I deadpan. "Kinda guessed that." I inhale through my teeth and try once more, running through the possibilities. "You were murdered by a man, leaving a bar, and dumped in water."

A piercing noise that sounds like something a banshee would

produce echoes through the house. Our hands fly to our heads, but as quickly as it started, it stops.

The television shuts off, and the woman blinks in and out one final time.

"What the hell was that?" Lanie yells, jumping up from the table, head spinning around the room, searching for something that she'll never find.

I blow out a breath, lips flapping at the force of air. "Sit down," I instruct, and she does. "I guess it's my turn to make a confession."

Corinne narrows her eyes on me.

"Christmas Eve, I saw a woman across the street, wearing a sparkly red dress. No shoes. I deduced by her appearance that she's spent some time in a body of water. Her hair was wet and matted to her head."

"You mean Char was right?" Lanie says, sounding amazed.

"It would appear so," I say. "I knew pretty quickly that the woman was a poltergeist. There were many similarities between her and Jenna Cruz."

"What similarities?" Corinne asks, kneading at her head.

"Just the way she presents herself. She never talks. Hardly moves aside from flashing in and out."

"That's . . . creepy," Lanie says, shoulders shaking.

I nod. "I've seen her a couple times since then, but more recently, she's been seemingly using the television to try to communicate with me." I glance over at the table where my journal is sitting. "Tonight, I believe she possessed me to send a message in my journal. I wrote *stop him* hundreds of times with no memory of it."

"That's . . . not good," Corinne muses, eyes narrowed as she appears to ponder this development.

"Do you know who she is?" Nina asks.

I shake my head. "I haven't gotten that far. Like I said, she's not come around much. With Ava around, I couldn't really investigate."

"Good call. We don't need to freak Ava out," Lanie says.

"I planned to bring it up tonight, but Lanie came here with a very specific plan in mind, and I kind of forgot."

"You kind of forgot about the poltergeist?" Corinne's mouth is wide, and she blinks several times, looking at me as though I'm the world's biggest idiot.

"What the heck is wrong with you? Those are not entities that you want to mess with," Corinne barks. "Help them and send them on their way." She throws her hand up into the air. "At the very least, cleanse your space and see if you can just get her to go away on her own."

"I know that. And I have been taking precautions," I snap.

Okay, so . . . maybe I haven't really taken any precautions, but the woman doesn't exactly scare me. Aside from looking creepy, she hasn't done anything that gives me the impression she will hurt me.

Aside from possessing my body.

"So far, the poltergeists I've come into contact with have been frightening, but not harmful," I explain.

"But that is not every poltergeist situation, Alyssa. Have you never seen *Amityville Horror*? Or *Poltergeist* for that matter?"

"Well . . . no . . ."

"You should, because you need to know what you're dealing with. They're not entities to mess with."

"You've said that," I say, and she cuts me off.

"They're angry, and anger fuels rage, and rage is how a human ends up hurt. If not worse. You could end up dead . . . killed by the dead people." Corinne's hard eyes stare into mine as if she's trying to burn her words into me.

My head falls back with a moan. "Okay. I got it." I huff. "I will look into it as soon as possible, but right now, I think that something great just happened, and nobody seems to have noticed but me."

"What good possibly came of that?"

"I've got to side with Cranky Corinne," Lanie says, making a face. "Poltergeist does not equal great."

I look to Nina. "It's good, because Ian didn't show up, which means he could be alive."

She blinks several times, and then a smile extends from one side of her face to the other. Her brilliant white teeth shine against the dark backdrop of the room.

"Oh my god. You're right, Ally." The relief is instantly visible. The color comes back to her face, and the creases at the corner of her eyes have diminished.

"That is great news," Lanie says, bouncing her head. "That I can agree with."

"So if that's the case, where do you go from here?" I ask Nina, not bothering to concern myself with whatever nonsense Corinne is going on about in the background. She's been harping on the poltergeist, and while I get the urgency to move the spirit along, right now, I just want to celebrate this win with my best friend.

"I head to Providence," she says. "I start my own investigation. If he's alive, someone there should know how to locate him."

"Why Providence?" Lanie asks. "If he's no longer a TA there, isn't it likely he's gone?"

"That's the place he was last known to be. I'll start there because I don't have any other leads," Nina says.

I take a deep breath. "I'm coming with you," I say. "Ava's leaving to head back to school. I have plans with Nick for New Year's, but any time after that, I'm good to go."

Nina nods, looking to Lanie.

"Nins, you know that I would, but I can't cancel all my classes on such short notice. If you think you're gonna be there for a while, I can try to cancel the following week."

Nina shakes her head. "No. Don't do that. There's no reason

for all of us to drop everything to go on a wild-goose chase." She sighs. "We have no idea where he is, or what he's up to. I don't want any of you to put your lives on hold to help me with this."

"I have nothing else to do," I say. "I'm coming, and that's all there is to it."

She smiles. "I'll be happy to have you with me."

"Good luck, you two," Corinne says. "I'm with Lanie. I can't ditch my clients." She taps her chin. "But we can help from back here. If you stumble across anything, and you need me to read cards or perform another séance, all you have to do is call."

"Thank you; I appreciate that," Nina says.

"Now . . . about that poltergeist," Corinne starts, scowling over at me. "Let's look and see if there are any missing persons in the area that match your ghost."

"I'll grab us all another round," Lanie says, popping up from the table and heading toward the kitchen.

"How old do you think she is?" Corinne asks, and I purse my lips.

"Early twenties, maybe." I think about the woman and the details I paid attention to. "Based on the dress she was wearing, it looks like she had been at a party. I don't know if the scene on the ID channel completely matches her situation, but the girl had been at a bar. So, let's assume that she's at minimum twenty-one, and at the oldest, I would say twenty-five."

Corinne pulls out her laptop and starts it up. "What does she look like?"

I search my memory and recall as many details as possible.

"Long brown hair." I suck air through my teeth. "Her eyes were black pits, so no clue on eye color." A shiver runs over me as I remember the most disturbing fact about her.

"When she was up close, it was obvious she had been in water. I don't know if she was drowned or dumped in afterward, but her skin was wrinkly, and her hair was soaking wet and sticking to her face."

"You mentioned the wet hair earlier, and that's actually very helpful," Corinne says, typing quickly. "That pretty much narrows it down to bodies of water. Based on how you're describing she was dressed, I can narrow the search down even further."

She continues to type away, not elaborating.

"What are you thinking?" I ask, when it becomes clear she has no intention of sharing yet.

"I think it's safe to assume she was at a bar or club close to the city. So I'm looking for missing persons around the harbor area. Feels like it would be a good start."

I don't ask any more questions, agreeing with Corinne. I allow her to work, utilizing her sleuthing skills to search the web for missing persons, while Nina, Lanie, and I concern ourselves with pouring more drinks.

It's going to be a long night for the Gin and Tarot Club.

Page of Cups

"I'M AFRAID THAT when I get back to school, none of my pants are going to fit me," Ava says, patting her stomach.

She's just managed to eat a double cheeseburger that was almost as big as her head.

Milly's is known for their burgers and large portions. People from all over New England come to town just to dine here.

"Don't be ridiculous. You have a metabolism I would die for," I reply, stuffing my mouth full of french fries. "Plus, what's life if you can't enjoy yourself?"

Ava sighs, picking up one more fry, and dragging it through a mound of ketchup before eating the red-coated potato.

"It's just so good. Milly's has the best food." She moans. "There's nothing close to it near campus."

I chuckle. "You have Sub Shack."

She eyes me with contempt. When your options are limited to one place, you quickly grow tired of it, and that's Ava's current predicament. Her love of turkey and cheese is ruined.

"I'll raise your meal-plan allowance if you're not using the gift card I got you."

She shakes her head. "I will. I just need a month—or two—break. I mean, they know me by name there."

"Not hard. The town isn't much larger than Knox Harbor, kiddo."

She sighs before taking a long sip of cola.

I chuckle, dipping my head toward her plate. "Eat up, girlie. It'll be a while before you're back."

Her lips turn down into a pout. "Don't remind me. I really wish I hadn't agreed to go to Sammy's. I want more time with you. It went too fast."

I smile. "Me too, baby girl, but it's an amazing opportunity. Sammy's family, from what I've been told, throws incredible parties."

At orientation, I met a few local women who were familiar with the Cartwright family. It's an honor to be invited, and something the local kids strive to achieve. It's about as big a deal to score an invite to one of their yearly gatherings as it is to rush on college campuses.

Their gated mansion rests on twenty sprawling acres of rolling hills and mature trees. It's old and ostentatious, having been passed down for centuries. Generational wealth that stems from railroad ties, apparently. Now they breed and train horses, many of which, I've been told, have been Kentucky Derby winners. Two even won the Triple Crown. Money is no object to the Cartwrights, and their parties showcase their wealth.

"From what Sammy has said, the party is going to be next level. The favors last year for the students were pairs of Birkenstocks. They had a whole room of various styles, colors, and sizes. Like . . . how?" Her eyes sparkle, and a broad smile lights up her face.

She leans forward, eyes scanning the area. "You don't think they're dirty, like Richard Dunbar?"

My head jerks back. "No. Why would you think that?"

I hate the rumor mill and the fact that Ava was filled in on all the details before I had a chance to tell her myself. The last thing I want is for Ava to distrust people.

She sighs. "I don't really think that, but how in the heck do people amass that much wealth without being crooked?"

I sit back in my chair, shrugging a shoulder. "Not everyone with money is a bad person, Ava. A lot of wealthy people work hard for what they have. Sammy seems like a great kid, and you like her, right?"

She bobs her head. "I do. She's one of my closest friends at school. And she isn't snobby or pretentious."

I smile. "Then that's all that matters. You'll have an amazing time."

We're quiet for a few minutes. Ava's focused on finishing the food on her plate while my eyes shift around the diner, taking in the few people eating around us.

The usuals are all accounted for, but there are a few unfamiliar faces seated at the counter bar.

Knox Harbor was recently featured in a magazine as one of the most idyllic small towns. Ever since, a string of tourists have descended, mostly East Coasters from nearby states, to check it out.

Christine and Milly are the only two working the floor, while Pete's in the back, manning the grill with his new assistant. I think I remember Milly saying his name was Brett, but I could be wrong.

"Everything okay?" Christine asks, making the rounds.

"All good here, Chris. I'll take the check."

She smiles and rushes off toward the server station.

"How are you doing, Mom?" I turn my head toward Ava, taking her in.

The worry I saw last time she asked me such a question is absent, which is a relief. I didn't want her worrying about me then, and I sure as heck don't want her worrying now.

I've come a long way since October, and I hope that she can see that. Seems as though she does.

"I've asked about Aunt Nina, but not you. She's like your sister, and I can only imagine how difficult it's been for you to watch her go through this." Her eyes lower to the table. "I've had a hard time dealing with what she's going through," she admits.

It hasn't occurred to me to have a deeper conversation about things with Ava. I'd hoped to brush it off and not concern her with the messy details. It was bad enough she knew. But Nina is her godmother, and I should have realized that Ava isn't a baby anymore. She deserves the truth.

"It's not easy to watch," I confess. "But your aunt is strong."

Ava toys with her cup, not meeting my eyes. "She is, but sometimes I wonder how much of it is an act."

Ava has always been so perceptive. Since she was a child, she saw things that most adults would have missed, too busy going about life to stop and look around.

I lean over the table, because talking about this out in public is dicey. Nobody needs to know Nina's business any more than they already do.

"She's an adult, and she doesn't want other people fighting her battles. I'm trying to respect that."

Ava offers a close-lipped smile, not liking that fact any more than I do.

"We only want to protect those we love," Ava says, sounding far too sad for my liking.

"I know, Aves, but it's not always possible. We just have to be here for her and follow her lead."

The door above Milly's chimes, and in walks a group of women, all wearing red hats.

"I think we should change the subject," I whisper, motioning with my head toward the door.

Her eyes enlarge and she makes a face in confirmation. Ava knows all about the Red Hatters and their penchant for gossip.

Today, however, there's a somberness to the typically chatty group of women. Their heads are bowed, and a sense of gloom hangs in the air.

"What's going on with them?" Ava asks, and I shrug.

"Alyssa. Ava," Nan Jenkins says, moving toward the front of the pack, face puffy and mascara stained. "It's so nice to see you two out and about."

This is just her way of digging in to see how I respond.

I know her games, and I refuse to play them.

My head tilts to the side, one eyebrow lifted as I take her in.

She's wearing a pair of denim overalls with a white-collared shirt underneath. Today, her red hat is understated—a ball cap with large white peonies across the brim.

"Is something wrong, Mrs. Jenkins?"

She sniffles, standing up straight. "It's awful. Truly awful."

I'm about to ask her what's awful, but she barrels ahead with a barrage of questions.

"How's Nina? Nick West?" Her whole demeanor shifts from melancholy to meddling in a matter of seconds.

"Fine," I say, looking around to her friends, who are all still rather subdued for the Red Hats.

"Just fine?" she asks, leaning forward as though I'll impart some secret to her.

"Holy moly," Ava hisses from across the table. "Get the hint, lady."

Mrs. Jenkins turns to her, and I smother a laugh.

"What was that, dear?"

Ava makes a point of looking down at her phone, trying to cover up her outburst.

"Sorry, I spoke out loud." She lifts her phone into the air. "My professor is sending emails during the holiday, and nobody is responding."

She shrugs and Mrs. Jenkins huffs, turning back to me.

"You know, you missed out on helping with the Christmas carnival."

Nope . . . didn't miss out on a thing.

They ask for help every year, but really, they just want bodies to do the work as they bark out orders. They aren't interested in ideas or changing things up.

I pass.

"You could always help us scout the area for the missing girl," she says, so nonchalantly I almost miss the remark.

"A missing girl?" She puckers her lips, nodding her head so aggressively that flowers detach from her hat, falling to the floor at her feet. She doesn't so much as flinch.

"We could use your help." I go to speak, but she raises her voice, pressing forward. "It's Esther Long's granddaughter after all."

I'm not familiar with Esther Long, but it's still sad to hear.

"I really wish I could help, but Ava leaves today."

She lifts her hand. "Say no more. Your time with her is valuable. It goes so fast."

I nod and give her a polite smile, hoping she'll leave it there.

"Maybe you can help with the Fourth of July festival?"

No such luck.

I suck air in through my teeth. "I'm going to be all tied up for the next few months. Probably all year," I amend. "I've started my own business—"

As soon as the words leave my mouth, I wish I could take them back. The last person that I need to know about my business, before it's even off the ground and running, is her.

"You did? I didn't see anything come through the chamber."

I take a deep breath and shove down my irritation.

"Because it's still in the creation process. When I'm ready, I'll inform the chamber."

It's an ordinance that every business being operated within Knox Harbor has to register with the chamber. It's just a way for them to siphon more money from locals and have their business in everyone else's.

She claps her hands together. "Very good. I'll eagerly await the details. You'll have to tell me all about it sometime. Right now, I'm going to go have lunch and console my friend." She glances over at their table. "We have a busy day ahead."

"Good luck. I hope you find Esther's granddaughter," I say, and Ava parrots my words.

"Alyssa Mann, is that you?" I hear yet another voice I was hoping to avoid today. Mrs. Hampson shuffles over, smiling wide. "You have to come next door soon. I have some new dishes I think you would love."

I internally cringe. The last time I bought anything from her shop, I ended up attached to a ghost that was less than friendly. He damn near ruined things between Nick and me before they even had a chance to begin.

"Another day. Ava's leaving to go back to school."

Ava looks at me crossly, knowing that it's an excuse.

She doesn't have a clue about what went down after that visit to Marmalade and Rye, because it's not something a young girl needs to be concerned with. Besides, Ava's made her feelings on the subject of ghosts known.

I give her a stern look that I hope reads *Keep your trap shut, kid*, and thankfully she appears to get the hint.

"I'm closed for the remainder of the day, so soon will suffice." She leans in, getting close to my ear. "I have a situation that I was informed you may be able to help with."

I lean back, narrowing my eyes in on the frail woman. "What situation exactly?"

"One we shouldn't discuss here, dear. It's . . . sensitive." She glances around the room, appearing skeptical of those around us.

"If it's important, maybe you should call the police?" I suggest, having no idea what I could possibly help her with.

"What does a donkey know about compote?" She waves a hand in the air. "No. This is a matter that only you can help with. I'll see you soon, Alyssa," she mumbles as she walks off, not even offering a goodbye.

Ava's eyes are trained on Mrs. Hampson's back, narrowed. "Did she just call you a donkey?"

I shrug, shaking my head. I've been called worse.

"In this instance, I don't believe I was the donkey." I chuckle, shaking my head.

The more I think on it, the more my gut tells me that someone has clued Mrs. Hampson in on my ability. Most likely Gloria.

Freaking fantastic.

✦ ✦ ✦

I HAVE AVA wrapped in a tight hug, not ready to say goodbye. We just did this back in October, but it never gets easier. While I'm proud of Ava and happy she's chasing her dreams, I miss her.

"Please drive carefully, and as soon as you get to Sammy's, call me," I say, giving Ava a stern look that's entirely unnecessary.

I shut the door and blow her a kiss. She returns the gesture, waving with one hand before backing out down the driveway. I watch her until she's out of sight, taking a piece of me with her, just like she does every time she leaves.

I need to do something. Otherwise, I'll end up crawling back on the couch and sulking because Ava's gone.

I quickly shoot off a text to Nick, deciding to invite him to dinner.

ME
Do you have plans for tonight?
Wanna have dinner at my place?

He doesn't respond, so I go about my day, cleaning up the house and doing laundry. An hour later, my phone dings.

NICK
I'd love to, but I have the flu.
Whatever Jack had . . . I've got it.

ME
Oh no! Can I do anything to help?

NICK
I'm good. Thanks for asking.
Jackie is here cleaning.

ME
Feel better!

If he's been throwing up, I'm sure he won't want to eat, but when he's feeling better, he will. I go through my pantry to locate things to add to a care package, shoving what I find into a weaved basket that belonged to Garrett's mother.

I'm just walking up the sidewalk when the front door opens and a female version of Nick steps out the door.

I've seen Jackie once or twice lately as she's come and gone from Nick's, but I can't help but notice how similar they look. She's quite a bit younger. Tall, dark hair, and beautiful blue eyes.

"Alyssa, right?" she says when she sees me.

I smile, offering an awkward wave. "Yes. Hi."

She returns the smile, running her eyes over me in a way that makes me feel a tad insecure.

"It's so nice to meet you. Nick's told me a lot about you."

My cheeks heat, and warmth spreads all over my body.

"I came to bring him a care package," I say, lifting the basket into the air.

She grins. "That's so sweet of you. The guy's house is completely bare. I was just running out to grab some things."

I look down into my basket. "I have soup, Gatorade, ginger chews, a cold compress, antacids, Metamucil, and lemon-ginger tea."

She whistles. "You covered all the bases. I can tell you're a mom."

I chuckle. "Guilty."

She looks back toward the house. "He's really at the end of this flu. He's weak but he hasn't run a fever or thrown up in twenty-four hours. I just disinfected, so you should be safe to go in. If you want."

That last part is said like some sort of challenge. As if she's sizing up just how serious we are, using my decision as the answer.

"Do you think he'll mind?" I say, pressing my teeth together.

Jackie grunts, waving a hand in the air. "Men don't care about that stuff. At least, Nick doesn't."

She's probably right. Garrett wouldn't have thought twice about allowing me to be around him sick, aside from the fear of me catching it.

"I'll take my chances."

She smothers a grin, bobbing her head. "Thanks for looking out for him. I . . . think he'll be set until tomorrow with all that," she says, gesturing to the basket. "Guess I'll head home."

"I'll let him know," I say, moving to the side to allow her to make her way down the steps.

She stops at the bottom, turning to look over her shoulder at me. "I'm looking forward to getting to know you better when he's up to it," she says. "Don't let him tell you he's fine. He's bored out of his mind."

I nod. "I'll sit with him."

She smiles widely. "See you around." She waves a hand over her shoulder, sauntering to her car with the grace of a dancer.

The snow-covered driveway would be enough for me to tiptoe, but she doesn't miss a beat, easily gliding over the slick white powder with ease.

Heading inside, I move straight to the kitchen, placing the perishables into the refrigerator and depositing the basket onto the table.

"Jack?" Nick grumbles from the couch.

I turn to find him facing the TV, sprawled out on the couch, under a blanket that appears to be made for a child. It's not, but due to his size, it's completely inadequate.

"It's me. Alyssa. I brought over some supplies, and Jackie asked me to sit with you for a while."

He turns around, offering a lazy smile. "She shouldn't have asked that of you. I'm fine."

I place a hand on my hip. "You're not. You look pale as death."

"That sounds ominous. Let's hope the stomach bug doesn't take me out. Not a manly way to go."

I smirk. "You had a different way of going out in mind?"

He makes a face. "Don't we all?"

My nose wrinkles. "Umm . . . no. A tad morbid and very premature to think about dying, don't ya think?" I tilt my head. "I've had enough death for a while."

He grimaces. "Well . . . when you put it that way . . ."

I smile. "Okay, sick boy, what are we doing? It's three o'clock, and I have some time to kill."

He licks his lips. "You really don't have to sit here with me. Jackie is overbearing as hell and bound and determined to play matchmaker, no matter how you feel about it."

I laugh. "Lucky for her, I kinda like you. And for the record, I was coming over here to check on you well before I ran into her." I glance around the room, looking for another blanket. One that will actually cover the man. "Where are your blankets?"

"What's wrong with this one?" he asks, lifting the small navy fleece.

"For starters, it's small enough to belong to Zoey."

He chuckles. "Fair point." He motions toward the hall. "You can grab my comforter. Jackie just ran it through the laundry. It should be on my bed."

I nod, heading toward the back of his house, until I find his room at the end of the hall. It's the only door that's open. The bed is made, but the black comforter is folded and draped at the end. Moving forward, I reach out to grab it when something falls, the noise coming from what appears to be the adjoined bathroom.

I peek around the corner to find a bottle of Tylenol lying on the floor. Jackie didn't mention when he last took medication, so I grab the bottle and the comforter on my way out.

"Have you taken anything lately?" I ask, lifting the bottle of pain meds.

He purses his lips. "No, actually. I'll take two of those. If you don't mind?"

I smile, making my way to the kitchen and grabbing a glass of water before offering the pills and water to Nick. When he's done, I remove the small blanket, draping his comforter over him.

"There," I muse. "Much better."

He sighs, lying back. "Thank you. This is better," he admits.

Nick points toward the massive TV hanging from the wall. "Wanna watch a movie?"

I take a seat right next to him on the couch, snuggling into the comfy cushion. "What are we watching?"

"You choose," he says, eyes trained on me. One corner of his lip is twitching as he suppresses a smile.

"Nope," I say, popping the *p*. "We have a rule at my house. Whoever is sick makes the choice."

His lips tip down, and he looks at me with a blank expression, as though his brain is foggy and he can't even drum up the name of a movie to suggest. He pouts his full lips, and it's adorable. I would imagine not many people have gotten to see Nick West like this. Vulnerable and laid back.

"What's something you've wanted to watch but never gotten around to?" I ask, hoping to spark an idea, because I do not want to have to choose. It'll take an hour for me to settle on something. It was a complaint that Garrett had often. If it wasn't movies I struggled to choose from, it was restaurants or paint colors. Really, any decision. For the most part, those days are behind me, because I have no choice. There's nobody to take the reins.

Except for today.

Nick chews on his cheek.

"A series, maybe? We've got time to kill," I offer.

His eyes widen. "*Lord of the Rings*? Would you watch those?"

I smile. "I'll definitely watch those."

I've seen them before, but it's been years. It's one of those franchises that Garrett would sometimes just have on in the background while he read or worked.

He pulls up a streaming app, searching for *The Fellowship of the Ring*, while I quickly check my phone, in case Ava texted.

She didn't, but I put the phone on vibrate so I'll be alerted if she does.

"You know, you don't have to sit clear over there," Nick says.

I glance at the small amount of space between us. If I move closer, I'll practically be on his lap. My cheeks warm at the thought.

"You're sick," I say, managing to scoot just a tad bit closer.

He frowns. "I'm not contagious."

"That's not . . ." I shake my head. "I only meant that I want you to be comfortable."

He pats the spot next to him. "I think I'll be rather comfortable with a gorgeous woman sitting next to me."

"Flatterer . . ."

"Is that a word?" he asks, grinning from ear to ear.

"Sure is," I say, smiling and sliding the few inches to seal the gap between us.

Our legs touch, and I just about melt into the cushion when Nick places his arm around me, pulling me farther in to his side. It's been so long since I've cuddled with a man, and it hadn't occurred to me how much I missed such a simple thing.

He lowers the comforter over our legs, and I settle in, completely comfortable and not at all awkward. I smile to myself, remembering my conversation with Ava surrounding said awkwardness. This feels good. It feels . . . right.

We're halfway through the first film when my eyes get heavy. I feel Nick's large arm pulling me down next to him, draping around my middle. We're sprawled on his couch, spooning. My hand is by my side, holding his.

This is the closest we've been, and it feels wonderful. It's something I've thought about on a few occasions—being with him like this, like a real couple. But reality is better than I could've imagined. Sadly, I'm too tired to bask in that for long.

"Close your eyes, Lyss. Get some rest."

Not long after he suggests it, I fall asleep, snuggled in Nick's arms.

Six of Cups . . . Reversed

MY EYELASHES FLUTTER, and I stretch my hands over my head, hitting a hard mass next to me. I pop open one eye.

"Boo." A woman with long, red hair is bent over me, smiling.

I screech, hands thrashing through the air as I twist and land on my back on the floor next to Nick's sofa.

"What?" Nick flies up, bending over the side, peering down at me. "What's wrong?"

I blink several times, trying to regain my composure. Light filters in from the floor-to-ceiling windows lining the back of his house.

It's morning.

We fell asleep and slept through the night.

"I . . . I'm not sure," I say, rubbing at my forehead, rising to a seated position on the floor. "A woman. She . . ."

I shake my head. "Sorry, I must've been dreaming."

Clearly, there was no woman. The house is empty of anyone other than us, ghosts included.

He chuckles. "You're a hazard to yourself. I should probably put bumpers up on your bed."

"Ha ha," I say, stretching once more and ducking my head so he doesn't see the way my cheeks are coloring. I can feel it. "So . . . looks like we had an impromptu sleepover."

Nick grins. "We did." He holds out his hand, and I take it in mine, allowing him to pull me to my feet and back down to the couch. "I hope there's more of those. Maybe next time, we can move to the bed. It's a little more comfortable."

My toes tingle, and a shiver races through me at the thought of sleeping in Nick's bed.

"Are you going to turn strawberry every time I mention my bed, Lyss? We could always get it over with. If that'll help." The wide Cheshire-cat grin doesn't fall from his face as his eyes sweep over me.

I choke on my own saliva. "I'm not shy. I just . . ."

He chuckles, shoulders shaking. "I'm just messing with you."

"You're awfully playful today," I say, pulling the comforter over me—a layer of protection against Nick's roaming eyes.

Not that I don't like it. I do. A lot. It's just my body is prone to cluing him in on just how much I like it.

"You make me laugh," he says, shrugging.

"It would appear you're back to normal." I pat his leg, and he smiles.

"You're my own personal elixir." He pulls me down and places a lingering kiss on my mouth. "Want breakfast?" His husky voice washes over me and my shoulders shiver as my eyes close, relishing the way he makes me feel.

I nod, unable to use words, completely lost on cloud nine.

"I need to freshen up," I say, moving to stand.

He points down the hall. "I have extra toothbrushes in a basket under the sink."

I narrow my eyes at him and prop one fist on my hip. "Are you trying to tell me something?"

"Nope. But I do plan to kiss you. Many times. So hurry up, will ya?"

I lick my bottom lip before rushing off, eager to get back to kissing. I'm about to enter the guest bathroom when Nick calls down the hall, "Use mine."

I continue toward the back of the house and his room. I was in here for only a minute yesterday, so I take my time looking around.

It's clean and very masculine. Gray walls and black accents everywhere else. There's not a pile of dirty clothes to be found. Then again, Jackie was here cleaning just yesterday. But something tells me that Nick isn't messy. His sister might be behind the organization, but he maintains it.

Under the sink, just where Nick said, I locate the extra toothbrushes, overflowing in a white, labeled basket. I grab the first package and start brushing, refusing to look at my rat's-nest hair, which will be the second order of business before breakfast.

I sigh, content with my fresh breath and prepared to work out my tangled hair, but when I look up into the mirror, the redhead from earlier is behind me, smiling like a lunatic.

"Who are you, and what do you want?" I say, grabbing at my heart and spinning around.

Her eyes are like saucers. "You can see me."

I grab the towel from the rack and hold it out in front of me, as if it's going to save me from the peppy ghost girl. I'm not afraid of her, just overwhelmed by her.

She's a spirit, but not the poltergeist I've been seeing. This one seems a little too happy for being dead.

"You can see me," she repeats, bouncing on her toes.

I tip my eyeballs north and nod my head. "Yes, I can see you, but how about you answer my question . . . Who are you?"

"My name?" she asks, biting her lower lip. "Let's call me . . . Pearl."

"Pearl?" I narrow my eyes at her. "Why do I get the feeling that is not, in fact, your name?"

She shrugs. "It is. It's even on my birth . . . and death certificate. At least, I guess it would be. Can't claim to have seen that one."

I purse my lips, taking her in. "Do you remember anything about how you died?" I ask, trying not to come across as insensitive.

She swallows, turning her head away from me. "I don't want to talk about that."

Her mood instantly changes. Gone is the girl who was just bouncing around. Her posture is tense, and her arms are crossed over her chest.

I take a step forward, prepared to place a hand on her shoulder, but pull away before making that mistake.

"I understand, but if you're here, you likely need my help crossing over," I say, voice calm and soft.

She shakes her head. "No. I don't. I choose to be here."

My head jerks, taken aback by her tone. "Oh, okay. You're choosing to stay with me or . . ." I let my sentence hang, hoping she'll fill in the blanks.

"I don't even know you. I'm not here for you," she says, rolling her eyes.

"Then who exactly are you here for?"

She huffs, seemingly annoyed with me. "Clearly, I'm here for him," she says, pointing out the door and toward where Nick is.

My head snaps to her face, and I run over every feature. And that's when the truth hits me.

"You're . . . Isla."

She narrows her eyes on me, sucking her teeth. "You know who I am?" she asks, and I nod.

"Of course I do. I've lived in this town for many years. I've met your mother on a few occasions."

The last encounter I had with her mother comes to mind, and I shiver, thinking about her less-than-friendly brother.

"I even helped Oliver cross over recently."

Her eyes widen. "What? What are you talking about? Cross over where, exactly?"

My mouth snaps shut.

She doesn't know. And how could she? Ghosts don't have carte blanche to roam. Whoever they're stuck with, or whatever they're tied to, determines where they go and what they see.

"Have you been here ever since . . ."

"No," she snaps, turning her head away from me. "For a long time, I traveled wherever he traveled. Until . . . recently."

I blink, trying to understand what she's not saying. Instead of pushing her and taking the chance of making her angry, I change the subject.

"When you said you choose to stay, what do you mean?"

She clears her throat. "I couldn't leave him. Especially after what happened in the following months. He needs me."

She's referring to the alcohol and how he crumpled into himself when she died.

"I'm sorry, Isla. I can only imagine how difficult that must've been for you to witness."

I mean every word, and she must recognize that, because her shoulders relax, and the deep frown she was wearing moments ago melts away. Her bottom lip trembles.

She lowers her head. "Especially since there was nothing I could do to help. I had to watch him fall apart, and it broke me." She huffs a humorless laugh. "If that's even possible for a ghost."

I offer a sad smile to the woman. "I lost someone I loved too. I can't claim to know how it's been from your side of things, but from this side, the survivor side, it's the worst pain imaginable."

One eyebrow lifts. "You did? May I ask who you lost?"

I bob my head, smiling sadly. "My husband and I were in a car accident, and he didn't make it."

Her eyes widen, and her hand lifts to her mouth. "That's terrible. I'm sorry . . ." She purses her lips. "What's your name?"

"Alyssa. Mann. I live next door."

"The widow," she says, mostly to herself. "I heard Jackie talk about you when she was here yesterday."

"That's . . . nice to hear," I admit, smiling a little too wide, considering the ghost I'm here with.

She rolls her eyes. "Don't get too used to it. He'll only push you away. He's bound and determined to be alone." She doesn't say this to be harsh. If anything, she sounds frustrated by it.

I tilt my head to the side. "And you know this how?"

She sighs. "Nick talks to me sometimes at night. He doesn't know I'm here, but he confides in me. Tells me his plans for the future, and how he wishes I were here to experience it all with him."

I swallow a lump that's formed in my throat. I know far too well what that's like. I often talk to Garrett about my day and my hopes for the future, for me and Ava.

"So . . . if you know who I am . . . do you know that we're . . ."

"Dating?" she says, and I nod. "I kind of worked that out while you slept next to him last night. Nick has never had another woman that isn't family here."

She looks around as if he's nearby and will overhear. She leans in. "Listen, I'm here to help. I think you have the best chance of making him fall in love with you."

I open my mouth to say . . . something, but find myself just blinking instead.

I lift my hands to stop her. "Whoa . . . Isla . . . nobody's falling in love here. We just started seeing each other."

She bats her lashes at me, pursing her lips. "While that might be true, I can help you move things along faster."

My nose screws up, and I shake my head. "Thank you, but that's not necessary. I'm happy where things are."

"Then you need to step aside and leave him alone."

She's back to stiff posture and that annoyed frown.

"What's . . . happened here? Why the shift?"

She bites her bottom lip. "I lied. I'm actually . . . stuck here."

It's my turn to frown. "You said you chose to stay. Now you're stuck? Which is it?"

She groans. "A part of me needs to know that Nick will find love again. And that part of me has the whole of me," she says, waving down the length of her body, "stuck."

Good lord. Why does the universe feel the need to make each and every case of spirits in my life disastrous? As bad as I thought it was to have Billy tailing me, having access to Nick's fiancée is worse. Much worse.

It feels wrong on so many levels.

"While I appreciate the confidence you have in me, I'm not on board with tricking him into love."

Her mouth drops open, and her head shakes. "Who said anything about tricking? I'm not sure you're the one either; I just want to help you along to see if you might be."

My eyes narrow in on the lovely ghost, wondering what I did in this life to deserve the crazy that seems to come my way.

"Alyssa? You okay?" Nick calls down the hall. "Food's ready."

"He cooked for you." She doesn't really say this to me. There's something sad about her words, and I want to ask, but think better of it.

I have no business knowing things about Nick's life that he himself hasn't chosen to share with me.

"I'm coming," I yell back, turning toward Isla. "Look . . . while I appreciate the situation you're in, I can't help you. You need to figure out how to get all sides of yourself on the same page and move on to the afterlife." I take a deep breath, because what I'm about to say will be hard for her to hear. "Your brother, Oliver—he recently passed."

"I know," she says, and my head juts back.

"But . . . earlier you acted like you didn't know," I say, confused.

"I knew, I just didn't realize that he stuck around," she explains. "Remember when I said Nick talks to me?" I bob my head. "He told me about my brother. Said he hoped we were together."

I sigh in relief, glad to not have to be the bearer of unhappy news after all.

"Well . . . he did stick around, because he had some unfinished business with your mom." Her eyebrows lift, and I press on. "He had money stashed that he needed her to find. I helped facilitate that."

Her face lights up, eyes bright with a light that hasn't been there since she first appeared. "Thank you. I . . ." She shakes her head, laughing lightly. "I can't thank you enough for that."

I shrug. "It was either help him or be forced to endure his wrath. No offense, but your brother was not exactly charming."

She titters, covering her nose with her hands. "Don't I know it."

"I gotta go," I say, motioning toward the door.

"Talk to him about the Jets. He's a huge fan," she says to my retreating back.

"I know nothing about the Jets. I hate football." It's not entirely true, but I'm not about to push this idea of matchmaking she has going on.

"Why? Football is fun." Her voice pitches, and I smother a grin before turning over my shoulder to look at her.

I make a face. "I find it boring."

She huffs. "Fine, then . . . ask him about his motocross days."

"What's motocross?"

Another way of pushing the idea of love out of her head. Of

course I know motocross. Garrett had his own dirt bike back in the day.

She takes a step back, eyes wide. "Okay, never mind. You're hopeless. I need to find the next contender."

"Sorry, Isla. Better luck next time."

She pats her heart and makes a frustrated sound.

I rush back toward the kitchen, thinking about all that I've just learned.

"Did you find everything you needed?" Nick asks, glancing up from the stove at me.

"Yes. Thanks."

His head tilts, and a lopsided smile spreads across his face. "You didn't find the hairbrush?"

"What?" I ask, patting my head and moving toward the oval mirror hanging on the wall.

Holy shit. I have a tangled mess on top of my head. I'd been so distracted with Isla that I didn't even bother to brush my hair.

"Wow. Yeah, I got tied up. Checking my phone." I shrug, baring my teeth in an awkward smile.

"That phone?" he asks, pointing to my cell phone that's sitting on the coffee table, right where I left it when I headed toward the bathroom.

I lift my arm, thanking god that I have on my Apple Watch. I hadn't looked at it once, but it's there and gets me off the hook with my little white lie. There's a text from Ava.

> AVA
> Remember the cheerleader that was
> drunk at the game a few years back?

My nose crinkles up as I try to recall who she could be referencing. Ava was never into Knox Harbor athletics, but Garrett took her to a game or two because there was an all-star quarterback that the entire state was buzzing about on our team. Garrett wanted to watch the kid play.

ME
Not really.

AVA
It was a big deal because her uncle
was a cop.

ME
Not sure, hun. What about her?

AVA
She's the girl that's missing.
The one Mrs. Jenkins and the hats were
looking for.

ME
Hopefully they find her.

I glance toward Nick, watching as he flips a pancake over.

"You made pancakes?"

He shrugs. "Everyone likes pancakes."

When I don't say anything, his face falls. "Do you not? Like pancakes," he asks, and I smile.

"I love pancakes."

A lazy smile falls over his face, and a sigh escapes his lips.

"Everything okay?" he asks, motioning toward my phone.

"Yeah. Ava was just telling me about a girl who's missing. Know anything about it?"

He lowers his head, turning his attention back to the pancakes. "Yeah, unfortunately. It's my captain's niece. She's considered a runaway though."

Either way, not knowing where your child is must be the worst feeling for any parent. I would be beside myself if it were Ava.

"Her parents must be worried sick. I would be," I admit.

"They are, but this isn't the first time that Chelsea has run off. She always turns back up."

Another text comes in, and I look down to see that Ava has sent me a photo. When the picture loads, my mouth drops open.

I stare at the photograph, a sinking feeling washing over me. The young woman captured in the image, smiling wide in her cheerleader uniform, is more than familiar. It's her, the girl in red, and the grim reality crashes into me.

She's dead.

"What's wrong?" Nick asks, placing the spatula down and turning off the stove.

I run my hands down my face, trying to formulate words. Nick knows about my ability. He asked me to use it to contact Charlie Dunbar while he was in his coma, stuck between worlds.

So why is it so hard to answer the question?

"Alyssa . . ."

I look up and push down my fears. Helping this young girl find peace and move on is more important than worrying what people will think of me.

"She's dead, Nick."

Eight of Swords

Nick

I SUCK IN a deep breath, taking in what Alyssa has just said. I can tell by the way she's looking at me that she's fearful I don't believe her.

I do.

I know she wouldn't claim this lightly. We're talking about someone's daughter, and Alyssa's not the type of person to purposefully hurt others. However, it could be easy to mistake Chelsea for someone else. Especially considering that it doesn't seem as though Alyssa knew her personally.

"Are you absolutely sure?"

She pulls her bottom lip into her mouth and clutches her elbow.

I lean forward, catching her gaze. "I believe you. I'm only making sure the ghost—or whatever you saw—was Chelsea. She's my captain's niece. It's important that I get this right."

She swallows, bobbing her head. "It was Chelsea. I saw her on Christmas Eve. Mrs. Fields did too."

My mouth slams shut, head moving back slightly. "Mrs. Fields?"

"That's why she was outside that night. She saw the girl staring at my house. She just didn't realize she was a ghost."

I place both hands on the counter, lowering my head. How the hell is Mrs. Fields seeing ghosts now? What's happening in this town?

"This is not good," I say, mostly to myself.

"No, it's not. It's a terrible tragedy."

I rub at the back of my neck, the stress mounting with every minute that goes by. This is going to be a total fucking nightmare.

"I believe she was murdered," Alyssa says, frowning.

My eyes widen, and my hands ball into fists. I'm not sure how my mind didn't immediately go to murder. I suppose I was hoping it had something to do with drinking too much, which I've been told has been an issue for her.

"She's shown up a few times, and the way she presents herself is very reminiscent of Jenna."

I remain quiet, allowing her to explain further.

"It's clear that she died in or was dumped into a body of water. Her hair is soaked and matted to her face."

"Shit," I curse under my breath. "Alyssa, this is a fucking mess for so many reasons."

She grimaces.

"What else can you tell me?" I ask, opening a drawer and pulling out a notepad and pen.

I need to jot this all down so that later, I can review everything she's said.

"Not much, honestly. Everything else would just be speculation."

"Humor me?" I say, writing down the description she gave of Chelsea's ghost.

"I believe she's trying to communicate through the TV. She'll turn to channels that show girls that resemble her leaving bars and being approached from behind. Whoever killed her was a stranger."

My eyes close, and I pinch the bridge of my nose. I'm not sure there's anything I can do that won't have the captain infuriated. You don't go around claiming someone is dead without a body.

"I can't take this to my captain. He won't believe it." I frown, apologetic that more people aren't open-minded about her ability. "He's not as receptive to things that can't be explained by science."

"I get it. You don't have to apologize, Nick. I'm not sure I'd fully trust it if it weren't happening to me." She smiles, and I know it's to ease my worry where her feelings are concerned. "So, what are you going to do with the information?"

I lick my bottom lip, peering up to the ceiling. "I'm going to call in a tip to Falls Haven PD. That's where she's been living and working and where she was last seen."

"I don't believe they took her far," she says, eyes narrowing to mere slits. "I'd suggest looking at the docks."

I grab my phone and make the call. It rings several times, and I'm just about to hang up and try again when a woman finally answers.

"Falls Haven PD."

"Hi. This is detective Nick West of Knox Harbor investigative unit. I've gotten an anonymous tip for an unidentified missing female."

"Go on," she says, and I can hear her typing on the other end.

"The caller said to check the docks area for the missing person. They insinuated whoever she is, she's deceased."

"Did the caller give any additional details on the missing person?"

"No. They only said I should reach out to Falls Haven with the information. I was unable to trace the call, unfortunately," I say, knowing that question was coming.

"I'll send someone out to check the docks. Thank you, Detective."

"Thank you."

The line goes dead, and I wonder if the woman will actually send someone out. The tip was so anonymous and generic, and with it being New Year's Eve, I'm sure they're busy as hell.

"When her body is found, it's going to send the captain into a tailspin. Especially with how busy we already are trying to tie up the Cruz case." My head falls back. "I can't imagine how hard this is going to be for her family."

"It's the worst possible thing that could ever happen to a parent. My worst nightmare."

I wince, seeing the way Alyssa's features are pinched. Even talking about this has her mind on Ava.

"It's moments like these I'm happy to not have kids. I'd be a nervous wreck. I'm not sure how you do it, Alyssa," I say, shaking my head.

"I won't lie; it's tough. Every time she walks out my door, I worry. Having her so far away makes it all the worse." She shrugs. "But I wouldn't change it for anything. She's made life so much better."

At one time I thought I'd have a whole houseful of kids. My life was mapped out with the white picket fence and Isla barefoot and pregnant. It wasn't meant to be.

"I wanted kids back in the day," I admit, catching Alyssa off guard, if her expression is any indicator. One eyebrow is lifted to the sky, and her mouth is gaped.

"Four boys and one little princess?" she says, and my head jerks back.

"What?"

She blinks several times, mouth opening and closing.

"Nothing, I was just thinking about what Garrett and I once discussed."

My breath quickens and my palms sweat.

What she's just said is exactly what Isla and I had talked about so many times. Down to the exact description. It was Isla's dream to have a big family.

Alyssa lowers her head. "That is now out of the question. No more kids for me." She doesn't appear sad, more worried when she delivers this information.

Does she think that would change things for me?

I'm forty-five years old; my days of wanting kids are long past gone. If anything, what she's said makes her even more perfect in my eyes. We're on the same page.

Not that children or marriage is even a topic of discussion at this point, but if she were saying she wanted those things, this would be over before we got started. I can't give her or anyone else kids. I took care of that right after Isla died. That would've been my life with Isla, but we were robbed of it, and I knew I wouldn't want that with anyone else. Ever.

She's chewing on her bottom lip, eyes misted.

"What's that look for?" I ask, leaning toward her. "I'm okay with it. I didn't really know how much time my work was going to eat up. I should've, considering my father was FBI, and I saw how much he worked." I place a stack of pancakes on a plate and slide it over to Alyssa.

"Syrup is in the cupboard." I jut my chin in the direction of said cupboard.

"I don't know how some people do it. Garrett and I were a team, and I know I couldn't have gotten through those early years with him gone a lot for work."

"Exactly. It's easy to create fairy tales until real life gets in the way. I would've hated leaving my family behind for work. Probably would've grown to despise it." I chuckle. "Funny how life works out. I can't imagine not being a detective. My work is so important to me."

She tilts her head to the side, bobbing her chin. "Your life could look very different, that's for sure." She locates the syrup and places it on the counter between us.

"I likely would've gotten out of law enforcement and gone into sales or something like that." I make a face, because the very idea of me wearing a suit and peddling products is utterly ridiculous. "I would've enjoyed my family but hated my work." I place my hand over hers, looking into her eyes. "Life has a funny way of knowing what we need more than we do."

My eyes bore into hers, and she flushes all over, eyelashes fluttering.

"I never would've thought I'd be standing in your kitchen. Not like this, that's for sure. But here I am."

I smile, walking around the counter, trapping her between my arms, leaning in. "Here you are."

I brush my lips against hers, and she sighs into it. Something crashes behind us, and Alyssa's head falls against my chest with a groan.

"What's wrong?" I ask, pulling back to look into her eyes, momentarily forgetting about the noise.

"I don't think you're ready for that information."

I frown. "Try me."

She looks up, cheeks coloring a pretty shade of pink. "Can we not talk about ghosts for a little while?"

My eyes widen. "Is it Chelsea? Is she here?"

Alyssa swallows, head shaking back and forth slowly. "Someone else." She sighs heavily. "I'll tell you soon, but for today, can we just enjoy the pancakes?"

I grin. "Yes. We're not letting perfectly good pancakes go to waste."

She smiles, her face instantly relaxing.

Her phone dings, and I glance down at the counter to see Nina's name lighting up the screen. She moves under my arm to grab her phone, and I take that opportunity to check my own.

I have a voice message from a number I don't recognize.

"Nick? Nick West?" I recognize the voice, vaguely, but can't place who the woman is. "Oh . . . sorry. Hi, Nick. This is your neighbor Patty Phillips. Could you give me a call, please?" She rattles off her number and I jot it down, realizing she's the middle-aged mom of three who peddles popcorn through the neighborhood with a uniformed second-grader every year.

I chuckle to myself at Patty's initial confusion. It's not like my recording doesn't make it clear that it's my voicemail.

Moving toward my hallway, I give her a call while Alyssa is occupied. It rings twice before she answers.

"Hi, Mrs. Phillips. This is Nick West, calling you back."

"Thank you for returning my call. I need your help. My Christmas sleigh, which I spent a lot of money on, was stolen from my front yard overnight."

"Do you have a door cam? Any idea who might've done it?"

I'm not even sure why I'm asking. This isn't my jurisdiction, and I'm off the clock. What I should do is give her the non-emergency number to the station and call it a day.

Old habits die hard, and one of mine is helping people even on my time off.

"Well . . . no. We don't have a camera. But our neighbor does."

I nod, even though she can't see me. "I'd suggest stopping by and asking if they can check their footage. Regardless, you should contact the station and file a report."

"Can't you head over and ask for the footage?" Mrs. Phillips asks, sounding annoyed with me.

"I'm sorry. There's not much I can do, honestly. I work in homicide."

She prattles on about not having time and how it's New Year's and she has plans. I inhale and exhale, rubbing at the center of my forehead, allowing her to vent.

"Mrs. Phillips, I'll stop by and see what I can do."

Her tone immediately changes. "Bless you, Nick. Happy holidays."

The line goes dead before I can respond.

"Happy holidays," I say, putting the phone back on the counter.

"Everything okay?" Alyssa calls down the hall, and I head back toward her.

"Another neighbor had something stolen from their yard. I need to contact the PD and set up patrol for our street at night."

"Yikes. I don't love hearing that."

"Thankfully, the thief hasn't attempted to break in. It's all been yard decorations taken. I wouldn't worry too much about it. Just take in anything you don't want stolen."

"I'll do that." She looks down at her phone, smiling wide.

"What are you smiling about?"

She lifts her head from her phone, placing it back on the quartz countertop.

"That was Nina," she explains. "We planned a girls' trip. We're leaving Wednesday for a week."

"Anywhere good?" I ask around a bite of pancake.

Alyssa's eyes are fixed on my throat, and I have to smother the grin that wants to spread across my face, recognizing the heat in her eyes.

I clear my throat, and she tears her eyes away from my neck, cheeks turning a dark shade of pink as she looks anywhere but at me.

"Providence."

I make a face, the word coming out of nowhere.

"That's where we're headed," she says to clarify.

"That doesn't sound like a fun getaway. It's freezing there." I take another bite of my pancakes.

"Let's just say that it's kind of like a job."

I lift an eyebrow but don't question her further. If she wants to tell me, she will.

"It's Nina's story to tell," she explains. "But if she's good with me sharing it with you, I will." She searches my face, likely trying to determine if I'm insulted.

I'm not. I know the drill, and I can appreciate her loyalty to her friends. It's an admirable quality. One that few people possess these days.

"Fair enough."

She blows out a breath, looking relieved.

My eyes catch on the wall clock, seeing that it's nearly noon. I need to run some errands before tonight, including to the dry cleaner to grab my suit. Thankfully, they're open today until four, so I have some time.

"We're still good for tonight, right?"

Her mouth forms an O. "Oh, shoot," she says, and I tilt my head to the side.

"If you have other plans, it's all good—"

She cuts me off. "Yes. I mean . . . no. I don't have other plans. I want to spend New Year's with you."

"Why do I feel like you're panicking?" I chuckle, watching as she looks at her phone.

"I don't have anything to wear. I need to run to the mall today." She stands, taking her plate to the sink.

"Leave it. I can clean up," I say, knowing that she's stressed.

I remember the days when Isla would act the same way, and it never failed—she always looked gorgeous. So will Alyssa. The woman could wear a paper bag and still manage to capture all my attention.

"Don't go overboard. Be comfortable. I'll like you in whatever you wear, Alyssa. I can promise you that."

My eyes roam over her appreciatively. She must notice, because that flush spreads over her neck.

"While I appreciate that, I want to find something new," she says, voice hoarse. "It's been a while since I've gotten dressed up and hit the town. I'm looking forward to it."

I grin, standing to move toward her. "Me too," I say, pulling her into me, leaning down to press my mouth against hers.

We're tangled up in each other when I hear clapping and giggling.

Alyssa groans, pulling away.

"Did you hear that?" I ask, brows furrowed as my eyes scan the area. Based on Alyssa's reaction, she did.

"Yes," she says gruffly. "I told you. We aren't alone."

I stagger back, blinking in disbelief.

I heard that. I . . . heard a ghost.

My head shakes. "How did I . . ."

"Hear her?" Alyssa shrugs. "No clue. Have you noticed a presence here? Heard anything before?"

"No. I mean . . ." My head shakes. "No. I haven't."

She smashes her lips together. "Interesting."

I take a deep breath, running my hands through my hair. "Who is it?"

Alyssa's shoulders sag, and I can tell she doesn't want to answer that. She pulls on her ear, biting the inside of her cheek.

"Alyssa," I drawl, and she blows air out of her mouth, lips flapping.

"Don't shoot the messenger, please." She grimaces, crinkles forming around her eyes. "It's Isla."

The wind whooshes from my chest, and I feel lightheaded.

"Sit down," she says, but I wave her off. "You look pale."

"I'm fine," I lie. "I just need a minute."

Or a lifetime.

There's no part of me that was prepared for Alyssa's admission.

It can't be Isla. There's no way. I'd have known if she were here.

"Nick," Alyssa begins, but stops, sighing heavily. "She's been here the whole time, but I only just met her today."

My head aches, and a million questions come to mind, but I can't formulate a single word.

"She's here because she wants to know you're okay and that you'll be happy."

I swallow down the emotion swelling within. I'm not an overly sensitive man. I can handle crisis and tragedy like none other. I deal with it on the daily. But this . . . this is too much.

"I just need time," I say, not knowing what else to say.

She nods. "Take as much time as you need. We'll cancel tonight. I don't need to—"

My head snaps up. "We're not cancelling tonight, Alyssa. We're going. I'm only asking for a couple hours to process this."

I take a step toward her, grabbing her hand. "This is strange, but it isn't your fault. You've done nothing wrong."

The relief that washes over her face makes me feel for her. I can't imagine how hard that was for her to tell me.

"Thank you, Nick."

I pull her into a hug, hoping to help ease her further. "I'll walk you to the door."

Without dropping her hand, I walk to the front of the house, opening the door and leaning against the frame, looking down at her. "I'm really looking forward to tonight."

She smiles, leaning up on her toes and placing a quick kiss on my lips. "See you tonight."

And with that, she's bounding down the steps, heading toward her house. I watch her until she's out of sight, not exactly thrilled to be headed back inside.

I'm not afraid of ghosts, and I'm certainly not afraid of Isla, but it's like I said . . . strange. What do I do? Do I talk to her? Assure her I'm all right and she can move on?

Do I even want that?

Yes.

Isla deserves peace.

I start to shut the door, but stop, frowning.

Someone stole my damn wreath.

The Hanged Man

"I'M SO EXCITED for you, Ally," Nina says, pinning a piece of my hair back. "Tonight is going to be good for you."

I watch through the mirror as Nina continues to tuck pieces into various places, looking like an expert as she does it.

"You should really have considered cosmetology. You're really good," I say, smiling at my friend through the mirror.

"Yeah, right. Can you imagine my mother's horror if I had suggested such a thing?" She looks up, widening her eyes and crinkling her nose.

"It's exactly why you should've."

She laughs. "Well . . . while I do enjoy occasionally dabbling in hair placement, it's not my calling."

I turn around to face my friend. "You do whatever you want. This is your life, and we only get one to live."

She nods. "It's why I plan to help women. It's something that I know will fulfill me." She blows a piece of her hair out of her face. "Despite my mother forcing me to get my PhD, I truly love what I do."

"I know you do," I say, smiling.

"So, tell me all about your plans for tonight," Nina says cheerfully. "Aside from the sleeping arrangements." She winks.

"Oh god. Did you have to remind me? I'm so nervous, Nina."

She tilts her head. "Why? It's not like you haven't had sex. You should be a pro by now."

I make a face, rolling my eyes. "It has nothing to do with that. It's so much worse."

She quirks a brow but doesn't speak, giving me the floor.

"This morning when I woke up at Nick's, I saw a woman."

Her eyes grow wide. "The woman in red?"

I shake my head. "Nope. This particular ghost is no poltergeist."

Her face relaxes and she chuckles. "Well, that's good. Isn't it?"

I level my gaze at her. "It's Nick's fiancée, Isla."

She splutters, mouth dropping open and then closing several times. "What?"

"She told me she believes she's stuck here because her spirit can't leave until she knows he's happy."

"Isn't he?"

I shrug. "She believes she needs to see him happily with someone else."

"That's . . ."

"Awkward?" I offer, smearing my top lip with a color called Bombshell.

"I was going to say morbid for her."

"That too," I say, tilting my head left and then right, marveling at how plump my lips look when I've finished.

"So, she's okay with you being with him?"

I grunt, turning back toward Nina.

"I don't know. She said she's feeling me out." I run my palm over my thigh, thankful I haven't put my dress on yet. "She doesn't like that I'm not a fan of football."

She purses her lips. "You don't *hate* football."

I shrug one shoulder. "I didn't tell her that. I don't want her interfering, Nina. It's . . . uncomfortable."

"What reason could she have for caring about your opinion on football?"

I shrug again. "Your guess is as good as mine. It's not like I could really drill her, considering Nick was in the house, right down the hallway."

Her eyes widen. "You didn't tell him?"

"No, I did."

Her breath hitches. "Oh god. What happened?"

My hands lift to my sides, palms facing the ceiling. "I mean . . . he about fainted."

She bobs her head, chewing on her nails. "This is bad. I can't believe he didn't call off tonight."

"I know. It shocked me too, but he was so good to me, Nina. He went out of his way to ensure I was okay, when it was him who had his world rocked."

"He's a good man," she says, patting my shoulder. "And you did nothing wrong. You can't help which spirits barge into your life."

I sigh. "We can't have sex tonight. She's attached to him." My voice pitches.

"Yeah . . . that would be a little more than awkward." She bites her top lip. "What are you going to do? You have to help her move on."

"I don't know. Honestly." I link my hands in an attempt not to touch my hair. That particular nervous habit would not serve me well tonight. "How do I get him to prove to her he's okay, without looking self-serving? I just feel like it's a conflict of interest that it's me that needs to send her on her way."

"I'm not following your logic," Nina says.

"What if he doesn't want her gone? What if he thinks I'm pushing him? I don't want him to resent me if she goes away."

Nina looks me in the eye and smiles sadly. "You'd want Garrett to stick around if he were here?"

My head shakes back and forth violently. "No. I'd want him to be in paradise with his parents."

"Then Nick probably feels the same way. Maybe you should see Corinne's mom. Have her help with this one."

My head jerks back. "Pass. She's intimidating."

"She's downright scary," Nina says, shivering.

In the end, having someone else help Isla move on might be in my best interest.

"But you might be right. If she has the answers I need, then I have to go to her."

She bites her lip, inspecting my hair and appearing to find something off.

"So, tell me about the party," she says, changing the subject to things that are less stressful.

"We're going to some hotel in Silverton. All I know is that we're being fed and the drinks are bottomless. They'll have a band until eight and then a DJ takes over until two a.m."

She snorts. "Does Nick know how much caffeine he'll need to feed you in order to make it to midnight?"

I laugh. "I'm not that lame. I can hang until midnight." I glance down at my feet, which are currently bare. "That's if my feet cooperate. The shoes I bought were not a good idea."

I glance at the offending shoes I purchased at the mall with contempt. They're beautiful and my legs look incredible in them, but they're killer and I'm not accustomed to wearing such a large heel.

"If I fall, I'll die."

She laughs. "If you fall, he'll catch you."

I sigh, watching that scenario play out in my head. There's nothing embarrassing about Nick holding me in his arms. But reality would not look like that.

"What are you doing tonight?" I ask.

I should have considered Nina when making plans for tonight. The least I could've done was spend this New Year with her. After all she's been through, I'm not sure she should be alone.

"Don't," she warns, and I look up at her, confused. "Don't feel bad for having fun, Alyssa."

"Who said I was feeling bad?" I ask, one eyebrow raised.

"I know you, and I know that face you're making." She huffs a humorless laugh. "I don't need you to sit around with me. I'm perfectly capable of picking out a book and pouring myself a glass of wine. You forget, I don't have FOMO over parties. I much prefer quiet and a good glass of merlot."

I smile because I know there isn't a shred of deceit in those words. That is Nina's ideal night, and I doubt she's been allowed to enjoy many of them until recently.

"You'll have a lovely night if that's what you're planning." And then I get an idea. "Why don't you stay here? I won't be home tonight. You can have my comfy bed and stay somewhere that doesn't feel like a prison."

Her eyes light up, and she smiles wide. "Are you sure?"

"Yes. I should've suggested it earlier. You are always welcome here, Nina. Hell, if you want, pack a suitcase and move in."

She blinks, and a tear runs down her cheeks. I quickly stand, pulling her into my chest.

"Nina. Don't cry," I coo into the side of her head.

"I couldn't do that to you."

I pull back, narrowing my eyes on her. "Why the heck not? I want you here."

"It's just . . ."

"If you're going to say it's my second chance, I might slap you. I'm an adult, and so is Nick. If we want privacy, we'll go to his house. It's not like it isn't very convenient."

She nods several times. “I’ll think about it.”

I lift my hand and place it on her cheek.

“I want you here. It’ll be good for me just as much as it will be for you,” I say. “I can’t take care of this place all on my own.”

Not entirely true, but I’ll say whatever I need to convince her. I know she needs to get out of that place, and why shouldn’t she move here?

“I’ll let you know soon.”

I nod, stepping away and looking back to the mirror to swipe away mascara from under my eye.

I glance at the clock. “Shit. I need to get dressed. He’s going to be here any minute.”

My phone pings, and I see Lanie’s name lighting up the screen.

LANIE
Is Nina there?

ME
Yessss . . . why?

LANIE
I need her tonight.

ME
Care to explain?

LANIE
Ugh. I will in 5 . . .

She doesn’t say anything else and neither do I, because I’m running out of time. I pull my dress from the closet. It’s a black, bodycon wrap dress that hits just below mid-thigh and shows just enough cleavage to be sexy, but not too revealing. It complements my figure perfectly and looks amazing with the red-soled shoes I spent far too much on.

When I'm dressed, I take a look in the mirror, twisting to see the sequins sparkling under the light.

"Wow, Ally. You look fantastic."

"I have you to thank for that," I say, pulling my best friend into a hug. "Thank you, Nina."

The doorbell rings and Nina squeals. "He's here."

I take a deep breath and grab my overnight bag from beside my bed, making my way downstairs, not bothering to put on my shoes yet. Not until I'm down the stairs and safe from falling to my death.

I pull open the door, and Nick's on the other side under the blinking porch light that clearly needs to be fixed.

My breath hitches at the sight of him in his black tux, hair slicked back, making him look like a movie star. He's absolutely gorgeous.

"You . . ." His words trail off, and a goofy grin spreads across his face. He leans in. "You are breathtaking."

My toes curl, and my entire body heats.

He's about to say something when Lanie comes racing up the stairs, practically pushing him out of the way. "Sorry, Nick," she says over her shoulder. "Where's Nina?"

I turn to point toward the kitchen, then turn back to Nick. "I'm sorry. She has zero manners."

He chuckles. "I've known Lanie Anderson long enough to know that when she's on a mission, you get out of her way."

I lift both brows, inhaling deeply.

"Are you ready?" he asks, continuing to sweep his cerulean eyes up and down my body.

I feel the heat spreading all over, and I have to swallow to collect myself.

"Ready."

He holds out his hand for my bag, and I give it to him. I place the killer shoes on my feet and don't miss the way Nick's eyes darken as he takes in the entire package.

"Bye, ladies. Happy New Year," I yell out, and hear it echoed back. I'd love to give them real hugs for the holiday, but based on the way Lanie arrived, they're likely in deep conversation. I do not have time to get involved in whatever that is. If it were important, they'd tell me before allowing me to leave.

Nick helps escort me to the car, which is very appreciated. There are still patches of black ice, and the last thing I need is to ruin tonight before it gets started by breaking my ass on the sidewalk.

He starts up the car and we're off. Nick keeps glancing at me out of the corner of his eye, and I wonder what he's thinking. Is he excited for tonight? Or are his thoughts still on what he learned today? I want to ask him, but his phone rings, cutting off my chance to speak. He glances at the screen on his dash and curses under his breath.

The screen is lit up with the name Grayson.

"It's my captain," he explains. "I've gotta grab this."

It's not a question, but he's staring at me like he's awaiting my permission.

"Of course," I say, sitting back into the car seat, getting comfortable for the thirty-minute drive we have ahead of us.

"Captain," he says by way of greeting.

I watch the side of Nick's face, but he doesn't give anything away. He's a stone fortress, holding in his thoughts on whatever is being said on the other line.

He mumbles words of understanding and agreement, and I think it's over when he says, "I'm very sorry for your loss, Captain. I'll catch the sonofabitch responsible."

They found her.

He presses the End button and sighs, glancing over at me, a look of regret shining through his stony features.

"I'm so, so sorry, Alyssa . . ."

He doesn't have to say another word. I already know what's coming.

"They found Chelsea." It's not a question. It was clear from the conversation.

He huffs, pulling the car off to the side of the road. His head falls against the headrest.

"It's all right, Nick. I understand," I say, hoping to alleviate some of the anxiety radiating from him.

He shakes his head. "They did, and you're right . . . it's bad."

I want to ask. I really want to, but I've learned in the short time I've known Nick that some things aren't meant to be shared in his line of work.

"They found her body in Falls Haven, and they suspect foul play," he says, which is more than I expected to get. He sighs heavily. "My captain is losing his shit."

I place my hand on Nick's leg, squeezing lightly.

"We knew this would be the case. I'm just glad they found her. I'd love nothing more than for Chelsea Grayson to move on."

He blinks several times, and I'm sure he wants to ask questions, but he doesn't.

"Captain wants me to head to the scene and work the case with the local authorities."

"You can do that? Work in another city?" I ask, recognizing there's still a lot for me to learn. Especially if I'm going to be starting a business where I cowork on cases.

"Captain got special permission since it's outside our jurisdiction. They agreed but specified that he can't work the case."

"He's too close to it."

Nick nods. "I'm surprised they're allowing me to assist." He blows out a harsh breath. "I was really looking forward to tonight. I feel like shit, ditching you."

"Like I said, I understand. You've got a job to do."

And I do. It doesn't suck any less, but this is his job, and considering Chelsea is a relative to the captain, what could Nick possibly do? It's not like he could refuse.

"I'll be fine. It appears that Lanie doesn't have plans, and I know Nina really didn't. I'll hang with them. Maybe we can try to get Chelsea to move on."

He grumbles something, running his hand back through his hair and messing up the carefully styled locks. "It's a fucking shame that nobody but me and your friends gets to see you in that dress, Alyssa." His husky voice and darkened eyes make my blood pulse in my ears.

"We'll just have to find another event for me to wear it to."

He smiles, leaning over and kissing me hard. I melt into him, opening my mouth to his tongue and relishing this moment. If it's all I get, I'll take it greedily.

He pulls away, head against mine as he groans. "I'm sorry."

Most would think he's apologizing yet again for needing to bail tonight, but I know that's not what he's referencing. I could feel the shift in his kiss. The way he was all in and then suddenly withdrew.

He thought about Isla.

He's likely wondering if she's here.

I clear my throat, pulling away and sitting up straight. "She's not here."

Nick doesn't speak, but I see the way his chest expands.

"I'll make this up to you. I promise," he says, and I wave a hand in the air.

"All good."

Nick turns back to the wheel, putting the car in drive and making a U-turn in the center of the next cross street. We're heading back toward my house, and the silence is heavy. Neither one of us says a word, making it uncomfortable.

He pulls into the driveway and puts the car in park, turning toward me.

"Thank you for being so easygoing about this. I know you're disappointed. I am too." His eyes shift, and his fingers tap against the steering wheel.

I can tell he wants to say something but is struggling with it.

"Nick, I—"

He cuts me off. "I didn't mean to act weird when we kissed. It's just a very tricky situation for me. Isla is gone, and I know that. Even if her spirit is lingering. But I'd be lying if I said a part of me didn't feel terrible thinking about her seeing me with someone else." He grimaces. "Does that make sense?"

I nod once. "Perfect sense, and I understand. Truly, Nick. It feels wrong to me too, and I didn't even know her."

He takes a deep breath, tapping the steering wheel again. "We'll figure this out."

I smile and grab my bag, opening the door to climb out.

"Be safe," I say. "Send me a text when you make it to your destination."

"I will." He runs his hands back through his hair again. "Happy New Year, Alyssa."

One can only hope.

Two of Wands

"WHY ARE YOU back?" Nina asks as I slink my way into the house, shutting the door behind me.

My shoulders slump as I drop the bag to the floor with a harrumph.

"He got called away to a homicide." It's all I offer, and neither one of them presses.

"So . . . no sleepover tonight with the hot cop?" Lanie purses her lips, pouting for me.

I shake my head. "Nope. That is on hold until further notice."

"I'm sorry, Ally," Nina says, rushing toward me to give me a hug.

I chuckle into her shoulder. "It's all good. I get to spend my night with you two now."

Nina pushes me to arm's length, inspecting my face. "You're allowed to be disappointed, Alyssa. Own your feelings so you can actually have a chance at a good night."

I huff. "Thank you, Dr. Nina. I shall endeavor to own my dissatisfaction."

She purses her lips, narrowing her eyes at me. "Sarcasm is not a good look for you."

I stick my tongue out before leaning forward and placing a kiss on her cheek. "I'm honestly good, Nins. If my plans were going to fall through, I'm happy to have you two here."

Lanie claps her hands together. "Great. We have another accomplice," she says to Nina, who raises her eyebrows and gives me a look that screams *You'd better run*.

"What are you needing an accomplice for? Do I even want to know?"

"Lanie had a dream," Nina says, widening her eyes for effect.

I turn to Lanie, whose head is lowered as she rocks back on her heels. "It was a nightmare. One that's going to come true if I don't heed its warning."

"You're shook by a *dream*?"

She glares at me, apparently picking up on my incredulity.

"It was more than a dream, Alyssa. It was a warning."

In all the years I've known Lanie, she has never been easily shaken. If anything, she's poked fun at Nina and I for acting the very way she is now.

"What was this dream about?" I ask, taking the cursed shoes off my feet and throwing them off to the side, happy to be done with them. Lanie takes a seat on the floor, and I make my way to the couch.

"I was tasked with completing a list of New Year rituals, and if I don't do it, my year will be catastrophic."

I smother a chuckle because Lanie is dead serious. It's as though Corinne or some other mystic told her these things personally and she's taken them to heart.

"Lane . . . it's not real," I say, trying to quiet her nerves. "It was a dream."

She throws her hands up in the air. "Exactly. Dreams can spell doom."

I pull my upper lip into my mouth and turn to Nina, hoping she can help calm our distressed friend. She shrugs, and I know she's leaving it for me to work out.

I huff, settling in for a whopper of a story. "What did these rituals include?" I say, opening myself up for a long night if Lanie's superstitious panic is any indicator.

"I don't remember," Lanie says, voice pitching. "I only recall that a scarecrow was involved. I have to burn it."

I can't help it. I laugh. "A scarecrow? Seriously, Lanie, are you hearing yourself?"

She shoots daggers at me with her eyes. "I know what I sound like, Alyssa. I'm scared. It's real. I can feel it."

"Tell us what we need to do, Lanie," Nina says, giving me a chastising look. "We'll help you beat this bad luck."

Nina is supposed to be the voice of reason. The one who helps us see the cracks in our foundation so we can get back on solid ground. She shakes her head imperceptibly, telling me not to rock the boat anymore. I throw my hands in the air. Apparently, we're going along with this.

"Fine." I huff. "How about we look up New Year rituals. I'm sure we'll find that a burning scarecrow is not involved," I suggest, offering a smile to hopefully mollify Lanie. "Then you'll know it was just a dream and there's nothing to worry about."

Lanie bobs her head, moving toward my office.

I fire up my Mac and start my search by plopping in the terms *scarecrow new year* and hitting Search. I'm biting my lower lip, trying not to make it obvious that I'm completing this search only to prove to Lanie that she's being unreasonable.

To my shock, I get a hit.

"New Year's Eve rituals to banish ill fortune and bad things," I read out loud.

Apparently, it's an Ecuadorian thing to set fire to scarecrows filled with paper at midnight.

"See," she screeches. "I told you."

"You probably read that somewhere," Nina says.

Now she wants to talk reason.

"I didn't. I swear. Something bad is coming for me. I know it."

This is so unlike Lanie that she's truly scaring me. She's damn near hysterical. I've never once seen her like this.

"Okay, so we're burning a scarecrow at midnight," I say, giving in because what other choice do I have? I don't want Lanie to spiral any further. "What else do you feel you need to do, Lane?"

She motions toward the computer. "Can I . . . search? I think I'll know when I see it."

I remove myself from the seat, standing aside so that Lanie can sit and scroll for as long as she needs.

"I'm going to go pour us some drinks," Nina says, motioning for me to follow her.

"I'll go change. I'm not wearing this getup," I say, twirling one more time to see the sparkle.

Nina heads to the kitchen and I follow, grabbing glasses while Nina opens the bottle of merlot she brought.

"What do you make of that?" Nina asks, and I lift both eyebrows.

"I was going to ask you that question. I'm a little shocked that you went along with all this."

She takes a little more than a sip of wine, sighing after she swallows.

"I'm a little caught off guard, if I'm being honest. This behavior is very odd for her."

I bob my head like a doll. "Very. What can we do?"

She shrugs. "Be here for her. And drink this," she says, lifting her glass to me. "I thought you were going to change."

"I am, but I think we're going to need a lot more of that," I say, pointing to her already empty glass and thinking about what's to come tonight. "Between my date being cancelled and Lanie, let's keep the drinks coming."

"I think we should run to the store and grab some champagne before everything closes. We can't burn a scarecrow at midnight without champagne." Nina laughs.

"No, we cannot."

By the time I've changed and we join Lanie in the office, she's compiled a list. I run over it, realizing that the night is going to be wacky for sure.

"Throw white flowers into the sea? We can't go to the Atlantic," I say, looking to Nina, who shakes her head, agreeing with my assessment.

"But we can put it in the harbor, and it'll make its way to the ocean," Nina suggests, and that seems to pacify Lanie.

Visit a cemetery is next on the list.

"For what?" I say, not bothering to elaborate on which item I'm referencing.

"I don't know . . . play with the dead?" Lanie barks.

"Honor the dead, maybe?" Nina suggests. "We could take some of those flowers and place them on the graves."

"That'll work," I say, turning to Lanie to see what she thinks.

She's nodding her head, which is a good sign.

"Where exactly do you plan to burn a scarecrow?" I ask. "The ground is covered in snow."

"That . . . I'm not sure," Lanie says, tapping her chin. "I'm also wondering where we'll even get a scarecrow, considering it's going to be January in a few hours."

"I have some options," I say, drawing Lanie's attention.

"Why?" she asks, sounding appalled by the idea that I would actually have the very item she needs.

My nose scrunches. "I'm an adult homeowner who likes to decorate for the holidays . . ." I lift a hand and look to Nina for support.

She's too busy reading the list to acknowledge me.

A smile spreads across Lanie's face. "Thank god one of us is an adulty adult."

Nina chuckles, finally joining the conversation. "I too have scarecrows. We might as well use mine, because I have no intention of taking half my shit with me when I pack up and move."

"Okay, so the plan is to stop by and grab Corinne, and then we'll head to your house," Lanie says, pointing to Nina.

"Corinne is coming?" I ask, sounding a little underwhelmed by the idea.

Corinne has fast become a part of our group, but there's a piece of me that loves the idea of simply hanging with my two best friends tonight.

"She's the DD. We're all drinking," Lanie says, as if I should've known that. "Dress warm," she says, heading up the stairs.

"Where are you going?" I ask, and she makes a face.

"To your closet. I need a sweater."

Tonight is going to be interesting.

"WE COULD ALWAYS go to the mortuary," Corinne says behind the wheel of my car, on our way to start our list of rituals. "My parents are gone until well into tomorrow morning, dancing the night away, buzzed up on champagne and gummies."

"Is that safe? To mix the two?" Nina asks.

Lanie makes a face. "Who cares?"

"Fine. Let's do that," I say, and Lanie's head snaps to me.

"Where do you think I'm going to get gummies at this late hour on a holiday?"

My mouth drops open, and my nose scrunches. "I was talking about going to the mortuary."

Her mouth forms an O. "Got it. Makes more sense."

I turn back to Corinne, shaking my head. "It'll be a lot safer than burning anything in the cemetery."

"Does this all need to be done before midnight?" Corinne asks, eyes trained forward.

It's pitch black and the roads, while mostly clear, are still a little slick.

"Yes. If it's not done before the final stroke of twelve, Lanie will burst into flames and join the otherworld." I grin, meeting Corinne's laughing eyes through the rearview mirror.

At least she finds me funny.

"You're an ass," Lanie spits, and I shrug.

Corinne pulls up to the docks, parking the car. "Get out," she barks. "Let's get this over with."

Nina and I roll our eyes at Corinne, and Lanie flips her the bird. I've become numb to Corinne's snark and sass. It's just who she is.

The place is empty, most of the boats having been stored for the winter months. Ahead of us is nothing but dark sky and still black water as far as the eyes can see.

"It's chilly out here tonight," Nina says, shivering next to me. She's wearing an NYU sweatshirt that looks two times too big for her. It hangs loosely, mid-thigh, against her black yoga pants. The only indication she realized it was winter are the gray-and-tan duck boots on her feet.

"Why didn't you wear a jacket?" I ask, watching her shoulders shake and hearing her teeth chatter.

"I was warm from the merlot. Now I'm not."

"Okay, let's get this over with," Lanie says, bundled up under a furry, oversize, green-and-cream-striped sweater jacket, holding a bundle of white flowers in her hand. "We're going to run out of time."

We all trail after her, making our way to the end of a dock, overlooking the dark water beyond.

"What should we say?" I ask, looking around at our little group.

"I've got this," Lanie says, taking a deep breath in and letting it out. "Mother Earth, universe, spirit guides, and angels, we bring to you a token of our appreciation; and with this gift, we benevolently ask for a prosperous New Year. May you bless us all with abundance and joy. Namaste."

"Namaste," Corinne and Nina echo.

Lanie gives me a pointed look, which I just barely see under the dim light from the pole overhead, and I rush out the word. "Namaste."

"Were you practicing that little speech the entire way over here?" Corinne says.

Lanie doesn't deign to answer, concentrating on passing out a few flowers to each of us. She places a kiss atop the petals of her small bouquet before tossing them into the harbor.

We all follow suit, and then stand and watch as the white flowers disappear into the pitch-black night.

"What the hell kinda hoodoo was that?" a man slurs, appearing out of nowhere.

He's wearing a large, tan fishing coat that's seen better days. His hair is disheveled, and he's clutching a bottle of cheap booze.

None of us had seen him before now, but he must've witnessed our whole ritual.

"We used to burn witches back in my day," he slurs, moving toward us at a snail's pace, dragging his right leg behind him. He's giving me *I Know What You Did Last Summer*–vibes, and I think it's time we go before we meet the same fate as the girl in red.

"Shut up, you old drunk," Lanie barks. "Go back into the hole you crawled out of."

"Lanie," Nina snaps. "Be nice."

"Yeah . . . Let's not provoke the scary guy. He might have an ax under that jacket," I whisper.

"Get gone before I call a priest," he shouts, and I grab Nina by the arm, pulling her along with me, Corinne and Lanie right on our heels.

When we're in the safety of the car, I let out the breath I'd been holding.

"Good grief . . . where did that guy come from?"

"Hell. It's another sign," Lanie says, far too serious for my liking.

"Don't be ridiculous, Lanie. That was no sign from Hell. If it were, you'd be thrown into the deep, strangled, and gutted."

My head snaps to Corinne, face screwed up. "Geez, Corinne. That's a bit much, don't you think?"

Lanie sighs. "She might be right. He was a sign that I need to get a move on. One ritual down. More to go."

"Better get moving before Superstitious Sally goes berserk," Corinne says, starting the car.

We're on our way to Wintersgate Cemetery to deliver the additional bundles of flowers we purchased from the grocery store, and nobody says a word. Everyone is focused on Lanie, watching her fidget in the front seat.

I think she needs to see Natalia. Whatever the horrible dream was, it has a hold on Lanie that isn't healthy.

"The plan is to get in and get out," Corinne tells the group. "We place the flowers on the first graves we come across and leave."

Lanie clears her throat. "No."

"No?" I say, head tilting to the side, staring into the back of Lanie's head.

"We need to place the flowers on specific graves," she says, voice far off. "We need to find graves of a person whose first or last name starts with a *g*, *u*, *y*, *l*, *i*, and *t*."

"Guylit? Why?" I say, my voice rising incredulously.

"We just do." The tone of her voice has me very worried. Lanie is clearly going through something.

"We should probably split up then," Nina says. "I'll take the *g* and *i*. Alyssa, would you take the *u*?"

I bob my head. "Sure."

"Corinne, you have the *t*, and Lanie, you have *y* and *l*."

We all agree with Nina's suggestion, wanting to get in and out. It would've been a great plan, but when we arrive, the gates are closed, locked by a chain.

"We really should've known that this would be the case. Not like they're going to leave the cemetery open for vandalization," Nina says, and she's not wrong.

We were not thinking.

"Now what? We can't get in there," Corinne says, turning back to look at Nina and me.

"Well . . . we could just throw them through the gates and be done. We've technically visited a cemetery," I suggest. "We'll just have to be okay with not finding specific graves."

"No, we must step foot on hallowed ground. And it must be done the way I said," Lanie says, and I shoot her a look.

"Where did it say that? I don't recall that as part of the tradition," I challenge, about done with catering to an idea that's bordering on insanity.

"It is. I know it is," Lanie snaps, eyes trained beyond the giant gates of the cemetery. "Just like we all knew you were telling the truth when you said you could see ghosts, I need you to stop questioning me and recognize that I know what I'm talking about."

I slam my mouth closed because she's got me there. Who am I

to question? Strange things have been happening to us all. Maybe this dream is something more. Something sinister.

"We could go to the crematorium and set the stove to begin at midnight. I know my dad has something that could break that lock," Corinne suggests, and I make a strangled sound.

"We're not breaking into the cemetery," Nina says, and I nod my head vigorously, grateful to know she's on my side.

"I agree with Nina," I say. "As much as it sounds like a cloak-and-dagger night of fun, it has bad idea written all over it."

"Cloak-and-dagger?" Corinne laughs. "Alyssa . . . I thought we had a conversation about your use of outdated phrases. Do better," she snaps, and I glare at her.

"Well whatever you want to call this idea, I'm not on board. There is no way I can go to jail for trespassing. It would ruin my future plans." I lean toward Lanie. "I'm sorry, Lane, but I can't do this."

She nods her head. "I understand. I'm not asking anyone to do anything they're not comfortable with. This is my problem, and I'll do it myself."

She opens the door and exits the car, walking toward the gate.

"Are we really going to let her do this?" Nina asks, glancing between Corinne and me.

"I don't think there's any stopping her," I admit, watching as Lanie fusses with the chain.

"You know . . . there's a better way."

My head snaps toward the voice, eyes widening when I see the ghost who should not be here.

Isla.

Six of Pentacles

"WHAT ARE YOU doing here?" I ask, finding Isla sitting next to me.

She squirms in her seat, a self-satisfied smirk adorning her pretty face.

"I've been here the whole time. Just decided to show myself to offer help," she declares, her tone brimming with confidence.

I shake my head, exchanging a glance with Corinne in the rear-view mirror, noticing her puzzled expression.

"Who's here?" she inquires, turning to look at the empty space beside me.

"Isla," I reply, gesturing vaguely. "She's here to offer her assistance, apparently."

Corinne turns back to Nina. "Who's Isla?"

"Nick's ex-fiancée," Nina whispers.

"Dead ex-fiancée," Isla corrects with a ghostly chuckle. I clear my throat, opting not to share that particular detail with Corinne and Nina.

"What's your suggestion then?" I ask, refocusing on the reason for Isla's appearance.

"If you walk around the cemetery, there's a shorter wall," Isla suggests, motioning toward the graveyard.

"How short are we talking?" I ask, eyeing the direction she pointed to.

"Short enough for all of you to scale over it with a boost. That tall girl out there could probably do it on her own."

"How is she here?" Corinne's head tilts to the side, a picture of perplexity.

"You shouldn't be here . . . but you are." I glance toward the cemetery. "Are you buried in there?" I ask, coming to the most logical conclusion.

"Yes, but that's not how you're seeing me," she says cryptically.

Nina turns around, her expression questioning, and I respond with a casual shrug, returning to the specter.

"So . . . enlighten me."

A mischievous grin stretches across her delicate features, and instantly my senses prick with apprehension. What is she up to?

"Check your purse."

I rummage through the contents of my purse, my fingers sifting through the usual clutter until they brush against something cold and made of metal. With a curious furrow of my brow, I extract the object, revealing a man's wedding ring.

"How . . . how did that get in here?" I murmur, my voice tinged with bewilderment.

Isla shrugs nonchalantly, an enigmatic gleam dancing in her eyes. "I put it there."

My eyes widen in realization, a sudden clarity washing over me. This is Nick's. Without uttering a word, I glance at Isla, and she responds with a subtle nod, a twisted glimmer dancing in her eyes. Her satisfaction is palpable.

"Why?"

"I had a theory." She picks at her pink fingernail, not elaborating, continuing to leave her motives shrouded in mystery. But I'm in no mood to speculate on her intentions.

"Spit it out, Isla," I snap, done with the games.

Her lips purse, a clear indication of her displeasure with my tone. Her confident demeanor slips, replaced by an air of uncertainty.

"I don't think it's Nick that I'm attached to, but the ring," she confesses, her gaze drifting down to the object in question, her smile tinged with sadness. "He wasn't supposed to see it until our wedding day. When I died, he took it. He's had it tucked away in his back pocket." She clears her throat. "Until recently. That's when I realized I couldn't follow him anymore."

I nod, understanding her train of thought. "So, by process of elimination, you concluded that it's the ring you're attached to."

She bobs her head in confirmation. "Yes. And I placed it in your purse so that I could attach myself to you."

"Why?" My voice is full of frustration. "Why would you try to attach yourself to me?"

"Because I have to know you. I have to figure out if you're the one," she explains earnestly.

"Jesus, Mary, mother of god, Isla," I exclaim, feeling overwhelmed. "We just started dating. What's with you trying to push?" My head falls back as I let out a sigh. "I'm not going to marry him anytime soon, if ever. You forget I'm forty years old, and I've already been married. We've just started dating," I repeat, trying to emphasize the point.

She shrugs, seemingly unfazed. "Call it a gut instinct."

"You shouldn't have instincts. You're dead," I snap.

"Ouch, that was harsh," Corinne says, head whipping around as though she'll get a peek at the affronted ghost. "What is she saying?"

"It's a long story. We don't have time."

Corinne harrumphs, twisting back around.

"I'm sorry, Isla," I say. "I didn't mean to be insensitive, but seriously, you've got to stop prying into Nick's and my relationship. And for the record, I don't think Nick would approve of me hanging out with you."

She waves a hand in the air. "Then don't tell him. He rarely knows what's best for himself. I'm here to help."

I close my eyes and inhale deeply.

"Why does it sound like there's a problem?" Nina asks.

"There is no problem. Just a misunderstanding," I assert, redirecting my attention to Isla and forcing a smile onto my lips. "If it's the ring you're attached to, then we simply need to figure out how to unattach you from it."

She shakes her head. "I don't think you can."

My head falls back against the car seat. "I'm going to tell Lanie about the wall," I say, exiting the car, desperate for fresh air.

I approach Lanie as if she's a wild beast, ready to turn on me at any moment. She kicks the gate, growling, only furthering my worry.

"Hey now, no need to alert the police before you've even stepped foot on hallowed ground."

She purses her lips, hands landing on her hips. "Are you mocking me?"

I blink a couple times, recognizing that it did sound like that, but it wasn't my intention.

"I'm sorry, Lane. I didn't mean to come off that way."

She gulps, her shoulders slouching. "I know this all sounds nuts, but I'm really freaked out, Ally. Like *really* freaked."

I take a tentative step forward and place a hand on her shoulder. "Is there something else going on? Something you need to tell someone?"

She stiffens, giving away that there might just be more to this dream.

"No," she snaps, jerking away from me.

I've known Lanie long enough to identify when it's a losing battle to pry. She's not going to tell me anything, and I have to be all right with that for now.

"I came out here to tell you that Isla says there's a short wall around the back. You should be able to scale it."

She narrows her eyes at me. "Isla? Who's Isla?"

"Nick's fiancée," I say, clenching my teeth together.

"The dead one?"

I pull a face, disturbed by Lanie's less-than-tasteful way of describing her. "Quiet. She'll hear you."

"What does it matter? She knows she's dead. Why is she here anyway?"

"She's attached herself to me," I say, sounding as though it doesn't bother me. "It's . . . convenient at times."

Lanie's face contorts. "Not." She takes a step toward me, leaning down to whisper, "Nobody wants to hook up with someone when his dead ex is hanging around." She looks around the area. "No offense, ghost girl."

"None taken," Isla calls out, appearing beside the gate. "Except, tell your tall friend to not call me that. It's offensive."

She's not being serious. I'm coming to find Isla sarcastic and witty, and it's no wonder she was to be Nick's wife.

I relay the message anyway, and Lanie scoffs. "Her very existence is offensive."

Isla titters.

"I'm sorry, but I'm still out," Nina says. "I can't take the chance of getting myself in trouble with all the Richard issues surrounding me. I've already got a spotlight on my back."

"She's right, Lane. There is no way Nina can do this, and we can't allow her to stay out in the dark alone." I tap my chin. "So I'll stay with her, and you two can go mingle with the spirits." I motion between her and Corinne, who's joined the party at the gate. She's clutching a bottle of champagne in each hand.

"Then you won't have completed the rituals, and your New Year will be crap," Lanie quips.

"News flash, love. You said it was your New Year in jeopardy, not ours. I'm simply doing this as a friend. One who loves you enough to tag along."

She grunts. "Fine. Cori . . . you with me?"

"I've scaled a wall or two. I'll play sidekick for the evening." She lifts her bottles of champagne. "I'll drink while you scour for your *guilt*."

I crinkle my nose at Corinne's random word.

"What is she guilty of?"

Corinne huffs. "Please tell me that I'm not the only one who worked out that the graves she needs to find are an anagram for *guilty*."

She isn't wrong, and that leads to a host of questions. Could the letters that Lanie seemed to choose at random not have been random at all? And furthermore, if she feels that she's guilty of something and this is to be her penance, what is she guilty of?

"Coincidence," Lanie says, waving Corinne's words off, but I'm not buying it.

"We'll stay out here, and if anyone comes along, we'll hoot like owls," I say, making the sound and drawing two looks of amusement and a snort from Isla.

"Classic," Isla chuckles. "You are definitely perfect for Nick."

I ignore her, refusing to feed into her delusions surrounding Nick and me.

"We'll see you two in a bit," Lanie says, grabbing Corinne by the arm of her black sweatshirt that says *I'm wicked* in bold white letters.

"What do we do?" Nina asks.

"First? Grab a bottle of the champagne from the car."

Nina nods vigorously. "We might as well not lose our buzz."

We take a seat on top of the car, and I pop the cork from the bottle, taking a sip and passing it over to Nina.

"This feels a lot like the summer before our senior year," she says, smiling. "Nights spent at the lake."

"It does," I say, bobbing my head.

I recall that summer with perfect clarity. It was a year that lives fondly in my memory. We spent nearly every night at our friend Liv's cabin, located down a dirt road, situated next to a small lake. We'd drink strawberry Boone's Farm and take reckless swims, oblivious to the danger of mixing the two. Looking back, it's a wonder we all lived to tell about those days.

I thank god on the daily that Ava is nothing like me. She's smart, but more important, responsible. These days a simple app allows me to monitor where she is at all times. Not that I check often, because I know she makes good decisions. She's typically at the library or in her room, and that gives me peace of mind.

"This is not how I envisioned tonight going," Nina says, looking up into the starless night. "New Year's has never been my favorite."

"That's why we need to make new memories." I pass the bottle back to her.

Her head lolls toward me, a lazy grin spreading across her face. "I'd say that tonight will definitely be a night I won't forget."

"Me too." I take a pull of the fizzy drink and sigh. "This is all a lot."

"Leave it to Lanie to come rushing in, freaked out by a dream."

"It's odd, isn't it? I mean . . . I'm not a therapist, but the way she's reacting, it seems a bit much."

Nina's quiet for a minute, and I think she's going to let my comment go, but she doesn't.

"There's something going on with Lanie. Her behavior suggests that the walls are closing in on her."

"What do we do? We have to help, right?"

She lets out a weary exhale. "I think this is something we need to allow her to come to us about."

Isla paces in front of us, head lowered to the ground as she mumbles something unintelligibly. "What's wrong with you?" I ask.

"It's just . . . I want . . ." She shakes her head. "Never mind. You wouldn't understand."

I sit up. "Try me."

She makes a strangled noise, and my eyebrow arches in curiosity. I haven't known Isla long, but she hasn't struck me as overly dramatic. Right now, her entire demeanor is theatrical.

"I know I'm dead. I've come to terms with that. But my body is in there," she says, jutting her hand toward the cemetery. "My final resting place. I'm right here, and a morbid part of me wants to see my gravestone. Wants to see what others do when they visit me." She sighs heavily. "Am I crazy for wanting that?"

I chew on my bottom lip, wholly unprepared to answer that question.

"I can't claim to understand, but who am I to say it's crazy? You should go in there."

Her face lights up. "You'll go in? You'll take me with you?"

"Umm . . . no. I didn't mean to imply that." I shake my head, angry with myself for not thinking my words through before voicing them. "I can't, Isla. It's illegal, and if I were caught, it would ruin my plans."

Her entire demeanor shifts, shoulders sagging in resignation. "I understand. I . . . shouldn't have asked that of you."

I lick my bottom lip, contemplating how I could make this happen for her without doing it myself. An idea hits me.

"If you're connected to the ring, you only need someone else to take it in there."

Her eyes light up, and she claps her hands together. "Who?"

"What's she saying?" Nina asks, head flopping from me toward the ghost she can't see.

"She wants to see her gravestone."

Nina's mouth pops open, forming an O. "Are you sure that wouldn't help her move on?"

My eyes narrow in on Nina. "She thinks she's stuck because Nick needs to be happy."

Nina purses her lips. "Seems to me that if she's connected to that ring, she might be here for a different reason."

My eyebrow lifts.

"Was she buried with her ring?"

I turn toward Isla. "Were you buried with your ring?"

She nods. "I'm sure I was. I wore it at all times."

"Maybe the rings need to be together?" I suggest, not having any clue if there's validity to the idea.

"You think? Could that be it?"

I shrug my shoulder. "I can't claim to have any clue about these things, Isla. But it's worth a shot. That is . . . if you want to move on to the next life."

She laughs, but it's full of sadness. "I don't want to stay here," she admits. "No offense to you, Alyssa, but as much as I want Nick to be happy, and I think you might be the person who could make him very happy, I don't necessarily love watching you two together. I try to put on a happy face and pretend that it's easy for me to push the love of my life toward someone else, but it's not. It's the hardest thing I've ever had to do, in life or death."

I swallow the lump in my throat, feeling terrible for Isla.

"I'm so sorry. I can't imagine what that must be like. It's not what I'd want for my husband to have to see."

She shrugs one shoulder. "No need to apologize. You've done nothing wrong. I'm not supposed to be here. I'm supposed to be on the other side, basking in the light with my baby brother."

I pull my mouth to the side, considering Isla. "Are you truly ready for that?"

She bites her lip. "I think so."

I glance at Nina and groan. "What do you think?"

Her eyes go wide. "I'm not sure that's a good idea, Ally."

"I'm not even sure if it will work, but I have to try to help her. Nick would want that."

Nina smiles sadly. "I think you're right, but I also think he'd want to know before you do it," she says, baring her teeth in an expression that tells me she's nervous about my reaction to her words.

I sigh heavily. "You're probably right. I'd be pissed if I missed out on a chance to potentially say a proper goodbye to Garrett."

She nods.

"I get it, and I agree," Isla says before I've had a chance to speak. "You're making the right decision."

I glance at my watch and groan. "Lanie's about to miss her window to burn the scarecrow."

Hopping down from the hood of the car, I open the back door and grab my purse, pulling my phone from the inner compartment I typically store it in for ease in finding it.

I have six missed calls from Lanie, and I quickly call her back.

"I need help," she says, voice trembling with fear. "Corinne twisted her ankle and can't walk. It's almost midnight."

I'm struggling to determine if it's Corinne's ankle or the time that has Lanie panicking.

"Where are you?" I ask, not sure how we're going to hoist Corinne over the wall if necessary.

There's a moment of quiet on the other end, but when she speaks again, her words hit me like a revelation. "We're right in front of Isla Craft's grave."

Is this some sort of sign from the universe that I'm supposed to take Isla to that gravestone after all?

No.

The universe is supposed to work with me, not against me, and me stepping foot in that cemetery cannot be for my greater good.

"We need help," she says, sounding frantic.

"What do you want me to do?" I say, resigned to the fact that we have to do something. We can't very well leave them trapped in the cemetery.

"Burn the scarecrow. But before you do, I need you to write out my words on the little pieces of paper I brought and stuff them inside."

I shut the car door and make my way to Nina, who's peering down from the hood of the car with a worried expression. She mouths the words *what's wrong*.

I close my eyes, shaking my head, hoping to convey I need a moment and then I'll tell her everything.

"What should I write?"

I hear her exhale. "*Fear* on one. *Let go of the past* on another. *Regain my power* on the third, and finally, *stop running* on the last."

The questions mount with each and every request she makes. What does she fear? What happened in her past, and most concerning, what is she running from?

"Alyssa, did you hear me?" Lanie bites.

"Yes. I heard you, and I'll do this. But, Lanie . . . you and I are going to have a long talk come tomorrow."

She doesn't say a word, and it's my turn to ensure she's heard me. "Okay?"

"Okay." It comes out a whisper, indicating that Lanie really doesn't want to have that conversation with me.

"What are you going to do with Corinne?"

"She'll be fine. She just needs to stop whining."

I hear Corinne grumbling in the background, quibbling with Lanie's words.

"We'll be back to the car as quickly as we can."

With that, the phone goes dead.

I relay everything I've just learned to Nina, and she doesn't speak, choosing to guzzle the remainder of the champagne left in the bottle she has clenched in her hands.

"How the hell are we going to burn this scarecrow?" I say, hoping to get a response.

"We can't do it on the ground. It's too wet."

I nibble at my bottom lip, trying to formulate a plan, but it's no use; my mind is blank.

"You could always burn it on top of that wall they climbed over," Isla says, drawing my attention to the gate. She's leaning against the steel bars, appearing human in every way except for the slight glow emanating from her.

Ten minutes later, we've written out the words that Lanie asked for, added our own to the stomach of the doomed scarecrow, and made it around the back of the cemetery to the wall.

I'm tall enough to reach the top, making it easy enough to light the stuffed ornament on fire.

"Someone help me lift her over," Lanie's voice sounds from the other side of the stone divider.

Nina and I share a look, and a part of me deflates knowing that one of us is going to have to put ourselves at greater risk for the group.

"I'll do it," I say, turning toward the wall.

A dainty hand lands on my shoulder, and I turn to see Nina.

"We're going to need someone on this side that can help lower Corinne. I'm not strong enough to do it on my own."

I purse my lips, preparing to scold her, but she shakes her head.

"I'm doing this." She moves around me, preparing to climb the wall. "Help me over."

I don't like this. Not at all. But I also know that determined look on Nina, and there is no talking her out of it.

I lift her up so that she can grasp onto the top of the wall and hoist herself over. On the boost up, I'm apparently a little too strong, and Nina damn near catapults over the wall, falling on the other side.

"Oh my god. Nina . . . are you all right?" I shout, a little too loudly for what's supposed to be a stealth operation.

"I'm fine, Hercules. Would you hurry up, Corinne? It's dark and creepy in here," Nina says, but I'm not entirely sure what's happening on the other side.

She's not wrong though. This entire place is dark and creepy.

"Alyssa, light that sucker on fire," Lanie commands. "It's 11:58."

I huff, dropping to my knees to rifle through my purse for the matches, when a bright light shines down on me.

"What do we have here?" a male voice says from behind me, and I freeze in place.

"Hurry up," Lanie shouts. "You've got to do it."

I do as she says, trying and failing to find the matches.

"Stop. Whatever you're doing, just stop," the man commands.

My arms fly up into the air, and I know that we're all in trouble.

Two of Swords

Nick

THE FALLS HAVEN harbor, usually humming with the activity of sailors and fishermen, is active for an entirely different reason tonight. There's a frenzied energy permeating the surrounding area as police rope off a section with tape, and a group of people work to prepare the body for transport.

"What do you make of this?" Chief Skiver of the Falls Haven homicide unit asks as he saunters up next to me.

I inhale a deep breath, the smell of seawater infiltrating my senses.

"Her family was concerned that she might have fallen into bad company," I say, recalling Chief Grayson's words days after the girl went missing.

He nods. "Wouldn't doubt it. Especially given her recent employment at Haven's Bard. That place is a mecca for trouble."

Haven's Bard is the local watering hole, but due to its location, it pulls in unsavory characters. Through the years, word of the troubles the town has with that place has spread as far as Knox Harbor.

The wind rouses, and shivers race down my spine, but it's hard to tell if it's the breeze coming off the water or the scene playing out in front of me.

The ominous black bag, a grim harbinger of death, is tightly zipped shut, concealing the lifeless form of Chelsea Grayson. The twenty-two-year-old vanished without a trace a week ago, leaving her family gripped with worry. But I knew her fate before tonight.

I just can't say that to Skiver or anyone else overseeing this case.

"What's your take?" I ask, looking away from the body bag.

"We know she wasn't working the night she went missing, and nobody at the Bard recalls seeing her that night," he says, detailing the conversations that were started upon Chelsea going missing.

"Any camera footage that can confirm that?"

He huffs a laugh. "That place doesn't have cameras. It's the kinda place that thrives on seedy shit. Can't have footage that would get the place closed down for good." He sighs. "Besides, based on what she was wearing, she wasn't at Haven's Bard."

"You sure about that? Maybe that's the very reason she's in that bag over there," I say, tipping my head in the direction of her body.

"You could be right, but I doubt it." He clears his throat, spitting onto the ground beside him. "Chelsea was smart. Too smart to be prancing around Haven's Bard in a dress like that. She knows the types of people who frequent that place. I just don't see it. That red dress is a stark departure from what anyone would wear in that area of town."

"Any place in town that would make sense for her to be that dressed up?"

"No." He shakes his head. "Falls Haven isn't that kinda place, Detective."

This whole damn night is raising unsettling questions about the circumstances leading to her disappearance. Nobody I've spoken to can place Chelsea anywhere around town that night. But clearly she was here, and I intend to get to the bottom of what transpired, leading to her being killed and dumped in the harbor.

I look down at my phone to find several text messages from Malone.

MALONE

Call me. It's important.

I turn to Chief Skiver. "Excuse me for a minute."

He nods his head, and I move off to the side, pulling up Malone's number. Eric sent that last text ten minutes ago. Hopefully shit didn't blow up in that time.

One of the main reasons I like Eric as my partner is that he's reliable. He respects my boundaries, refraining from unnecessary interruptions when I'm off duty, unless the situation is truly urgent. And when I'm deep in a case that takes me away, he employs all available resources to resolve an issue before reaching out to me. So the fact that he's texting and calling me at damn near midnight on New Year's Eve tells me something is wrong.

"Buddy, we have a problem," he says by way of a greeting.

"Fucking spit it out, Malone. I'm dealing with a dead body over here."

He sighs heavily down the line. "Fine. I'll just haul her ass to jail, and then you can fuck off with your bitching because I called and you were too busy."

Her?

Now he has my attention. There isn't one person I can think of that he'd call to get my permission to take in.

"I'm listening," I drawl.

"Man, don't shoot the messenger, but I was doing my rounds at Wintersgate Cemetery, and found a vacant car at the gates. I decided to investigate, and, well . . ." He blows out a breath, and I'm about to snap at him to hurry up with his long-winded story, but his next words come and knock the air from me.

"There were trespassers, and one is Alyssa."

A range of emotion rushes through me before settling on confusion.

"She wasn't actually in the cemetery, but the others were." Eric stops, clearing his throat. "And they were attempting to burn a scarecrow."

My face screws up, and I shake my head. "What?"

I'm not even sure what I'm asking. This whole conversation has me entirely baffled.

"Who's with her?" I ask, but really, I know before he even answers.

There's only one person who could've led this charge, and my bet is on Corinne Moradi. That woman has been nothing but trouble since landing in Alyssa's path.

"The culprit appears to be Lanie Anderson."

"That's also not surprising." I groan. "What's this about a scarecrow?"

"I'm going to let you talk to Alyssa," he says, and I hear some muffled voices on the other end.

"Hi, Nick."

Her bubbly voice despite the situation has me smothering a chuckle.

"Alyssa," I drawl, allowing her name to hang in the air.

"Nick, listen, don't be mad. I can explain," she rushes out, not taking a breath between words. I can tell she's had a bit to drink based on the semi-slurred words. "It's just . . . I don't think we should do this over the phone. Wait . . ." Her words trail off, and I'm about to speak when I hear the incoming request to switch to a video call.

Despite my better judgment, I accept the call and wait for a moment while the phone switches modes and Alyssa's face pops up on the screen.

"Can I take this over there?" she asks Malone, but he's too busy flirting with someone just out of my view to bother answering.

She walks out of earshot and takes a deep breath.

"What are you doing at the cemetery, Lyss? It's midnight," I say, shaking my head in exasperation.

"New Year rituals," she says, as if that explains it. "Lanie had a dream. It's a long story."

I grunt, not at all surprised that a dream would have Lanie trespassing. "She could've gotten you arrested. You realize that, right?"

She nods her head. "It's not Lanie's fault entirely. I came freely of my own will."

I smother a laugh, tilting my head. "Are you drunk?"

Her eyes widen, and her hand flies to cover her mouth. "No. I mean . . . I've had some champagne."

My head falls back as I groan. "Alyssa. Not only is that trespassing, but it would also be drunk and disorderly."

"Nick . . . there's more, and you're not going to like what I'm about to say," she starts, and my eyes close.

"Go on. It's been a long night." I pull the phone away to hide a yawn.

I'm exhausted and in over my head with Chelsea's investigation, with no leads to go on.

"Isla put your wedding ring in my purse so that she could attach herself to me."

The blood rushes to my ears, and my head spins.

"She attached herself to you? With my ring?" I rub at my forehead.

"Yes, and she wanted me to take her to her grave to see if she could move on."

I catch about every three words.

Isla.

Ring.

Grave.

Move on.

"Alyssa . . . please tell me you didn't."

My heart is pounding, attempting to dislodge from my chest. My vision swims with red, and I know that I'm moments away from lashing out, which I don't want to do. I can't process what she's saying. Can't think.

Every part of me is locked up, awaiting Alyssa's unspoken words.

She wouldn't do that, right?

She sighs heavily. "I didn't. There was no way I was going to make that decision without you."

The breath whooshes from me, and my hand flies to my chest, rubbing out the phantom pain. "Thank you. You have no idea what that means to me."

Maybe she does. Having her own loss, she might be the only person who could ever understand.

"Nick, I—"

"Alyssa, it's all good. We'll talk about this more later." I blow out a breath. "Can you give the phone back to Malone? Please?"

She swallows, bobbing her head. She calls for Malone, and he comes onto the screen, eyes animatedly wide.

"And now do you see why I called?"

I nod once. "Are any of them sober?"

"Yeah, the crazy-hot other brunette."

"Corinne," I say, shaking my head at my partner.

"She's their DD."

"Get them all in the car and follow them back to Alyssa's. Make sure they're in the house before you leave."

"Roger."

"And, Malone," I say before he hangs up. "Thank you for calling."

He nods once more before the call ends, leaving me reeling with all that's just unfolded.

My respect and admiration for Alyssa just increased tenfold. The fact that she is willing to be stuck with Isla for my benefit is something I'll never forget.

I groan, head tilting to the sky.

I've yet to completely come to terms with the fact that Isla stuck around. I've done my best to shove it as far from my mind as possible, because no matter how much I believe Alyssa, this is hard to swallow.

But I can't dwell on any of that right now.

I have a dead girl on my hands and no suspects.

It's going to be a long day.

Seven of Cups

IT'S BEEN TWO weeks with little communication from Nick. We've exchanged several text messages back and forth, but he's been so consumed with the Grayson case that we haven't had time to discuss my New Year's Eve shenanigans. Or Isla, for that matter. The only text he's sent that alluded to that night was him telling me how much he appreciates that I didn't act upon Isla's wishes.

NICK

You'll never know how grateful I am that you didn't listen to Isla.

ME

I'd never do something like that without involving you.

NICK

I don't deserve you.

I've reread that exchange more times than I care to admit.

Nick's belief in my abilities is something he struggles with. He's seen the proof, but it lacks all reason, and for him, that's a tough pill to swallow. Telling him I see Isla is another thing entirely. The fact that he never questioned me, not once, just shows how good a man he is.

I'm sure hearing that she's still around isn't easy for him to handle.

"Are you all right, Ally?" Nina says, bending down to peer into my eyes.

I look up and smile. "Fine. So, what's the plan?"

Her pursed lips and hard stare tell me that she's less than impressed with my pathetic attempt to change the subject.

"I'm all right. Really. Still a little weak, but I'll survive."

I ended up getting the stomach bug that Nick had. It took me out for forty-eight hours, but that was a week ago, and I know it's not what Nina is asking about.

She takes a deep breath and settles into her no-nonsense stance.

I throw my hands up. "Okay . . . It sucks. What else do you want me to say?"

Her features soften and she takes a seat across from me, looking like the consummate therapist.

"Would you like to talk about it?"

I pinch the bridge of my nose, counting to ten in my head. "No, but I appreciate your willingness to listen if I were," I say, hoping this appeases her. She frowns. "I wish that we could talk. Get something figured out about Isla."

She bobs her head. "I understand, but he's not avoiding you, Ally. He's been busy." She blows a piece of hair out of her face.

"Do you think he wants her to stay?"

She makes a face. "No, Alyssa. Nobody wants their loved one to be stuck here. He's investigating a murder. One that's very important, considering it's his chief's relative." She sighs heavily, rubbing at her forehead. "Chelsea was so young. Such a well-loved girl. The pressure he's under must be crippling."

News of Chelsea Grayson's murder has been the talk of the town. She was a Knox Harbor grad, so the local chatter has been nonstop.

"I know you're right. I just wish there was some way for me to help." I kick up my feet, turning my attention back toward the TV.

"In fairness, you can't do much spending your day like this." She motions to the TV, where yet another Hallmark movie plays in the background.

"I'm only watching it because you haven't been ready to make a move," I say. "We're in Providence, and school's back in session. Let's start asking about Ian."

She sits back with a huff. "We will. Later today."

We've been in Providence for three days, staying at an Airbnb just off campus—a little loft with one king-size bed, a bathroom, and a small kitchen with the bare necessities. It's cozy and the bed is comfortable, which is all I care about these days.

Nina spent a few hours at the campus library asking around. She said it was likely that back in Ian's days here, he would've frequented the stacks for research.

"I have a lead," she says, and I perk up at the news. "Another TA that shared a place with Ian is now tenured. I sent him an email after leaving the library on Saturday, and he answered a couple hours later." She pulls something up on her phone and then looks at me. "He's agreed to meet."

"How did you find out about him?"

"The librarian at the front desk. She's an older woman. Recognized Ian by name and said Professor Drake might have information."

"Are you prepared to use your ability if needed?"

Her cheeks pinken, and she shakes her head. "No. I haven't used that on purpose yet, and I don't plan to."

"Why not?"

She chews on her bottom lip. "For one, I'm not exactly sure how it works. Do I just touch someone and see random things? Or can I actually tune in for something specific?"

I shrug. "You won't know unless you try," I say, leaning forward and offering her my arm. "Try it on me."

She blinks. "How?"

I chew on my bottom lip. "Think of something specific you want to know before touching me and see if it works."

She blows out a breath and appears to formulate her question, if her furrowed brows and pinched expression are any indicator.

Nina reaches out and touches my arm. Her eyes are closed, and her lips are smashed together.

She gasps and jumps back as though I've stung her.

"Did it work? What did you see?"

She clears her throat. "It didn't work . . . exactly. I thought of a specific thing I wanted to see, and it didn't show me that, but I did see something . . ."

I make a face for her to spit it out.

"I saw Chelsea."

My breath hitches.

"You saw her?"

"She was standing by your refrigerator door, just staring at you."

I get a tingly feeling of spiders crawling over my body that has me wiggling in place.

"Creepy."

She nods but remains quiet. There's something she's not saying. I know Nina, and I know when she's holding back. This time, it appears as though she's working something out in her head.

"What else did you see, Nina?"

"I could see into her head." The word comes out a whisper.

I blink, unable to fully grasp what she's claiming.

"She was in a speakeasy of sorts. Something that's hidden from locals." She rubs at her head, wincing. "She was dealing drugs."

That was *not* what I was expecting.

✦ ✦ ✦

WE DIDN'T HAVE much time to deliberate on the whole Chelsea-was-a-drug-dealer shock, because Nina's meeting with the professor is approaching, and we needed to make our way across campus.

"I know you haven't figured out how to use your ability, but this is one of those times where you absolutely should try to use it, Nina. If he isn't able to give you anything, touch him and see what comes through."

She groans from beside me as we practically power walk across the courtyard toward the history building, where Professor Drake's office resides.

"I don't want to go around touching strangers. It's weird."

"We came all this way, and if touching a stranger leads to uncovering Ian's whereabouts, isn't it worth it?"

She swallows, bobbing her head. "If I have to in this meeting, I will," she promises.

"I'm coming in with you."

Nina skids to a stop, whirling on me. "That's not necessary, Alyssa. I'm more than capable of having a conversation."

"I know that, but I want to be there. I might pick up on something that you don't."

We've stopped at the base of what appears to be one of the oldest buildings at Providence University, Rexton Hall. It towers above us, its imposing stone structure adorned with hanging buttresses. A plaque, standing a foot taller than me, explains that Rexton Hall is a black-foliated building dating back to the 1800s.

Originally a church, it was acquired by the university in the early 1900s and became the first building to house classes for Providence University, formerly known as Hathor University, named after its founder, Arin Hathor.

"This place is . . ."

"Petrifying?" Nina says, staring up at the Gothic monstrosity.

"It's a bit creepy."

The clock tower bell chimes, signaling it's ten a.m. and we need to be meeting with the professor.

We burst through the weighty doors, our footsteps echoing as we race up the stairs to the right, making a beeline for the third floor, where the professor's offices are situated. By the time we reach the landing, we're breathless, and to our humiliation, the professor is already waiting outside his door, a faint hint of amusement dancing in his eyes as he witnesses our panting.

"Hello, ladies." He greets us with a smooth, almost suave tone that sets my instincts on edge. "Come in." With a polite gesture, he steps aside, allowing us to enter.

The room is sparsely furnished, dominated by a basic oak desk positioned across from two empty chairs. Cream walls adorned with an array of framed certificates and awards lend an air of academic authority to the space.

"How can I assist you?" he inquires, taking his seat and intertwining his fingers beneath his chin.

"Thank you for agreeing to meet with us, Professor Drake," Nina begins, her tone polite but tinged with underlying tension.

"Dillon is fine, please," he interjects, flashing a toothy grin.

"Dillon," Nina corrects with a smile, maintaining her composure. "I realize this may seem rather unorthodox, but I'm in search of someone, and I was hoping you might be able to provide some insight." As she speaks, I can't help but notice the slight raise of his eyebrow.

"And who would you be seeking?"

"Ian Whalen."

His eyes widen momentarily before he swiftly masks his expression, adopting an air of indifference. "I'm afraid I'm not certain how I can assist you. It's been quite some time since Ian was associated with Providence."

"I'm aware," she says. "But you were roommates. Surely, you've remained in touch."

"I haven't been in contact with him since he left."

His right eye twitches, and his fingers tap on his desk. Two signs that tell me he isn't being truthful.

"Do you have any idea where Ian might've gone? Another university?" she asks, and he slams his lips together, shaking his head.

"I'm sorry. I have no information. I wish I could be more help."

Nina's expression falls, indicating she's giving up, but I won't allow it. I subtly nudge her foot with my own, silently urging her to continue with her questioning. She glances up at me from the corner of her eye, and I tap her foot again, hoping to convey the importance of making physical contact with him. After a deep breath, she leans forward and places her hand on top of his, halting the rhythmic strumming. Although he eyes her hand with curiosity, he doesn't move his hand out from under hers.

"Are you sure he never mentioned where he was going? He must have said something," I press, noticing the bob of his throat as he prepares to fabricate another lie.

"I'm sorry. I don't have any information," he repeats, finally withdrawing his hand.

Rising from his chair, he moves toward the door. "If there's nothing else I can assist you with, I'm afraid I must make my way across campus for my next class."

Nina straightens her shoulders and follows suit, making her

way to the door. As she extends her hand, he accepts it, looking apprehensive.

"Thank you, Professor. You've been most helpful."

She offers no further explanation, marching out of the office with me close behind.

"Florida," she whispers as we make our way down the hall.

"So . . . care to tell me what you saw when you touched the professor?"

She places her phone down and turns to me. "Ian's mother is in a retirement village in Florida. I saw the sign that said *The Communes* and then his mom on a patio, sipping something from a mug."

"That's a great lead," I say, picking up my pace to stay next to Nina. "Do you think Ian's there too?"

"No. But I think she knows where he is. Seems like Dillon only has contact with her."

"What's the next move?"

"I'm leaving for Florida, as soon as possible. I need to book my flight."

I twist my mouth. "And you weren't going to take me with you?"

She expels a weary sigh. "I don't want to keep you away from your own stuff, Alyssa."

"You're going to sunshine and warmth. Why on earth would you think I'd want to pass on that leg of the journey?"

She smirks. "Well . . . in that case, I'll book two tickets?"

I bob my head.

Florida, here we come.

Nine of Swords

As the dimly lit bar buzzed with conversation, a beautiful girl sat alone at the end of the bar, bathed in the soft glow of overhead lights. Her gaze fixed on the liquid swirling within her glass. With every sip of her gin and tonic, she seemed lost in thought, her mind a universe of its own, at least to the curious onlooker.

There was a quiet intensity about her as she glanced around the room with a calculated gaze, her eyes darting from one customer to the next, waiting for the right moment to unfold.

A handsome stranger met her eyes, catching her off guard. She wasn't supposed to be seen or noticed, but that wasn't likely to happen. The girl was gorgeous, drawing more attention than she realized. She moved her long, blond hair over her shoulder, pulling her eyes back to her drink and away from his penetrating stare. She waited.

An hour later, the time had come. She slipped an envelope discreetly across the worn wooden surface of the bar before casting a quick glance around, ensuring that no prying eyes caught her clandestine exchange.

The bartender accepted the envelope with practiced ease, slipping it swiftly beneath the bar top with a subtle nod of acknowledgment. He knew what to do.

With her task completed, the girl nonchalantly finished the remnants of her drink, the clink of ice against glass barely audible over the music pouring from the jukebox in the corner. Without so much as a second glance, she rose from her seat and headed toward the exit.

A sense of unease prickled at the back of her neck, and her steps quickened ever so slightly. But it was no use. A strong arm wrapped around her waist, pulling her back with startling force. A hand clamped over her mouth, muffling the scream that threatened to escape her lips.

In the darkness, a struggle ensued, the girl's heart pounding against her chest as she fought against the unknown attacker. Panic surged, her heart hammering against her rib cage in a desperate rhythm. Darkness enveloped her, swallowing her whole.

I sit straight up, hands flying to my neck as a scream bursts from my chest.

"Alyssa? What's wrong?" Nina's concerned voice rings through the dark room, instantly bringing me back to my senses.

It was only a dream.

My breathing begins to regulate, and my heart rate slows considerably.

"Holy shit . . . that was intense," I say, hand held to my heart. "So real."

The lamp next to me flicks on, and the dark room is bathed in light. Nina's standing over me, dressed in navy-and-white plaid pajamas. The shorts are barely visible under the button-down.

I peek up at her, grimacing. "I'm sorry for waking you."

"You were screaming. Scared the hell out of me," she says, running her hand back through her hair. "I thought someone was murdering you."

"Were you still up?" I ask, recognizing she hadn't been in bed.

"No. I fell asleep on the couch watching *20/20*. Which didn't help."

Despite the heaviness still lingering from that awful dream, I laugh.

"Care to tell me what that was about?" Nina asks, taking a seat on the bed.

I relay everything I can remember and allow her to sit with it for a few minutes. Recalling the specifics only drives home the point that it was the strangest dream I've ever had. It was so real. Like I was watching through a camera lens, waiting for something to go down.

"You weren't in the dream? Nobody you know was in the dream?" she asks, and I purse my lips thinking about it, which doesn't take long.

"No. There were three people that I remember, and I know none of them."

She bites on her cheek, eyes narrowed. "That's strange . . . right?"

I huff, sitting back against the headboard. "What isn't strange anymore, Nins? Ever since my birthday, things have taken a turn for crazy town, and we seem to be driving the train."

She nods, blowing out a harsh breath. "Have you considered that maybe it wasn't a dream?"

I turn toward her, gaze narrowed in on my friend.

"Humor me for a moment," she says, and I arch a brow. "What if it was a prophecy? Or a vision?"

I'm thoroughly speechless. This is Nina speaking—an educated therapist, who would typically have an entirely separate explanation for my dream.

Oh, how times have changed.

"Don't look at me like that," she snaps.

"Like what?" I lean to the side, reaching for my glass of water sitting on the nightstand.

"Like I'm talking foolish. You and I both know that these things are real."

I gulp down the rest of the glass and turn toward her.

"I'm just surprised to hear you say it. That's all," I explain, smiling to calm her temper. "I see ghosts, Nina. I don't see visions."

She huffs. "I touch people and see visions. Why is it hard to believe that you can see visions as well as ghosts? It's entirely possible to have more than one ability, Ally."

I consider what she's suggesting, finding that I have no rebuttal.

"I've been doing some research," she says, pulling the blanket over her legs. "Trying to understand my ability. And through that research, I read a lot about people with abilities like ours. It's not uncommon to have more than one. In fact, it's less common not to."

While I've been preoccupied with shoving my abilities aside, Nina has been dedicated to unraveling the mysteries of our capabilities—a pursuit I should have been actively engaged in as well.

How many latent powers could be lying within me?

"Let's assume that you're correct," I say, arching an eyebrow. "What can I do with the dream?"

Her tongue protrudes from the side of her mouth while she appears to concentrate.

"I think it's very important for you to write down every single detail while it's fresh. And then, you should probably try to connect with the girl, because it's likely she's already dead."

Anxiety coils in my stomach as I entertain the morose possibility. "Do you think?"

Her grim expression says she absolutely thinks it's possible.

"If it's a vision and what you saw has already transpired, then yes, she's likely deceased. However, if it's a prophecy, you might be able to save her."

I blink repeatedly, replaying her words in my mind.

"How? If she's not a spirit, I can't connect with her."

Her gaze locks onto mine, and I detect a hint of sorrow lingering within her icy irises.

"Don't you see the similarities between Chelsea Grayson and the woman in your dream?"

I'm not even sure what happened to Chelsea. All I have to rely on are a few movie clips depicting the demise of other girls.

"There's likely a connection," she remarks, and I wonder if she could be right.

I don't have to ponder for long because in the dim corner of the room, not one but two ghostly figures flicker in and out of sight, their faces twisted in silent screams. The girl in the red dress, unmistakably Chelsea Grayson, is one of them, but the blond girl, with hair tangled and matted, wearing the same outfit she wore in my dream, remains nameless.

"Who are you?" I whisper, knowing deep down not to expect a response.

Poltergeists don't communicate with words. If anything, they assault your senses with a deafening banshee cry.

"You were right," I say, not taking my eyes off the specters. "She's dead, and they are connected."

I hear her intake of breath. "You need to call Nick."

She's right. He needs to know that there's another victim.

I grab my phone from the nightstand and make the call, paying no attention to the fact it's two a.m.

"Hello?" His craggy voice is full of sleep, and I instantly feel bad for waking him. "Alyssa?" he says when I don't speak.

"I'm sorry to wake you, but we have a problem."

There's a rustling on his end, and I envision Nick springing from bed, his concern overriding any remnants of sleep. "What's happened?" he asks, sounding every bit the detective.

"There's another victim. Her death was much the same as Chelsea's," I say, knowing he's going to need much more than that. "I don't know who she is, but she's blond and young like Chelsea."

"How do you know this? Did she come to you?"

"Yes. She appeared beside Chelsea, which is why I know it was the same person who killed her."

He sighs heavily. "What else do you have that I can use to find her?"

"Her body was dumped in water too, so I'd start by the docks."

I pause, trying to decide whether to tell him about the dream. Seeing ghosts, I've proven, but the dream part is new even for me. In the end, I decide to trust that he won't rebuff me.

"I saw her in a dream before she came to me in life," I admit. "She was at an underground speakeasy, running drugs."

"I'll check for local missing persons and see if I can match the description you've given with someone." He huffs. "Is there anything about the speakeasy you can tell me?"

I search through my memories of the dream, finding nothing of use. I'm about to tell him that when I remember that the bar napkin had a symbol on it.

"There was a symbol. I'm not sure if it's random or part of the club, but it was a triangle with an eye in the center. Well . . . the oval shape of an eye with another upside-down triangle interlocked with a half triangle."

"Half triangle," Nick says, mostly to himself.

"It didn't have the bottom line. Instead, the ends of the intersecting lines looked like inverted feet."

"Wait . . ." he says, words trailing off. "I'm sending you a photo. Can you confirm that this is the symbol you saw?"

My phone pings, indicating a text, and I pull it up to see exactly what I was attempting to describe. At least in part.

"That's it, if you put the eye around that and center the eye in the middle of a full triangle."

"That's helpful, Alyssa. Very helpful."

I smile, even though he can't see me. I'm just happy to know I've given him something to work with.

"How are you doing? Has . . . have you seen Isla?"

"No. I haven't. I actually left the ring back at my place," I admit, feeling guilty for purposefully leaving her behind.

It's no offense to Isla—she's lovely—but I wanted to focus on Nina while we search for Ian.

"That makes sense," he says around a yawn. "Well . . . I hope you and Nina are enjoying your trip. I . . ." His words trail off, and I wonder if he's going to complete the sentence, and then he does. "Miss you."

A smile spreads across my face. "I miss you too. Hopefully we can both wrap up our mysteries and get back to that date that seems to evade us at every turn."

"I'd like that." He sighs. "I should probably start looking into your blonde. Get some sleep, okay?"

"I will. And if I learn of anything else, I'll let you know."

"Thanks, Lyss. I'll talk to you soon," he says before ending the call.

"That went well," Nina says, swiping through her phone.

"It did, but I know I put so much more on his plate. Another body is going to make this case all the harder for him." I sigh.

She doesn't comment on that because she knows I'm right. With every additional piece of information that was dragged to the surface revolving around Richard, things got more difficult. Sometimes, more isn't better when trying a murder case. There's too much room for a mistrial, which means that one family is likely to get screwed out of justice.

Five of Pentacles

WE'VE JUST ARRIVED in Florida and our first order of business is to buy groceries, since we'll be here for a week.

We've split up, each with our own list of items to grab.

I've just finished my list when I spot Nina in the produce section, eyes fixed on a cucumber. Her shoulders are slumped, and I don't miss the way her hands shake.

Even from a distance, it's clear she's upset.

"Dammit," I say under my breath.

I've only been away from her for fifteen minutes. What the hell could've happened in that short amount of time?

I lean over my shopping cart, swerving around people like a seasoned race car driver. Random shoppers call out greetings as if they know me. I offer a half-hearted wave to a few, but my focus is on getting to Nina.

As soon as she spots me, her demeanor shifts instantly, relief flooding her features. I'm overcome with the urge to pull her close, to offer comfort in the midst of whatever turmoil she's facing.

But I know drawing attention to her would only exacerbate the situation.

I tamp down the emotion swelling within me and put on my cheeriest face.

"Hey, Nins. What's up with the cucumber?"

She looks down at the misshapen vegetable with contempt. "Nothing. I . . ." She stops mid-sentence, placing the cucumber in her small, black basket, glancing at the shelves once more. She grabs a package of celery before turning back to me.

"Since when do you cook with celery?" I ask, one corner of my lip tipped up.

She despises celery. Claims it lacks flavor and finds the crunchiness pointless. Nina gazes down at her hands, grimacing slightly before returning the package to the shelf. There's a noticeable swallow, and I catch the subtle quiver of her bottom lip.

Lowering my voice even further, I edge a little closer. "Look at me. Take a deep breath." She blinks repeatedly, then inhales and exhales, a sigh of relief escaping her lips. She appears calmer than she did just moments ago.

"What's wrong?"

"Richard is contesting the divorce. My attorney just called."

I see red, the need to throttle his smarmy ass so intense I'm practically choking on it.

"Can he do that?" I say a little too loud, drawing attention to us.

I'm sorry, I mouth to the elderly gentleman next to us. He offers a tight-lipped smile, going about his business.

"He can definitely draw it out and make the whole process miserable." She shakes her head. "I'm not sure why I'm surprised."

"While that's not great news, it's not the end of the world. We'll fight this. I'll be right by your side."

She clears her throat, standing up straight and appearing more like Nina. "You're right. We're not going to talk about that man and his bullshit. We're here to find Ian."

"Let's go," I say, wrapping my arm under hers and steering my cart with one hand.

"What are we cooking tonight?" I ask, to get her mind off Richard's antics.

"I don't even know," she says. "I haven't gotten half of the things on my list."

"Not a big deal," I say. "Let's make some lasagna and garlic bread." I glance at her out of the corner of my eye. "Comfort night like we used to have in college."

She snorts. "That happened like one time."

I shrug. "Still happened. You helped me get over a devastating breakup by way of food. Let me comfort you in the same way."

She smiles. "I'm not devastated about my divorce."

"Obviously," I say, making a face. "Good riddance."

Nina chuckles, shaking her head. "Dinner sounds perfect." She slows her pace a little bit, and I follow her lead. "I think tonight is a wine night. What do you think?"

"Of course it's a wine night."

She squeezes my arm. "Thank you, Ally. You don't know how much I appreciate you."

I smile, her words warming my heart. "I'm going to grab the ingredients we need and a couple bottles of wine."

"I'll get dessert," she offers.

I clap my hands together, drawing the attention of an elderly woman currently inspecting the back of a jar of peanut butter.

"Perfect. I'll see you in a bit."

Nina turns around to head in the opposite direction, bumping right into someone. She screeches and jumps back as though the lady electrocuted her.

"Nina?"

My eyes narrow in on the petite woman, decked out in a neon tennis skirt and white tank.

Recognition dawns, and I realize it's Jill Kincaid, a woman Nina and I went to college with.

Nina's eyes are wide, and she rubs at her chest. "I . . . I'm fine." Her head drops, shaking back and forth. "Sorry, I didn't mean to run into you. What are you doing here?"

"It's absolutely fine," Jill says, placing a hand on Nina's shoulder. "It sounded like you were hurt, if anything."

Nina does a good job at trying to hide the wince, but I see it.

She saw something when they touched.

"No. No . . . it was just static," she says, taking a step back and disconnecting herself from Jill. "I hope I didn't zap you too."

Jill waves a hand in the air. "I'm fine. It was my fault we collided. I'm hardly paying attention. I'm just coming from pickleball and I'm rushing around."

"Pickleball," Nina says, nose wrinkling.

"Well . . . yes. It's the thing to do in The Communes."

"Hi, Jill," I say, approaching the pair.

Jill's eyes widen. "Oh my god, Alyssa. How are you?"

"Fine. What a shock to see you here," I admit. "It's been ages."

She bobs her head. "It has. I've lived here for the last ten years. My husband retired and wanted to move south." She shrugs nonchalantly. "This place is a wet dream."

Nina snorts, mumbling, "That's one way to put it."

"What was that?" Jill asks, leaning forward.

My eyes are trained in on Nina, wondering what her comment was about. Thankfully, Jill doesn't seem to have heard her words.

"Sorry, nothing. I just . . . I've gotta get going. Just saw the time and realized we have places to be."

Jill nods her head, glancing down at her fitness watch. "Me too, actually. Are you two in town for a few days?"

"Yes," I say, and Nina shoots me a look, suggesting I should've kept that to myself.

"Fabulous. You two must join me tomorrow on the pickleball courts."

I always liked Jill, and some exercise would be good for me.

"I'm in," I say, glancing to Nina.

She shrugs, offering a close-lipped smile. "Sure. Why not."

"Wonderful. Meet me at Rockwood Center at eleven."

"We'll be there," Nina says, and Jill leaps forward and pulls her into a hug. "We have a lot of catching up to do, missy."

Nina's entire body stiffens, but I can't see her face.

"I want to hear all about your life. I'm sure it's been fab," Jill says, glancing toward me, and my hand flies to my throat. There's a tightness there.

It's clear she doesn't know a thing about Richard.

"Oh . . . it's been fab," Nina says, pulling out of Jill's grip. "See you tomorrow." Nina turns toward me. "I'll finish up here and meet you at the front in five."

And with that, she's rushing off, leaving me standing in the middle of aisle five with Jill staring at me like someone stole her candy.

"How are you? Truly?" Jill asks. "I can't imagine how hard things have been for you."

Clearly Jill knows about Garrett, and she seems to care.

"It's been tough, but I'm slowly transitioning to my new normal. Not easily, but one day at a time it's improving."

"I'm just so sorry."

I swallow the lump forming in my throat. It's never easy encountering someone for the first time since Garrett's passing.

"I appreciate it, Jill."

"You ladies need to experience The Communes in all its glory. Let your hair down and party until everything closes down at nine."

Laughter bubbles from her chest. "The after-hour parties are the best." She winks, and I have to wonder what goes on at these after-hour parties.

"You look great, by the way," she compliments, her smile widening as she glances down at my legs.

I fidget in place, feeling awkward.

What she's seeing is a very well-designed pair of yoga pants that make me look like I lost five pounds instantly, as they suck everything in.

Ava bought them for me for Christmas, and I will be getting at least two additional pairs.

"Thank you. I appreciate that," I reply, resisting the urge to divulge the secret behind my seemingly trim figure. I'm eager to steer the conversation away from this increasingly strange topic.

"We'll make plans tomorrow. You girls have a good night," she says, waving a hand in the air. "See you at eleven."

She saunters away, her hips swaying in a manner that seems deliberately attention seeking. It's classic Jill Kincaid—she's always been a glory hound and total hell-raiser. Looks like not much has changed.

I shake off the discomfort caused by Jill's overt appraisal of my body and head straight for the wine aisle. I grab three bottles, but then decide to grab another one.

We're definitely going to need it.

"THAT WAS DELICIOUS," I say, slumping back into the cream wingback chair, stuffed to an uncomfortable degree.

"It's been a long while since I've had lasagna," Nina comments, likely remembering all the times that her dipshit ex scolded her about her food choices. "The perfect comfort food." She sighs contentedly.

We've enjoyed ourselves through dinner, keeping the conversation light, with me doing the bulk of the heavy lifting. I've caught her up on my time spent with Ava before she returned to school and the party that she claims nobody has stopped talking about.

"When is her spring showcase?" Nina asks, tapping her mouth with a red napkin.

"April, but I can't remember the exact date off the top of my head."

"That's exciting. I bet hers will be the best."

I smile, thinking about all the work she's put into her project already. She hasn't allowed me to see it, but she's told me about every single hour spent piecing it together.

"It's going to be quite the ordeal," I say, wiping my mouth with my napkin. I set it on the table, prepared to shift the conversation to her.

"What happened back at the store with Jill? You clearly saw something you didn't like."

Nina takes a dainty sip of her merlot, licking her lips once she's swallowed. "Caught that, did you?"

I tilt my head and smirk. "Spill the details," I press, but she only chuckles, keeping her secrets.

My impatience shows as I make a face, hoping she gets the message. Eventually, she gives in, sighing and placing her hands in her lap.

"When I touched her . . . I saw a montage of her sleeping with half The Communes." She clicks her tongue, squinting one eye. "Both men and women."

I snort. "Awkward. Now you're being subjected to X-rated peep shows? What kind of gift did you get cursed with?" I chuckle, but her lips are smashed into a thin line, signaling she doesn't find any humor in it.

"Yeah . . . you're right. It's not funny. Sorry."

She shrugs. "It's her business. Not mine." She clears her throat, leaning in as though to share a secret. "She's into some pretty kinky things."

I attempt, unsuccessfully, to stifle my laughter at Nina's appalled expression.

"Kink shaming, Nina? I didn't think you of all people would be so scandalized. You lived with Richard Dunbar, king of orgies back in the day."

She grimaces. "That was before my time. And I'm not kink shaming. To each their own. I'm just saying that hers are a shade darker than what I'm accustomed to."

My eyebrow lifts in question. "Just what are you used to?" I tease, watching her cheeks flush with color.

She shakes her head. "Not me personally. From movies."

"Riiight," I drawl, earning myself a severe scowl.

I raise my wineglass to my lips, observing her nose scrunching as she chews on her cheek. "I don't think I could even bend my legs like that."

I choke on the wine, spluttering as she looks on in confusion.

"Are you all right?" she asks.

I bob my head. "Yes, of course. I was just thinking how it doesn't seem right that some women can bend themselves like pretzels while the rest of us are hardly able to bend at the hips." I smirk and she smacks her lips together in pure irritation.

I suck on my teeth, thinking about Nina's situation. What we need to determine is how this ability of hers works.

"How often is this happening? Is there anything that seems to trigger it?" I ask, watching her neck roll.

"It's happening far more often than I'd like," she admits. "When I touch someone, I typically see *some*thing."

"Is everything you see bad?"

She's quiet for several moments, seeming to contemplate my question. Likely by running through what she's seen.

"Yes," she finally says. "Even when I touched the professor and saw Ian's mother, it was a vision of her being very sick."

"We need to consult Natalia about this. She should have some insight. At least I hope so, for your sake."

"In the meantime, I guess being a town outsider will have its perks after all. When people avoid you, it's hard to touch them."

I purse my lips, not liking the way Nina's downplaying something that is clearly painful. It's not like her, which I'm adding to my growing list of things to address.

"I know way too much about Knox Harbor and the people who live there. They're all hiding things. Some darker than others." She visibly shivers. "I do not want to know any of it."

"Sounds to me like there are a lot of people throwing stones while living in glass houses around Knox Harbor," I grumble. "Maybe the next time someone looks at you weird, you should go ahead and touch them. Let them know that they're not as perfect as they like to pretend."

She laughs. "Maybe you're right. Maybe I should give them a taste of their own medicine."

We both laugh, thinking about that scenario. It would certainly make things interesting around there, but it would also put more of a spotlight on Nina. They'd simply find a way to turn it around on her.

"But you won't, because that's not you," I say, and she nods.

"I wish I had the nerve. I wish I wasn't so scared of what people think of me."

"There's nothing wrong with being a good person. Don't change who you are, Nina. Richard could make anyone bitter, but I don't want to see you turn into that."

"That's the problem, Ally. I don't even know who I am," she says, slumped over the table. "I spent so many years putting on a front." She huffs, shaking her head. "I've been wearing so many masks that when I look at myself in the mirror, it's like I'm looking at a stranger. All the hopes and dreams I had growing up, I threw aside."

I lean over my plate, getting as close to her as I can. "You keep telling me about how this is my second chance. Well, you have one too. You're not stuck in this life, Nina. You can change your fate."

"How?" She practically whispers the word, but I hear the way her voice breaks.

"One day at a time," I say. "Make a list of non-negotiables. What is it you want out of life? What will you absolutely not put up with? Write it down, and every day commit to it."

"That . . . sounds like a good idea."

"Now . . . about tomorrow," I say, remembering our plans to meet Jill. "Do you know anything about pickleball?"

She makes a disgruntled noise. "Not much. And for the record, this was all your doing. If this goes sideways, I'm blaming you."

I smirk. "Deal. But what could go wrong with a game seemingly made for senior citizens?"

She shoots me a look that suggests a whole host of things could go sideways.

"Either way, you'd better be prepared, because I am not about to lose to Jill Kincaid."

Their rivalry apparently lives on.

Five of Wands

THE SUN BEATS down on the pickleball court, causing sweat to drip from places it should not. My boobs are smashed into one of Nina's sports bras that's a size, maybe two, too small, because the last thing I anticipated while packing for a getaway to Florida was an intense game of pickleball and thus the need for a boulder holder for sports.

Nina and Jill were dubbed captains, not that it was necessary. In no way was I potentially playing with a stranger who, within minutes of meeting her, made it clear that this was her sport.

Jill and her friend Sandra came in matching outfits: neon pink skorts with white racerback tanks, and matching white sneakers with pink swishes. They swore total domination, and honestly, I believed them. I was ready to fake an ankle sprain and bail before the game even started. But then I saw Nina's eyes light up with that competitive fire—she was in it to win it, and there was no turning back.

Her determination is evident in every swift movement, every lethal swing of her paddle. She plays like she's been at this for decades, which leaves me sputtering profanities every time Sandra nails the ball right at my face.

"Shit!" I shriek as the yellow missile rockets toward me. I barely avoid it, but I don't miss Nina's exasperated groan, which is quickly smothered by cheers.

"Nice call, Ally," she shouts.

She doesn't bother to explain, so I'm left assuming the ball must have gone out of bounds. I'd do about anything to make my own exit at this point.

"You're up," she says, handing the ball over to me, apparently my turn to serve.

I've been watching the three women, who seem to know the game like the back of their hand, and think I have the method figured out. The key is to get it in the big rectangle, but over the part called the kitchen.

I make my move, and the ball is in motion, flying back toward me. I allow it to bounce, then hit it back over the net. My feet move me instantly up toward the net, next to Nina.

The pickleball court crackles with energy as the intense match continues. The ball pings back and forth, creating a noise that is beginning to grate on my nerves. From the sidelines, an outsider might mistake me for a pickleball prodigy, but let's be real. It's my sheer terror of losing the game for Nina that fuels my surprisingly competent performance.

I have to admit, Jill and Sandra make for a dynamic duo, playing with seamless coordination, anticipating each other's every move. Meanwhile, Nina and I are faking it until we make it. Or at least I am. I'm clinging on to the idea of beginner's luck carrying me through this shit show.

We're in the middle of a long rally that stretches on as both sides refuse to yield an inch.

I'm simply trying to not let Nina down.

Sweat glistens on Jill and Sandra's brows as they dart across the court, their focus unwavering amidst the intensity of the game. With every volley, the tension mounts, the stakes growing higher with each passing moment.

As the game progresses, it becomes apparent that Jill and Sandra aren't just playing to win; they're aiming their shots directly at Nina with the precision of vengeful sharpshooters. Each time they hit their mark, it feels like the court is about to turn into a full-blown war zone.

Nina stops mid-play, throwing her hands up in the air, apparently done ignoring the deliberate targeting. "What's with all the aggressive shots?" she calls out, frustration lacing her voice.

Jill smirks, her eyes glinting mischievously. "Just having a bit of fun. Aren't we, Sandra?"

It's clear by Nina's stance that she isn't having it. "Well, it's not fun. It's bullshit and I'm done," she snaps, turning on her heels and walking toward the exit.

I immediately see red for my friend. If I'd known Jill would still be a jealous drama queen all these years later, I would've steered clear of this athletic torture—and the unnecessary emotional damage for Nina.

"Seriously?" I say, lifting my hands. "You invited us here, and this is how you're going to act?" I shake my head. "It's a bit disappointing to see that some things never change, Jill."

Jill's expression softens as she glances toward Nina. "You're right. Nina," she calls out. "Come back. We're sorry." There's a hint of sheepishness in her tone, and Nina must recognize it because she stops and turns around, stalking back toward us.

"I'm sorry, Nina, I didn't mean to upset you. Can we—"

"Save it, Kincaid," she cuts in, shooting me a look that could freeze lava as she storms by.

"Let's finish this," she says to me, not addressing the other two at all.

They shrug, getting into position, the game starting back up on game point.

Sandra hits the ball toward Nina, appearing to use every ounce of strength to catapult it toward her, putting a spin on it that I fear will be hard to return, but Nina manages without effort, sending it directly to the back line, making it difficult to tell if it will be in or out.

Sandra looks and makes the decision it'll be out, but she's incorrect. The ball hits the line and game, set, match.

"Ahh. We won," Nina says, acting like it's no big deal, when I can tell she wants to break out into a full-on dance. "Looks like your plan didn't work. Never does, but you don't seem to learn, do you, Jillian?"

Jill's face flushes, and I wait for shit to hit the fan. She hates to be called Jillian. Loathes it. And Nina has always wielded it as a weapon. Instead, Jill tips her head back and starts laughing, and soon, Nina joins her.

Sandra looks on, horrified and confused, but I just shrug.

This is how Jill and Nina were in college. They had a love-hate relationship that often ended in explosive arguments after a night at the bar. Too many drinks were typically to blame, but maybe it was their personalities all along, the alcohol only exacerbating things.

Jill places her arm around Nina's shoulder, walking her off toward the benches in the shade.

"Might as well join them," I say, motioning toward the exit.

We sit for over an hour, catching our breaths and talking the paths our lives have taken.

Jill's gaze drifts to the ground, her expression pensive. With a heavy sigh, she finally looks up, her voice tinged with a hint of melancholy.

"You know, I had the biggest crush on Richard back in college," she admits, her words laced with a mixture of nostalgia and regret. "I thought he was the one, you know? I wanted to marry him, but in the end, you won his heart."

Nina and I exchange a knowing glance, sensing the weight behind Jill's confession. Nina reaches out a comforting hand, offering silent support to Jill, knowing the bombshell she's about to drop.

"I remember that early on, you liked him. But I thought you changed your mind," Nina replies softly, her tone gentle. "You dodged a bullet. Richard is a horrible man."

Jill's eyes widen in surprise at Nina's blunt assessment. "What do you mean?" she asks, seeming caught off guard by Nina's declaration.

Nina takes a deep breath, her words measured yet firm. "He was the worst husband, Jill. He cheated on me. He lied." She shakes her head, chuckling darkly. "He made my life miserable," she admits.

A flicker of concern crosses over Jill's face as she absorbs Nina's words.

"He's in jail for murder."

Jill's head snaps up, her eyes blinking rapidly. "What? Are you serious?"

Nina fills Jill in on all the details, and she sits quietly through it all. A moment of understanding passes between them, the tension from earlier on the court dissipating as the weight of Nina's revelation settles in.

Eventually, the sun dips below the horizon, casting long shadows across the court as we sit together in silent solidarity.

"We should meet up again sometime," I suggest, breaking the silence. "But let's plan something less . . . physical."

Jill and Nina exchange a glance, nodding in agreement. "For sure," Jill says, a genuine smile playing on her lips. "Tonight, and I know the perfect place."

"I SWEAR TO god, if we end up at an orgy, I'm going to kill you," I say to Nina as she finishes applying her lipstick.

"You really don't think . . ." Her words trail off as her eyes get larger. "I'm texting her to ensure that's not the plan."

I can't help but chuckle at Nina's obvious discomfort at the mere mention of sexual debauchery. The thought of her reaction to being dragged into something like that is quite amusing. But I'm not concerned. Jill knows that sort of thing isn't our scene.

She dabbled in some questionable activities in college, and we made it clear back then that we weren't interested. She never pushed. We'll likely be enjoying a lively night out on the square, as Jill suggested.

As I finish applying the last layer of mascara, I step back and appreciate my reflection in the mirror. A smile spreads across my lips as I notice the results of my new nightly skin care routine. The fine lines around my eyes seem less pronounced, a testament to the effectiveness of the absurdly priced products I've been using.

I've been contemplating Botox, but only for my forehead. The lines there are too deep for any cream to make a significant difference. It's not a necessity, but it's something I want for me, and I have the means to afford it. There shouldn't be shame for a woman investing in herself. I refuse to let anyone's opinions on it dictate my choices. Often, others' views are a reflection of their envy. Nothing more. If they had the money, they'd likely do it too.

Twenty minutes later, we're out the door and in the square where we agreed to meet Jill.

The Communes sprawl before us like a utopian oasis for retirees. It's reminiscent of other retirement communities in Florida, but with an air of exclusivity that sets it apart.

Jill, ever the social butterfly, is surrounded by a group of people, chatting animatedly while sipping an amber cocktail. I catch her eye, and her face lights up, hands flying into the air, alcohol spilling over the side of her plastic cup.

"You made it," she cheers, pulling Nina into a side hug. "I was afraid you two would pull your typical shenanigans and ditch."

Her lips smash together, and Nina laughs.

"We were looking forward to it."

Jill smirks, leaning in close to us. "As long as the dicks and chicks remain clothed."

Nina splutters, and I smother a grin.

"You were always up for testing boundaries," I say, my shoulders shaking with laughter.

She offers a toothy smile, waggling her eyebrows before grabbing Nina by the elbow and pulling her toward a group of people.

Jill had a knack for attracting the attention of wealthy men, and tonight appears to be no exception. They swarm to her like bees on honey, each vying for her attention in ways I find a bit pathetic.

"Let's dance," I suggest to Nina, and she nods, appearing eager to get away from Jill and her harem.

A cover band is playing nineties hits, which seems to please the diverse crowd. It's definitely what Nina and I would've chosen. We dance and sing along to the songs, having a great time.

"Here," Jill says, reaching between us to place plastic cups full of liquor in each of our hands. "Drink up. We got the invite of the year."

Nina and I share a glance, and Jill rolls her eyes.

"Don't clutch your pearls just yet, Nina Joy," Jill says, a Cheshire-cat grin lighting up her face. "We've been invited to an underground poker tournament. A very exclusive invite."

Her eyes travel over to a group of regal men who reek of too much money. A salt-and-pepper-haired man with piercing blue eyes smiles at Jill, lifting his chin slightly.

"Who is that?" I ask, not immune to the charm he emanates, even from a distance.

"That's Harlan Abbott. He's part of the investment group that built The Communes." She turns toward us. "And our ticket to fun."

Within five minutes, Nina, Jill, and I are escorted into a decked-out golf cart with the most comfortable seats I've ever sat upon.

"Help yourself to anything in the cooler, ladies." Harlan's deep brogue curls around me, and I shiver in response.

Not because it's sensual and manly, which it is, but for a reason I can't quite pinpoint. He has me a bit on edge, especially considering we know nothing about this guy, and Jill hasn't always been the best judge of character.

He drives down the golf-cart path for a good forty-five minutes, steering us toward the far end of The Communes, where the nature reserves begin. He pulls the cart onto a small hiking trail, just wide enough for the cart to traverse. Branches scratch against the pristine metallic finish, and I grimace at the horrific sound. Harlan doesn't seem bothered that his fancy cart is being scratched to hell.

The ride is bumpy, and I'm just about to ask how much farther it is when the trees open up and a set of massive iron gates with a giant M in the middle greets us. Beyond the gates sits an old, abandoned house, straight from a horror movie.

"Nope," I say, shaking my head. I lean into Nina, whispering, "I did not come here with you to get axed."

She grits her teeth, looking about as comfortable with our current situation as I am.

"Welcome to the old Montgomery Estate," Harlan says, as the gates creak open by some unseen force.

I peer up to the dark manor ahead, not a light to be seen.

Jill squeals, clapping her hands in excitement. I turn toward her, face screwed up in a mix of emotional distress and confusion.

Harlan turns back toward Nina and me and takes a breath. "I don't think I need to say this considering Jill is your friend, but I'd be remiss if I didn't ensure that you understand that you are never to speak of this place. Not to anyone." He looks at Nina and then at me. "Can I trust that anything you see tonight will never be shared outside of these gates?"

I nod, and so does Nina.

"Of course," I say, because what is the alternative?

He smiles. "Very well."

I'm pulled from the safety of the golf cart and dragged by Nina toward the dark house that looms over us. The front door squeaks open and we enter, not a sound to be heard.

My concern is growing, the hairs on my neck prickling to attention.

We're led to the back of the house, stopping in front of a large fireplace surrounded by a bloodred wall.

"Are we waiting for everyone?" Jill asks, no hint of apprehension evident in her tone.

Harlan smiles, and it does nothing to ease my racing heart. He steps forward and touches the side of the fireplace, over a stone that's a shade darker than the others. The fireplace wall springs out, opening to a set of stairs. The fireplace had been an illusion, hiding a secret passage to god only knows where.

"After you," Harlan says, sweeping his hand out, gesturing for us to move down the steps into the dark abyss.

This whole scene brings to mind my first encounter with Natalia. That ended fine. This will too.

Jill is already halfway down the steep flight of stairs before my foot has hit the first step down. The only thing visible is the light shining from Jill's phone.

We walk down a long tunnel that's nothing but brick and mortar.

"What is this place?" I whisper, but Harlan hears me.

"Montgomery Estate was built in the late 1800s. During prohibition, the owners, Francis and Alta Montgomery, hosted many underground events here," he says.

"They surely didn't build tunnels in that time," Nina says, looking around.

Harlan chuckles. "No. The tunnels were constructed during the original build. The home was built by Francis Montgomery's grandfather August Montgomery. He was . . . rather eccentric, from what I've been told. As a child, he lived through the Civil War, and that experience led to the tunnels."

"Safety," I say, mostly to myself.

"Exactly," Harlan answers. "He wanted a way to hide his family in the event that war was to ever take place on American soil again."

We finally reach a set of double iron doors, a keypad fixed to the wall next to the entrance. Harlan quickly taps in a code, and the doors open to a room bursting with activity.

We enter the clandestine venue, where anticipation crackles in the air. The rich aroma of cigars mingles with the sound of chips against the felt-covered tables. Men and women, dressed in their finest, gathered around poker tables, their faces masked with confidence.

I watch in awe as the games unfold around me, the stakes high. The tension in the room is palpable as the players inspect their hands. Each card dealt has the ability to make or break the person's bank.

The entire place is glamorous and exciting, and highly illegal. Whoever is behind these games is certainly turning a profit. I can't shake the feeling of unease that gnaws at the back of my mind, knowing that we shouldn't be here. This could put Nina and me in a very bad position if we're caught.

"Ladies," Harlon coos, placing his hand at the base of Jill's back. "Grab yourselves a drink from the bar and join a game. If poker doesn't pique your interest, there are billiards in the next room. Or you can always join the ladies in the parlor that's through the curtains beyond the billiards room."

Jill leans up on her toes, whispering something into Harlan's ear, and his eyes darken, his tongue swiping slowly across his bottom lip.

"Yes, I think you're right, Jill." He smiles down at her. "Can I offer you two any . . . party favors?"

"No, thank you," Nina says, sounding calm and sure. "I have a big day tomorrow. Need to keep my head about me."

Harlan bows his head, turning toward me.

"Unfortunately, I'm with her tomorrow, and will also need to refrain from party favors. But thank you for the hospitality." The words are acrid leaving my mouth.

I wasn't born yesterday. Jill the idiot suggested that he offer us drugs, and she finds herself far too funny, if the expression she's attempting to hide is any indication.

"Billiards?" Jill asks, eyebrows lifted and face pinched with unmasked humor.

I roll my eyes, grabbing Nina by the elbow and steering us in the direction of the curtain separating the billiards from the poker tables.

We spend the next hour playing darts and watching as Jill takes on other women from The Communes in various card games that I'm not familiar with. This room has remained free of the men, our own little female sanctuary, and I have to admit, I've had fun.

"Let's go get a drink," Nina suggests, and I nod.

"Grab me one too, would ya?" Jill calls out, never taking her eyes off her cards.

We head back into the mayhem, the place more packed than it was when we first arrived. I have to wonder how many people know about this place, and how it remains a secret from the police. When this many people are privy to something, it's only a matter of time before the news is slipped.

My eyes scan the area, landing on Harlan. He's speaking to the bartender when a mysterious figure approaches him. The guy looks like a corpse, devoid of any hint of color in his pallid complexion. His jet-black hair accentuates the starkness of his appearance even further. Nina moves us closer until we're standing at the bar, right next to them.

They're speaking in a low murmur while surreptitiously glancing in our direction. Is it to shield their discussion from eavesdroppers, or does it pertain to us directly? I can't help but feel a smidgen of curiosity, wondering what secretive conversation is taking place.

Harlan's demeanor shifts subtly as he listens, his expression growing more serious with each passing moment. Whatever the stranger is saying seems to carry weight, and I find myself straining to catch even a snippet of their conversation.

"I'll be there in a moment," Harlan mutters in response, his voice tinged with a sense of urgency that sends a ripple of unease through me. The stranger nods curtly before slipping away into the shadows.

Turning toward us, Harlan offers a strained smile. "Are you enjoying your night, ladies?" he asks, though his words seem streaked with distraction as he glances around the room keenly.

"Yes, thank you," Nina says. "It's been a lovely night."

He nods, not bothering to look at Nina as he rolls up his shirt sleeve, uncovering a tattoo on his forearm. I'm fascinated by the symbol etched into his skin. My eyes narrow as I take in every detail, a wave of recognition washing over me. It's the exact symbol from my dream: a labyrinth of interconnected triangles, a vigilant eye dead center. A chill tumbles down my spine as the significance dawns on me.

"What's that tattoo?" I ask, before I've thought better of it.

He turns toward me, chewing on his cheek, seeming to contemplate my question.

"Just something I did as a stupid teenager." He brushes me off with a dismissive wave of his hand, but I'm not buying the fabricated nonchalance.

He took too much time to consider me before I witnessed the mask drop into place.

"It's quite detailed," I say, deciding to double down and see if I can get him to talk about it.

"The ideas of a drunk teenager." He shrugs. "Nothing special."

Lies.

It's not hard to detect when he refuses to meet my eyes, and the moment I made mention of it, he lowered his sleeve, covering the marking, making it feel even more mysterious. A brand of secrecy he's uncomfortable discussing.

"Please excuse me. I have some business to attend to," he says, voice low and menacing.

Nina slides in closer to me. "Why do I get the feeling like this business might include roughing someone up in a back room?"

I turn toward her, eyebrow lifted. "Or worse."

Her mouth drops open into an O.

"What can I get you?" the middle-aged bartender asks, sliding two bar napkins across the lacquered top.

"Two gin and tonics," I say, and Nina makes a face.

I shrug. "I'm going to need it, and Jill is getting the same thing."

Nina smirks. "Make that three. I guess it's that kind of night."

We grab our drinks and head back toward the parlor, finding Jill still in the same seat we left her in, sweeping the table of what appears to be well over one hundred dollars.

"I'm on a roll, bitches. Please tell me you brought me a . . ." She looks over her shoulder, smiling wide when she sees the drink in my hand. "That's my girl."

She reaches out her hands, waggling her fingers, signaling she wants the drink. I hand it over, rolling my eyes at Jill, who goes right back to the next hand of whatever they're playing.

Nina and I find a seat, sipping quietly as we watch the game. My mind lingers on the tattoo. It's a puzzle waiting to be solved, and I'm itching to get started.

I pull out my phone and start a search for tattoos with triangles and an eye. I get a bunch of hits, but nothing close to what I saw. Grabbing a pen from my purse, I make quick work of sketching out the symbol on my napkin, staring at it for far too long.

My glass is empty, and the girls have started yet another game. This time, Nina joined, and they're working to explain the rules to her. I take the opportunity to head for another drink and see if I can find out any information on Harlan.

"Another gin and tonic?" the bartender asks, and I nod. "Tad's the name," he says. "And yours?"

"Alyssa." I greet him with a smile, settling into the seat beside a woman bedizened in diamonds. Her left arm boasts a bracelet outshining even my engagement ring, gleaming under the golden lights. She glances my way, a forced smile spreading over her lips before she dismisses me, flipping her bleached blond hair over her shoulder. However, I can't ignore the symbol that currently haunts my thoughts—it's right there, tattooed behind her ear.

What in the world is happening?

Leaning in slightly, I lock eyes with Tad. His gaze flickers open just a fraction, his head subtly shaking as if warning me not to start up a conversation with the rude woman.

My curiosity is beyond piqued. My head is screaming at me to pay attention. There's no such thing as coincidences these days. I saw that symbol in a dream, and here it is, right in front of my face, and more than once. It means something, and I have to uncover what.

I scan the room, searching for more clues, but I don't find any. I'm not sure what I was expecting. A roomful of people sporting triangle tattoos?

Exhaling a frustrated sigh, I let my head slump back against my shoulder. The woman glances in my direction, her nose wrinkled in disdain. She then pivots toward her companion, uttering something that prompts him to cast a similarly disdainful glance my way before they stand, vacating their seats without so much as a backward glance.

"Good riddance to you too, assholes."

"You know, you really should be more careful," he says, wiping the bar down with a white towel. "You don't want to make enemies of that woman." He motions toward the blonde, who's now across the room, with a slight tip of his head. "She has a lot of pull around these parts."

I take a sip of my drink, sighing heavily. "Lucky for me, I'm not from these parts, and I don't care who she is."

He smashes his lips together, leaning closer to me. "She has pull in many places." He stresses the word *many*, lifting both eyebrows as if he's imparting something very important to me.

"Who is she?" I ask, voice equally low.

"A socialite from New York. Moved here about two years ago. She frequents this place often."

I clear my throat. "What's with the tattoo behind her ear? It's the same one that Harlan had on his forearm," I say, recognizing a little too late that I'm walking a very dangerous path.

Tad freezes in place, arm suspended in midair. He blinks several times, and I know that bringing up the tattoo here was not in my best interest.

He gets right in my space, placing his hand over mine. "Why are you here?" he asks, glancing around as if to see if anyone is paying attention. "Who are you?"

I pull my hand out from under his, eyebrows tilted inward. "I told you, I'm Alyssa, and I'm not from here."

"Are you with the police?" The words are just above a whisper.

I make a face. "No. I'm not."

His face appears to relax, and he nods, signaling he believes me for some reason. He goes about making my drink, sliding it toward me when it's ready.

"They're part of a secret society," he murmurs, his voice tinged with fear.

"Like the Illuminati?" I ask, completely baffled by this.

"I guess. They have their hands in everything, but nobody knows who they really are," he explains, continuing to search the area, likely ensuring we're not caught gossiping about things we have no business discussing.

"You do not want to cross them, Alyssa. Be very careful with the questions you ask. Poking your nose around here will not end well for you or your friends," he warns, casting a glance toward the back room where Nina and Jill are.

I nod my understanding.

My heart races as I realize the gravity of what I have stumbled upon. This is no ordinary illegal poker tournament—it's a gathering of the elite, the powerful, the secretive.

People who could've been involved in the murder of Chelsea Grayson.

But how?

We're in Florida. She was killed in Massachusetts, and the woman with the tattoo is from New York.

Could this society have roots in the New England area?

"Whatever you're thinking, don't," Tad cautions. "Enjoy your drink, and when you leave, put this place as far out of your mind as possible."

I ponder everything that he's said, knowing that I won't turn my back on what I've learned here. I was shown that tattoo in order to help solve Chelsea's murder, and I will use whatever knowledge I have to do just that. While it's unlikely these individuals were directly involved in her death, the presence of that tattoo strongly suggests someone within their circle might be.

I take a sip of my drink as Tad busies himself pouring more drinks and occasionally wiping down the bar, shooting me cautious glances in between. I'm about to order one more and head back to the girls when I feel a presence beside me. I look up and my breath hitches.

Harlan leans over the bar, but beside him, a spectral figure flickers in and out of existence, glaring menacingly at the side of his head. The apparition appears to be that of an elderly gentleman, the signs of age evident even in his ghostly form. I estimate he's in his mid- to late seventies.

My spine straightens as the ghost turns to me, a sinister smile spread across his wickedly cold face. Except I don't know who he is.

"Tad, could I get my usual?" Harlan requests, completely oblivious to the ghost that seems to wish him harm.

"Of course, sir," Tad replies promptly, springing into action.

A bead of sweat collects at Harlan's temple, and he swipes away at it.

"Are you all right?" I ask, unable to peel my eyes from Harlan or the ghost, just beyond him.

He tilts his head. "Fine. Just need that drink," he says, chuckling.

I smile, forcing a small laugh. "You and me both." I lift my now-empty glass into the air, and Harlan smirks.

"And another for the lady, Tad."

Tad bows his head slightly, not looking up from the drink he's pouring.

The ghostly figure remains fixed on Harlan's profile, his gaze unwavering even as he flickers in and out of existence. I can't shake the feeling that I've stumbled into something far more dangerous than a simple game of poker. It's clear that the secrets of The Communes run deep and that uncovering them could come at a price.

A price that this spirit might have paid personally.

Wheel of Fortune

AS SOON AS Tad had handed Harlan his drink, both he and the sinister ghost disappeared. Thank god.

I took Tad's advice and refrained from asking any additional questions surrounding the tattoo and the supposed secret society attached to it. Instead, I joined my friends in the other room and allowed the women they'd been playing with to teach me how to play spades.

We had a great time, laughing and drinking into the early morning hours. I even managed to forget about that angry spirit that had been present.

Harlan stopped into the lounge to ensure we could find our way home. He promised to have a golf cart waiting. Thankfully, Nina stopped drinking hours ago in anticipation of being our driver. Ever the good friend and mother hen. That was the last of Harlan we saw for the rest of our time on the Montgomery Estate, and I can't say I'm sad about it.

"Are we almost there?" Jill whines as we stumble our way back through the tunnels, finally ready to call it a night.

The sun will be rising before too long, and Nina and I have an important afternoon ahead of us. We need sleep.

"It shouldn't be far," Nina calls out as she leads the way.

"Wanna come back to my place for a nightcap?" Jill slurs, and Nina looks over her shoulder, face pinched in something like disbelief.

"It's three a.m.," Nina squawks. "I'm going to bed."

I bob my head in agreement. "I'm beat, and we have things to do."

We're finally climbing the rickety stairs, headed out of the secret tunnel. The house is dark and eerily quiet. The musty odor of mold and decay permeates the room, a detail I hadn't noticed earlier. The air feels heavy, and every hair on my body stands on end.

"Let's get out of here," I suggest, growing increasingly uneasy.

When we make it out front, Harlan's golf cart has been replaced by a generic one he'd promised Jill would be waiting for us. We pile in with Nina behind the wheel and Jill sitting shotgun. I'm in the back, my gaze involuntarily drawn toward the looming silhouette of the decrepit home, its weather-beaten façade appearing as though it could collapse at any moment.

The engine roars to life as the golf cart sets off along the winding dirt path, gradually leaving the eerie place behind. Despite the distance, the unsettling feeling that had gripped me refuses to dissipate. While the other girls engage in lighthearted conversation and laughter, oblivious to my growing apprehension, I remain on edge, my senses heightened.

A figure emerges from the shadows. Squinting against the dim moonlight, I lean forward, my heart pounding in my chest, questioning whether my eyes are playing tricks on me.

But there's no mistaking what I see.

It's the elderly ghost, its ethereal form shimmering in the moonlight. A shiver runs down my spine as he emits a bone-chilling wail.

"Drive, drive!" I yell, panic rising in my voice as Nina slams her foot down on the accelerator.

The golf cart lurches forward, but the spirit is relentless, his wraithlike form floating effortlessly behind us as we speed through the night.

"What's happening?" Nina shouts, over the howl of the wind and the hum of the motor.

I look up to meet her concerned eyes in the rearview mirror, mouthing the word *ghost*.

Nina grips the wheel tightly, her knuckles turning white as she navigates the winding path, desperately trying to outmaneuver our pursuer, whom she can't even see.

"Why are you driving like a bat outta hell?" Jill's voice pierces through the chaos, a hint of fear punctuating the words. With a firm grip on the seat, she struggles to maintain her balance, and I worry she'll be thrown from the cart at this rate.

"Hang on, everyone," Nina yells, her voice determined.

With each twist and turn, the ghost gains ground, his wails echoing off the trees like a haunting melody.

Jill's eyes are wide with terror as we hurtle through the darkness, the wind whipping through our hair.

"What is that noise?" Jill cries out, her head whipping back toward the banshee cry.

She can hear him.

"I don't know, but we need to lose it, fast," Nina shouts, her voice tinged with urgency as she scans the area for an escape route.

"We're not going to make it," I say, my heart racing as the ghost charges toward us, his eyes blazing with malevolent fury.

We zoom through the labyrinth of trees and bushes, and just when all hope seems lost, the path straightens and the lights of the main street glimmer in the distance like a beacon of safety.

Just a bit farther.

Nina guns the engine, propelling the golf cart forward. As soon as we break through the trees onto the street, the ghost emits a furious wail, vanishing into thin air as if it collided with an invisible barrier.

Jill's scream slices through the air, and I quickly raise my eyes just in time to witness Nina execute a sharp turn, swerving to avoid colliding with a parked car on the side of the road.

"I'm sorry," Nina shouts, her eyes darting between the road and the rearview mirror.

"It's okay. We're . . . okay," I manage, my breath ragged and heart pounding. "He's gone."

Nina exhales heavily, easing off the accelerator and sinking back against the seat.

Jill's hands shoot up in the air, and she erupts into cheers as if we're fugitives who narrowly dodged a capture in a high-speed chase. Apparently oblivious to the fact we were being hunted down by a ghost with ill intentions.

"That. Was. Awesome," she exclaims, clapping her hands enthusiastically, while both Nina and I can only shake our heads in disbelief.

That's Jill for you—the friend who thrives on adrenaline rushes.

The remainder of the ride home is silent, save for the soft snoring of Jill from the front.

As we skid to a stop in front of Jill's condo, Nina and I exchange relieved glances.

"That was too close for comfort," I say, rubbing at my chest.

"But we made it." Nina's voice is filled with relief as we share a collective sigh. "What was that, Ally? Was it a poltergeist?"

My lips press together as I think through the specifics. "It was a regular ghost, but one who wasn't good in life or death if I had to guess."

"You don't want to go back there and help him on to the afterlife?" Nina asks, one side of her mouth tipped up slightly.

"No," I say, shaking my head. "My life means more to me than that. I'm coming to learn that messing with things I don't understand isn't in my best interest."

She nods her head. "I'm happy to hear that. You need to keep yourself safe."

For Ava, I won't take chances without having the right people with me to help navigate the unknown. That spirit back there will have to stay put.

"What are we going to do with her?" I ask, tipping my chin toward the sleeping beauty who hasn't so much as moved since she fell asleep.

She chuckles, shaking her head. "Let's carry her in."

✦ ✦ ✦

AS WE STUMBLE into the rented condo, something we found online, exhaustion weighs heavily on me, but the events of the night refuse to be brushed aside. I lead Nina into the living room, eager to piece together what happened at the abandoned estate.

"The ghost . . . the one that was chasing us," I start, trying to organize my thoughts in a way so as to not confuse Nina. "It was with Harlan earlier tonight at the bar, drilling holes into the side of his head."

"Harlan?"

I nod, swallowing hard as the memory of the ghost's haunting gaze floods back to me. "I think it's connected to Chelsea Grayson's death."

Nina's brow furrows as she listens intently. "Connected? How is that possible?"

I take a deep breath. "Remember the dream from the other night? The one with the stranger?" I ask, and she tilts her head to the side. "On the napkins at the bar in my dream, there was a strange symbol—one with triangles and an eye."

Her mouth opens and then shuts. "I do remember the dream. But what does that have to do with tonight?"

"I saw that same symbol on Harlan's forearm and behind a woman's ear at the bar."

"The exact symbol or a similar one?"

"The same," I say, eyes boring into hers. "The bartender told me that it's linked to some secret society."

She chews on her bottom lip, eyes narrowed in concentration. "I hear what you're saying, but it's a big leap to connect them to a murder back home."

"The woman at the bar with the tattoo, she was from New York. What if they have ties to New England?"

Nina's eyes widen with realization. "You think this secret society is widespread, and some force is bringing it to light here so that you'll work the case."

I nod gravely. "Yes. I think we need to find out more about them and just how widespread they are."

"Do you think Chelsea was involved with the society?"

I shrug. "I'm not sure, but I want to have Nick check her for a tattoo."

"What if we have Nick look into Harlan?" Nina suggests. "He has access to ways of digging up information that we don't. He might be able to connect the dots between the secret society and Chelsea's death."

"I also think we need to have a talk with Jill. She should really stay away from Harlan and that place. I don't have a good feeling about either."

She nods in agreement, and I feel a bit better about our chances of uncovering something.

"That's a great idea."

I send off a quick text to Nick, needing to get the ball rolling on the investigation of Harlan and the society.

ME

When you get up, call me.

My phone rings almost instantly.

"It's Nick," I say, glancing up at Nina, who's curled up on the couch.

She lifts a brow as if to say, *Are you going to answer it?*

I click the button and take a deep breath. "Hey. What are you doing up already?"

He sighs down the line. "I haven't been getting much sleep. A lot happening around here," he confesses, his voice husky and deep. A shiver runs down my spine as I listen, captivated by the enticing sound. "What's going on? Everything okay?"

A lazy smile spreads across my face, and when my head lifts, I find Nina staring at me in amusement. I roll my eyes.

"Everything is fine. Well . . . not exactly fine, but I'm fine—"

"Lyss," he says, bringing my rambling to a halt. "What's happened?"

I heave a breath. "How do you know something has happened?"

He chuckles. "You tend to talk in circles when you're trying to avoid sharing something you think I'll have a hard time believing."

"Huh," I say, recognizing how quickly Nick West has come to know me.

"You can tell me, Alyssa. I'll always believe you."

My body tingles from the tips of my toes to my scalp. His words envelop me like a warm hug.

"Thank you, Nick. I appreciate that." I take a deep breath and dive into my suspicions.

When I've finished relaying every last detail, Nick's quiet on the other line.

"What is he saying?" Nina whispers, and I shake my head.

"Tell her I'm thinking," he says, humor in his tone.

I smirk, relaying the message. Nina harrumphs, sitting back into the cushions with a yawn.

"Do you think you could draw up a sketch of the tattoo?" he finally says.

Chewing on my bottom lip, I quickly retrieve the sketch I made earlier from my purse. With a few taps on my phone, I send it over to Nick.

A tense silence hangs in the air before Nick speaks again. "Listen, Alyssa. I need you to get out of Florida. Now. It's not safe for you there."

I hesitate, weighing his words carefully. "We can't leave yet. We're meeting Ian's mom tomorrow afternoon."

"I've seen something similar to this before, and the people it was attached to are dangerous, Alyssa." I hear him curse under his breath, and then he says, "These are the sorts of people that won't hesitate to silence anyone who tries to out their secrets." Nick's voice crackles over the phone, laden with concern.

I nod, even though he can't see me. "I understand. I'll proceed with caution."

"I don't think you do understand. I'm serious, Alyssa. These people play by their own rules. You're playing with fire."

"Nick," I say, voice hard and determined. "I hear what you're saying, and I do recognize the danger. I appreciate you and your words, but I promise, I can take care of myself."

There's a resigned sigh on the other end of the line. "Fine. But please be careful, Alyssa. I mean it. They have connections in high places."

I wonder if he's alluding to the government, but I don't ask, understanding his deliberate ambiguity.

"We'll catch the people behind this. I promise you that." I can hear the determination in Nick's voice as he vows to uncover the truth.

"Has the second body been discovered?"

"No. Nothing yet. Have you seen anything else that could tell us who she is?"

"Unfortunately, no," I reply, stifling a yawn.

"Get some rest. Call me if you find anything else that could be helpful."

"I will. Good night, Nick."

As we hang up, a sense of purpose washes over me. First, we'll find Ian, and then I'm going to help Nick take down Chelsea's murderer.

Ten of Cups . . . Reversed

Nick

LITTLE ZOEY WIGGLES in my arms, trying to break free despite my hold on her. Today is her first birthday, and I got cleared for a day off so that I could be here with my family to celebrate.

She's an animal, zipping all over the place, getting into shit she shouldn't. Which is why I'm holding her while my mom and sister prepare the birthday dinner.

"You can put her down, Nick. She'll be fine," Jackie says, pulling homemade pizza from the oven. "She's far steadier on her feet than you'd expect."

"Where's Joe and Dad? Surely, they'd love to pull themselves away from the TV to watch her," I tease, knowing exactly the kind of reaction we'd get by even suggesting it.

Joe also has the night off, and that man never gets shorted his breaks. And rightfully so. He works hard. Both men will inevitably grumble when Mom insists that we all join her around my sister's dining table that she's worked tirelessly to make a showpiece worthy of HGTV in honor of our favorite toddler's big birthday.

"No way. Don't interrupt them." Our mom rushes toward me. "It's my turn. Come here, Zo-bug," she coos, arms outstretched.

Zoey looks up at me with the largest cerulean eyes I've ever seen. Her full lips are puckered as if to say, *Don't you dare let go of me.* I hand her over reluctantly, hating the way her puppy-dog eyes appear to plead for me to keep her.

"I wasn't being serious. And for the record, I like holding my niece," I say, as she's snapped from my hold by my domineering mother.

I've been so busy lately that I have hardly seen her. When they say time flies, they aren't kidding when it comes to kids. I swear Zoey was just born yesterday, and here she is already walking.

"Aww . . . did you have fun with Uncle Nicky?"

My nose scrunches. "Don't call me that."

The only person who's able to get away with calling me Nicky is Shirley Clementine, and that's only because she saved me from myself.

"I gave you birth; I'll call you whatever I want," Mom blusters, all the while shooting daggers at me with her eyes.

"Why are you so grumpy today?" Jackie asks, placing a pan of breadsticks on a hot pad in the center of the kitchen island and blowing a wayward piece of her brown hair from her face.

There's quite a spread accumulating. Not that I'm surprised. These two don't do anything in half measures.

"Nicholas?" Jackie presses, and I look up, waiting for her to continue. When it's clear she has nothing new to say, it occurs to me that *I'm* the supposed grump.

"I'm the grump?" I ask, pointing a finger at my chest.

Mom rolls her eyes. "Obviously."

"I'm not grumpy," I say, instantly wincing at the tone of my voice.

Even to my own ears, I sound exactly that.

I slump back into the barstool that's less than comfy. "You really need to spring for more comfortable chairs, Jack."

"See. Grumpy," she says to my mom, who bobs her head in agreement.

"I'm just tired. It's been a really long month with Richard's case and now the new one."

Neither one of them comments. With Jackie's husband being in law enforcement and my father retired FBI, they're both more than familiar with the need for confidentiality.

Jackie purses her lips and lowers her head, rocking back and forth on her feet.

"I'm glad to hear there isn't trouble in paradise. When you didn't ask to bring Alyssa, I was afraid that it was over before it got started."

I grimace, wanting to throttle my sister and her big mouth. She's managed to open an entire can of worms, and she knows damn well what she's done. The smirk she tries to hide gives her away.

Mom's white-haired head whips toward me, and I shoot Jackie a glare that promises revenge in some capacity.

"Who's Alyssa? Are you in love?" she asks, teeth bared in a smile that tells me she's already planning a wedding in her head.

The palm of my hand slaps against my forehead as I groan. "Mom . . . why do you always jump straight to love?"

She leans forward, barely registering that she's got too loose a grip on Zoey. "Well . . . if you're dating someone . . ."

"Would you hold her tighter?" I snap, pointing toward Zoey, whose little head, half-cloaked by a headpiece, complete with an obnoxious bow, is bobbling all over the place.

She waves me off, rolling her hazel eyes. "I'm more than capable of taking care of a baby, Nicholas. I raised you two perfectly well."

"Debatable," I say, popping an almond into my mouth.

"I'm going to try to pretend you didn't say that," she singsongs, placing a kiss into Zoey's thick, dark curls.

"I'm going to pretend you aren't trying to marry me off to someone you've not even met," I say, voice pitching in exasperation.

"Stop avoiding my question. Are you or are you not dating someone?"

I groan. "It's new."

"Hallelujah," she bellows. "Praise Jesus."

I make a face. "When was the last time you were in a church, Ma?"

She tsks at me. "I attend worship in my head every day."

Jackie titters and I harrumph.

"Doesn't count. And why don't we stop acting as though I'm a lost cause, shall we?"

"Nobody said that, Nicholas. It's just been a while." She coos into the side of Zoey's head, missing the scowl I direct to her.

"Yeah . . . because my fiancée died."

My mother's face falls, and Jackie drops a pair of metal tongs, the sound reverberating off the stove.

"I'm sorry, Nick. I didn't—"

I shake my head, lifting my hand. "I know. It wasn't fair of me to say that."

Her chin quivers, and now I feel like a complete shithead. My mom has been the most supportive person through everything, and she didn't deserve the way I just snapped at her. Albeit innocently. I wasn't even truly mad. My tone said otherwise.

Grumpy might be accurate.

I guess I'm just feeling a lot of pressure, and there's no one to blame but myself.

Things with Alyssa happened so quickly, but we haven't even had the time to really move forward. This case is bleeding me dry. Richard Dunbar is a fucking snake, and for the first time in my career, I'm nervous that the criminal will weasel his way out of the charges he deserves.

All because of money.

Then there's Chelsea's case and the body we've yet to find.

But none of that compares to the knowledge that Isla is nearby. Stuck at Alyssa's, not in paradise with her brother like she should be. That fact haunts me more than anything.

"I understand why you haven't dated. I'm just worried about you. I want to see you happy again," Mom says, pulling me out of my dark thoughts. "We miss her too, ya know."

I swallow down a lump, needing to change the subject. "I know, Ma. I know."

My mother loved Isla. She was a daughter to her and a sister to Jackie. She fit into this family perfectly, and I know the day I lost her, they all did too.

I want to give my mom a hug. To promise her a wedding and babies and all the things she always dreamed of for me. But that's not in the cards.

Not because I can't see things progressing with Alyssa, but because I'm forty-five years old, and those days have long passed me by. Maybe I could be convinced to have a civil ceremony one day, but outside of walking down the aisle and closing the deal, I've been there done that with all the planning and festivities leading up to the big day.

"What all did you make?" I say, trying to lighten the conversation.

"Stop deflecting, Nick," Jackie fusses. "Tell Mom about Alyssa."

Mom nods like a bobblehead, and I sigh, knowing they won't stop until I give them something.

"It's very new," I start, and Jackie's hand rolls in the air for me to get to the good part. I scrunch my nose and bare my teeth at her.

"We haven't even been on a date."

"But she did go to his house to take care of him when he was sick," Jackie says, practically giggling.

"She did? That sounds . . . serious."

I don't even bother reminding her for the umpteenth time that this is new.

"Alyssa is the widow next door," Jackie explains to Mom, whose mouth forms an O, and her eyes widen.

"The pretty one. With the blondish strawberry hair?"

I pull a face at my mother. "How do you even know anything about my neighbors?"

She sits back, holding Zoey close to her chest, running a hand down her back.

"Oh, you can never be too careful." She averts her gaze. "I had your dad pull some strings with some friends. Had to find out everything when you moved to that neighborhood. You never know about everyone who lives around you. They could be bad."

"You ran reports on my neighbors?" I ask incredulously. "I moved in next to Char and Bob. Tell me you didn't pry into their life."

She purses her lips.

"Ma," I groan. "I'm an adult. Not to mention, I'm a detective. I'm more than capable of taking care of myself."

She shrugs one shoulder. "A parent's concern never ends. Right, Jack?"

Jackie smothers her laughter, pursing her lips like a duck and nodding.

"What are you smiling about?" Mom asks, looking at Jackie out of the corner of her eye. "Whatever I do for him, I do for you too. I don't trust the director of that day care you're taking our little Zoey to."

The smile immediately drops from Jackie's face. "There is nothing wrong with Kensley. She's a great director."

Jackie's defense of the woman falls flat. The way she pinches the skin of her neck only furthers my suspicion.

Mom's lips thin out in an expression that says she's not impressed.

"What did you dig up on Kensley?" I ask, now curious who's watching over my niece, while simultaneously enjoying Jackie's irritation.

"She was tough to crack. Had to get access to her expunged records. She was quite the party animal in college."

Jackie's shoulders relax, and the lines on her forehead retreat. "So was I," she says, throwing her hands up in the air. "If only you knew the shit I got away with."

Mom covers one ear with her hand. "I'm not listening. You were a perfect angel."

"She was a demon," I say, popping another almond into my mouth. "Remember that time when you—"

"Shut it, Benedict," Jackie snaps in my direction.

I grin around a mouthful, just happy to have the conversation off me for a bit.

"You two are so gullible. I didn't pull any strings. That would be illegal."

Jackie and I share a look, unconvinced by Mom's claim of innocence.

"Back to your Alyssa," Mom says, ending my reprieve quicker than I thought possible.

I groan, head falling back. *My Alyssa?*

Caroline West is a seasoned manipulator of emotions when it comes to her children and their love lives.

"*My Alyssa* happens to be amazing. She's smart, witty, caring . . ." My words trail off when I get a glimpse of Mom. She's one step away from a cartoon character with heart-shaped eyes bugged out of their sockets.

I can practically see the cogs in her head drumming up all the details of how to ensure Alyssa Mann never escapes.

I clear my throat. "Anyway. Like I said . . . it's new."

Mom waves a hand in the air. "Semantics. Your father and I fell in love in a week."

"You were at Summer Jam, Ma. I'm not sure love factored into that week."

She glares at me, and I have the good sense to snap my mouth shut.

"Your father is a retired FBI agent; we did not partake in the weed."

My eyebrows shoot into my hairline, and Jackie chokes on air.

"The weed?" Jackie snorts. "Good god."

"Who said anything about weed, Mother?" I say, smirking.

She blusters for several minutes, turning as red as a beet. "Nobody. I just meant . . ."

It's my turn to mimic her. I wave a hand in the air and purse my lips. "Oh, Carol, nobody said you were smoking it." I glance at my sister, who's two seconds from bursting into a fit of laughter. "Did we?" I ask.

Jackie's head moves back and forth. "But I'm not so sure you didn't have a contact high." She taps her chin. "That's likely what's wrong with Nick."

I clap my hands, mocking my sister. "Good one, Jack."

She bows low, popping into a curtsy.

"You two are not funny," Mom says, shaking her head. "And don't think for one second this discussion about Alyssa is over. You will tell us everything over dinner."

I slam my lips together and smile wide. "Great. Can't wait."

And this right here is one of the very reasons I didn't even consider asking Alyssa to join me. There is no way in hell she's ready for Caroline West and all her probing questions.

My dad might be a former special agent, but he has nothing on my mom. Her interrogation skills are topnotch.

Scary, even.

She'll have your entire history spilling from you within minutes. Tears falling as she gets you to open up about every pain point in your life. She's the mastermind of the West family, keeping us all on our toes and in line.

My phone vibrates in my pocket, and I excuse myself to take it. Mom half rolls her eyes, not at all pleased with the interruption. She grumbles about it to Jackie until I'm out of earshot.

"This is West," I say, answering the unknown call.

"Nick?" I recognize the voice, vaguely, but can't place who the woman is.

"Yes."

"It's Lanie. Anderson," she says to clarify. "Thank god you answered. Someone broke into my house. I need you to investigate."

Lanie lives in downtown Knox Harbor, not an area prone to crime. It's a small town with lots of eyes and ears. Criminals don't stand a chance of going undiscovered because there isn't a camera in the world that's better at providing details and timelines than the people who reside in town.

The Red Hats might as well be part of the sovereign citizen movement. On many occasions, they've taken it upon themselves to conduct citizen's arrests in the name of keeping Knox Harbor "safe from riffraff"—their words. They have been helpful a time or two, but mostly, they're a giant pain in my ass and the captain's. They tend to think that age and the amount of time they've lived in Knox Harbor give them special privileges. I've had to remind Nan Jenkins on several occasions that wearing a red hat and living in town does not make her exempt from the laws. That conversation has never gone over well.

"Do you have cameras?" I ask, jumping right into detective mode.

"They were disabled," she grits out. "We're dealing with professionals. I need you."

I pinch the base of my nose. "You do know that I'm a homicide detective, right?"

She huffs. "Which is ridiculous. I'm sorry, Nick, but this town doesn't have enough homicides to justify your job."

My head tilts to the side, and my eyes roll. "Considering your best friend's husband is in jail for multiple murders, you might want to rethink that stance."

She snarls. "He's an idiot. But my stance remains. You might want to consider a career change. Something with stability."

"Noted, but for the time being, it is . . . my job . . . which means I don't handle break-ins. I can make a call to Malone and—"

"No," she says, cutting me off. "This requires discretion, and Malone is a tireless flirt who blabs his mouth if I flutter my eyelashes at him. I need someone who can solve a crime and be quiet about the details."

Malone is a lot of things, but he doesn't talk about cases. I'm not about to fight Lanie on that, though. She'll have me on the phone forever, and based on the stink eye my mom is hurling in my direction, I'd be smart to wrap this convo up.

"Lanie, I'm sorry, but—"

"For your love of Alyssa, please help me."

I close my eyes and count to five, kneading at my forehead, a headache building.

Everyone seems bound and determined to make this love, and we haven't even had a proper date. However, I do care about her, and this is her friend.

"All right, fine. I'll help you out, but it won't be until later. It's my niece's birthday."

She sighs. "No rush. I'm leaving town. I'll shoot you a text with the code and we can chat via phone," she says, ending the call.

I clench my teeth, wondering if I should just head over there now and save myself the inquisition to come from my mom.

"What was that about?" Mom asks, eyes narrowed in on me.

"Someone broke into Alyssa's friend's place. She asked me to take a look around."

Mom's eyes light up, and a shit-eating grin spreads across her face at the mere mention of Alyssa. "You really like this girl." It's not a question, and I know a drilling is about to commence.

I sigh. Might as well spill my guts and admit my feelings for a woman I'm just getting to know. It was Christmas not long ago, and I've yet to give Mom her gift. What could be better than the hope that one day I might at the very least give her a wedding?

To most that would seem a major stretch, considering we've only started dating. But not for good ole Carol.

She'll be picking out her mother-of-the-groom dress by dessert.

A text comes in, and I consider ignoring it, sure it's Lanie, stressing the need for help with her discreet issue, but decide to check anyway.

> SKIVER
>
> Another body was located at the East Fork docks. Similar situation. Young girl. When can you get back to town?

My blood runs cold as Alyssa's premonition comes to pass. I've been waiting for a body to show up, and now that it has, it makes what she says all the more real. *Everything* that she says.

Isla included.

ME

Do you have an ID on the victim?

SKIVER

Not yet. Body was just discovered.

ME

I'll be back tonight. It won't be until late.

SKIVER

Safe travels. See you in the early am.

My appetite is gone, and my mood has plummeted. So much for a fun family birthday celebration.

The Chariot

AS WE PULL up to the small ranch home, I turn to Nina, watching her closely.

She fidgeted the entire ride here, her nerves getting the best of her.

"Are you okay?" I ask, peering at the side of her head.

She takes a deep breath and lets it out slowly. "I'm nervous. She has no clue we're coming. What if she sends us away? What if . . ." Her words trail off, and her eyes well with tears. "What if he's gone, Ally?"

Grabbing her hand, I squeeze, hoping to reassure her. "Don't think like that. Let's not go there until we've spoken to his momma. Okay?"

She sniffs, nodding her head. "I just need a minute."

I offer a smile, allowing her whatever time she needs, turning my attention toward the house in front of me, painted in an earthy taupe tone.

Nina made a stop at the town center when we first arrived, looking up Angela and Steven Whalen. That search came up short.

With a quick Google search, we were able to determine that Steven, Ian's father, passed several years ago. That led Nina to search for Angela under her maiden name. She'd want to fly under the radar anyway, especially if Richard had been snooping around.

And that's when she found her. Angela Burch resides at 19501 Windemere Lane in the community of South Port in The Communes.

The home's classic brick façade is complemented by an array of beautiful flowers in an assortment of colors, making it easy to see what draws a person to The Communes for retirement. The neatly manicured lawn leads to a sprawling porch, decorated with cozy rocking chairs situated toward the east. A perfect setup to watch the sun rise every morning with her cup of coffee and The Communes' paper. Assuming that's a thing.

"I'm ready," Nina says, drawing my attention to the front of the cart. At some point while I was lost in the details of the place, Nina moved and is now waiting for me to join her. It's time.

As we stand on the porch, ringing the doorbell repeatedly, an unsettling silence greets us. Did we make a mistake coming here without notifying Angela?

Nina peers into the house, looking for any signs of life, then sighing heavily, signaling she's giving up.

"She's out back," a foreign male voice calls from behind us.

We twist around to find an elderly man, walking his small dog on a leash.

"She's always out back this time of day," he says, motioning toward the back of the house.

A sense of relief washes over me knowing that she's here, and Nina will get some answers.

We call out our thank yous as we make our way around the side of the house. And just as the man had said, she's there, sipping sweet tea under the shade of an umbrella.

Her eyes widen with surprise, and the teacup slips from her grip, shattering on the pavers. She doesn't jump to picking up the broken pieces; her hands are over her mouth, tears streaming down her face.

"You shouldn't be here, sweet girl. It's dangerous for all of us," she cautions, rising from her chair and heading straight to Nina, pulling her into a tight embrace.

"He's in jail, and hopefully going to stay there for a long time. I won't allow him to hurt you anymore."

My heart sinks at the reminder of Richard's actions and the havoc he has wreaked on their lives.

Angela pulls out of Nina's grip, looking her over. "You have grown into such a beautiful woman, Nina." Her smile is wide, her eyes cloudy with tears. "I always knew you'd do great things."

Nina squeezes her shoulder. "Sit. Let's catch up."

And they do. For the next thirty minutes, they talk all about what Nina's been up to these last twenty-plus years and her plans for the future. The only topic left untouched is Ian. While I expect Nina to let Angela take the lead on that conversation, I'm not entirely convinced she will.

"I'm so proud of you," Angela says, beaming at Nina. "And I'm so incredibly sorry for what that evil man did to you."

Nina's head tilts to the side. "What do you know?"

Angela sighs heavily. "It's no secret that he forced you to marry him." Her face turns hard, and she shakes her head. "When I found out you were going to go through with it, I knew he was blackmailing you. You'd never fall for someone like him."

Nina nods solemnly. "He did. But that's all in the past."

"Bull," Angela retorts sharply. "Even now, he still has a hold over you. I can see the fear in your eyes, Nina Joy." Her fists clench at her sides, her face flushed with anger, a vivid display of her emotions.

Nina leans forward. "I promise you, I'll be fine. They're working to put him away for life, and I have faith they'll find a way to do it." Nina takes a deep breath, and I know what's coming. "I need to know what happened to Ian. Did Richard do something to him?" she inquires, her voice trembling with emotion.

Ian's mom shakes her head, her eyes filled with sorrow. "No, but he threatened it. I was scared, so I begged Ian to get out of Providence, to assume a new identity," she explains, her voice heavy with regret.

Nina's gaze drops, guilt weighing heavily on her shoulders.

"Don't do that. Don't blame yourself, Nina. This is all on Richard. That bastard ruined all our lives." She huffs a humorless laugh. "At least he tried. Ian's smart. He's fine."

"You know where he is." It's not a question. It's clear from the way Angela said it that she does.

Angela shrugs, feigning obliviousness. "If I had to guess, New Orleans. But I don't know. I haven't spoken to him in years because he was trying to keep me safe," she confesses, her voice choked with emotion.

"This is all my fault. I should've stood my ground years ago."

Tears well up in Angela's eyes as she reaches out to comfort Nina. "No, sweet girl. He would've only made all our lives worse. You did nothing wrong aside from falling in love far too young," she reassures her, words filled with compassion. "Now. Let's spend some time together. It's been too long."

Nina smiles, nodding her head in agreement.

We settle into a game of gin rummy, our cards clicking softly against the table as the sun casts its golden glow upon us, painting the sky with hues of orange and pink. With each passing moment, the air grows cooler, a gentle breeze sweeping through the patio as the sun dips below the horizon. Despite the cooling temperatures, the warmth of our companionship envelops us, offering comfort in the midst of uncertainty.

Ian is out there. The only hint that Angela will provide is New Orleans. What will happen if Nina pops up out of nowhere? Will he be as open to seeing her as his mom has been? Or will he turn her away, blaming her for all the hurt that Richard has caused?

As Nina prepares to leave, Ian's mom offers her a final piece of advice.

"If you find him, don't let him stay hidden." Her eyes bore into Nina's. "If Richard has gotten himself into trouble, Ian will be the last thing on his mind. It's time to stop running. Time to stop hiding," she urges, her words resonating with conviction. "I'm not getting any younger. I want time with my son before I go."

A strangled cry bursts from Nina, tears streaming down her face as she moves toward Angela, pulling her into her chest. Both women cling to each other desperately, like two lost souls grasping onto a glimmer of hope. Hope of being reunited with someone they both have love for.

"I will do everything in my power to bring him home to you," Nina vows.

With a heavy heart and renewed determination, Nina says goodbye to Angela. My mind is racing with thoughts of Ian and the life they once shared. Could they have a second chance at love after all this time?

It's clear that no matter how long has passed, Nina has carried a torch for Ian Whalen. It seems that torch still burns brightly.

As I drive away, I can't shake the feeling that the time for hiding is over for all of us. We all have our dragons to slay. Perhaps it's time to face our demons head-on.

My phone pings from the cup holder, and I pick it up to see Lanie's name lighting up the screen.

LANIE

Nina won't answer her phone.

What's the address to the condo?
I just got off the plane and I need the address.

I glance over at Nina, who appears lost in thought. "Did you know Lanie was coming here?"

Her eyes narrow as she turns toward me. "No. Not a clue. Why?"

"She's here and asking for the condo address."

Another text comes in.

LANIE
I'm tired and in need of a drink.
Address . . .

I quickly type out the address and hit Send, turning to Nina. "She's grabbing an Uber and heading to the condo."

Her eyebrow lifts into the air. "I could use a few drinks," Nina says. "Better stop off at the liquor store."

I nod, veering toward the town center.

Leave it to Lanie to pull a sneak visit last minute. She can't possibly have known how much Nina is going to need us tonight. Or maybe she did.

✦ ✦ ✦

LANIE'S ARRIVAL WITH a small bag in hand is met with raised eyebrows and curious glances from Nina and me, because Lanie Anderson does not pack light. Ever. This can only mean she was in a major hurry to skip town. The question is . . . why?

"I'm here, witches. Let's see what The Communes is all about," she announces with a mischievous grin.

Nina darts forward, wrapping Lanie in a tight embrace. "I'm so happy you're here," she practically whispers.

Lanie steps back slightly, studying Nina's expression. "Are you okay? I can't imagine how hard today must've been for you." Nina shrugs, a half-hearted smile tugging at the corners of her lips.

"I will be soon."

"Let's get you settled and open a bottle of something strong," I suggest, motioning toward the bedroom. "There's only one bed, but the couch pulls out. You can keep your stuff back in the bedroom."

Lanie nods. "Sounds perfect to me. I'm just happy to be out of Knox."

There's something that Lanie isn't saying, and while I want to get to the bottom of her unspoken reasons for rushing to Florida, now isn't the time. She just arrived, and I don't want to ruin the night before it's even started. Nina needs our support, and if Lanie doesn't want to share her secrets, then I won't pry. For now.

Nina has been working to create a serene setting, complete with soft instrumental melodies playing in the background and the lights replaced by an array of candles she found in a closet in the hallway. I attempt to lend a hand, but she gently shoos me away, assigning me the important task of ensuring our wine is at the perfect temperature and we have plenty of reserves.

After a quick shower, Lanie emerges wearing a mismatched ensemble that seems more suited to Nina's taste than her own. It's a practical combination of shorts and a button-down shirt, showing Lanie's sophistication and maturity, which isn't something she typically embraces.

"Looks like someone's been busy," Lanie observes, her eyes sweeping over the room.

"Are those mine?" Nina inquires, gaze lifted from the candle she'd been lighting to focus on Lanie's pajamas.

Lanie looks down and shrugs nonchalantly. "No clue. Found them in my drawer."

A chuckle escapes me as Nina's expression shifts, her nose wrinkling in apparent recollection of when she misplaced them.

Lanie expertly uncorks a bottle, the satisfying pop signaling the start of our wine-night ritual. Our glasses are filled to the brim with ruby-colored liquid, the rich aroma wafting through the air.

The condo is filled with chatter and the clinking of glasses as we settle in for our much-needed wine night. The stresses of the day melt away as we sink into the comfort of one another's company, the glow of candlelight casting a warm ambiance around us.

Lanie regales us with tales of her latest yoga adventures, complete with the addition of a goat from Miller's Farm. Her animated gestures only make the story better.

"The damn thing peed all over the place. It was like a goat fire hose, and to top it off, it decided my snake plant was the perfect spot to drop a deuce." She scrunches up her nose. "It was an absolute menace, so I took it back to Jack Saunders and demanded my money back."

"I bet Jack had a good laugh," Nina says with a chuckle.

Lanie shrugs. "Couldn't care less. His goat is broken."

"I'm still trying to figure out why on earth you'd think bringing a farm animal into a building would be a good idea?"

Lanie makes a face. "Sharon Goldstein has been talking about some goat-yoga class in Silverton as though it's the best thing on earth. It was making my regulars consider making the trip out there." She shakes her head, appearing haughty. "I couldn't allow that."

"Well . . . looks like that worked out well for you," Nina chimes in, and I smother a giggle at the glare Lanie sends her way.

Nina takes a sip of wine and clears her throat, signaling our conversation is about to drift to more serious matters.

"I'm so happy you're here, Lanie, but can you please enlighten us on what compelled you to flee town so abruptly that you resorted to borrowing my pajamas and a bag we all know won't even accommodate your nightly skin care routine?"

Lanie grimaces, hinting at the discomfort she's trying to conceal. "Someone broke into my place. I couldn't stay there, thinking they might come back."

Nina's gasp echoes through the room, mirroring the shock reflected in my own wide-eyed expression.

"They didn't take anything, as far as I could tell, which only adds to the mystery," Lanie explains, her voice tinged with frustration.

"What possible motive could someone have for breaking into your place?" Nina questions, her concern evident in her furrowed brow.

I don't say a word, thoughts swirling in my mind. It was clear to me from Richard's scandal that Lanie has been entangled with some bad company. She turned down a proposal from Marcus Wells, and although he's behind bars, his associates, whoever they may be, aren't. Marcus was so caught up doing Richard's dirty work that someone had to be doing his. At least, that's what my intuition is telling me.

"It's all good. I have Nick on the case," Lanie says, and my head snaps up.

"Nick? How the heck did you get him clearance to take on a break-in?" I ask. "Especially considering how busy he is with Chelsea Grayson's murder."

Lanie bobs her head. "It took a bit of persuasion," she admits. "Let's just say he's looking into things on his own. It wasn't reported to the police."

"Why the hell not?" Nina crows, clearly distressed by this. "You need to report it."

Lanie throws her head back and groans. "Don't start nagging. Nick has been debriefed on my reasoning, and he's looking into things. While he does that . . . I'm here. With you two." She looks between Nina and me. "Can't that be enough information for now?"

My eyes narrow in on Lanie, and while I said I wouldn't pry, I feel like I need to, now that the door has been cracked.

"No, Lane. Something has been going on with you, and I'm worried. Why won't you confide in us?" I ask, my voice laced with worry. "You've seemed really on edge lately, especially since New Year's Eve."

Lanie's response is quick, almost too quick, as if she's been rehearsing her answer. "Oh, that was nothing," she attempts to assure us, but her tone is strained. "I was just going through a weird time, you know? Being overly superstitious and all that. It was just a dream, nothing more." Her words ring hollow.

"So you're fine with the fact we didn't even finish the ritual?" I interject, trying to determine if she's being honest. "Remember, the scarecrow never burned?"

"All good." Her voice trembles slightly, giving her away.

Lanie's reaction speaks volumes. Despite her attempts to mask her fear, I can see the telltale signs—the slight tremor in her hand, the haunted look in her eyes. Fear. It grips her tightly, refusing to let go, and I can't help but wonder what she's hiding behind that carefully constructed façade.

I peek over at Nina to find her face pinched and lips smashed into a thin line, a sign she's not buying Lanie's story either.

Lanie closes her eyes and inhales deeply. "Fine," she snaps. "You wanna know what's wrong? My past is catching up to me, and I'm worried."

"Does this have something to do with Marcus?"

Her head moves back slightly, confusion evident. "Wells? No. This is pre–Knox Harbor, things I did in my youth that I thought I got away with. I made some enemies of some dangerous people."

"Lanie." Nina's voice softens. "What can we do? How can we help?"

She huffs a humorless laugh. "Nothing. We allow Nick to investigate, and hopefully he finds something before he has to rush back to Falls Haven to deal with that second body."

The atmosphere grows heavy as Lanie drops the bombshell, her words hanging in the air like a heavy fog. My entire body locks up, eyes blinking uncontrollably as a chill creeps up my spine. The gravity of the situation sets in.

"Oh my god," Nina says, head snapping to me. "It's happened."

Lanie's eyes squint. "What's going on? What's wrong with her?" she asks, pointing to me.

"How do you know there's another body?" I ask, eyes trained in on Lanie.

She makes a face, looking back and forth from Nina to me as though we've lost our minds. "It was on the news."

The heaviness that was pressing down on me lifts immediately, and I have to wonder where my mind went that had me feeling so tense.

Was I questioning Lanie's character?

No. Never.

I trust her with my life. It has to be something else. Something I'll have to worry about later.

"I dreamed about another victim," I admit, and Lanie inhales sharply. "Who is she?"

She swallows, pulling out her phone. "Sierra Montgomery. A young girl from Knox Harbor."

She turns the iPhone around, and there she is, the girl from my dream, standing next to a smiling Chelsea Grayson.

We pepper Lanie with questions, concern etched into every line of our faces. She doesn't have much information, just that the body of Sierra was discovered at the docks, just down the road from where Chelsea was found.

"Do they think she was in Falls Haven searching for Chelsea?"

Lanie shrugs. "No clue. They're not really speculating. All they've said is that her death bears a striking resemblance to Chelsea's, and they're not ruling out a potential connection."

"Ally," Nina says, turning to me, drawing my attention. "Doesn't it strike you as odd that Sierra's last name is Montgomery?" I furrow my brow, not quite grasping her insinuation. "You know, considering our questions about the secret society and Chelsea's death," she clarifies.

I tilt my head, indicating my continued confusion.

"The place with the ghost was called Montgomery Estate. Could there be a connection between her and the society?"

Dread settles in the pit of my stomach. It may seem far-fetched, but if there's one thing I've learned, it's that spirits don't appear to me without reason. There's something more to all of this. There's a connection.

"What am I missing?" Lanie asks.

We fill her in on the party at the estate, the mystery surrounding the dream, and the symbol I saw. I describe the tattoo that Harlan and the snobbish woman both had, and how the bartender let it slip that there's a secret society. Lanie is speechless, taking it all in.

"This tattoo, can you find it online?"

I shake my head. "No. I've looked. But I did make a rough sketch."

Pulling up the picture I sent to Nick, I turn it around and show Lanie.

"That's . . . an interesting symbol," she says, tilting her head to the side.

An idea sparks in my mind. "Should we call Corinne? Have her look into it on the dark web?" I suggest, and both Lanie and Nina agree.

"Hey, Corinne," I greet when she answers the call. "Lanie and Nina are here with me, and we need your investigative skills."

"This should be good," she drawls. "What do you need?"

"Can you look into the symbol I'm sending through text?"

It's quiet on the other line for a moment before Corinne calls out, "Got it. I'll search the web and get back to you."

She ends the call without a goodbye, which is typical Corinne.

We eagerly await her call, each passing minute heightening our anticipation. Finally, the phone rings, and I hang on Corinne's every word as she unveils the revelation she's unearthed.

"The group behind that symbol is called the Order of Providence."

I'm staring at Lanie while Corinne delivers this news, and I don't miss the way her eyes darken and her throat visibly tightens.

She knows something about the Order of Providence.

I wait for her to spill what she knows, but instead, she dons a mask and pretends to be oblivious to what it represents.

I'm hurt and confused.

We've been friends long enough that I should absolutely call Lanie out on this. But I don't. Because the only reason Lanie Anderson would keep secrets is to protect me. She's just like Nina in that sense.

A hush falls over the room as the weight of her words sinks in. The name makes every hair on my body stand at attention, conjuring images of clandestine meetings and dark secrets lurking beneath the surface.

"Can you look into something else for me?" I ask, and Corinne grunts down the line.

"I need you to look into Chelsea Grayson and Sierra Montgomery's friendship. What were they into?"

"I can do that. Anything else?" she asks, and I can hear the excitement in her tone.

Corinne lives for this as much as the rest of us. There's a sense of satisfaction that comes with uncovering hidden agendas and crimes.

"Can you see if there's a connection between the owners of the old Montgomery Estate right outside The Communes in Florida and Sierra Montgomery's family?"

"I can tell you already that I won't be surprised to discover a connection with the Montgomery name. The news has reported that Sierra was a wealthy socialite whose late grandfather was connected to illegal gambling and extortion."

Holy shit.

Nina and I share a glance.

That's exactly what Montgomery Estate is—illegal gambling at the very least.

As the pieces of the puzzle start to come together, I can't help but feel a sense of unease. What led Sierra to Falls Haven? And does it connect to Chelsea's death?

"I'll loop in Darian to help," Corinne says. "He's a little too familiar with the shadowy side of New York City. If that woman tied to the Order is from there, he might be able to learn a bit about her and the Order itself."

Excitement bubbles within me as Corinne reveals her plan to tap into her brother Darian's connections. I'm hopeful that we'll soon uncover the answers we seek.

With the death of Sierra coming to fruition, our quest takes on new urgency. The Order of Providence may hold the key to unraveling the murders, and I'm more determined than ever to uncover their secrets and bring justice to those young girls.

The Moon . . . Reversed

I WAKE UP in a cold sweat, the remnants of the dream I just had still clinging to my mind like cobwebs. It felt so vivid, so real. Mrs. Fields, my quirky neighbor, was wandering through the night, peering into windows and snatching ornaments off neighbors' yards while they slept.

Eventually, she returned to her house, almost in a trancelike state, depositing her stolen treasures in her garage like some sort of shrine to her nocturnal thievery.

It was unsettling, to say the least.

Shaking off the icky feeling, I leave the bed and head to the kitchen, craving the comfort of a cup of coffee.

I shoot off a quick text to Ava, checking in on her. I've spoken to her every day since she left, but the past couple of days it's all been via text. She's got her head down, diligently working on her piece for the spring showcase. She still has two months, but I'm told the project is massive.

It's all she'll give me. The whole thing is meant to be a huge surprise to everyone outside of the school, and Ava's done her part in keeping her lips zipped.

"Whatcha thinking about?" Isla says, catching me off guard.

I whip my head over my shoulder and heave a breath. "Where have you been?"

She snickers. "Around. Mostly just watching like a creep. Not much else to do since you keep wandering off and leaving me here."

"I'm sorry. I've had some important stuff going on with a friend, and I had to concentrate on her. Having . . ."

"A ghost around isn't conducive to life?" she says, smiling to show she's playing with me. "I get it. I'm just ready to be somewhere else."

I run both hands down my face, feeling terrible that Isla is stuck sitting around while the rest of us go about life. It's not fair that she wants to move on and can't.

"I'll talk to Nick," I vow. "I'm not sure how it'll go, but I'll do what I can to get him on board with helping you."

Her face lights up, and she wiggles in place. "He's home now. No better time to send the spirit home." Her hands are lifted into the air, and she shimmies her hips.

I chuckle at her antics. "I said I'll discuss it with him, but I can't promise it'll happen today." I hold her stare. "Please be patient with me."

She sucks her teeth, rolling her eyes heavenward. "Fine. I'll calm myself down and prepare to be stuck looking at these walls a bit longer."

I glance out the window and find that she's right; Nick's car is in the driveway. It's a sight I haven't seen since returning from Florida. He's been stuck in Falls Haven, working closely with the local detective and FBI.

Now that there's a double homicide in the small town, both too similar to ignore, they've brought in the feds.

I quickly shoot him a text, suggesting lunch at Milly's Diner.

NICK

Good morning, beautiful.

A smile spreads across my face as I lift my arms into the air, stretching out the kinks.

"What did he say?" she asks, clapping her hands, looking far too giddy.

I wave her off with my hand, watching the bubbles on the screen that tell he's typing.

NICK

You're speaking my language. Milly's it is. What time?

ME

Eleven?

He agrees to eleven, saying he'll meet me there because he has to head back to Falls Haven afterward. It's just as well, because I need to stop into Marmalade and Rye to check on Mrs. Hampson. The last time I ran into her, she alluded to needing my specific set of skills for a private matter, and I'd be lying if I said I wasn't curious about that.

"Wanna join Nick and I at Milly's?" I ask, thinking it can't hurt to have her tag along for a public date.

She bobs her head animatedly. "Heck yeah. Let's go."

At exactly eleven on the dot, I step into Milly's, greeted by the familiar chime of the bell announcing my arrival. Scanning the room, I spot Nick seated in a booth at the back. He acknowledges me with a lifted chin and a grin, causing a flutter in my chest. It's surreal to think that he's here just for me.

"Aww look at that. He's got it bad," Isla says, with no amount of bitterness evident. "He looks good. Happy," she says, a smile in her voice.

She isn't wrong. He does look good.

Nick is my dream. His salt-and-pepper hair adds a touch of sophistication to his rugged allure. With a strong jawline, straight nose, and impeccably sculpted features, he's effortlessly captivating.

He exudes an undeniable confidence that leaves me speechless every time I'm in his presence. But it's his dimples—oh, those dimples—that could melt even the coldest of hearts. They make my knees weak and my belly flop like a teenager's.

He possesses a presence that commands attention, yet there's a softness in his gaze that belies his tough exterior, making him all the more irresistible. It's as if he stepped right off the pages of a magazine, bringing my ideal man to life.

"Hi, Alyssa," Christine calls from her computer. "You can sit anywhere."

"She's with me." Nick's husky voice rings through the small space, drawing the attention of every local in Milly's.

They all share curious glances, and I know without a doubt the rumor mill will be going strong later today.

"Uh-oh . . . you just went Knox Harbor official. That's about to be front page," Isla teases.

Christine, ever the romantic, flashes me a wide grin before playfully winking and giving a thumbs-up. Suppressing a laugh, I return her smile and stride over to join Nick.

"Have you been here long?" I ask, removing my coat and taking a seat across from him.

He shakes his head. "Nah. Just got here."

Isla takes a seat next to him, and I see his shoulders shake a bit. "It's cold in here," he says, but I don't comment.

It's not cold; it was his reaction to Isla. He just doesn't know it.

"What can I get you to drink?" Christine says, placing a cup of coffee in front of Nick.

"I'll have one of those." I motion toward the mug. "Maybe bring a whole carafe. I could use it today."

"God, do I miss coffee," Isla groans. "Nothing better."

Christine nods, her ponytail bobbing as she turns away. "Coffee coming right up," she chirps, disappearing behind the counter.

"Didn't sleep well?" Nick's concern is evident as he studies my face.

"I had a bizarre dream. That's all," I reply, shrugging my shoulders nonchalantly. "Mrs. Fields was wandering around at night, snatching things from people's yards and putting the stuff in her garage."

Nick lifts an eyebrow, his interest piqued as he takes a sip of his coffee.

"It was strange," I continue, my brow furrowing in concentration. "Garden gnomes, angels, a wreath . . ." I trail off, trying to recall the details. "And a Christmas sleigh."

Nick's eyes widen as he splutters slightly. "A sleigh?"

I nod firmly. "Yes, a sleigh. I told you—it was strange."

"What did the sleigh look like?" Nick leans forward.

I pause, my mind replaying the dream. "It was red, with gold stenciling along the sides," I say, my voice trailing off uncertainly.

Nick's head shakes and he whistles. "That's the exact description Patty Phillips gave me of her missing Christmas sleigh. What're the odds?"

I purse my lips, considering the possibility that this dream could be like the last.

"A sleigh's a sleigh," I say, shrugging my shoulders.

"Yet, a dream is never just a dream with you," he says playfully, but I hear the hint of truth in his voice.

"Oh my god. I have butterflies," Isla says dreamily. "Can ghosts have those?" She purses her lips and taps her chin.

I ignore her, focused in on what Nick's just said.

"You don't think . . ." I allow my words to trail off, not wanting to embarrass myself by assuming Nick truly thinks the missing items in the neighborhood could've been Mrs. Fields's doing.

"Never say never," he says. "I'll check in on her. Doesn't hurt to stop by."

"There's a lot going on these days around here," he says, placing his cup down and intertwining his fingers. "Break-ins, theft . . . murder." He shakes his head on a huff. "Chelsea and Sierra may have been killed in Falls Haven, but they're both from Knox Harbor. That can't be a coincidence."

I offer a sad, tight-lipped smile. "No, I don't suppose it is," I admit. I lean forward, not wanting to be overheard. "I think they're involved with a group called the Order of Providence."

His eyes narrow, and he bites the bottom corner of his lip, appearing to mull that over.

"What gives you that impression?" he finally asks.

I have to think about that for a moment, compiling all that's happened leading me down that path.

"The combination of what Chelsea's ghost showed me, mixed with my dream about Sierra. That's when I first saw the symbol. I wouldn't have thought about that again, but it's likely not happenstance that it popped up again at Montgomery Estate."

He nods. "Then there's the fact that Sierra had that tattoo behind her ear too."

My head jerks back. "What? She did?"

He sucks on his teeth, nodding his head.

"What about Chelsea?"

"She didn't. But they were friends. Whatever Sierra was into, she likely roped Chelsea in too."

I exhale heavily, feeling a pang of sadness for the girls. They were too young to be caught up in something dangerous enough to lead to their deaths.

"Wow," Isla states. "There was truth to these secret societies after all."

My eyes narrow in on Isla, and I want to ask her what she's talking about, but refrain because of where we are. Thankfully, she gets the hint that I'm curious and continues.

"My brother always said that the people running drugs through Knox Harbor were part of a much bigger organization. Something like Illuminati." She shrugs. "I always thought he was just talking nonsense. Maybe not."

Interesting.

So this society might have roots here. If they do, Nick will uncover them.

The conversation shifts to Nick's family, and my heart warms as he shares stories about them. His niece just turned one, and he recounts the celebration they had over the weekend. I met his sister only briefly, but I know without a doubt we'll get along well. I can sense the love he holds for his family. It's evident in the way his smile never fades when he speaks of them, and in the sparkle in his eyes as he talks about his niece, Zoey. The entire time he talks, Isla is focused on his words, smiling so wide.

You can tell she cared deeply for all of them too. Even if she didn't know Zoey, she looks like a proud aunt.

We've just cashed out and are heading toward the exit when Nick grabs my hand. There's a collective sigh behind me, signaling that Milly's patrons have all been watching us. No doubt they're preparing their stories to spread far and wide the moment they leave the restaurant. Just as Isla said.

That's Knox Harbor for you. Small towns thrive on gossip, but they *live* for romance.

Nick's grip on my hand tightens, and he looks down at me, a smirk playing on his lips. "I guess I made a statement today."

"Yeah ya did," Isla says from behind us, sounding like our own little cheer squad, but I don't turn around, wanting to capture this moment with Nick.

Those dimples pop, and my breath hitches. I inhale, pulling myself together so that when I speak, my voice remains steady despite the effect this man has on me.

I grin, and nod once. "It's official, West. You're off the market and likely walking down the aisle this afternoon."

He throws his head back and laughs, knowing that I'm only teasing. I think we're both on the same page about where we are in our relationship.

I come to a stop in front of Marmalade and Rye, ready to part ways.

"I'm going to head in and see Matilda," I say, nodding my head toward the store. "She needs my help with something."

"I have some time. I'll come with you," he says, pulling us toward the door.

My feet dig in, and Nick turns to me with a blank look.

"You really don't have to come with me. It'll be boring for you."

Nick lifts an eyebrow. "Are you trying to ditch me, Lyss?"

I take a deep breath, feeling my cheeks puff out slightly, then exhale slowly, biting my lower lip in contemplation. "Maybe?"

He chuckles. "What are you and Tilda up to exactly?"

I heave a heavy sigh, recognizing that if I'm going to tell him what's happening, he might as well come with me.

"Let's go," I say, pulling him into the shop.

Matilda Hampson is decked out in her typical blue pantsuit, silver hair pinned up in a tight French twist.

"Man, these people never change, do they?" Isla says, taking Matilda in.

"Alyssa," Matilda calls, flouncing toward us. "And Nicholas. To what do I owe the pleasure of your visit?"

He looks down at me and shrugs. "I'm here with her."

She tilts her head, her expression thoughtful. "With her . . . interesting," she muses aloud, then turns to me. "Can I speak freely?"

I glance up at Nick, moistening my lips nervously, waiting for some sign that he won't bolt out of here.

"Pretend I'm not even here," he says, flashing me a reassuring smile.

I turn back to Matilda. "What can I help you with?"

She nods eagerly, holding up a hand and hurrying toward the back.

"Should we follow her?" Nick asks, and I shrug uncertainly.

Less than a minute later, she's scurrying toward us with what looks like a wand of sage gripped in her hand.

"What the hell is that?" Nick whispers.

"Sage," Matilda says, having heard him. "For cleansing the area."

"Do you think that could move me along too?" Isla asks, hope lacing every word.

I grimace, shaking my head just enough that nobody else should notice.

Isla's smile disappears and she harrumphs, placing her hands over her chest.

Nick grunts, and I look up in time to see his eyes close in a pained expression.

"I know I said to pretend I wasn't here, but I really have to suggest you not light that in here," Nick says. "It's a fire hazard and a code violation. You're in town, and the whole of Main Street could light up like a torch if this goes wrong."

Matilda brushes off his concerns with a wave of her hand. "You don't need to be crazy to be smart, but you need to be a little smart to be crazy."

"What does that have to do with this situation?" Nick asks, looking between Matilda and me.

"Eccentric ways are called for in this situation, Nicholas. We'll be fine." She turns to me. "Do you know what to do with this?"

"Yes," I say, tilting my head to the side. "But I can sense that you do too. So why call on me?"

Matilda straightens, placing one hand on her hip. "One hand is not enough to catch a flea," she says, gritting her teeth and lifting both eyebrows skyward. It's clear she's trying to relay that the flea is in fact a ghost, without using those words.

"Got it," I say, holding my hand out for her to pass over the sage. "Nick, since you are law enforcement, would you be willing to wield the sage for us?"

He rubs at his full bottom lip, inspecting the sage like it's a weapon of mass destruction, eventually reaching out to take the bundle.

From Matilda's back pocket she pulls a grill lighter, large enough to get the sage burning hot.

"Follow us and wave the sage in the air, making sure to cleanse all the items," Matilda instructs Nick. "I'm unsure what brought the unruly spirit into my space."

I can't help but stifle a laugh as Nick reluctantly waves the sage bundle in the air, his eyes bugged out like a startled rabbit. Matilda stands beside him, chanting in a language that sounds like a mix of ancient incantations and gibberish, while Isla, unbeknownst to anyone but me, dances in and out of the smoke, holding onto hope that the sage will send her on.

"To the window, to the wall," I say under my breath, drawing a deep chuckle from Nick and a look of confusion from Isla.

"What was that?" Matilda asks, looking over her shoulder.

"Never mind," I say, smothering my laughter. "Please continue."

She purses her lips. "I need you to repeat after me, Alyssa. Otherwise, this won't work."

I bob my head in understanding.

"*Spiritus qui intra haec parietes habitant, non gratus estis,*" she calls out.

I join in with the chanting as best as I can, trying to keep a straight face, because I have to admit I'm not entirely sure what I'm saying.

Nick's dimples are on display as he bites his lower lip. He's getting too much enjoyment out of this.

We continue to move around the room, periodically speaking in what I now recognize as Latin.

Nick's discomfort is unmistakable, his movements awkward and stiff as he follows Matilda's lead. He shoots me a pleading glance, silently begging me to end this bizarre ritual. But I can't help but enjoy the absurdity of the situation, especially seeing Nick, the epitome of stoicism, being dragged into the world of spiritual cleansing.

She stops in the middle of the store, head tilted toward the ceiling, hands raised out to the sides. "Spirits who dwell within these walls, you are not welcome." She turns to me. "It is done."

"What? Nothing happened," Isla says, irritation clear in her tone. "Nothing was even here. The kook has lost it."

Nick and I breathe a collective sigh of relief that it's over, watching as Matilda lifts a vintage tin canister up toward Nick. He drops the sage bundle like it's a hot potato, his expression a mixture of relief and humor. She quickly moves to the back with the tin and sage, leaving Nick and I alone in the shop.

I can't help but burst into laughter, the tension of the moment dissipating in the ridiculousness of it all.

Nick shakes his head, a wry smile playing on his lips as he looks at me. "Remind me never to let you drag me into anything like this again."

I grin, feeling a sense of camaraderie between us. "I gave you an out." I shrug one shoulder, pursing my lips.

"Alyssa," he drawls, grinning as he moves toward me.

He pulls me into his chest, and I look up into his eyes, sighing contentedly.

"Deal. But admit it—you secretly loved every minute."

Nick rolls his eyes, but there's a twinkle of amusement in them. "Yeah, yeah. Let's just hope we haven't invited something to attach to us."

I feign shock, lightly swatting at his chest. "Nick West, are you turning into a believer in the supernatural? Embracing the unexplainable?"

He smirks, pulling me in closer and placing a kiss on my forehead. "I believe in you."

I melt into him, basking in his words and the warmth of his body.

His earlier words soak in.

Let's just hope we haven't invited something to attach to us.

Nothing out of the ordinary happened during the cleansing. But his former fiancée is here and well and truly attached. I know I need to broach that topic, for her, but I also don't want to ruin the moment.

I step out of Nick's embrace, glancing around the room. Isla is nowhere to be seen, but Matilda materializes, holding something in her hand. She seems visibly relieved, which should soothe my unease, but it doesn't.

"In gratitude," she says, presenting me with a Turkish bowl. It matches the set I bought earlier in the year. It's now back with Gloria Craft.

"Thank you, Mrs. Hampson."

"Matilda," she corrects. "And thank you. The space feels lighter."

"This isn't necessary," I say, holding up the bowl. "I'm concerned it didn't work. Nothing happened . . ."

She lets out a breath. "You don't feel that?"

I make a face, shaking my head. "Feel what exactly?"

"The heaviness is gone. Whatever entity it was, it left." She takes a step toward me, placing a hand on my shoulder. "Not every cleanse will result in a show. Most ghosts aren't trying to fight to stay."

I narrow my eyes at the woman. "You seem to know an awful lot about this stuff, Matilda . . ."

She harrumphs. "I watch a lot of movies."

It's evident that's a cover story for her knowledge of spiritual occurrences, but I don't call her out on it. I've heard the rumors of the Red Hats dabbling in rituals.

"Let's get that packaged up and you two on your way," she says, moving us toward the back room.

Her office is a chaotic assortment of antiques waiting to be cataloged and shelved. The air is thick with the scent of age-old leather and the faint aroma of dried flowers. Layers of dust coat the surface of every space, apart from her desk.

Matilda moves among her prized possessions with the grace of a connoisseur, her eyes gleaming with appreciation for the historical significance of each piece in her collection as she searches for something out of view.

My eyes roam the space, landing on an old photograph pinned

to the wall above her desk. It's a black-and-white picture of five men standing in a line, dressed in T-shirts and jeans. They look like greasers from the fifties.

I move a little closer, inspecting the image. I've always been obsessed with the past. It's strange to think that mere decades ago, life was so different.

I'm about to turn away when I notice the triangle symbol tattooed on one man's arm. My eyes move quickly from one guy to the next, finding that all of them have the same tattoo, located exactly where Harlan's was placed.

The Order of Providence.

"Who are these men?" I ask, drawing the attention of Matilda.

"That's my Joseph and his brothers," she says, smiling sadly.

"Five boys? His mother had her hands full," I say, continuing to inspect the photo.

"Not biological brothers," she titters. "Only Carl was biological. The rest were his brothers by choice."

Fraternal.

The Order of Providence.

"What is this tattoo they all have?" I ask, pretending that I'm seeing it for the first time.

"Something Carl drew up that they all decided to ink their arms with," she says, rolling her eyes. "I never liked the thing."

"Do you know what the meaning behind it is?" I press, hoping to get something from her about the Order.

"No clue. I never cared much about what those boys got up to. Their business."

It's clear I won't get anything more from her on the subject, so I drop it.

She packages up my bowl and walks us to the door, thanking me once more for my help. I can't get out of Marmalade and Rye fast enough.

Outside, I take a deep breath, soaking in the fresh air, the scent of sage clinging to me and Nick.

"Let's hope that worked. Otherwise, I might wake up with a Billy Garet replacement at the end of my bed," I say, half jokingly.

"You're safe. You reek of sage. No spirit is going to come within a mile of you."

Nick chuckles, but there's a flicker of uncertainty in his eyes. "Maybe we should bathe you in sage," he says, his tone suddenly more serious. "I'm worried about what could attach itself to you."

I bite my lip, a nervous laugh escaping me. "I can't avoid spirits. And besides, I have one back at my house that you and I need to discuss soon."

Nick's demeanor shifts, his expression growing guarded. "Yeah, we probably should," he agrees, his tone clipped.

"I'm sorry, Nick. I didn't mean to—"

"No." He shakes his head. "Don't apologize. I didn't mean to come off like an ass." He rocks back on his feet, looking wholly uncomfortable. "It's just awkward to discuss Isla like this. I haven't come to terms with it all."

I bite my cheek, uncertain what to say.

"I know we have to help her move on. I'm just . . ."

"Not ready," I say, and he nods. "I'm letting you call the shots here."

"Thank you," he says, and I offer a tight-lipped smile.

"I don't want you to be angry with me, but she's ready, Nick. She said so today."

"Soon." It's all he says, so I take it that it's time to change the subject.

"What do you make of Carl and Joseph Hampson?" I whisper the names, not wanting anyone to overhear.

"I'll look into them. See if I can find any connections to the

Order of Providence," Nick offers, glancing down at his phone. "I gotta get going."

He leans in, pressing a gentle kiss to my lips. He feels distant. Reserved. I can't help but think it's because of our conversation about Isla.

It's completely understandable.

The situation is undoubtedly tough for him to wrap his mind around.

The woman he once loved is lingering, unable to find peace in the afterlife.

If I were in his shoes, I'd be torn between wanting Garrett to stay and knowing that he needs to move on.

The time will come when he's prepared to let her go again, and until then, I'll respect his need for space to process everything.

What else can I do?

The Hierophant . . . Reversed-Ish

AS WE STEP onto the bustling streets of New Orleans, the air thick with the scent of spices and the sound of music, excitement surges through me. Lanie, Nina, and I have been looking forward to this trip for days, and we're finally here.

Our primary objective might be to track down Ian, but you don't come to New Orleans and pass up the opportunity to bask in all the city has to offer.

The colorful façades of buildings embellished with whimsical artwork only add to the city's enchantment. I find myself craning my neck to take in every detail, unwilling to miss a single square inch of the place. The entire time, I'm thinking about eating, because the food in New Orleans might be my favorite part. I'm going to savor each bite of flavorful gumbo and decadent beignet placed in front of me.

"Are you hungry?" Nina asks, shoulders shaking with jollity.

I lift a brow, caught off guard by the accurate assessment. Did my stomach growl?

"What makes you ask that?"

She smirks, looking down at our intertwined arms.

My eyes widen as the realization sinks in. "You read my mind?"

As soon as I say the words, Nina's expression morphs into shock. She hadn't even realized what she'd done.

It wasn't a bad vision she saw, but my internal thoughts.

"How . . ." She trails off, her voice barely a whisper, echoing the bewilderment in her eyes.

"I really think we need to prioritize meeting with Corinne's aunt Bee. She knows we're in town," I suggest, recalling how before we left, Corinne had suggested we look up her aunt, who typically sets up shop in Jackson Square, reading tarot for whoever asks.

"You might be right," she says.

A commotion next to us has Nina and I halting our conversation to see what's going down. Of course, we find Lanie in the center of the controversy.

"Get your damn hands off me before I break your arm in two," she snaps. "I already told you no."

Nina and I rush toward Lanie, hoping to pull her from the intoxicated man's grasp. He's clearly had one too many drinks—his speech is slurred and his movements are unsteady—while his friends stand by, finding amusement in his inappropriate behavior.

Nina grabs the guy's arm, narrowing her eyes. "Does your friend over there know you're sleeping with his fiancée?" she confronts him, her tone laced with accusation.

The man recoils, taken aback by Nina's blunt revelation. He mutters a half-hearted apology before slinking away into the crowd before Nina can out him to his friend.

"Jerk," Nina barks to his back. "I think we should head toward Jackson Square and see if we can find this Aunt Bee."

I nod.

Jackson Square isn't as crowded as Bourbon Street was. There are tables and tents set up around the perimeter of a park. We walk the line in search of Corinne's aunt, who's sure to be every bit as eccentric as her mother.

Bee's presence is unmistakable, her table adorned with mystical trinkets and a deck of tarot cards laid out in front of her. As we approach, we catch the tail end of a reading, the girl in tears of joy as she embraces Bee.

"Thank you so much," the small, dark-haired girl whispers to Bee.

With a warm smile, Bee waves the girl off. "Go . . . revel in your newfound happiness."

The girl bobs her head and smiles before darting off toward her friends waiting off to the side.

As soon as the girl is out of earshot, Bee turns her attention to us. "Poor girl. She's about to get engaged all right, but she'll leave him for his brother."

My head snaps toward the girl practically skipping away, happily reciting all that Bee shared about her future.

"Why didn't you tell her?" I blurt out, unable to mask my incredulity.

It seems cruel to withhold such critical information, especially when it could drastically alter someone's life trajectory.

"She didn't ask," she states matter-of-factly, as though it were the most natural thing in the world.

Her casual dismissal plants seeds of doubt about her true intentions. It's as if she views people merely as pawns in some cosmic game, oblivious to the gravity of her readings and the profound impact they could have on lives. The thought leaves a bitter taste in my mouth, tarnishing the hope I had for this meeting. It's entirely the opposite of what I wish to do with my abilities.

Her sharp gaze lands on me, scrutinizing me in a way that only raises my hackles more.

"Corinne Moradi sent us," Nina says, likely hoping to establish a connection.

As for me, I simply want to turn around and find someone else.

The mention of her niece's name sparks recognition in Bee, and she regards me with renewed interest.

"You . . . you're the one with powers," she murmurs, her voice tinged with awe.

"That's what we came to talk about," I reply, feeling torn about how I wish to proceed with the woman.

"Can you tell us how our abilities work?" Nina asks, taking the decision out of my hands.

"Your abilities? You have them too?" she says, sounding skeptical.

Nina nods her head.

"I'm heading to grab beignets. When you're done, meet me at Café du Monde." Lanie doesn't wait for us to respond before she's heading off.

Bee's expression softens, and she gestures for us to follow her.

"You don't need to be here?" I say, pointing toward her table.

She waves me off. "Nah. It'll be fine."

She walks us across the street and down a short alley, unlocking a door that opens to a steep set of stairs.

"Welcome to my home," she announces, raising a host of questions.

I find myself silently wondering how she can afford such prime real estate in the heart of New Orleans.

Bee turns to me with a knowing smile. "My family had money," she explains casually, as though it were the most natural thing in the world. "It was passed down through generations, allowing us to maintain this place."

I feel a flush of embarrassment rise to my cheeks at being caught in my silent inquiry. It's a reminder that around people like Bee, my thoughts are not my own. I tuck that away, a reminder to be careful not to allow my mind to wander to places I shouldn't among such company.

Bee's residence is a chaotic labyrinth of curiosities, each item telling a story of its own. Piles of ancient tomes teeter precariously on overflowing bookshelves, their weathered pages whispering secrets from centuries past. Dusty artifacts and mystical trinkets adorn every available surface, their origins shrouded in mystery. The air is heavy with the scent of dried herbs and incense, mingling with the musty smell of old parchment.

"Take a seat," she says, motioning toward a wingback chair sitting across from a cluttered desk.

I motion for Nina to sit.

"I'll be fine standing," I say, wanting to feel like I have the upper hand, standing taller than the small-statured woman who's now hunched over the desk.

Bee purses her lips at me but doesn't insist that I sit.

"Why have you come to me?"

I recount my experiences communicating with ghosts and the recent emergence of prophetic dreams. Bee stares off into space for several quiet minutes, and I wonder what she's thinking.

"It appears you are a medium with enhanced psychic abilities." She taps the desk with her fingers. "Mediums can communicate with spirits who choose to communicate with them. You'll receive only the information they choose to share."

I huff. "That's not helpful. Why not share everything so I can get them sent on their way?"

She bites her tongue. "Spirits are stuck between worlds. Their memories oscillate between what they remember from earth and what they know from before. They're confused. That's why they're coming to you. They're hoping you'll straighten things out."

Nina and I share a look.

"What about the dreams?" I ask, trying to keep us moving along.

"The precognitive dreams are part of your abilities. They're typically a more advanced skill that comes once a person has mastered the art of communicating with the spirit world. Think of them as a link between you and the divine."

"I'm not following."

She purses her lips. "The universe is sending you messages of things to come so that you can stop them or intervene. Pay close attention to the details and write them down immediately." She leans forward, eyes boring into me. "You have the ability to call upon dreams."

I squint, nose scrunched, but I don't get a chance to ask for clarification as Bee marches on.

"Before you lay your head on your pillow, ask the universe to send you a sign. Be very specific about what you want. If there's a message meant for you, it'll come."

"And you?" she says, turning toward Nina. "What are your gifts?"

Nina shares her journey of touching people and uncovering their secrets, which has evolved into the ability to read minds. Bee listens raptly.

"This is interesting indeed," she clucks. "Clairvoyance and psychometry. Very cool."

Nina's nose wrinkles. "What does that mean? How do I shut it off?"

Bee huffs. "You don't shut it off, ding-dong. You embrace it. Use it to help your—others," she amends, deciding not to out herself as selfish.

She's clearly looking out for number one, utilizing the things she learns to better her circumstances. I don't need to be psychic to see that.

"Your gift requires focus. If you want to know something about someone or any object, you simply have to touch it to gain answers."

"I've tried that, and it didn't work. I only see things at random."

She rolls her eyes. "That's because it's too new. You haven't conquered it yet. That will require months of meditation and practice."

Bee stares at Nina intently, as though she's working something out, likely trying to read Nina's mind. "No wonder you're flustered by this power. It appears as though your mind fixates on the obscene."

Nina's face flushes bright red, and she stammers, "That's not—I see into the minds of the people I touch! I've seen all kinds of thoughts—it's not always—"

Bee bursts into laughter, clearly amused by Nina's discomfort. I can't help but smirk at the scene. This is the first time I'm meeting Bee, but there's something oddly familiar about her demeanor—something reminiscent of Corinne.

Bee's expression softens slightly, but she remains with a teasing edge. "Relax, Nina. It's all part of the process. Everyone's mind has its quirks. If you're seeing things that make you blush, it's probably because people's thoughts are just as chaotic as you're finding them."

Nina takes a deep breath, still visibly embarrassed. "Fine, but I'm going to need a lot of practice if I'm going to handle what I see without feeling like I need to take a bath in holy water."

I snort, barely able to contain my laughter. Nina's frustration is clear, and her look practically screams, *I'm serious. This stuff is filthy.*

Bee meets her glare with a perfectly straight face. "Well, I suppose a cleansing ritual might be more effective than trying to scrub it all away with the church's less-than-blessed holy tap water.

Though, at this point, you might need a full exorcism to clear out the mental clutter. Or, you know, maybe just keep your hands to yourself and refrain from peopling until you've got this under control."

"Oh, great. Maybe I should just wrap myself in aluminum foil and make a grand entrance as the world's most neurotic human," Nina snaps.

I sense the brewing storm and realize it's time to step in before this turns into a full-blown catfight. "Okay . . . Time to go."

Bee stands from the desk, walking to a bookshelf against the wall. She scans the shelves until she finds what she's looking for. She pulls not one but three books from the shelf and places them on the desk in front of us.

"Here. Take these and read up." She slides the books across the desk. "When you're done, please return them. My address is on the inside of each book, along with my phone number. Call if you have questions."

"Thank you," we say in unison, Nina sounding a bit more relaxed than moments ago.

From this meeting, I've learned how important intention and seeking guidance from the universe will be if I want to utilize my gifts in full. There's so much potential, but it's not going to come to me overnight. I'll need to work to nurture my abilities.

As the sun sits low over Jackson Square, we leave Bee's place feeling enlightened and empowered, armed with newfound knowledge to navigate the complexities of our abilities.

We meet Lanie and shove copious amounts of fried dough into our mouths, completely content to call that our dinner for the night. We're tired and need to check into our rooms.

The sun is beginning to dip below the horizon as we arrive at the old, historic bed-and-breakfast nestled in the heart of New Orleans's Garden District. The house looms before us, its ornate façade adorned with intricate carvings and latticework. Ivy creeps up the sides of the building, adding to its charm.

"This is . . . an interesting choice," Nina says, sliding up next to me.

"I love it," Lanie says, clapping her hands in excitement. "It's got all the vibes."

I chuckle, shoulders shaking at Lanie's enthusiasm.

The wrought-iron gate creaks open as we step onto the cobblestone pathway, leading us to the grand Victorian mansion that will be our home for the duration of our stay.

Entering the foyer, we are greeted by the smell of aged wood and potpourri. The interior is a testament to the house's storied past, with antique furniture and vintage decor in every corner. It feels as though we have stepped back in time.

"May I help you?" A stout woman wearing an apron and hairnet looks up at us from behind a desk.

"We're checking in," I say. "Two rooms under the name Mann."

"Do you happen to have a third room? Even for one night?" Lanie asks.

"You can stay with me," Nina says, but Lanie shakes her head.

The woman flips through a bulky book, indicating that the Ramada House hasn't modernized its check-in procedure, opting to maintain a traditional approach.

"They're on the third floor," announces a woman emerging from the back, clad in a black jumpsuit with bleached hair neatly pulled back. She doesn't appear to be too much older than we are. "Thank you, Rosie. I'll take it from here."

The older woman bows slightly, rushing off, mumbling something under her breath.

"My name is Adeana Ramada. This is my parents' place," she explains. "What brings you to town?" she asks, as she searches through a drawer behind the counter.

Nina, Lanie, and I share a look, each likely trying to determine what to tell her.

"Just a visit," I say.

The woman looks up at me, expression pinched as though she knows I'm not being honest.

"We do have an extra room, but only for the night," she says to Lanie.

"That's fine. I'll take it." She turns to Nina. "Is it okay if I bunk up with you come tomorrow?"

Nina nods her head. "Of course."

"Perfect," Adeana says. "Follow me," she requests, walking out from behind the desk toward a large set of winding stairs.

As she shows us to our rooms, she points out various things about the place. Where the bathrooms are located. Where to find extra towels and linens if we should need them. Basic things typical of a bed-and-breakfast.

Each room is uniquely decorated with plush furnishings and luxurious wallpaper, adding to the character of the place.

"Your room will be right this way," she says, leading me to the end of the hall.

My room overlooks the lush gardens below, the moonlight casting a soft glow through the lace curtains. The overhead lights flicker, and I turn to see Adeana's eyes trained on the light.

Her head lowers, and she smiles. "It's something old houses do. Nothing to be concerned about." There's something in her tone and in the way her eyes crease at the corners that leads me to believe there's something she isn't saying. "Well . . . good night." She bows slightly, closing the door behind her, leaving me to turn in circles, inspecting the incredible room.

I practically throw myself onto the bed, sighing at how comfortable it is. Mentally ticking off my to-do list before I can finally relax leaves me fidgety. First order of business: return Ava's missed call, and tackle the dreaded conversation with my mother. She doesn't call often, but when she does, there's typically bad news to be shared.

An hour later, I've managed to complete everything on my list. My call to Ava went unanswered but was quickly followed up with a text letting me know she's at the library studying for a quiz. We said our good nights because she wasn't sure how long she'd be there.

My chat with my mother was brief. She called to express her regrets about missing Ava's showcase. I reassured her that the important people would be in attendance and urged her to reach out to Ava. That landed like a lead balloon, but I don't care.

I'm done with the nonsense that family is defined by blood. Ava and I found our family in Lanie and Nina, and we're happier for it.

I've just finished removing my makeup and brushing my teeth when a sudden chill fills the air, accompanied by a ghostly breeze that seems to swirl around me with an otherworldly presence.

The hairs on the back of my neck stand on end as the cool air brushes against my skin. It's as if the very atmosphere of the room has shifted, filled with an eerie energy that I've experienced before.

A spirit is here.

My heart pounds in my chest as I prepare to uncover the ghostly entity and what it wants with me.

"Who are you?" I say, moving in a circle, inspecting my surroundings.

My question goes unanswered, nothing materializing or making its presence known outside of the shifted air. It's an old bed-and-breakfast with drafts, to be sure. Maybe I'm imagining it?

Suddenly, Lanie bursts into my room, her eyes wide with terror.

"Something is in that room," she says, jabbing a finger in the direction of where she just came from. "I'm not sleeping in there."

I smother a smile, recognizing that I was just having my own moment and shouldn't tease her.

"Come on in. You can sleep with me," I say, pulling back the covers and patting the mattress.

Without hesitation, she crawls into bed.

"I refuse to spend another moment alone in that haunted-ass room," she barks, yanking the covers up to her chin. "My closet door kept creeping open. I even put a damn chair against it." She shakes her head, shoulders shivering. "It flew across the room."

My eyes widen. "Seriously?"

She nods. "Maybe not clear across, but it definitely moved away from the door."

"Let's get some sleep," I suggest, lying down and getting comfortable.

Lanie follows suit and, despite the unsettling events, is able to relax, cuddling up next to me. We huddle together in the safety of my room, and before long, our breathing slows and my eyes close, the ghostly presence of the house seeming to fade into the background.

I'm not sure how long I'm asleep before I'm jolted awake by the sensation of the bed shaking beneath me. Confusion clouds my mind as I glance around the room, only to see the chandelier above us swaying ominously, and the lights flickering on and off erratically.

"Are you feeling this?" I whisper, turning to Lanie, who is also wide awake, her face reflecting the same mixture of disbelief that I feel.

Before she can respond, the trembling intensifies, causing the floorboards beneath us to creak and groan as if under immense pressure. Panic seizes me as I realize that this is no ordinary occurrence. This is one very pissed-off ghost.

With trembling hands, I reach for my phone, my fingers fumbling as I struggle to illuminate the room with its weak glow. The dim light casts eerie shadows across the walls, adding to the sense of foreboding that fills the air.

"We have to get out of here." Lanie's voice shudders as she speaks, her usually confident demeanor shaken by the supernatural events unfolding around us.

Without another word, we scramble to our feet, our movements frantic as we stumble toward the door, desperate to escape the haunting presence that lurks within the confines of this room.

As we burst into the hallway, the shaking subsides, leaving us breathless and shaken. We exchange glances, our minds racing with questions and uncertainties. What just happened? And more importantly, were we the only ones who experienced that?

Not another soul is to be found in the hallway. Nina is seemingly fast asleep in the comfort of her bed.

We rush to her door, banging our fists against the wood when we find it locked.

"Nina, wake up," Lanie calls through the door.

When it finally swings open, Nina stands in the dark, dressed in a pair of shorts and a Nirvana T-shirt. She rubs at her eyes, dazed and unsure what's happening.

"What?" she says, voice full of sleep.

"You didn't feel the house shaking?" Lanie asks incredulously. "The place just about came down with us in it."

Nina blows air out of her nose, making a sound between a grunt and a huff. "No."

It's all she says, clearly still asleep.

"Well, there is something here. Something dark," Lanie says, looking to me for confirmation. I nod my head.

"Whatever it is, I'm not sure it's a ghost," I confess. "This felt different, worse than a poltergeist. It felt evil."

The realization settles heavily in the pit of my stomach, filling me with an overwhelming sense of dread. "I don't want to stay here," I declare, my resolve firm as I glance nervously around the room, searching for any sign of the malevolent presence.

Despite not experiencing the unsettling phenomena firsthand, Nina seems fully awake now, her senses on high alert.

"Do you think it's a . . ."

"Don't say it," I snap. "Don't give life to whatever it is."

Something within me is screaming to run. To turn away from the foreign entity.

We rush to the front desk and explain to Adeana that we need to leave.

"I'm not sure that's a good idea," she says. "With the festival in town, finding another room could be near impossible." There's something in her tone, a hint of underlying motive that makes me uneasy.

"What do you think?" Nina asks me, and I shrug. "I think it's worth taking our chances. I'd rather catch a red-eye and head home than stay in this place another night."

"You felt them," Adeana murmurs.

"Them?" I repeat, with no shortage of frustration. "What is it?"

She sighs heavily, closing her eyes. "A year ago, we allowed two viral YouTubers to record their ghost-hunting show here. They did a séance with a Ouija board, and something . . . came through and stayed."

My head lolls back on my shoulders. "What were you thinking?"

"I wasn't here," she cries. "I found out after they left. The place was closed to visitors so that I could clean it up, and all hell broke loose."

"Literally, if I had to guess," Lanie deadpans, shaking her head.

"Can you help me get rid of them?" she asks.

I share a glance with my friends. Lanie shakes her head, signaling we should leave while we can. Nina, on the other hand, is looking at me like I couldn't possibly desert Adeana in her time of need.

"Yes, but if there are multiple spirits here, I'll need some help."

"I'm out," Lanie says, throwing her hands into the air. "You said not to say it, and here you are doing exactly that. I'm not playing with the devil, Alyssa."

I run a hand back through my hair. "They're angry ghosts, Lanie. Not demons. Geez. We'll call on Bee tomorrow first thing and get rid of whatever is here."

"How do you keep me safe?" Her voice pitches. "I might die before tomorrow."

I roll my eyes. "We'll take precautions. Everyone will sleep in Nina's room. It seems to not be as active."

Nina bobs her head.

I reach for my phone, dialing Nick's number, completely forgetting what time of the night it is. Walking to a private corner of the place, I wait for Nick's voicemail to kick on.

"Alyssa? What's wrong?" Nick doesn't sound like he's been asleep at all.

"I'm staying at a very haunted bed-and-breakfast, and if I'm being honest, I'm spooked." I begin to pace, recognizing just how much this encounter has me on edge. "I'm sorry for calling you at this hour. I'm not even sure why I did."

He blows out a harsh breath. "When you say haunted . . ."

"I mean something evil that's proving to have a lot of energy."

He's quiet for several moments, likely contemplating what to say to such a thing.

Poltergeists are unsettling and bring a chill with them. This brought foreboding. It's a spine-tingling darkness that whispers promises of torture and death. It's pure evil.

"You can't stay there," he says, and I huff a laugh.

"I don't have a choice. I have to help." I shuffle on my feet. "I'm not sure why I called. I guess . . . I just wanted to hear your voice," I admit.

"I'm not gonna lie. A wicked part of me is getting too much satisfaction outta the fact you called me in the middle of the night because you're scared."

I bark a laugh. "You are wicked. Getting pleasure out of my fear."

"No, darling. I'm getting pleasure outta the fact you gave me the chance to save you."

I smile, shaking my head. "I don't need saving, *darling*," I say, mocking him. "I'm perfectly capable of ending this angry spirit myself."

He chuckles. "That, I do not doubt." He's quiet for a moment, voice serious when he continues. "But I can't allow you to do this yourself. If you're fighting evil, I am too." He sighs. "I'll catch the next flight out. I'm on break for two days."

"You made me promise not to drag you into something like this again," I say, reminding him of his words at Marmalade and Rye.

He barks a laugh. "That only pertained to Matilda and her sword of sage."

I giggle, trying not to be too loud.

"If you insist on coming here, be prepared. This is different, Nick," I say, hoping he hears how serious I am.

"I'll see you tomorrow. Good night, Lyss."

As I hang up the phone, a sense of determination washes over me. We may have stumbled into a nightmare, but I can do this. I know I can. Having Nick here will only add a bit of comfort and a warm embrace to snuggle into after.

"Is there anyone else staying here?" I ask Adeana, who is watching me carefully.

She shakes her head.

"Good. Put on the *No Vacancy* sign. We're having ourselves an exorcism tomorrow."

The Fool . . . Reversed

Nick

I'VE BEEN REPLAYING the events of the past few days in my mind, particularly the visit to Lanie's loft. Despite thoroughly searching the place, I found no evidence of a break-in, no signs of forced entry, nor any indication that someone had trespassed. It's perplexing.

Did a break-in actually occur, or was it merely a figment of Lanie's imagination?

She sent me a photo of a note she supposedly found taped to her refrigerator.

It's never okay to turn your back on family.

It's a cryptic note typed out onto a piece of printer paper. It sounds more like an affirmation than a threat, and it makes me wonder who'd take the time to enter Lanie's apartment without making it obvious just to deliver that message.

The neighborhood theft rate has increased, and people are even reporting on KnoxNeighborWatch that someone has been tapping on their windows at night and smearing a dark residue all over their doorknobs. It sounds more and more like teen activity, which narrows the list of suspects down considerably.

Regardless, it's getting out of control, and I don't have the time or energy to investigate it any further. I had to hand it off to another department; they've upped the patrol on our street. That hasn't stopped the calls and texts from concerned neighbors overtaking my phone and sanity right along with it.

As I wait for my flight, I check my emails, finding one from my friend Greg, the private investigator I connected Alyssa to.

I asked him to check into the Hampson brothers and see if he could dig up any information on the Order of Providence, among other things. My hands are full, and the sooner Alyssa makes it back to Knox Harbor and gets her own PI business up and running, the better. I could really use her set of skills.

She's been so busy trying to help Nina find this Ian guy that I haven't wanted to press for her to contact the dead for more information.

For fuck's sake.

Who am I and what is happening to me?

Since when do I openly admit to believing in such things? Let alone internally bitching because I can't request a séance to get an audience with a dead girl, skipping over the tedious investigation. Oh, how times have changed.

My father would have a coronary if he knew I was tapping into the spirit world for answers.

I open the email from Greg to try to take my mind off ghosts and Alyssa for a little bit.

Nick,

I've got some info on the Hampsons. Turns out they were known as the Knox Harbor mafia. They had their hands in drugs, counterfeit money, you name it. Every time the DA got close to pinning them to something, they got off. Never spent a minute in jail.

Carl Hampson was found dead in his home with a gunshot wound to the head. It was ruled suicide but was later changed to suspicious. I've attached my findings to this email. Joe Hampson died of natural causes about ten years ago. The other three in the photo were their friends, Gerald (Jerry) Hoven, Buck Sauder, and Frank Montgomery.

Sierra Montgomery is connected to the Montgomery Estate. Her grandfather was the previous owner. His background is very similar to the Hampson brothers, and in fact, he was one of their friends in the photo you sent. Fucking odd if you ask me.

As for the Order, I'm still looking. The dark web doesn't seem keen to discuss that society, which makes me question how far you really wanna go down this path. These societies are known for staying a secret by all means necessary, if you catch my drift. I'll let you know if I dig up anything. Assuming I'm still alive . . .

Lastly, I paid a personal visit to Providence U. Spoke to Professor Dipshit, who spilled the details when I mentioned I had proof he's sleeping with his student, Felicity Baden. Ian Whalen has changed his name to Connor Fulton. He's living at 123 Magnolia Avenue, New Orleans, LA 70113, with his teenage son, Chase. –GE

Chuckling, I close my email. Greg's a jokester, but he's also the best PI I know. He doesn't mess around, and that's another reason

I asked for his help with things. He uses tactics I can't to get the answers I need quickly.

I glance over the attachment that details his findings on Carl Hampson's death. Forensic evidence suggests that the angle of the wound and the position of the gun do not match typical patterns of suicide. There were also discrepancies in witness statements regarding Carl's mental state and his behavior prior to his death.

I'm reeling from the news that one of the five men in the photo is a Montgomery. I snapped a photo of that picture when Matilda's back was turned, hoping it would be useful down the road, and it would appear it already has been.

I sigh, running a hand back through my hair. My mind is racing with all the information. I type up a quick text to Lanie, ready to move on from one of the many open cases I've gotten myself tied up in.

ME

Your note is with forensics.

If we find a print, I'll let you know.

Otherwise, I didn't find anything.

LANIE

Didn't figure you would, but thanks for looking. See you soon!

ME

See you soon.

I shut down my phone and place it in my bag, eager to board the plane and use the next four hours to rest. I'm anxious to get to Alyssa and relieved to have something to present to the girls when

I arrive in New Orleans. This news will get Nina the reunion she's been looking for and Alyssa back in Massachusetts.

This calls for a celebration. I'm going to make that past-due date happen.

✦ ✦ ✦

AS I APPROACH the Ramada House, a chill washes over me, despite the balmy New Orleans afternoon. This place is unlike any other bed-and-breakfast I've encountered. I can't put my finger on what exactly I'm feeling, but a heavy, oppressive energy pushes down on me.

Ghosts and demons? It's the stuff of nightmares, not police investigations. Yet here I am, stepping into a world I never imagined I'd believe in. Not to solve the case, but to be here for my girl.

My girl.

Damn, I love the sound of that. I didn't think I'd be ready for a serious relationship anytime soon, but Alyssa changed the game. She makes me want more than a simple fling.

She makes me think of the future. A future with her by my side.

I shake off that thought, needing to be prepared for whatever's happening in the creepy fucking place in front of me.

The sound of a wail has me running up the stairs and through the front doors. What I find inside is pure chaos.

A dark-haired woman dressed in a black cloak stands amidst swirling incense and sage, waving a cross in the air. The place is full of smoke, making it hard to breathe as the floors tremble beneath my feet and the walls groan ominously. It feels like the whole place could collapse at any moment.

"Get out," the woman's deep, throaty voice reverberates through the room.

My finger flies to my chest, eyes narrowed in on her as if to say, *Me?*

She rolls her eyes, shaking her head as if I'm the biggest idiot she's ever encountered. Turning her back to me, she continues waving her cross in the air, shouting out commands for the demon to leave.

The place is alive, bellowing and groaning with every demand the witchy woman makes.

Instinct tells me to grab Alyssa and get her out of here, but I know better. She won't leave.

"Alyssa," I call out, taking my chances of pissing off Madame Hocus-Pocus or worse . . . a demon.

"Over here," she yells, above the phantom howls.

I make my way through the smoke in search of Alyssa, my ears ringing with every scream of the house. I can't tell where the sound is coming from. It's everywhere and nowhere.

Fucking anarchy.

When I finally find Alyssa, her determined gaze is fixed on the woman wielding the cross, her eyes blazing with a fierce resolve that both impresses and worries me. I keep my distance, giving her space to do what she feels she needs to do. But my eyes remain steady on her at all times. I won't intervene unless I know her life is in danger.

While the exorcism—or whatever the hell you call this—continues, Alyssa's demeanor shifts.

"This isn't good," she says, eyes scanning the room. "There are several spirits here. A horrible ghost that we encountered in Florida apparently didn't leave us."

"Oh my god," Nina's voice pitches. "The one that chased us down the path at the Montgomery Estate?"

Alyssa bobs her head. "He doesn't want us to send him or the others away."

I exchange a concerned glance with Nina and Lanie, who are huddled in the corner, practically on top of each other.

Alyssa turns to me, her voice trembling with urgency as she says, "One of them is Carl Hampson."

"What?" Lanie, Nina, and I all say in unison.

"Carl from Knox Harbor?" Nina asks, and Alyssa nods her head.

"Why would he be here?" Lanie asks, looking at me as if I'll have all the answers.

"I believe he attached himself to me the other day at Marmalade and Rye," Alyssa explains to the girls. "Matilda asked for my help to move some spirits on. He had to have been there."

"I knew Matilda was into witchery," Lanie says, smiling deviously.

"Quiet," the strange woman hisses, with a hint of an unidentifiable accent. "I need all of you to concentrate your energy on banishing this angry ghost. Tell him that he's not welcome here."

I try to concentrate, channeling my inner zen amidst all the noise. But it's like trying to meditate in the middle of a rock concert. The piercing scream of the demon—or whatever is in this place—threatens to derail my focus at every turn.

"There's a woman and a child here too. They aren't angry. They're stuck," Alyssa calls out to the group.

With furrowed brows, I attempt to envision banishing the unseen ghosts, but my mind keeps wandering to mundane thoughts. A mental list of things to do in the Grayson case. Did I pack the right clothes for this trip? Can that demon possess me?

"Focus, West," I scold myself, attempting to clear my mind once more. But just as I start to feel a semblance of calm, someone carelessly bumps into me, nearly causing me to topple over a candle.

"Sorry," comes a voice from behind. I turn around to find some random girl. Her blond hair is coming undone from her low bun and flying all over the place. Her eyes are wide, and her teeth chatter.

She dashes around me, rushing out of sight.

Who the hell was that?

Trying to banish an angry ghost feels more like summoning a taxi than anything else. But in New Orleans, I'm sure stranger things have happened.

"Bee, he's getting stronger," Alyssa says, and I have half a mind to call this whole thing off and make them all vacate this haunted hellhole.

"He's working with another male spirit. Concentrate," the woman named Bee demands, and everyone in the room, aside from me, closes their eyes, seemingly taking Bee's advice. "Buck Sanders. Saunders . . ."

"Buck Sauder?" I ask, eyes narrowed in on Bee.

Her eyes widen. "You know him?"

"I know of him," I say, growing more concerned by the second.

If Carl Hampson and Buck Sauder are together, that can't be good.

I slam my own eyes shut, taking my chances at a sneak attack on Buck Sauder or Carl Hampson, who's either pissed off about being murdered or still struggling with his inner demons. In my mind, I make it very clear to both that my body is not open for takeover. I witnessed that once between Corinne and Charlie, and absolutely fucking not. No way. Stay the hell back.

One minute the place is moaning and threatening collapse, and the next it's silent. I peek one eye open to find all the women sharing glances that I can't read.

You could hear a pin drop as Alyssa and Bee scour the area, searching for any signs of the spirits.

"They're gone," Alyssa says.

There's a collective sigh from all of us. I breathe for what feels like the first time since entering the place, coughing on the smoke still lingering.

Lanie and Nina scramble up from their huddled position, jumping in to help the tall blond woman from a few moments ago, who materializes from behind the desk, looking like she got into a catfight and lost. Not only is her hair sticking up everywhere, but her mascara is also smeared down her face.

"Bee, do you need help with that?" Alyssa says, pointing to the incense and sage.

Bee waves a hand in the air. "I can handle this, and then I need to head out. My table needs to be set up."

Whatever the hell that means.

Alyssa rushes toward her friends, pulling them into a group hug.

"Are you two all right?" she asks. Nina nods her head while Lanie shakes hers.

"I will never recover from whatever that was." Lanie doesn't even sound like herself when she delivers her answer.

I've come to know her as strong and independent. Unshakable. Right now, she seems every bit the young one of the group. Her eyes are wide and mouth set in a grim line. She's rattled. But who the hell isn't, after that?

"We'll be fine," Nina says. "Go." She tips her head in my direction, and I offer an awkward wave in return.

Nina smirks, shaking her head.

I look over at Alyssa, still trying to wrap my head around what I just witnessed. She makes her way toward me, jumping into my open arms. I hold her for a moment, surprised she seems to be holding up all right. She's not even trembling.

"Well, that was nuts," I say, shaking my head incredulously.

Alyssa looks up at me, grinning. "Tell me about it. I still can't believe Carl Hampson showed up."

"And Buck Sauder," I say, drawing the attention of every woman in the room.

"Who's Buck?" Lanie asks.

I look to Alyssa. "Remember the photo from Matilda's office? The one with the five men?" She nods, head tilted to the side. "Buck Sauder was one of them."

"What? How? None of the spirits that were here resembled anyone from that photo aside from Carl," she says, and I shrug my shoulder. "Your guess is as good as mine. Maybe he died older, and you don't recognize him because he doesn't look the same?"

"If Buck is the older spirit, that's the one that came from Montgomery Estate. How the hell could Buck Sauder, a man attached to Carl Hampson, have been conveniently hanging around an illegal poker game in Florida?"

That has my mind racing with questions. How did Buck get there? Why was Carl Hampson sticking around his brother's wife? And what role does Matilda Hampson play in all of this? It's clear that there's more to uncover. I make a mental note to look into Buck and Matilda when I get back to Knox Harbor.

"I don't know, Lyss. Seems to me that this poker game is connected to Carl and Buck's past dealings. Sounds like they were involved in illegal activity that spanned the US."

Alyssa's eyes close on a heavy sigh. She's exhausted, and I have an urge to sweep her into my arms and get her home.

"I'm glad you're here," she says. "I'm sure you're swamped, and this will likely have you working twice as hard."

I look down at her and smile. "Captain ordered me to take a couple days. I'll be fine."

She visibly exhales. "That's good."

I step back, looking between her and her friends. "I have some news. Ian's changed his name. He goes by Connor Fulton here. My PI was able to locate an address for him."

Nina's hands fly to her mouth, eyes bright with unshed tears. "I don't think I believed that he'd actually be here. I just assumed it would be another step on a wild-goose chase," she admits, chin dropping as the first tear slides down her cheek.

Lanie pulls her into a hug, whispering soothing words into the top of her head.

"Are you going to head that way?" Alyssa asks, and Nina's head pops up.

Her expression is unsurprisingly hesitant. "I don't think I'm ready to see him tonight," she admits, her voice tinged with indecision. "After everything we just went through, I need some rest, and time to think over my plan."

Alyssa nods, rubbing her temples as if to soothe a headache creeping in. "Yeah, it's been a long day," she agrees. "We didn't get any sleep last night, and all this smoke is making my head spin."

"Let's get out of here for a bit," I suggest, but Alyssa hesitates, her gaze flickering back to where the blonde and the others are still gathered.

"I'm not sure I can just leave them here," she murmurs, her concern evident in her voice. "Not after everything that happened."

I can't help but feel a twinge of disappointment at her reluctance to leave, but I understand her reasons.

"We don't have to be gone long," I offer reassuringly. "Just a quick walk to get some fresh air. They can come with us."

Alyssa seems to mull over the idea for a moment, but before she can respond, Nina speaks up. "We'll be fine," she insists, her tone firm. "We're going to help Adeana and Bee clean the place up, and then get some rest. I have a big day tomorrow, after all."

"I should help too—"

"Alyssa Mann . . . go," Nina says, cutting her off. "I could use some quiet time." She blows a piece of blond hair out of her eyes. "Besides, I think today would be a great time to make my list of non-negotiables."

Alyssa grins at her friend, and I have to wonder what that's all about.

"Fine. You work on that, and I'll be back as soon as possible," she says, looking up at me and smiling.

"Don't rush back," Lanie says, waggling her eyebrows. "Have a glass of wine and relax." A mischievous grin spreads across her face, and I'm almost afraid to hear what's about to come out of her mouth. "Don't wake me up." She winks, turning on her toes and heading off toward the blonde, who's currently pouring water over the sage.

Alyssa's eyes close on a sharp inhale, her cheeks turning a bright shade of pink.

If I were a better man, I'd dismiss Lanie's suggestion in order to make Alyssa more comfortable. But I'm not. If I have my way, the whole place will be awake when I finally get her alone.

Knight of Cups

TONIGHT HAS TURNED out to be just what I needed. Nick talked me into leaving the bed-and-breakfast, and it turned into an impromptu date. We indulged in a hearty meal, the savory flavors still dancing on my taste buds.

We're strolling hand in hand through the French Quarter, swaying to the sound of the jazz music playing all around us. Despite the heaviness that lingers from our earlier brush with the supernatural, the simple joy of being with Nick has my cup overflowing.

We come across a row of tables where various psychics are offering their services, and I don't miss how Nick's steps pick up, a sure sign he's trying to avoid any more mystical encounters.

"You scared about what they'd have to say?" I tease, earning a playful glare from Nick.

"No, I just want to spend time talking to you and not some wannabe playing god."

I quirk a brow, looking up at him with a challenge. "You don't believe in them, but you believe in me?"

"That's right," he says without hesitation. "You've more than proved your ability. These people are preying on those who want nothing more than to experience a touch of magic."

"A touch of magic, huh?" I grin, and Nick's mouth slams shut.

"Is it the detective or inherent skepticism talking?" I ask, biting my bottom lip, watching Nick squirm with every word I speak.

"Both?" He shrugs. "I was raised to ask questions. To look beyond the surface."

"But you're not," I dare say. "You've taken one look at these people and determined they're fakes."

Nick's head jerks back and a hurt expression crosses his face. "I have not. Have I?"

I purse my lips, shrugging one shoulder.

"Okay . . . fine. Pick one out," he says, and I smile.

"I'm only playing with you, Nick. You have nothing to prove."

"Yes, I do." He stares into my eyes as he says this. "You're right. I need to give people a chance."

I bob my head, looking around before I find a woman shuffling a deck of tarot cards.

Grabbing Nick's hand, I pull him toward her table. The woman is wearing at least five colorful scarves draped around her neck, her hair hidden under a burnt orange turban. An assortment of crystals are scattered on her table, along with at least ten decks of tarot and oracle cards.

"For whom am I reading this evening?" she says, glancing between us.

"Him," I say, motioning toward a stoic Nick.

His posture indicates he's not at all comfortable with this, yet he's humoring me.

The woman bows her head, motioning for him to take a seat. He slinks down into the cheap folding chair, nearly breaking the thing. The woman purses her lips before making a show of running her hands over all her decks until she's landed on *the* one meant for Nick's reading.

She shuffles the tarot deck with dramatic flair, and I can't help but stifle a giggle at her theatrics. With a flourish, she lays out the cards, and I find myself leaning in to see what she's drawn.

"What is this deck?" I ask, nose screwed up in a mix of confusion and cynicism.

I understand that there are an endless number of tarot decks available by extremely talented artists, but this one is just plain weird.

"Ah, the Card of Eternal Socks," she proclaims dramatically, pointing to a card depicting a pair of mismatched socks floating in a sea of bubbles. "This represents your past, a time of lost socks and misplaced keys."

I exchange a bemused glance with Nick, who raises an eyebrow in disbelief. The psychic continues, undeterred by our suppressed laughter.

"And now, the Card of Cosmic Cheese," she declares, gesturing to a card featuring a block of cheese with stars and planets orbiting around it. "This signifies your present, a time of cosmic contemplation and cheesy revelations."

I struggle to contain my laughter as Nick looks on, clearly unimpressed by the absurdity of it all.

"The Card of Chaotic Chihuahuas. It represents your future and revolves around unexpected disruptions and frenetic energy."

This card takes the cake in kooky. A tiny chihuahua is running amok in a whirlwind of colorful confetti.

She shuffles the deck once more, flipping through them quickly before one card flies from the deck. She flips it over, revealing walruses frolicking in a whimsical underwater scene.

"Oooh," she coos, "this is rather interesting."

I cross my arms over my chest, waiting with bated breath for whatever revelation of brilliance she's about to impart on us. "This card symbolizes what's to come if nothing changes," she explains. "You can expect unexpected twists and playful energy." She waggles her eyebrows.

I clear my throat, ready to ask questions to better understand Nick's spread.

"What does any of that mean?"

The woman opens and then closes her mouth. "Well . . . I don't know. Only he does."

My head falls back with a groan.

The psychic's over-the-top delivery was the only thing that made the money I'm about to hand over worth it. The fact that she can't explain the meaning, beyond what the little book that accompanies the cards says, makes it abundantly clear that Nick was right. She's nothing more than a charlatan.

"Okay," I say, placing the twenty-dollar bill on the table. "Thank you very much, but we're going now."

I motion for Nick to follow me away from the fake psychic before things get any weirder.

His laughter is deep and throaty as he steps up next to me, shaking his head as his chest shakes.

"Shut it, West," I snap playfully. "Those cards meant something. It's not their fault the woman wielding them is clueless."

"Oh yeah? Please enlighten me on the hidden meaning behind the Card of Constant Cheese," he says, voice cracking as he bursts into laughter.

I slap his stomach. "It was Cosmic Cheese, not Constant." I can't help but contain my own laughter.

"It refers to your current contemplation about how to release your former love so that you can step into this new relationship with both feet."

Nick and I both snap our attention to a man shrouded in

shadow down the line of tables. As we continue toward him, a small table light sitting beside him illuminates his features. The man's intense stare is focused on Nick.

"Excuse me?" Nick says, eyes narrowing in on the slender man seated behind a black-clothed table.

Much like the woman's, his is filled with mystical trinkets and multiple decks of cards.

"The cards she drew weren't the problem. It's her lack of ability," the man says. "But you already knew that."

I blink, thrown off guard by the man.

"Come. Sit," he says, motioning toward his vacant chairs. "I'll interpret her reading and add my own twist."

"No, thank you," Nick says, continuing to walk past the man's table.

I can tell by Nick's posture that the man has him on edge.

"I can help you. If you'll only listen," he calls to Nick's retreating back.

I'm not about to force Nick into anything more tonight. I'd only been kidding before, and he was a good sport for going down the rabbit hole with me. But this man's mention of Isla is something else entirely. I won't interfere in this.

Nick's steps falter, eventually stopping. He doesn't move, seemingly contemplating what to do. When he turns around, it's clear he's decided that the man's promise of help is something he wants to pursue.

He takes a seat, not looking at me once. It stings a little, but with the subject being Isla, I can only imagine how uncomfortable he is, especially having this discussion in front of me.

"I'll just be over here," I say, turning to walk away to give him privacy, but he reaches out, hand grazing my arm.

"No. Stay."

It's all he says, but I can tell he doesn't want me to go. I nod and take the seat next to him, determined to act as a source of support for whatever's to come.

The man folds his hands together and places them on the table. "Tell me, what were your cards? Say them in order if possible."

Nick looks to me, and I search my memory. "Eternal socks, cosmic cheese, chaotic chihuahuas, and something about walruses," I say, unable to recall the last one in any greater detail.

He takes a deep breath. "Whimsical Walruses," he says, bobbing his head as if that somehow makes sense.

He takes a few minutes to close his eyes and concentrate. Nick and I share a glance, both curious about where this is going. When the man opens his eyes, they're a deeper blue than they'd been moments ago.

"Your past was a series of unfortunate events. You lost someone special, only to lose yourself."

Nick stiffens next to me but remains quiet. The man has so far hit the nail on the head, and I know this is going to be a life-changing reading for him.

"Presently, the one you lost has made a return, but not for long. They need closure that only you can provide, but you're hesitating." He stares into Nick's eyes. "Why?"

Nick swallows, head tilting to the side. His mouth opens, and he's about to speak, but the man's hand flies up, stopping him.

"I see it now. They're not of this world entirely."

My mouth drops open. This is going beyond a card reading. This man is a gifted psychic.

"You understand things will never be what they were, but you're struggling with the knowledge that, in a sense, they'll leave you again."

My stomach twists, pain gripping my chest at the thought of how Nick must be hurting. Without thinking, I reach out, placing my hand on top of Nick's shaking hands. I squeeze, letting him know that I'm here. That I understand.

"But they must go. They want to go. And only you can make that happen," the man says. "You need to say whatever it is you never had the chance to say and send them on their way."

"What if I can't? What if it doesn't work?"

"It will," the man says confidently. "When you do, a new love will take root and grow. It'll be unlike anything you've experienced before." He purses his lips and looks to the sky. "But the road to that love won't be without its struggles. It appears you will have many obstacles to face together before you get that happy ending."

Nick looks to me and offers a smile that I return.

"Is there anything else that I should know?" Nick asks, and the man closes his eyes again.

"You have gifts that you suppress. Open your mind and heart, and they'll manifest."

Nick's face screws up. "That, I doubt." Nick shakes his head. "I'll leave the gifts to others."

I exchange a look with Nick, feeling a mixture of excitement and curiosity. What powers could Nick have that he's refusing to use? Can he be persuaded to one day drop that wall and allow himself to fully embrace that this world isn't what it seems?

The psychic turns to me, his eyes piercing my soul. "You are surrounded by spirits," he says solemnly. "Not everyone can be helped, and you must be prepared to tell some to move on. Closure isn't granted to all."

His words feel like a punch to the gut. What's the point in having this ability if I can't help them?

"Do you have any idea how many spirits are roaming the streets of New Orleans?" the man says, grabbing my attention. "Too many. It would take you your lifetime to send even a portion of them on. It's impossible, and you'll only wear yourself down quickly trying. Take precautions and know what your body can handle." He narrows his eyes. "Angry spirits are something you shouldn't trifle with. Allow someone who understands dark arts to tackle those in the future."

I swallow, feeling entirely too exposed by this man. How does he know so much about us when we've only just met? Could I one day do the same?

Nick stands, holding out his hand to me. "Thank you, sir. We appreciate your help."

He throws a fifty-dollar bill onto the table before pulling me to my feet. "We appreciate your time."

I follow Nick down the road, but my mind is stuck back on that strange man who knew far too much.

"Do you want dessert?" Nick asks, and I turn to look at him with a pinched expression.

"I couldn't eat if I wanted to right now."

He nods his head. "Let's head back to the B and B. We've had enough for one day, I'd say."

A heavy breath bursts from my chest, exhaustion taking over. He's right. It was too much.

I DON'T EVEN remember the walk back to the Garden District. We were both silent, lost in our own thoughts. I can only guess what held Nick's attention, but mine was stuck on the fact that I have to pick and choose who I help. That feels like a heavy burden to bear. How can I turn spirits away, knowing that someone will likely be left here on earth to suffer? It's heartbreaking to think about.

We're in front of the Ramada House when Nick turns to look at me.

"Are you angry with me?"

I move back a step, looking up at him. "Why would I be angry with you?"

Air expels from his open mouth. "You haven't said a word since we left that guy. I just assumed . . ." His words trail off.

"I'm not," I say, shaking my head. "I've been too busy thinking about what he said. It's bothering me to think about turning a spirit away who just wants closure."

His head moves up and down. "I get it." My eyes narrow in on him, not because I'm skeptical, but because I'm curious about what he's thinking. "I have three filing cabinets back at the station full of unsolved cases. Families left wondering what happened to their loved ones. So, when I say I understand, I truly do, Alyssa." He takes my hand and brings it to his lips, planting a gentle kiss. "All we can do is try to help as many as we can. It has to be enough."

"How do I choose?" I whisper.

He shrugs. "For me, I felt a special calling to homicide. I didn't have a personal connection. As stupid as it sounds, I watched a true-crime documentary, and it stuck with me. I put myself in the victims' shoes and knew that if someone ever hurt my family, I would die getting to the truth."

"Maybe I should take Bee's advice and ask the universe to send me the people that need my help the most."

He raises an eyebrow. "Where did she come from anyway?"

"That would be Corinne's aunt," I respond, a smirk playing on my lips as I notice the slight wrinkle of his nose.

"That makes sense," he chuckles, though the humor fades from his expression swiftly. "About Isla . . ."

I shake my head gently, not wanting to pressure him into discussing her. "You don't owe me any explanations. I understand, Nick. If I were in your shoes, I'd feel just as torn."

He grimaces, glancing around. "Is she . . ."

"No. The ring is back in Knox Harbor. She isn't here," I vow, wanting him to feel comfortable, and that knowledge clearly helps.

His shoulders relax, and his features soften. "I feel guilty." My head tilts to the side, but I allow him to continue. "If I don't fight sending her on, won't she think I'm trying to get rid of her? Won't she think I've replaced her easily with you?"

I place a hand on his shoulder, smiling sadly. "I promise you, that's not something to worry about. The woman was trying to coach me on how to win your love."

He splutters and coughs, finally breaking into laughter. "What? Oh god. What did she say?" The smile that spreads across his face is almost blinding. It's like the weight of the world has been lifted by a single truth.

"Hmm," I say, tapping my chin. "Let's see . . . I was supposed to ask you about the Jets. And motocross." He lifts a brow. "When I told her I didn't care for either, she was rather horrified. She said I needed to step aside so that she could find someone more compatible for you." I chuckle and he grunts.

"That . . . definitely sounds like Isla." He shakes his head. "So she's trying to set me up."

"Oh yeah. She wants to see you happy, Nick. It's all she wants for you."

He takes a step toward me so that we're chest to chest, looking down at me with a lazy grin. "It's my dad who likes the Jets. I could give two fucks about football." He shrugs. "Motocross almost killed me in my thirties, so those days are over." He pulls me flush against him, staring down into my eyes. "A lot's changed since Isla died. I've changed. I'll always be the man she fell in love with, but I'd like to think I've evolved, like men are supposed to."

I smile up at him, my eyes roaming over his handsome features, getting lost in his beautiful gray-blue eyes.

"I want you to know me," he says, eyes penetrating mine. "The person I am now. Not the guy who lost Isla, but the man who's falling for you."

My breath hitches, my entire body light and tingly.

"Because I am, Alyssa. I'm falling hard, and I hope you're right there with me."

I feel a flutter in my chest, a sensation that's become all too familiar in Nick's presence. It's as if every word, every glance, every touch between us ignites a spark, drawing us closer together.

"I am, Nick. I'm right there with you."

Nick's lips crash against mine, and a surge of electricity shoots through me, igniting every nerve ending in my body. His kiss is bold and passionate, leaving me breathless.

His hand gently cradles the back of my neck, his touch causing goose bumps. Our lips move together in perfect harmony, the connection between us deepening with every minute that passes.

Time seems to stand still as we lose ourselves in the moment, the world around us fading into the background. It's just him and me, our hearts beating in sync as we share this intimate embrace.

Until some idiot passing by decides to ruin the moment. "Do us a favor and get a damn room."

I pull away, placing my head against Nick's chest, feeling his heart beat a mile a minute. He chuckles into the top of my head.

"No need to be embarrassed, Lyss. The guy looks more bitter than anything," Nick says, loud enough for the guy to hear.

"Yeah, fuck you, man," the guy yells, continuing to make his way down the street.

"Let's go," he says, leading me into the B and B.

The place is empty, Adeana nowhere to be seen. We make our way up the stairs and down the hall to my room. I find the key buried in my bag and unlock the door.

Nick lightly pushes me inside, closing the door behind us. I turn to face him, my heart racing as I take in his heavy breathing and the intense desire in his heated gaze.

He moves toward me with measured steps, gradually guiding us backward until the backs of my knees hit the soft mattress.

"If you're not ready for this, we can take things slow," he says, searching my eyes. "I'll follow your lead."

My head shakes back and forth slowly. "No." The word comes out breathy, my hand lifting to grasp his T-shirt. "I want this."

With those words, all hesitation fades away as I pull Nick toward me. His lips meet mine, igniting a firestorm of desire between us. There's no doubt or uncertainty, only the overwhelming pull to him.

Nick slowly lowers me to the bed, taking special care not to put his full weight on me, never breaking our kiss. He explores my mouth like he's been here a million times before but wants to uncover something new. It feels familiar but is mixed with that brand-new thrill. The chills and butterflies are all present and doing a number on my senses.

With every moment that passes, each kiss we share, I feel myself falling deeper for him, my emotions swirling like a whirlwind inside me. It's as if we're creating our own little world, a place where nothing else matters except us.

He pulls back just slightly. "I . . . don't have a condom," he says breathlessly.

There's something about knowing he came here without the intention of taking things further that makes my heart swell. It shows that this means more than that to Nick. What we have runs deeper than physical attraction. It's there, absolutely, but it's not all this is. We're building an emotional bond that is so much greater.

"I had a vasectomy, but . . . I never followed up to confirm it worked," he admits, looking sheepish.

I grimace at what comes next. "It wouldn't be a good idea," I admit. "I'm not on birth control because . . . well . . ."

He presses his lips to mine, cutting off my awkwardness.

"I think we both know that a baby is not in our plans."

I chuckle. "Yeah. No babies."

Nick falls over to his back on a groan. "I could run to the corner store," he says, but a thought occurs to me.

Lanie's here, and if anyone would come prepared for anything, it's her.

"I'll . . . be right back," I say, refraining from explaining my plan.

It's going to be embarrassing enough to ask her, knowing she'll be right across the hallway, knowing exactly what we're doing.

And that thought has me stopping before my hand has even touched the knob. I turn back to Nick, teeth clenched and forehead wrinkled.

He laughs. "Having second thoughts about asking Lanie?"

My eyes widen. "How did you . . ."

His head tilts and he grins. "If you're leaving this room, it's for one thing, and Lanie seems like the best chance."

"But then she'd know, and it would be weird . . . right?"

His eyes roam over my body and darken. "Personally, I don't give a damn who's across the hall and what they know." His shoulder does a half shrug. "But I want you to be comfortable. So it's your call."

My head falls back, frustration mounting.

I'm an adult. I shouldn't feel awkward about this.

"Fuck it," I say, recognizing that I've just let the mother of all curses slip, as I make my way through the door and across the hall, Nick's laugh following me the whole way.

I lift my hand to knock, and it swings open before I've had a chance. Lanie is decked out in a ruby, long-sleeved satin jumpsuit with a deep V-neck, banded waist, and tapered pants. She's already taller than me, but the nude, open-toe pumps have her towering over me.

"Going somewhere?" I say, eyeing her up and down.

She pops out her hip, pulling her nude clutch against her chest. "I didn't come all this way to sleep."

"I'm not trying to sound like your mother, but I don't like the idea of you roaming around New Orleans by yourself."

She rolls her eyes. "First of all, if I had a mother worth mentioning, you'd sound just like her. Secondly, I'm going with Adeana."

My eyebrow lifts. "Ah, that's . . . fun."

She nods enthusiastically. "She has the hookup to some incredible club. Nina's passed out, and you're . . . well . . . preoccupied. Figured you wouldn't even know that I'm gone."

I smile. "I'm glad to know you're not going alone. Be safe."

She nods. "Did you need something?" She's grinning as though she knows a secret.

I rock back on my heels, feeling the awkwardness creep its way back in.

She grunts, opening her purse and producing exactly what I came for. "Your face gave you away," she says, holding it between two fingers. "There's more in the top drawer," she says, motioning her head toward the lone dresser in her room. "Get it, girl."

She hands me the condom, smiling wide as she walks past me, leaving me standing in her room as she makes her way down the hall.

I sigh. At least she won't be here, and Nina's asleep.

I grab a couple more from the drawer just to be safe and rush back to my room, finding Nick on his back, peering up at the ceiling.

I close the door quietly, making my way to join him on the bed.

He turns toward me when he feels the bed dip. "Everything okay?"

"Yeah. Lanie was headed out for the night. She's going with Adeana to some club."

"Adeana?" Nick asks, sounding a tad skeptical.

"The blonde you met briefly. Her parents own the place. They're meeting her friends."

He nods as if this news satisfies his concern.

A loud, obnoxious yawn breaks free from me, signaling to Nick that I'm beyond exhausted. And I am. I didn't sleep last night, and it's caught up with me.

Nick pulls me against him, kissing the top of my head. "You should sleep."

"No," I whine. "I'm fine."

Nick tries to cover his own yawn, but it's no use. I can see how exhausted he is too. His eyes are glassy, and the lines around his eyes are more pronounced than usual.

"Looks like we're both beat," I say, chuckling. "I'm sorry."

"For what? I get to hold you all night." He grins. "Sweetheart, I'm not disappointed to sleep next to you. Not one bit." He places a kiss on my mouth, allowing his lips to linger for a moment. "There will be plenty of nights for us. Tonight, let's sleep."

We get ourselves comfortable, me curled into Nick's side as his breathing evens out. He was more tired than he let on, and I'm happy I didn't push. He's right—we have all the time in the world to be together intimately. There's no rush. This right here, me being snug tight in Nick's arms, is all I need.

Ten of Pentacles

AS WE PULL up to 123 Magnolia Avenue, Ian's home, I can feel Nina's tension thickening, morphing into a cloud of doubt and fear.

Nina, Lanie, and I stare up at the regal Greek Revival home, quiet and contemplative.

The place stands proudly amidst a canopy of sprawling oak trees, ivy gracefully climbing the walls, adding a touch of rustic charm. Its imposing façade, a pristine white hue that appears recently painted, keeps the place timeless. The towering columns and pedimented portico evoke a sense of grandeur and elegance. It's the type of home that makes New Orleans's Garden District so special.

"What if it's not him?" Nina murmurs softly, continuing to look forward.

"Then we keep looking," Lanie declares, and I nod my head in solidarity with that plan.

"What if it is and he turns me away?"

I shift my gaze to Nina's profile, observing the delicate lines etched around her right eye, and the subtle downturn of her lips.

There's a sense of vulnerability in the way her features soften, as if revealing a glimpse of the inner turmoil she may be experiencing.

"Then I'll rap him upside the head," Lanie vows.

I lean forward, shooting her a disgruntled look. "There will be no rapping. We're not Richard," I snap.

"She's right," Nina says. "Ian's been running because of threats."

I turn toward Nina and offer a tight-lipped smile. "Take this one step at a time, Nins. Knock on the door and give him the chance to say his piece. It'll be okay. *You'll* be okay."

She hesitates for a moment before finally moving toward the front door and lifting her hand to knock. The sound echoes through the quiet neighborhood, but there's no immediate response. For a fleeting moment, I wonder if Ian will even answer.

"Maybe we should come back?" Lanie suggests, but the door creaks open.

Nina's breath catches, and I know it must be Ian.

In his late thirties, he exudes a sense of maturity tempered with a youthful charm. His light hair, tousled in a casual yet intentional manner, frames his angular face, accentuating the sharp lines of his jaw. But it's his eyes that draw you in—bright aqua orbs that seem to hold a world of depth and emotion within them. They sparkle with intelligence and warmth. Despite the passage of time, he clearly recognizes Nina, his expression locked on her in a mixture of shock and something else I can't pinpoint in the moment.

Nina's face pales as she takes in Ian's appearance, the weight of years of separation and unanswered questions hanging heavy between them. "Ian," she murmurs, her voice barely above a whisper.

He stares at her for a long moment, his eyes scanning her face as if searching for answers. "Nina," he finally replies, his voice barely audible.

The air is thick with unspoken words as they stand there, grappling with the past and the memories that bind them together. Lanie and I stand awkwardly, fidgeting in place, wondering if we should do something, say something to help our friend along.

Finally, Nina finds her voice, her words coming out in a rush. "Richard is in jail," she blurts out, her voice trembling slightly. "Murder. He'll be going away for a very long time."

Ian's eyes close, a pained expression crossing over his attractive face.

When he opens them again, there's nothing but determination shining back at us. "Good. I hope the son of a bitch rots."

Nina swallows, bobbing her head more times than necessary. She's back to staring wordlessly, appearing far too self-conscious for the likes of her.

Nina is smart and incredibly beautiful. She has nothing to be worried about, yet I can tell that's exactly what she's doing. I have to help her.

"I'm Alyssa," I say, stepping forward. "Nina's best friend."

Lanie shoots a disgruntled glare in my direction. "One of her best friends," she says haughtily. "I'm Lanie. The third wheel." She wrinkles her nose in a teasing manner, smiling at me and Nina.

Ian chuckles. "Nice to meet you, ladies." He steps back from the door, returning his gaze to Nina. "Would you like to come in?"

We all speak at the same time, agreeing to his offer.

As I step through the grand double doors, I'm immediately struck by how well kept the place is. The foyer boasts towering ceilings with intricate crown molding. A stunning staircase spirals gracefully upward, revealing just a bit of the second floor through the rounded landing.

"Wow," Nina says, moving in a circle to take the place in. "I can't believe this is your home."

He shrugs. "The back of the house is my living space. This part is open to the public certain times of the year. It's part of the Historical Society's parade of homes."

Ian motions for us to follow him.

Sunlight streams through tall windows, casting a warm glow over the polished hardwood floors. Ornate chandeliers hang from the ceiling throughout, their crystals catching the light and casting shimmering reflections across each space we pass through. Antique furniture, richly upholstered in velvet and brocade, fills the rooms, each piece a testament to the owner's care in preserving the past. The walls are adorned with oil paintings and gilded mirrors, adding to the sense of opulence and grandeur.

He walks us through the stately home to the backyard, where a small carriage house sits at the back of the property.

"This is where I spend most of my time," Ian says, opening the door to a cozy home that looks far more lived in. "Take a seat."

Nina, Lanie, and I all take a seat on the couch, our legs touching.

"How did you find me?" he asks Nina.

"I had some help from Alyssa's boyfriend. He's a detective."

Ian nods his head. "I've gotten pretty sloppy the last five years," he admits. "I took a job at Tulane in the history department and couldn't use my alias. They allow me to work under Connor Fulton, but I knew having that information out there would eventually lead someone to my door if they looked hard enough." He huffs a humorless laugh.

"I didn't mean to intrude on your life, Ian. I only wanted to ensure you're all right and to tell you that it's safe for you to resume your life."

"This is my life," he says, arms lifted as he gestures around. "Ian Whalen died a long time ago, Nina."

Nina makes a strangled noise, and I can see the guilt she harbors.

"You shouldn't have had to run from him," she cries, hands coming to her face to shield the tears streaming down her face. "This is all my fault," she whispers.

Ian's eyes widen in disbelief at her words, and for a moment, he seems unable to comprehend what she's saying. "It was never your fault, Nina." He falls to his knees before her, grabbing her hands away from her face. "I didn't run for me," he begins, his voice thick with emotion. "It was never about me."

Ian stands, walking toward a table near the television. He grabs a picture frame and a box of tissues, holding them out to Nina.

Her eyes narrow in on the offering, first grabbing a tissue and then the frame.

"I couldn't allow Richard to find our son."

Nina gasps, her hands gripping the frame tightly as she stares at the photo of Ian and a young man. The closer I look, the more realization sinks in.

Her son has been with Ian this entire time.

"You knew?" she whispers, her voice barely audible.

Ian nods, his eyes filled with sadness and regret. "Your mother . . . she went to my mom," he explains, his voice barely above a whisper. "She told her everything. It was my parents who adopted him. We've been raising him all these years."

As the weight of Ian's words sinks in, a flood of emotions washes over all of us.

Nina's mother, the woman we all love to hate, ensured Nina's son was safe and with his father. It might've been the most important thing the woman has ever done, aside from give Nina life.

The truth, long buried beneath years of secrecy and silence, is finally laid bare. Nina weeps next to me as I pat her leg, offering the only comfort I can in the moment. Her tear-filled stare is fixed on the photo of her son. A boy she handed over at birth and hasn't seen since.

And as we sit here, facing the truth together, I can't help but feel a glimmer of hope for Nina's future. Yes, she's missed out on a large part of his life, but she gets a chance to know the man he's become. The man his father raised.

I stand, offering my seat to Ian. Nina needs him in this moment. They need each other.

"His name is Chase," Ian says. "He's twenty-four and in his senior year at Tulane. It's why I took the position." He chuckles. "Our son is brilliant, but there's still costs."

Nina's face is a mix of emotions—shock, sadness, and a hint of longing as she processes the news. "Tulane?" she repeats, her voice craggy. "What's he studying?"

Ian nods, a sad smile tugging at the corners of his lips. It's clear he can see how hard this is on Nina. "Psychology," he replies, his voice tinged with pride. "He's always wanted to work in a school setting. His plan is to help with students' academic and social-emotional development. A mix of his mom and dad," he says, smiling sadly as he peers into Nina's eyes.

The mention of Nina's influence on their son brings a bittersweet smile to her lips. It's clear that despite the years of separation, the bond between mother and son runs deep.

I catch Lanie's attention and motion for her to join me in the corner.

"I think we should give them some time alone."

She nods her head. "What should we do?"

"I think I'm going to head back to Knox Harbor with Nick. There are some things I need to help him with."

I can see the disappointment flicker across her face. "I'll stay here with Nina until she's ready to head back," she says.

"Are you angry with me?"

She shakes her head. "No. I get it. I just wish you were staying." She glances at Nina and Ian, whose heads are together as they look through an album. "I'll be spending some time with Adeana, if things go the way I'm envisioning."

I smile wide. "That'll be a good thing. Nina's happiness is all that matters right now."

She makes a face. "Obviously. But please allow me a moment to mope about my abandonment."

I roll my eyes and pull her into a hug. "If I could stay, I would. But murders are occurring at an alarming rate. If I can help, I have to."

She nods her head. "Yes, you do, my little spirit talker."

"I'm older than you," I say, mouth forming a tight line.

"But I'm taller," she singsongs.

"What's going on over there?" Nina asks, voice full of amusement.

I'm happy to see her mood has shifted. She looks good. The sadness from earlier has been replaced by something resembling hope.

"I'm heading back to Knox Harbor. Lanie will stay back with you."

She offers a smile. "I need to stick around for a few days." She glances at Ian. "I'd like to meet my son, if that's all right?"

"Of course. I don't understand how Chase has waited this long."

A beaming smile takes over her face, her eyes alight with happiness, and that's exactly how she is when I've made my way out of the carriage house, heading to the B and B to get my things and Nick. On the short walk back, I look up the flight Nick said he was on later tonight and see there are still seats available. I make the purchase and pick up my pace, as we'll need to leave for the airport in the next couple hours.

It's time to get back home and get to work on catching the Falls Haven killer.

✦ ✦ ✦

AS WE FINALLY pull into Nick's driveway, exhaustion threatens to pull me under. It was a long day, between witnessing the reunion between Nina and Ian and traveling back home.

Nick shuts off the car and turns to me. "Wanna stay at my place tonight?"

His suggestion is tempting, especially since Isla is likely roaming the halls next door at mine. After the last couple days we've had, I could use a ghost-free night of sleep.

"I'd love that," I say.

"Do you need to head over there to grab anything?"

I shake my head. "Nope. I have everything I need in my suitcase."

Once inside Nick's house, we drop our bags beside the door and make a beeline for the couch, sinking into its inviting embrace. Nestled in Nick's protective arms, I feel a sense of contentment wash over me, like a warm blanket on a chilly night. His touch is gentle yet deliberate as he lazily draws random patterns on my bare arm with his fingertips. This is a form of happiness I could get addicted to. The events of the day melt away as our bodies meld together in the dim light.

"How did today go?" he asks, continuing to trace absently along my skin.

It's driving me crazy in the best way. My stomach tingles, flipping and flopping with anticipation for more. I want his hands all over me.

"Fine." The word comes out breathy, and my cheeks warm with embarrassment when Nick chuckles, signaling he noticed.

"Things are going to be good for Nina. I know it."

"That's good," he says, voice tinged with a sensual, throaty quality that causes me to shiver in response. "Are you cold?"

"No." I snuggle up closer to him. "Just content."

He places a kiss to the shell of my ear, and I can't contain the exhale that makes it very clear that I love what he's doing.

He turns me to face him, mouth lowering to mine. The world outside fades away as we become lost in each other, our senses consumed by the heady rush of desire and the way our tongues move in sync effortlessly. Time seems to stand still as we surrender to this moment.

His hand moves under my shirt, slowly rising to just below my chest, resting on my ribcage. He pauses as if to ask permission but doesn't stop kissing me. I place my hand over his, guiding him until he's palming one full breast, a single finger circling my nipple and pulling a groan from deep within me.

I haven't been touched like this for so long. I'd thought that sensation would be long gone at this stage of life, but it's alive and well, the sensation sending shock waves down my body, landing firmly in my core. I forgot how something so simple could feel so damn good.

Heat pools in a place it hasn't for years, and I want his attention there.

Just as I'm about to move his hand south, his phone chimes with a notification that's reserved to alert him that someone is at his door.

He breaks contact, swearing under his breath.

"Who the hell would be here at this hour?" he says, rising from his spot on the couch and grabbing his phone from the coffee table.

He pulls up the security camera, and his expression changes from one of annoyance to concern.

I peer over his shoulder to see Mrs. Fields slinking away from his front door, her movements erratic and confused.

"Fuck," he says, jumping up and darting for the door.

I'm right behind him, grabbing our coats from the chair where we discarded them.

Neither one of us takes the time to put on shoes, our feet destined to be soaked and cold when this is all over. But that's not what's important right now.

We find her standing on the sidewalk, disoriented and claiming to be lost.

"I . . . don't know where I am," she says, looking around as if she hasn't yet noticed Nick or me right behind her.

Nick approaches her cautiously, likely not wanting to startle her.

It's clear something isn't right.

"Mrs. Fields," he says, touching her shoulder gently.

She turns to look up into his face. Her head tilts to the side, confusion evident in the way her eyes squint and nose wrinkles up.

"Who are you?" she says, taking a step back. Fear replaces the confusion from mere seconds ago.

I take a step around Nick, wondering if seeing a woman would make the situation less stressful for her. Her expression morphs into a semblance of calm when she gets a look at me. I don't think she recognizes who I am, but clearly, seeing another person has her less stressed.

"Can I offer you a cup of tea?" I ask, trying to direct her toward Nick's home.

She bobs her head. "Yes . . . tea. That would be nice," she says, allowing me to steer her into Nick's house. I have her take a seat, placing a blanket over her legs. She's shaking, the cold finally registering.

Her teeth clatter and her hands shake. "Let me help you," I say, grabbing another blanket from a nearby sofa and wrapping it around her body.

"Thank you, Alyssa."

At the sound of my name, my head snaps toward her. She blinks, obviously recognizing that she, in fact, does know who I am. I watch as a series of emotions flicks across her face.

"Where am I?" she finally asks.

"Nick West's, Mrs. Fields. We found you outside in the cold."

She bursts into tears, and I'm not sure what to do. The only thing that I can think is to pull her into an embrace and allow her the moment she needs. It's clear that the confusion has her rattled.

"Mom?" a foreign male voice says, drawing our attention.

A man just barely taller than my five-foot-seven height stands just inside the door, looking toward his mother with tears in his eyes.

He rushes forward, and I step back, allowing him to take my place.

"I knew Tom was in town. His car was in the driveway when we got home," Nick says, wrapping his arms around me and pulling me back against his chest.

There's a knock on the door, and Tom calls out, "That's likely Abby. She was getting dressed to come help." Nick lets a petite brunette in, and she offers a sad smile before joining Tom and Mrs. Fields.

"Thank you so much for calling. We should've put alarms on the doors months ago," Tom says. "We were asleep. Had no clue she left."

"I'll take her back and get her settled. I'll sleep with her tonight," Abby says. "Thank you both."

"Please, take the blankets. I'll get them another time," Nick says, as Abby attempts to fold and put the blankets back on the couch. "It's too cold out there."

Abby nods, smiling, helping Mrs. Fields out of the house.

"We just found out that she has sundowner's," Tom explains. "We were looking for an in-home caregiver, but we're struggling to find anyone that will work out." His head lowers. "She's too far progressed."

"I'm really sorry to hear that, Tom. I wish there was something I could do to help."

"You've done enough, Nick. I appreciate you and"—he looks up at me—"I don't think we've met. I'm Tom Fields."

"Alyssa Mann. I live next door."

His eyes widen. "Ah, another neighbor. Great to meet you. I wish it was under different circumstances, but still, it's a pleasure."

"It's great to meet you too," I say, offering a small smile.

He sighs. "We plan to put the house on the market next week and move her into an assisted living facility close to us," he says. "We just have to move all the junk. Mom has become a bit of a hoarder lately. I'm not sure where she's getting all the shit." He runs a hand back through his hair. "The garage is full of trinkets."

The dream I had of Mrs. Fields comes to mind. "There wouldn't happen to be garden gnomes and a red Christmas sleigh among the trinkets? Maybe a wreath or two?"

Tom's eyes narrow in thought, and he bobs his head. "Now that you mention it, yes. Abby loved the sleigh. Thought about asking Mom if she could keep it."

I grimace, glancing at Nick.

"There's been a string of thefts on the street in the past couple months. Lots of reports of missing lawn ornaments and decorations," Nick says. "My wreath was among those things taken."

Tom's eyes widen. "You don't think . . ." He groans, head falling back. "Mom was taking those things at night."

"I'm afraid that might be the case," Nick admits.

"Will she be arrested?" Tom's voice is full of concern, and Nick is quick to reassure him.

"Absolutely not. I'm sure any doctor could provide evidence of her sundowner's, which would be grounds for any case to be dismissed. Besides, we live in a great neighborhood. Anyone who had items taken would just be grateful to get their things back."

"Nobody would choose to press charges," I add. "Not knowing the situation."

Tom's concern melts away, leaving him to look exhausted. He nods. "I'll put something on the neighbor group explaining the situation. We'll make sure everything is returned."

Nick nods. "That will take care of it."

"I'm going to head back and help Abby," Tom says, making his way to the door. "If you happen to know anyone in the market and wanting to move into the neighborhood, please send them my way."

"Will do," Nick says, saying good night to Tom and closing the door on this night.

Nick leads me back toward his bedroom, pulling back the covers and helping me to get comfortable. I watch as he tears his black T-shirt over his head, discarding it in the corner. My mouth waters as his gray pants lower to the ground, leaving him in a pair of black boxers that hug him tight, his impressive bulge on full display. I look away, feeling like a voyeur.

Nick crawls in behind me, pulling me against him. "One mystery solved," he says, placing a kiss on my shoulder. "It's too bad about Mrs. Fields. I wouldn't wish that end of life on anyone."

"Me neither," I agree. "It's heartbreaking."

"No more talk about sad stuff for tonight. I just want to enjoy this time with you before I have to go back to Falls Haven."

I turn toward him, pressing a kiss to his lips. "I agree."

"I like you in my bed," he whispers against my lips.

I sigh contentedly. "Me too."

So very much.

Six of Swords

AS THE FIRST light of dawn breaks through the darkness, I lie wrapped in Nick's arms, unwilling to move for fear I'll wake him and the moment will be over.

I slept better than I have in months, and it had everything to do with the man next to me.

As if he can hear my inner thoughts, he rouses, his arms moving away, leaving me cold.

I audibly whine, and Nick chuckles. "My arm's asleep," he says, voice extra husky. "How did you sleep?" he asks, and I sigh.

"Like a baby. When do you have to leave?"

He clears his throat. "Early Wednesday."

"How did you manage to get so much time off? I'd think they'd want this solved quickly considering the victim is your captain's niece."

He runs his hand back through his hair, mussing it in a way that has me itching to touch him.

"This break was ordered by Falls Haven's captain." He huffs. "He's calling it a mental-health break." He shakes his head. "I think he knows I'm incapable of truly cutting off the detective in me. It seems more likely he wanted me back here poking around without drawing attention."

"Why?"

"My captain. He doesn't want him knowing the details because of his connection to the victim. It muddies the investigation when emotion plays a factor."

I guess I understand the logic.

He takes a deep breath and blows it out in a huff. "I . . . have a favor to ask you."

I sit up, turning to face him. "What's up?" I say, seeing the conflict in his expression.

He swallows, takes a deep breath, and looks me in the eye when he says, "Will you help me help Isla move on?"

"Of course. Whatever you need."

AS WE WALK into my kitchen, I'm met with the sight of Isla sitting at the counter, looking ready to climb the walls.

"You know, you really suck for leaving me here. It's been so damn boring," she says, directing her complaint at me.

"I know, and I'm sorry. I had to focus on my friend and didn't think it would be a good idea to drag you to New Orleans."

She purses her lips, glaring at me. "I've never been. Wouldn't have minded the change of scenery. Maybe I could've rubbed elbows with a few famous spirits."

"I'm sorry," I say, grimacing. "She's been bored," I explain to Nick, who nods in understanding.

"He knows I'm here," she murmurs, mostly to herself.

I take a deep breath, knowing I need to facilitate the conversation between them, since Nick can't see or hear the dead. "Isla, Nick is ready to help you move on," I tell her gently.

She looks at Nick, her expression softening. "I knew he'd come through. When do we do it?"

"Now?" I say, shrugging one shoulder, in a way to indicate I'm on their schedule.

She jumps up from the chair, heading toward the door like a golden retriever ready for its walk.

"What are you waiting for? Send me packing."

I chuckle, shaking my head. "She's in a bit of a rush," I tell Nick.

He smiles. "Sounds like her."

Isla's shoulders sag, and she turns back to Nick, her gaze fixed on him with a sorrowful smile gracing her lips, the love she held for him still shining through.

"Can you tell him that I'm only in a hurry to get to my brother?"

I relay the information.

"Then let's get her to him."

We pull through the gates of Wintersgate Cemetery, driving as close as we can get before our feet will have to carry us the rest of the way.

Nick is just ahead, with Isla right next to him.

As I walk through the snow-covered paths of the cemetery, I can't help but be struck by the eerie beauty of the place. Tombstones rise up from the earth like solemn sentinels, waiting to greet the newest addition to their ranks.

Despite the chill in the air, there's a strange sense of peace that permeates the atmosphere, as if the spirits of the departed are watching over the place, keeping vigil.

When we finally make it to Isla's grave, all three of us stand still, looking at Isla's name etched into the stone.

"You were the best part of my life," Nick says, his voice filled with emotion. "A piece of me died with you that day."

I remain silent, allowing Nick this time to say all that's left between him and Isla, hoping it brings him peace as much as it does her.

"But I've come to terms with that season of life ending, and I'm ready to move forward," he declares, looking over at me when he says, "I've found happiness again."

Tears well up in my eyes as Isla's spirit nods. "I'm happy that you're happy," she whispers. "There's no sadness or jealousy in my heart. Only love." She turns to me. "Treat him right." She smiles, and I return it.

I take the time to share with Nick all that Isla's said. It's clear that a heavy weight has been lifted. He knows she doesn't feel replaced or hurt. She's happy.

I hand Nick the ring, and he bends over the grass where Isla's remains rest.

"Goodbye, Isla. I'll carry you with me always."

She places a ghostly hand on his shoulder. "And I'll carry your love with me to Heaven. Goodbye, my love."

With that, Nick buries the ring. A bright light surrounds us, and I look up in time to see Isla's head tilt toward the sky, a look of peace on her face that can only mean she's on her way home.

"Thank you, Isla, for helping mold Nick into the man he is today," I say, earning one final smile before she moves on, leaving the earth behind.

I give Nick a few moments of silence, allowing him time to grieve her loss again. When he's ready, he turns and moves past me, steps quick.

"We need to do some research on Matilda Hampson," Nick says, his voice grave as he looks over his shoulder at me.

"Umm . . ." I have questions, but I don't want to voice them.

Maybe this is how Nick copes, by pushing it down and getting back into detective mode.

"Carl Hampson's tomb was right behind Isla's," he explains,

but I'm still at a loss for why he's bringing this up now. "That symbol—from the Order of Providence—it was on his tombstone."

My steps falter. I didn't see it, but then again, I wasn't exactly looking at any tombstone but Isla's.

"Seeing it reminded me that I have questions for Matilda," he says. "There has to be a reason why his spirit stuck around and decided to attach itself to his brother's wife, of all people."

I'd wondered the same thing.

"Especially considering Carl Hampson was likely murdered."

My head snaps up to Nick. "Murdered?"

He nods. "Gunshot wound to the head that was originally ruled a suicide. When I dug into the records, it was considered that based on a statement made by Matilda. She claimed that his behavior had been erratic leading up to his death and that he'd told her he was considering taking his own life." He shakes his head. "Statements given by his doctor and others say the exact opposite."

It's hard to fathom Matilda being embroiled in anything unsavory. Her husband and brother-in-law might have had their share of shady dealings, but surely not her. She always seemed so innocent and naive, tending to her garden and baking pies for all the festivals. But then again, appearances can be deceiving, and in this town, secrets run deep, or so it would seem.

We walk through the front door of Marmalade and Rye and head straight to the back, finding Matilda hunched over her desk, reading through what appears to be a catalog of antiques.

"Well hello, Alyssa. And Nick," she says, her voice tinged with surprise. "To what do I owe this pleasure?" She tilts her head, and her face falls. "Please tell me you didn't take what was here home with you." Her eyebrow lifts, and I understand her insinuation.

"Actually, yes," Nick says, and my head snaps to his.

That's not the direction I thought this chat was going to go.

"Carl followed us to New Orleans and caused quite the stir at a bed-and-breakfast," he says, voice laced with reproach. "Him and Buck Sauder."

Matilda's slight frame shakes at the mention of Carl and Buck. Her shocked expression slowly morphs into something else. Something resembling fear.

"They're gone," I say, hoping to calm her nerves. "We sent them on to the next life." Her eyes widen in astonishment, a flicker of relief mingling with lingering disbelief.

But as the weight of the news settles in, I notice a subtle shift in Matilda's demeanor. Gone is the warmth and familiarity, replaced by an air of unease and apprehension. Her eyes dart nervously between Nick and me, as if searching for answers she's not sure she wants to find.

"Did they . . . speak to you?" she asks, and that simple question doesn't sit right with me for reasons I can't pinpoint.

Nick shrugs, sucking on his teeth. He's slipped into Detective West right before my eyes, and this is a side of him I've never seen.

"Carl mentioned something about the Order of Providence, but nothing he said made sense," Nick lies.

He's probing for information, testing the waters to see how much she knows.

Matilda's response is guarded, her words carefully chosen as she feigns ignorance, denying any knowledge of the society. "I've never heard of such a thing. Sounds like fiction to me."

"We just paid a visit to the cemetery. Carl had a strange symbol etched into his tombstone. Are you familiar with what I'm referring to?"

She purses her lips, shaking her head. "No idea, Detective." There's a bite to her tone, one that suggests she doesn't like Nick's line of questioning.

With a firmness I've rarely seen from him, he warns Matilda. "This society has come up a lot recently in connection to murder cases. If you know something and choose not to help, you could be brought up on charges for obstructing justice."

"I'll keep that in mind, Nicholas," she says patronizingly. "But as I said, I've never heard of such an order. So if there's nothing more you wish to ask me, you can show yourself out. I'm rather busy." She motions down to her catalog.

"One more thing, and then we'll get out of your way," he says, shoulders straightening. "I'm reopening Carl's case. It would appear that suicide seems unlikely."

She nods. "I'm sure that's why he was hovering about. The man would not be content until his murderer was brought to justice. Please keep me in the loop. As his only surviving relative, I'd like to be informed if you find anything."

Nick nods. "Of course. Thank you, Matilda."

We're walking toward the front of the store when I hear Matilda say, "It's sometimes better to let sleeping dogs lie."

I turn over my shoulder, and my eyes connect with Matilda's. They're hard and cold, something I've never seen on her.

She knows something. Something dangerous.

Nick turns to me, a thoughtful look on his face. "You did good back there."

I chuckle. "I didn't do anything. I watched you lay the law down on Mrs. Hampson like she was the villain you're trying to catch."

He shakes his head. "No. She's no villain. I know one when I see it." He sighs. "She knows more than she's letting on, but for now, her secrets aren't my concern."

"It would've been helpful to have Nina back there. One touch, and Nina would uncover whatever she's hiding."

"You know, the two of you together could make a great team. I could use your services on a lot of cold cases."

I huff a humorless laugh. "I doubt I could convince Nina to

ditch her plans. And besides, it'll be some time before I'm up and running."

He bites his bottom lip. "I probably should let Greg tell you this, but he mentioned something interesting," he says, his voice tinged with excitement.

I wave my hands in the air, gesturing for him to spit it out.

"He's considering closing down shop. Says he's getting too old for this. He'd be interested in taking on a resident manager role, which means you could apply for a Watch, Guard, Patrol Agency License."

My brows are furrowed as I try to rack my brain for what that means.

"You could skip over the part of working for someone else. It would give you the opportunity to start your own business now."

I'm stunned by the revelation, my mind racing with the possibilities. I wrap my arms around Nick, pulling him close and kissing him fiercely, not caring who sees.

He chuckles against my lips. "If I knew that's what I'd get for simply sharing good news, I'd have done it sooner."

I place another kiss on his lips, smiling.

"Maybe I just like to kiss you," I say.

"By all means." He pulls me back in, pressing his mouth against mine again.

With Nick by my side, anything feels possible, and I can't wait to see what our future holds.

Three of Pentacles

Nick

I'M JOLTED AWAKE by the sound of Alyssa gasping. Her breathing is labored, and she's drenched in sweat. I reach out to touch her arm gently. "What's wrong?"

Alyssa's eyes snap open, shining bright with anxiety. Her head is shaking back and forth erratically, fear gripping her.

With everything she's been part of lately, it's not a wonder she's having nightmares.

Murder. Cover-ups.

Then you add in ghosts and poltergeists, and that's too much for anyone.

It's my job to deal with strange events and gruesome murders. Alyssa's a mom, a former advertising executive. This foray into detective work is all new to her, and it's clearly taking a toll.

"I had a dream . . ." Her head shakes, face pinched. "A vision," she amends, her voice trembling. "Another girl is dead, or will be."

I slump back against the headboard, contemplating what she said. If any other person were to tell me that someone has died or is about to be killed based on a dream, I'd laugh at the absurdity of it. But I know Alyssa has abilities beyond human comprehension. I trust her implicitly, even if it goes against everything I've been raised to believe.

Evidence.

That's what my father drilled into me. Yet, I'm about to go down this rabbit hole of dreams being reality.

I feel a surge of urgency coursing through me. The need to solve this case is damn near crippling.

"Tell me everything," I urge, my mind already racing.

Alyssa jumps up from the bed and begins pacing, her movements frantic as she recounts the details of her vision.

"A dark-haired girl, petite, and likely in her early twenties," she rattles off, as though she's reading down a checklist.

The description already fits the Grayson and Montgomery cases.

"She was sitting alone at a crowded bar. The bartender leaned over, and she slid an envelope under his hand."

"Could you tell what was in it?"

"Money," she says, almost as if in a trance. "It was thick. I couldn't see the cash, but I know that's what it was."

"What else?" I press, knowing the sooner we get this all out, the more accurate the details will be.

"She stood to leave, but a man sitting next to her asked to buy her a drink. He was tall, thin." Her eyebrows tilt inward. "He had a full-sleeve tattoo. Red flowers intertwined with an octopus." Her eyes catch on something past me, and she gets caught in a near trance. I'm about to speak when she goes on. "She finds him attractive, so she says yes." Her eyes meet mine, and I can tell she's shaken. "Somehow, I can feel her inner thoughts, Nick. She had reservations. She knew she should leave. She's thinking about how they wouldn't like her sticking around."

My eyes narrow. "Who's they?"

She shakes her head, shrugging both shoulders. "I don't know," she admits. "She just refers to them as *they*, but I can tell you it refers to multiple people, not a pronoun preference."

I nod, not bothering to question how she knows that. Her abilities are morphing into something more. Something that even Alyssa doesn't understand.

"At some point, her vision becomes fuzzy. She's feeling off and begins to panic. While the guy is in the restroom, she leaves. She's walking quickly toward a black car when someone grabs her from behind." Alyssa takes a seat on the edge of the bed, putting her head in her hands. "I feel her fear. Hear her thoughts. She knew she was going to die." She looks up at me, eyes filled with tears. "Then the vision ended."

I have questions, but I'm struggling to ask them. I don't want to push Alyssa when she's this upset.

"The car," she says, as if reading my mind and answering the questions I have. "It's hard to tell in the dark from this far away, but I'm pretty sure it's a black Toyota Camry. When we were buying a car for Ava, it was between the Camry and Corolla. I looked at a lot of those cars."

I grab my phone, queuing up my Notes app and recording the most important details.

Noting that Alyssa seems calmer, I take a chance and ask a lingering question.

"Did you get the feeling that *they* were whoever grabbed her?"

I don't have to elaborate on my use of *they*. Alyssa knows I'm referring to whoever the girl was thinking wouldn't want her to stick around.

Alyssa's quiet in thought for several moments. A range of emotions crosses her features, from confusion to curiosity, and finally landing on certainty.

"I don't think it was the same people. I'm getting the feeling that she was working for the people who would've wanted her to drop the cash and leave." She blows out a breath. "But I also think she knew who grabbed her." Her head tilts to the side. "Not the actual person, but the group the killer is tied to."

My mouth slams into a thin line as I take in everything she's just said.

Even if I asked how she knows this, she wouldn't be able to put it in words. It's a gut feeling. An intuition. A new ability that has me downright speechless.

"We need to act fast," Alyssa declares, her tone resolute. "We need to reach out to the spirit of this girl. To see if she's dead."

"You think there's a chance she's still alive?"

She bites her tongue, eyes squinting. "I'm . . . not sure." She grabs her phone from the nightstand. "I need to reach out to Corinne for help. A séance typically requires more people."

"I'll check in with Chief Skiver in Falls Haven. He needs to know I'm chasing a lead here in Knox Harbor. It should buy me a day."

Let's just hope he doesn't press for information. I can't exactly tell him my sources are dreams and dead people.

"DARLING NICK, YOU simply must sit next to me," Natalia purrs. Corinne's eccentric mother pats the spot beside her with a dramatic flourish.

When Alyssa reached out to Corinne, she was informed that they'd need more help, and since Lanie and Nina are still in New Orleans, Corinne called in her mother.

Alyssa warned me that the woman was next level, but I am now finding that depiction to be a colossal understatement.

I take a seat, and Natalia leans over toward me, placing her hand on my thigh. "I'll keep you safe." She squeezes my leg, and I cough, squirming in place.

My eyes dart to Alyssa, who meets my gaze with an amused twinkle in her eye. She mouths the words *good luck*.

I grit my teeth, suppressing the urge to beg her to intervene. This entire situation is odd enough, but I'm not sure I'm prepared to be felt up while dealing with the dead.

What the hell have I gotten myself into?

"Scoot closer. We'll need to share energy," Natalia coos, and Alyssa coughs, trying to smother her laughter.

I bare my teeth in a grin that promises retribution, but it doesn't even faze Alyssa. She's getting too much joy out of my discomfort.

It's moments like these that remind me why I'm so drawn to her—her easy confidence and lack of jealousy only add to her allure. Except that in this one instance, I wouldn't mind a bit of possessiveness. Anything to put some space between me and Natalia.

"Mother," Corinne snaps, drawing the woman's attention away from me. "I'm going to need you to focus."

Anything negative I've ever said about Corinne, I take back as she rolls her eyes, making it clear she's onto her mother's antics and won't allow it to go too far.

"Who are we calling upon?" Corinne asks Alyssa.

"I don't have a name, but any spirit of a young, dark-haired girl who visited my dream who wants to come through."

Corinne smacks her lips together, staring at Alyssa like that's the dumbest thing she's ever heard. She's obviously less than happy with this spirit request.

"That is a little too broad. It could bring about spirits we don't want," Natalia says, and Corinne appears to agree when she nods at her mom.

"I'll know if it's her when she comes through," Alyssa says, and Corinne huffs in response.

"I know this isn't preferable," Alyssa says, speaking directly to Corinne. "But I have to know if the girl from my dream is dead. I don't have a name. Only a description."

Corinne sucks her teeth for a moment, considering Alyssa before placing her hands on the table for her mother and Alyssa to take hold of.

"God, Goddess, Mother Earth," Corinne begins, launching into an over-the-top dialogue with the air.

She's calling out to the spirit world, asking for a dark-haired woman connected to Alyssa's dream to come forward. Aside from her animated voice, she's not overly theatrical. If anything, I expected more of a show from her. I'm surprised to find that my skepticism of the woman is waning. Every second I spend in her presence, it decreases a little more.

Now that I know abilities like Alyssa's aren't fantasy, I have to recognize that it's likely that Corinne isn't the fake I made her out to be. While I was grappling with Alyssa's truth, I made Corinne the villain in my head, and now I'm not so sure I was correct in that assumption.

She's a no-bullshit straight shooter, which I appreciate from the men I encounter, so why should it be any different with her?

Generational patterns are hard to shake, and I vow to do my best to have it end here and now. Not every detective is good, and not every person who questioned power dynamics, gender roles, and social tensions in Salem was a witch.

Corinne is allowed to be hard-nosed and blunt; it doesn't mean there's something wrong with her. She's not a criminal just because she questions and defies the norms.

After several tense minutes, nobody shows, and everyone in the room is quiet and contemplative. Just when I think the entire séance will be called off, Natalia charges ahead, spouting off in a language that sounds like a cross between pig Latin and Martian to my untrained ears.

Natalia's sitting there, swaying back and forth like a palm tree caught in a hurricane, and I'm half expecting her to jump up from her seat and break into the "Thriller" dance. This is the kind of spectacle I was anticipating from Corinne, but it would appear that the circus acts are reserved for Natalia.

As quickly as her wacky behavior started, it's over, her body going slack. She's completely still for well over a minute, and I'm about to check for a pulse when her eyes pop open and she's back to normal.

"Someone is here to speak," she says, voice shaky. "Are you open to conversing with a Chelsea?"

Alyssa and I share a glance, both of us shocked to hear that name.

Alyssa bobs her head. "Yes. Can she show herself to me?"

Upon Alyssa's request, Chelsea must've appeared, because Alyssa's eyes widen fractionally, her shoulders straightening as she looks over Natalia's shoulder at what appears like nothing to me.

I watch in fascination at the one-sided conversation.

"Interesting," Alyssa says. "Is Sierra with you?"

My head moves back and forth between the empty space and Alyssa, curiosity over what's being said about driving me crazy.

"Shit. Tomorrow?" Alyssa rubs at her forehead. "Where were you going the night you were taken? You were dressed up." She listens intently to whatever is being said before saying, "Wow . . . this runs deep."

"What runs deep?" I ask, and am immediately shushed by Natalia.

"Chelsea is sharing very important information with us," she says, eyes trained on the blank space where Chelsea must be.

I sit back in my chair, disgruntled that Natalia is privy to the conversation when I'm not.

"Sucks, doesn't it?" Corinne drawls, slumped back in her chair, arms crossed over her chest, annoyance clear as day with her downturned lips and narrowed eyes.

I sigh, nodding in camaraderie with Corinne in our moment of being on the outside.

Several moments pass as more information appears to be shared. When Alyssa says, "Thank you," I know Chelsea has left the room.

She turns back to the table, taking a deep breath.

"Sierra's uncle approached Sierra about an opportunity to make a lot of cash by running drugs and washing money for a man that remained anonymous. Sierra brought Chelsea and another friend, Ashley Evans, into the fold."

"Ashley is the girl from Alyssa's dream," Natalia interjects, and my eyebrows lift.

"Dead?" I ask.

Alyssa shakes her head. "Not yet, but she will be tomorrow, most likely. Thursday is the day they deliver the money to a set of bars who are in on the money-laundering part of things."

"Let me guess, a bar in Falls Haven?" I say, and Alyssa nods once.

"We've gotta go," I say, preparing to stand from the table, but Natalia lifts her hands to stop me.

"There's more that's crucial to this investigation, Detective."

Gone is the flirty tone and inappropriate touching. Now, Natalia is all business, determined to relay the information that Chelsea Grayson found important enough to share.

"Chelsea said that they'd recently started getting threatened by an unknown person. The person used voice-altering technology, so she can't even say whether it was a man or a woman. But the person accused the girls of encroaching on their territory. She said that Sierra's uncle was warned, but he brushed it off like it was no big deal. She thinks whoever's territory it was is who killed them."

"Turf war," I say, to nobody in particular. "Do you think this has something to do with the Order of Providence?"

"Chelsea was working for the Order. She doesn't know the members or who was at the top, but Sierra's uncle definitely knew something." Alyssa looks to me when she says, "Sierra's uncle is Harlan Abbott. The man from the underground poker deal in Florida."

"Florida? He's managing these girls from Florida?" I say in disbelief.

This is much bigger than we thought.

"She was working at another underground poker lounge in Falls Haven. One that sounds awfully similar to the one under the Montgomery Estate," she says. "There's a guy there who goes by the name of Rocco. He gives them the envelopes before they leave the secret poker site on Thursday morning. They don't want them moving around with wads of cash for long."

"Did she tell you what happened to her? The coroner's report says that she had blunt-force trauma to the head," I say, and Alyssa nods.

"She was flirting with a guy that sounds like the same person from my dream. She started to feel lightheaded and said she was going to leave. The last thing she remembers is waking up on a boat. She thinks she was hit over the head. She doesn't remember anything after that."

"He's drugging them," I say, and Alyssa's eyes darken, as though she hadn't put that together yet.

"Where's the site of the poker games in Falls Haven?"

Alyssa's face falls. "She wouldn't tell me, because she said my life would be in grave danger if she did."

My eyes close, frustration mounting. "You've already been exposed to one of these places that's likely linked. How are you not already in danger?"

"They haven't pieced together that I'm any more than a friend of an important friend. Apparently, Jill must be having an affair with Harlan, so he trusts that she's vetted us. We know Jill from college, not Knox Harbor. He likely has no idea how close I am to their other operations."

I rake my hand back through my hair. "This is all so damn convoluted. What the hell are the chances that you'd run into some underground activity in Florida that's connected to home? Connected to deaths that you dreamed about?"

Natalia laughs, but it lacks humor. "Welcome to the complex cosmos, where embracing your talents often means becoming a pawn for some cosmic puppeteer."

Alyssa's face pales, and my own stomach twists uncomfortably.

"And this is what you want for me?" Corinne exclaims. "Why do you hate me?"

Natalia purses her lips, not bothering to humor her daughter with a response. Instead, she looks to Alyssa. "The universe is guiding you to where you need to be in order to help these spirits. The source, god or whatever you choose to call it, demands karmic justice, and you are being used to enact it." She shakes her head, appearing almost sorry for what she's communicating to Alyssa. "Nothing in your life moving forward is a coincidence, my dear. Much of what occurs is meant for you to use to right a wrong."

"How will I know the difference?" Alyssa asks, sounding far too calm for someone who's just been told she's a glorified pawn in a real and very dangerous game of chess.

Natalia shrugs one delicate shoulder, her oversize yellow sweater slipping down her shoulder. "I never leave home without my tarot deck. It's very useful when needing to commune with the universe."

"I'm not well versed in tarot," Alyssa says, and Natalia scoffs. "Get yourself a deck that comes with a book. You'll find that the more you use them, the clearer the answers. From what I've gathered of your abilities, you should be able to read them intuitively."

"Thank you," Alyssa says before turning to me. "We need to go if we want to save Ashley."

"One more thing," Natalia says, her hand and one finger lifted into the air. "These . . . groups," she murmurs, eyes narrowing when she says *groups*. "This Order of Providence . . . It's bigger than Knox Harbor. Bigger than the whole of Massachusetts," she explains. "Be sure you've considered your life and that of your daughter before you go chasing after something you know nothing about willy-nilly, Alyssa. There are times when, even if our gifts are urging us to intervene, we must refuse the calling. For our own safety."

Alyssa stares at Natalia for several moments, throat bobbing as she digests the words.

I won't allow Alyssa to put herself in danger. She's made it clear how important it is for her to help, but I hope she heeds Natalia's words and understands that her life is more important than going down dark paths.

I'll do whatever it takes to ensure Alyssa remembers that.

I won't lose another woman I care for.

Natalia and Corinne both make their way toward the front door, but before Natalia steps onto the porch, she turns.

"You'll need your friend. The one that was with you when you visited Bee. She'll be necessary in uncovering some of the missing pieces." And with that, Natalia is gone.

Ten of Wands

THE MOMENT CORINNE and Natalia had left my house, I called in an SOS to Nina, telling her I needed her help. Thankfully, she and Lanie had just landed in Boston and were headed home to Knox Harbor.

I didn't give too many details, thinking it best to have that conversation in person. I explained that Nick and I were going to check into a hotel in Falls Haven and that big things were about to go down. She promised she'd be to my room first thing today, and in true Nina fashion, she didn't let me down. Seeing that Lanie had joined her was a surprise.

"You two are the best, seriously," I say, pulling my two friends into a group hug.

"She didn't really give me a choice," Lanie deadpans. "I was threatened with my life."

Nina pulls away, rolling her eyes at Lanie, who winks in return.

I smile, grateful for this moment of levity before we get into the heavy stuff.

"What made you come back so soon?" I ask, directing the question to Nina.

She shares a glance with Lanie, who shakes her head. "Nope. You get to tell her."

Lanie crosses her arms over her chest, and my eyes ping-pong between the two.

"Someone tell me what's happening," I say, starting to feel as though whatever I'm about to hear, I won't like.

Nina sighs. "We have more important things to worry about, but since you asked . . ."

"Spit it out, Enamored Nina," Lanie teases.

"I've come back to find an apartment or house for rent and arrange for a moving company to pack up my things. It's time."

I smile, nodding my head. "That's great news." I turn to Lanie. "But why are you acting a bit salty over it?"

She looks at Nina, pursing her lips and tilting her head as if to say, *You're still up.*

"I'm heading back to New Orleans for the next month or two. I want to spend time with Chase . . . and Ian."

"We all know you won't come back," Lanie says, and I hear the sadness in her tone more than the bitterness.

"You don't know that," Nina says, but it lacks conviction.

Lanie's probably right. Chase attends Tulane, and Ian works there. They're settled, whereas Nina isn't. It would only make sense for her to move to them.

"I'm happy for you," I say, offering my most sincere smile to my best friend.

She leaps forward, crushing me to her chest. "Thank you, Ally."

When we've all had a moment to process the fact that Nina is leaving, it's finally time to discuss what's happening and why I called Nina in the first place.

I'm sitting across from my two best friends, sharing what I learned from the brief encounter with Chelsea Grayson. The entire time I share what she said, Nina sits enraptured and visibly shocked by it all, whereas Lanie seems tense, almost paranoid, and it occurs to me that this isn't the first time she's gotten strange at the mention of the Order.

"I need to ask you something, Lanie. But I need you to not get defensive," I say, holding her gaze. Her eyes narrow in on me, and she bites her cheek. "Do you know something about the Order of Providence?"

She runs her tongue along her bottom teeth, hard eyes trained on me.

She's not happy with my line of questioning, which just further proves she's keeping secrets.

Nina peers at the side of Lanie's head before turning to me, a look of confusion marring her face.

"Why would you ask something like that?" Nina asks, but I don't address her, refusing to look away from Lanie's cold stare.

Never in my life have I been on the receiving end of that glare.

"Because two different times when the Order has been mentioned, Lanie has gotten weird," I explain, turning away from my stare-down with Lanie. "We have the ability to save a young girl, but we can't go running into this with a half-assed plan that could get us all hurt. If she knows something, she needs to speak up."

"Do you know who this group is?" Nina asks.

Lanie takes a deep breath and huffs out a humorless laugh. "I am familiar with the legend of the Order of Providence, but I only know it from whispers among criminals as being a society that pulls all the strings on the East Coast. If they exist, they have been said to have had a hand in some of the biggest events that have occurred on our side of the US."

My head moves back slightly, not following Lanie.

Lanie sighs. "If something happened in Washington or New York that was big news, we as civilians might not know the truth behind that event," she explains. "Maybe certain things didn't play out the way the public was led to believe. Maybe there is truth in the crazed conspiracies that float out there on numerous happenings." She shrugs. "The Order of Providence was positioned as a thing of myth . . . not reality."

"And how were you hearing about it?" Nick asks, voice smooth, but I don't miss the subtle hint of accusation as he enters the room carrying a tray of coffees. "I'm a detective. My father is former FBI, and this is the first I'm hearing of such a society."

Lanie's eyes close on a long exhale. "Pre–Knox Harbor, I was a different girl. I ran in a bad crowd and got pulled into some shit I never meant to get involved in." She takes a deep breath and looks at me and then Nick. "I'm asking that you don't press on the specifics, as they're not relevant to this. But mark my words—if the people I was tied to were scared of what they deemed lore, the knowledge that it's real should scare the shit out of all of us."

I see the way Lanie's hands shake and the sudden concern in Nina's eyes.

"If this changes things and you don't want to get involved, knowing the risks, I understand," I say to both my friends. "I don't want to put you in harm's way."

"I said I'd help," Nina states. "Just tell me what I need to do."

"Me too," Lanie parrots.

We spend the next hour running down everything that Nick knows about Haven's Bard, the bar we believe is one of the drop points.

"Every dream or vision I've had, it's been dark outside, so we need to be there and in place before nightfall," I say, picking lint off my black joggers. "Nina, your objective is to locate a spot at the bar next to the man with the tattoo sleeve, assuming this plays out like my dream."

"Got it. Touch him and concentrate on uncovering who he is and who he works for," she recites her part for tonight.

"If you're unable to make it happen for any reason, just protect Ashley. Keep her in the bar at all costs. As of right now, we have nothing to hold the guy on, which means we need to focus on keeping Ashley alive."

Lanie and Nina nod.

"Lanie, you don't have to do this," I say, because she still looks a little pale from all the talk of the Order.

"I'm going." It's all she says, and I leave it at that.

Tonight, we could use all the help we can get.

"Remember, this isn't official police business," Nick says, meeting each of our eyes. "I have nothing substantial enough to take to Chief Skiver. We're on our own. We have to do this carefully. The guy is innocent until we have proof that he's up to no good."

We all nod our understanding, moving to get ready. To anyone at the bar, we need to look like three friends out on the town for the night. Nick will try to remain in the background unseen, so if he needs to intervene, the suspects won't see it coming.

"LANIE, WHAT THE hell?" I say, looking down at her feet.

Nick and I left the hotel early to scout out the bar while it was still daylight, leaving the room open for the girls to get changed. I'd told Nina on my call to dress for a night out on the town, so they came prepared with a change of clothes.

Nina has on a pair of black leather Spanx and an oversize, off-the-shoulder cream sweater with a pair of black booties. Lanie, on the other hand, looks like she missed the memo that it's nearly February and we're trying to save a life, not spend the night line dancing.

"We're not in Nashville," I say incredulously.

"What?" she says, curling her lip. "We're going to Haven's Bard, and these are my shitkickers. Anyone gets out of line, I'll take them down easily with these bad boys."

I take a deep breath, closing my eyes. "I said to dress for a night out on the town, but to be inconspicuous. You will not go unnoticed."

She shrugs. "I never do, love."

"Okay," Nina drawls, "we've got work to do." She turns to me. "Ready?"

I nod, moving forward and pushing open the door.

As we step into the bar, my heart sinks.

This isn't the place.

Haven's Bard is huge, flooded with harsh fluorescent light, completely opposite of the dimly lit bar I saw in my dream.

The place we need is smaller. The bar in here spans the length of the back wall, wrapping into a half-moon. High-top tables are off to the right, while a large dance floor takes up the left all the way to the start of the bar tables.

To Lanie's credit, she dressed perfectly. The dance floor is filled with women dressed similarly to Lanie, dancing the tush push.

"This isn't it," I say dejectedly.

Nina furrows her brow. "Are you sure?"

"Positive. The place we're looking for is smaller. Darker."

Nick glances around the room, scanning the crowd. "I don't see anyone that matches your description of the guy, or the photo we found of Ashley online either."

The music shifts, and the sound of screeching women scratches at my senses. I have to get out of here.

A woman walks by, and Nina's hand darts out, stopping her. "Excuse me," she says, smiling sweetly at the twenty-something blonde decked out in rhinestone shorts and white cowboy boots. "Is there another bar in town that's a bit smaller? Maybe with less lights?"

The girl narrows her eyes in on Nina, nodding her head. "I get it, girl. Just work on blending; you'll get to a point where you won't be afraid to show your face."

Nina drops her hand from the girl's arm, blinking rapidly, hand lifting to her face.

"You're probably wanting Muddy Mermaid. It's a dive bar close by. Good luck." She offers a toothy smile before heading to the dance floor to a group of girls that cheer when they see her.

"What the F . . ." Nina's words trail off. "Is my makeup bad?"

"No. You look great."

"I'm not even wearing foundation. How the hell could I blend better?"

I chuckle. "The girl is already a bit past drunk, Nins. She's probably seeing two of you."

"Yeah, well . . . I wonder if her girlfriend knows she's been in the bathroom making out with the redhead sitting at the bar."

My eyebrows lift into my hairline. "Any other night, I'd say raise the roof on this place, but we have more important things than to get back at Little Miss Drunk-and-Confused."

"What do we do?" Nina asks, her nose scrunching up as her head shakes.

I glance in the direction she's looking and find Lanie in the middle of the dance floor, leaned back, the entire top half of her body gyrating to the music.

"Good grief," Nina says. "I'll go grab her while you two plan our next move." She takes off toward the dance floor, eyes trained on Lanie and her antics.

I pull my phone out and start searching for bars close by. Muddy Mermaid comes up, but so does another that sounds like it's just as much a dive bar.

"There are two within five minutes of Haven's Bard, but in opposite directions. It's a coin flip, and we're out of time. It's nearly sunset, and we're not in position," I say, panic rising as Ashley's life hangs in the balance. My head drops with a groan. "I don't know what to do," I admit to Nick. "I'd just be guessing, and what if I choose wrong?" I shake my head. "I think we should split up."

"Not happening," he says, voice stern. "We're talking about a murderer, Lyss. I'm not leaving you."

I step toward him, grabbing his hands. "We have to. Otherwise, that girl is going to die. I can't live with that."

"Do you remember what Natalia said? You can't save them all, Alyssa." Nick's eyes lock on to mine with intense focus, but I notice a crack in his armor that reveals his vulnerability. He couldn't bear the thought of her dying any more than I could. The first chance he gets, he'll be rushing out of here to try to intervene. He's only trying to protect me.

"Trust me, Nick. Please."

I watch as he appears to war with himself before nodding. "Do you promise you won't do anything that puts you in danger? If you see her, you'll do what you can from inside to keep her from leaving. But under no circumstances do you leave that bar."

"I promise," I say, willing to make that compromise.

She might not even be there to begin with.

He sighs. "Who's going with me?"

"Lanie," I say, knowing that I can't worry about corralling her tonight.

He lifts a brow, frowning. "Sticking me with the wild card."

"She'll listen to you," I say. "I can't be worried about her and finding Ashley. I know you'll keep her safe. Nina, I don't worry about. She'll be by my side the whole time."

He bobs his head. "I think it's the best plan. Where are Lanie and I headed?"

"Muddy Mermaid."

He grins. "Sounds shady. I think we have the winner."

I smirk. "I'm not so sure. We're off to Rebel Roost."

"Is that a biker bar?" he asks, pulling out his phone, likely to search it up.

I shrug, not having a clue. Neither has a website, as far as I could tell.

"Yeah . . . no," he mumbles. "We'll take Rebel Roost. I remember that place. There was a double murder there a couple years ago. Rival biker gangs. You're not going there without me."

"All right," I say, not apt to fight when we just need to make moves. "I'm going to grab Nina and head to Muddy Mermaid. Keep me posted on what you find," I say. I turn to leave, but he reaches out, stopping me.

I'm pulled into his strong embrace, melting into him.

"Be careful, Lyss. I mean it." He places a hard kiss on my lips before pulling away and stalking toward Lanie, who's still on the dance floor.

I know he hates this. I can tell by his posture that he's not comfortable with the arrangement, but he's a good man, and he won't allow Ashley to die if there's a chance that we can stop it.

As we step outside, the cool night air hits me like a slap in the face, the realization of what we're about to do washing over me. I have no idea what's to come, and that thought is more than a little unsettling.

Nina speeds down the road, driving like I've never seen her drive before. She's weaving around slow traffic and honking for people to get out of her way.

We're pulling up to Muddy Mermaid in record time, and I know immediately that this is the one and we're not too late.

Ashley's black car is parked in the corner, just where I saw it in my dream.

"She's here," I say, quickly sending a message to Nick, telling him to head this way.

"I don't know about this," Nina whispers, her eyes wide with apprehension.

I twist in my seat, placing a hand on Nina's shoulder. "We're in this together. I won't leave your side, and we won't do anything that puts us in danger."

She takes a deep breath, nodding her head once. "Let's go be heroes."

I grin, loving Nina's positive outlook. We're going to be fine. Ashley is going to be fine.

I'll keep repeating that in my head until it's reality.

We push through the creaky door of the lounge bar, and it's exactly as I remember. The low light casts a golden glow over the place. There is a row of booths off to the side, but it's hard to make out the faces of the people occupying the seats. The lighting in here is not great.

We stand just inside the door, scanning the area for any sign of Ashley. She's perched on a stool almost dead center of the bar.

"That's her," I whisper, pointing to her back.

Except it's not a man with a tattoo sleeve sitting next to her, but a girl. They're chatting animatedly, only the back of the woman visible. She has stick-straight black hair that hangs to the top of her jeans, only the sleeves of her white T-shirt visible.

The woman turns to look over her back toward the door. It's hard to tell her age from this distance, although it's clear she's younger than me. Her full, pouty lips, heart-shaped face, and nose with a slight dorsal hump are hard to miss. Her catlike green eyes land on me briefly, but she doesn't seem to give me much thought, turning back toward the bar.

I'm about to suggest to Nina that we head that way, when the door opens behind us, and in walks the man with the tattoo. The octopus surrounded by roses stands out starkly against his alabaster skin, running from his shoulder to his wrist, inky vines slipping onto the top of his hand.

The woman turns, subtly tilting her head in a gesture that might escape notice by most, but not me.

"That's him," I whisper into Nina's ear. "And that woman is involved."

Nina's eyes narrow in on the girl with Ashley, eyes turning hard.

"It takes a special kind of evil to be involved in this," Nina says under her breath.

She's right. Whoever this woman is, she's vile.

We both watch as the woman rises from her seat, exchanging words with Ashley, who responds with a smile, looking over her shoulder at the man. It's obvious that Ashley finds him attractive, her eyes sparkling and her smile widening with a hint of mischief.

"Oh my god," Nina says, pulling my attention toward her. "She just dropped something into her drink while her head was turned."

The woman strides toward the restroom, leaving Ashley alone at the bar. The tattooed man slides into the now-vacant seat. Ashley says something to him about it, because he feigns ignorance, making to move, but she stops him, tapping the seat, signaling for him to sit.

That's when my dream plays out in front of us.

"Let's go," I say, pulling Nina away from the door, realizing we've been standing here for too long.

The last thing I want to do is draw attention to us.

We move to the far end of the bar, where I send another text, checking in with Nick.

ME

Where are you? He's here.

NICK

About to pull in. I'll keep watch out here.

I give his message a thumbs-up and wave down the bartender.

"Can I get a gin and tonic?" I turn to Nina. "What do you want?"

"I'll have the same," she says. "Make mine a double."

The orange-haired man laughs. "Rough night?"

"You could say that," Nina admits, and I don't miss the way her hand shakes at her side.

She's nervous, and I don't blame her. I'm surprised by how calm I am considering a murderer is right down the bar from me.

We stand at the bar watching the man closely for several minutes, the woman never returning.

"What do you think that woman's doing?" Nina asks, taking a sip from her glass. "She's been back in the bathroom for some time."

"Unless . . ." My words trail off as the thought crosses my mind.

I wave down the bartender. "Is there an exit back by the restrooms?" I ask, and he nods.

"Yeah. You can use it. There's no alarm."

Nina and I share a look, and I quickly send off a text to Nick.

ME

Female suspect may have left out a side exit.

Long black hair, white T-shirt.
Did you see her?

NICK

No. Haven't seen anyone.

Where did she go?

I'm lost in thought about the whereabouts of the woman, and I almost miss the most crucial moment.

The man spills his drink right onto Ashley, and she yelps as the contents soak through her forest-green dress. She jumps up, swaying a bit, showing signs that the roofie is kicking in.

That's when I piece together how this all works.

Seven of Wands

Nick

MY PHONE PINGS, signaling I've received a text message.

> ALYSSA
> Ashley's heading your way.
> She's not in good shape.
> The woman is likely hiding out in the shadows.

Not even two seconds later, Ashley Evans is walking out of the bar, alone, but I remain in my car. Alyssa said she was drugged, and that the woman will likely present herself.

I could intervene now and get her to safety, but that's just a temporary fix. I need a reason to arrest whoever comes after her, and giving away my presence is unlikely to accomplish that.

Ashley's moves are slow and unbalanced. I'm concerned that she's going to face-plant into the stones.

"What are we doing?" Lanie says. "Should we help her?"

"Not yet," I say quietly, watching Ashley closely.

Out of the shadows from the side of the building, a woman emerges, moving up behind Ashley. She's too messed up to even hear the woman's approach. She wraps her hand around Ashley's mouth, but I'm not sure it's necessary. Ashley's too disoriented. The woman is having a hard time holding her up.

"Holy shit," Lanie says, voice shaking. "Nick, we have to—"

"Look," I say, dipping my head forward, pointing out the man exiting the bar.

"That's him," I say.

He's heading toward the girls, steps quick and assured. He doesn't even bother scanning the area. He exchanges words with his accomplice before bending down and picking a now-limp Ashley up off her feet. The woman rushes off toward a truck.

That's when I jump into action.

"Need some help?" I say, slamming the car door behind me.

The man's head snaps to me. "I've got it handled. My girlfriend is just a little drunk. That's all."

Ashley fidgets in his grasp.

"Not . . . girl . . . fend." Her words are choppy and slurred, just barely audible.

"Do you know him?" I ask Ashley, knowing I'm unlikely to get a response.

But I need to do things by the book; otherwise, I'll have nothing.

Ashley's head shakes, just barely.

"It appears as though she doesn't know you," I say, eyes lasered in on the man.

"Use your fucking eyes, man. She's wasted."

I shrug. "Doesn't matter. If she says she doesn't know you, I'm gonna have to insist you put her down."

"Who the fuck are you? Get lost, douchebag."

I pull my badge from my back pocket, lifting it to the man's face. "Police, asshole, and I said to put her down."

I hear footsteps approaching from behind.

"It's me," Lanie calls out, rushing up to my side.

The man drops Ashley, and Lanie jumps forward, falling to her knees on the stones, doing her best to provide a softer landing for Ashley.

She's got to be hurt, but I can't worry about it right now. The guy is sprinting toward the truck.

Gunshots are fired, and I dive forward, tackling the skinny piece of shit to the ground. The truck tires squeal, peeling out of the bar parking lot, headed south down the road.

"Fuck," I say, pain lancing up my back from the impact of securing one of the suspects. "You're under arrest for obstructing justice and attempting to flee the scene," I say, cuffing the son of a bitch.

"What can we do?" Alyssa says, rushing toward us.

Half the bar is outside, checking out what's happening.

"We heard the gunshots," she says.

"Help Nina with Lanie," I instruct, the man underneath me trying to wrestle his way out of my hold.

The bartender rushes up, helping me contain the man while I search his pocket for an ID.

"Austin Barlow," I say, reading the name off his license.

"The police are on their way," the bartender says, pushing a knee into Austin's back, holding him in place.

"Do you have a first aid kit?" Nina directs to the bartender. "One of the girls has a pretty deep cut on her knee and a gash on her head." She turns to look over her shoulder. "The other girl needs to get to the hospital. She was drugged."

The bartender hops to action, racing off toward the bar, waving for the other patrons to get back inside and allow me to do my business.

Exhaustion is pressing down on me.

I'm getting too old for this shit.

Nina bends down, peering into my eyes. "Can I?" she asks, and I nod, giving her space to use her ability.

I watch as she bites her tongue, eyes narrowing, then darkening.

"He was contracted by a group known as KVS. He wasn't part of it in the beginning. The woman was. He was just supposed to help dispose of the girls. Turf war," she says, shaking her head. "He's a nobody piece of shit."

"Anything else?" I ask, and she touches him again.

"What the fuck?" he snaps. "Get your hands off me, she-devil."

"If he didn't do it, he'd be washing up to shore right along with her. Seems like our man here owed a lot of money to someone high up in the KVS."

It's going to be a long night.

✦ ✦ ✦

"NICE WORK, WEST," Chief Skiver says, patting me on the back. "How about next time you get a hunch, you call in for some backup?"

"I'll consider that next time."

He chuckles. "Get some rest. We'll take it from here."

I nod, standing to my feet and stretching.

Austin admitted to it all. He said he'd entered a poker game and bet money he didn't have. So far, he's agreed to give up the location of where this underground betting is happening and anything else he knows in exchange for a plea deal.

He doesn't know who runs the poker games, but when he couldn't pay up, he was dragged into a room where the woman, who we've come to learn is Olivia Rossi, told him he could die or pay off his debt. It was on him to kill and toss the bodies of those they deemed threats to their operations. He said that after the death of Sierra, they initiated him into the group, branding him with the outrageous tattoo.

Turns out that Olivia Rossi is wanted by the feds for multiple heists. The FBI is taking over the case, meaning I can finally go home and tell the captain that I've brought Chelsea's murderer to justice.

I walk out of the station to find Alyssa leaning against my car, looking down at her phone.

"You've been here this whole time?" I ask, and she looks up.

"Just got here. I've been at the hospital with Lanie and Nina."

My eyebrow lifts. "Everyone all right?"

She nods her head. "They will be. Lanie has a fractured patella, and she's not happy about it."

I whistle. "I bet. Makes it hard to lead yoga classes if you can't do yoga."

"It's more than that," Alyssa says, appearing lost in thought. "She's acting so strange. Paranoid. Scared. They gave her a sedative."

I pull my top lip into my mouth, bobbing my head, not at all surprised that Lanie Anderson is a tough patient. "What do you think is wrong? Just too close an encounter with a near death?"

She shakes her head, eyes narrowing. "No. It's something more."

I can tell Alyssa's bothered, and I wish there was something I could do. But Lanie Anderson is a tough nut to crack, and it's likely she's just overwhelmed by tonight and unwilling to admit it.

"Lanie will be in a brace and will have to do some physical therapy, but she'll be fine. They got her all cleaned up." Alyssa yawns. "When she's discharged, they're going to check into the hotel to get some sleep."

"Looks like you should too," I say, pulling her into my chest and rubbing her back. "You look exhausted."

"I am. But I wanted to wait for you."

I get her into the car, heading toward the hotel. We're both quiet for several minutes when I ask, "How's Ashley?"

Alyssa's head falls to the side. "They have her on an IV. A police officer is stationed at her door for when she's better. Her mom was causing quite the scene when they showed up."

"She's going to jail," I say, shrugging. "But I'm sure they'll make a plea deal with her, and she won't be in there long."

"That's what I said. The most important thing is to bring down the Order and whoever this KVS is."

I nod. "Skiver and the FBI will do anything to uncover the people associated with KVS and the Order," I vow, knowing that's their objective.

"Now what?" Alyssa says, voice tinged with sleep.

"We get some rest and head home tomorrow."

"I'm pretty sure Chelsea's spirit has moved on. I don't feel her anymore."

I turn to look at Alyssa. She's shrouded in darkness, but as we pass under a streetlight, making our way into town, her face is illuminated.

God, she's beautiful.

Even exhausted, she takes my breath away.

"That's good," I say, clearing my throat when my words come out all husky.

"It is." She sighs heavily. "Do you think when we get home, we can put the investigating on hold long enough to actually date?"

I laugh. "I promise you; we'll make it happen." I place one hand on her thigh. "You and me. This thing's official, yeah?"

She turns her head to look at me, a lazy grin plastered across her face. "Definitely."

That one word has the ability to turn an otherwise shit day into one that I'll remember forever.

Alyssa Mann is quickly becoming my happiness. The woman I want to spend every minute with.

The woman I want to introduce to my crazy family.

And that scares me more than the KVS or Order of Providence.

Epilogue

The Tower

TWO MONTHS LATER . . .

NINA, LANIE, NICK, and I are gathered at the exhibit hall, standing in front of Ava's mixed-media masterpiece, titled *A Curious Case of Tentacles*. It commands our attention. Its sheer creativity leaves me speechless, tears welling in my eyes.

But it's also captured me in a chokehold, sucking the air from my lungs.

A giant octopus, its tentacles reaching out in all directions, dominates the center of the piece, overlaying a page from *Alice in Wonderland*. Each tentacle is adorned with shimmering crystals that catch the light and bathe the room in rainbow hues. The octopus's expression steals the show, its eyes gleaming with a sinister intensity. A Cheshire-cat grin makes it appear even more menacing.

In one of its tentacles, the octopus clutches a large eye, seemingly choking the life out of it.

The octopus.

The eye.

Words Natalia Moradi spoke to me not long ago replay in my mind.

Nothing in your life moving forward is a coincidence, my dear.

"Do you like it?" Ava asks, holding my hand.

I turn to her and nod, a tear falling down my cheek. I swipe it away quickly.

"I'm in awe, Ava. This is so beyond my expectations."

And it is. It's truly incredible. The detail. The symbolism. This is more than just a school project—it's a work of art, a reflection of Ava's endless talent.

I couldn't be prouder of her in this moment, but it's also packing on a host of questions I can't ask.

"How did you decide to do this?" Nina asks, her voice thick with emotion.

Ava shrugs. "I wanted to create a piece using a passage from *Alice's Adventures in Wonderland* in the background. The overlaid image was originally the Mad Hatter as the focal image, but I always felt like it was wrong." She sighs heavily, shoulders sagging. "The pieces needed to be connected by something other than the book itself. Otherwise, it just felt unoriginal."

"What made you choose an octopus?" I ask.

She stares at her piece, a dreamy quality taking over her expression. "They're mysterious and cunning. They're known to be playful and creative. The passage I chose embodied all those things."

Maybe this is truly a coincidence.

"Thankfully, we got a new teacher a few weeks ago, and he suggested the octopus when I told him my concerns. He helped me re-create my project in record time." She turns to me. "That's why I've been so MIA."

Lanie, Nina, Nick, and I all share a look.

"Who's your teacher?" I ask, glancing around the room. "I thought it was Mrs. Woods."

"He's a student teacher, Mr. Oaks." Ava's head swivels around as she lifts up on her toes. "There he is," she says, pointing toward a man conversing with another family about their child's project.

He turns to the side, scratching at his arm. The sleeve of his black smock lifts, and there on his arm is an octopus tattooed on his skin.

Nina sees it too, because her eyes are wide as she turns back to me. It's clear that we've arrived at the same conclusion.

The KVS knows that we've been snooping around, and nearly took down one of their own. They're sending a warning.

"I'm going to go see a friend's piece. I'll be back," Ava says, smiling at all of us before bouncing away.

The four of us huddle together, voices lowered. "What the hell?" Nick nearly growls.

Lanie blows out a harsh breath. "She has to come home. Somewhere we can keep her safe."

"You can't exactly pull her from school without explaining your reasons. And you can't tell her the truth," Nina says. "Her knowing anything puts her in more danger."

I close my eyes, my heart pounding out of my chest. "Guys, we have to be looking at this wrong. We just learned about the KVS. What would be the chances that this has anything to do with them? What if his tattoo is mere coincidence? I mean, it's not exactly like Austin's."

"I think she's right," Nick says, running a hand back through his hair. "Get me all the details on this teacher, and I'll look into him. He can't have a record; otherwise, he wouldn't have gotten this job."

I bob my head, starting to feel slightly better.

I'm obviously still on edge. Knowing that secret societies exist and that I had a hand in putting away some people who could potentially bring their whole group down has me nervous. Add the fact that I've been to one of these underground poker locations, and it's hard to not feel like I have a target on my back. Not only with the KVS, but the Order could be watching us too.

"Everyone, let's just calm down," Nick says, addressing my friends.

Lanie looks ready to tackle Mr. Oaks to the ground, brace or no.

"He's right. We're really just overreacting. It's a tattoo. Octopuses are popular. They're not limited to criminal organizations."

My phone vibrates in my purse, and I hear both Lanie and Nina's do the same.

We all pull our phones from our bags, staring at our screens.

UNKNOWN

We're watching you and those you love.

Give Lanie my regards. xo OR

I blink, rereading the text several times.

"What is it?" Nick asks.

I hand him my phone, looking first at Nina and then at Lanie. "What does yours say?"

Nina turns her phone toward me, showing me her screen.

UNKNOWN

Touch one of ours again and die

"Lanie?" I say, peering up at her, wanting to see her screen.

Her head shakes back and forth as she backs away from us.

"This can't be happening." It's all she says.

I grab Lanie by the arm and pull her away from the throngs of people, Nina right behind us.

I refuse to make a scene. The last thing I want is for Ava to realize there's a problem. I won't ruin this day for her.

"What do you know?" I snap at Lanie as soon as we're out of sight from anyone else. "And don't you dare act like you know nothing."

I lift my phone, putting the screen right in front of her face. "OR? Who is OR?"

She closes her eyes, swallowing hard. A pained expression is frozen on her face.

"Olivia Rossi." The name slips from her mouth in a whisper, as though saying it louder will lead to her materializing.

"Why?" I bark. "Why is she bringing you up as if you know each other?"

"Because we do," she cries. "She's part of my secret past. The person I ran from." She shakes her head, looking pathetic, something entirely foreign for Lanie. "I knew she was coming. I dreamed it." She grabs my shirt, holding tight. "I didn't burn the scarecrow, and now she's coming to take away everything that I love."

Her nightmare.

I know that some people have the ability to see things before they occur through dreams. I'm one of them. And now it would appear that Lanie has that ability too.

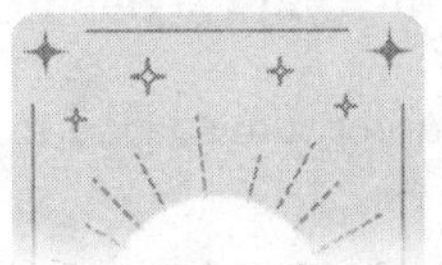

Acknowledgments

Thank you, readers, for the incredible outpouring of support for this series. It means everything to me that you've embraced Alyssa, her friends, and the entire fictional town of Knox Harbor.

A heartfelt thanks to my forever friend Jill O., for allowing me to use your name for a questionable character. You're a good sport and I love you forever!

To Jackie F., you rolled in like a hurricane of fun, and I'll never let you leave me. You've been my rock these past few years and I know you will be for many more to come. Love you, mean it.

To Kristin P., thank you for providing a safe space to share my thoughts and feelings. You'll never know how comforting it is to know that I'm not alone.

A huge thank-you to Kai for all your help these past few months—I couldn't do this without you.

To all my English teachers who fostered my love for reading and writing, you may not realize the profound impact you've had on me (even if it didn't always seem that way).

Thank you to my father; I'm so glad to have the relationship I do with you.

A huge thank-you to my Berkley team—Esi, Genni, and everyone else who had a hand in making this book a reality. And to my incredible agent, Carrie, who made this all possible: you're all stuck with me if I have a choice in the matter!

And lastly, to my family—#14, Z, A, and G—my world doesn't spin without you.

Keep reading for an excerpt from Melissa Holtz's

An Enchanting Case of Spirits

Available now from Berkley

Five of Cups

ANOTHER SPOONFUL WILL dull the painful truth.

My youth is gone.

A carton of ice cream is gripped between my legs like my life depends on it not slipping from my clutches. A cool autumn breeze flits through the open window next to my whitewashed sleigh bed, and I shiver as it races up my exposed arms.

I consider closing said window but refrain, too comfy to move from under the heavy down comforter and matching gray sheets I'm currently curled beneath.

My lips wrap around a tarnished silver spoon—a wedding present from my mother—and a chill settles over me. Whether from the draft or cold dessert, I'm not sure, and I couldn't care less either way.

Less than nine hours remain of my fortieth birthday, and I'm alone, eating my ice cream as though it's my last supper.

My eyes are fixed on the harvest-yellow walls, a color I adored once upon a time but now resent because I'm no longer the carefree wife and mother who chose that cheerful shade.

Birthdays come and go, and the next may not be promised, but it's just a day. Tomorrow, all the calls and messages will stop. I'll be one year closer to my own death, with nothing but wrinkles and cellulite to keep me company.

Dramatic much?

My phone chimes from the nightstand and I ignore it. It's been going off all day with messages commemorating a day I'd rather skip from family and friends who know this yet refuse to oblige me.

Almost immediately the phone rings, and I know that either I answer or risk a wellness check from the police, courtesy of my well-meaning friends. There's no doubt it's Lanie or Nina on the other end of this call. Both of my best friends are dogs with a bone, and neither will stop until I shut off the phone or scream down the line that I'm alive.

Sighing, I grab the black smartphone and push accept.

"I'm breathing. You can stop calling," I drone, sounding pathetic even to my own ears.

"Well, that's a relief." Lanie's dry tone just barely hides the irritation she works so hard to conceal. "I thought you'd managed to drown yourself in Chocolate Salted Fudge Truffle or that nasty riesling you adore." I hear Lanie's deep breath before she continues. "Alyssa, you can't hide from your birthday."

"But I'm going to give it my best try," I say, eyeing the now-empty ice cream container with contempt, sending a thanks up to the gods that she didn't attempt a video chat. If Lanie Anderson saw my current condition, she'd stage a full-on intervention.

All traces of irritation and worry vanish when she says, "Ava called."

I groan, silently cursing my far-too-perceptive daughter for calling my overprotective best friend. This wouldn't be the first time. In fact, it seems to be happening far more often than reasonable.

I know Ava doesn't want me to be alone today, but I don't want her worrying when she should be focusing on studying for her exams. She's a little over an hour away at a prestigious boarding school for the arts, and if it were her choice, she'd give up her dreams and come back home.

"She shouldn't have done that. I told her I was fine."

"She doesn't think you are, Ally. You haven't left your house for more than a grocery run this week. It's your fortieth birthday and you aren't celebrating, when we all know that birthdays are a big production with you."

"I left my house," I say indignantly, blowing a wayward piece of hair out of my eyes.

"Don't be cranky. It's unbecoming of a woman in her prime." Her teasing lilt is meant to make me laugh, but I don't.

"I'm not cranky and I'm not in my prime."

"Sure you are!" she says far too cheerfully when moments ago it was all doom and gloom. "Forty is a prime number."

"It's not."

"It isn't? Hmm . . ." she murmurs, and I can see her clearly in my head, full lips pursed and one perfectly microbladed eyebrow cocked in contemplation. "Well, I guess you're right. Nothing prime about forty."

"I hate you."

"You don't," she practically purrs.

She's right. I cherish our friendship. Even more for her part in picking me up off the floor on numerous occasions over the last two years. Lanie has been a constant friend. One who hasn't allowed all of me to break into the million tiny pieces it wants to. A fate my poor heart didn't escape.

Two years ago, my soul was crushed, and it wasn't with one hard knock to my front door.

The harsh reality is that I was sitting next to my husband Garrett the day he died. My head hit the side window, and the last thing I remember is a bright light and the color red. For over a year, I relived the accident nightly. I didn't have dreams; it was always the same nightmare. One I couldn't wake up from.

Garrett died. I survived. And that truth has haunted me for a long time.

My eyes catch on Garrett's ashes, which sit in a generic, unmarked container on top of my dresser. Too cliché for a life as beautiful as ours had been.

A tear slips down my cheeks unbidden, and I swipe it away.

Not today, Satan.

My current grief is brought to you by my birth. I only have room for one trauma at a time.

"Earth to Ally," Lanie sings through the phone.

I shake my head, clearing my mind. "What did you say?"

"It's your birthday, and it's Thursday wine night. I know you said you didn't want to celebrate, but you must. Nina and I are headed out, and you're coming."

I chance a glance into the floor-length mirror resting against my wall and grimace. My wavy strawberry-blond hair is matted at the crown of my head, and I have dark circles underneath my bloodshot eyes. The entirety of my face is blotchy and swollen, a byproduct of crying.

I'm a hideous beast today.

"No, thank you."

My spoon scrapes the bottom of the empty ice cream carton, and the tears stream briskly down my cheeks.

It's been two years and I know this breakdown isn't about him. It's about a number. Forty always sounded ancient and here I am living it and feeling every ache and pain that decided to start on this very day.

How convenient.

"I . . . I'll be . . . fine," I cry. "I'm just so . . . ugly." The wail that accompanies that last part resembles that of a dying animal, and I'm sure Lanie is beyond concerned about my mental state.

"You're not, babe. You need us." The tenderness she uses is so unlike her.

She's my bossy, no-nonsense friend, who's more likely to slap the sense back into me than to allow the moping.

"As much as I don't want to be the overbearing friend on your day, this isn't a situation that I'm going to back down from. I'm coming to you."

"No, I—"

It's no use. The line is dead, and I know without a doubt that Lanie and Nina will be here at some point regardless of any protest on my part.

Forty wasn't supposed to look like this. I'd had every intention of marching out of my thirties with my head held high, ass tight and no lines to be found from the corners of my eyes to my hairline, seventeen years into a blissful marriage.

Exactly none of those things are my reality.

I have tracks deeper than an off-road path lining my forehead and a scar that runs from my temple to the corner of my right eye, a permanent reminder of all I've lost.

Lanie is right. I'm wasting away in this room.

If Garrett were here, he'd tell me to pull myself together, get dressed, and plan on a headache in the morning. But he's not here, so I'll eat my ice cream and feel sorry for myself until the birthday hijackers I call friends arrive.

AT FIVE O'CLOCK on the dot, I hear the key turning in the lock in the door. I gave spares to both Lanie and Nina in case of emergencies. Apparently, my breakdown earlier constitutes an emergency.

Seated in a dark corner of the living room, with a clear view of the front door, I watch Lanie pop her head inside. The sun has long set, and darkness blankets the room, shielding me from her view.

"Alyssa?" she calls out, as though she cares about my privacy. "We're coming in."

Lanie flips a switch, and the overhead lights beam down around us. Lanie's brown eyes are wide, one black-and-white-Converse-covered foot still in the door as if she fears what she'll find. I'd laugh if I wasn't having too much fun watching these two tiptoe around like some ghost is about to pop out at them.

Nina's head peeks around Lanie's body, her blond hair hanging loosely over one shoulder, and our eyes lock. My lips tip up in amusement.

"Hi, love," Nina says, pushing Lanie through the door when she sees me sitting in my comfy chair.

I raise my hand and wave, not wanting to speak for fear I'll start laughing and pee myself, which has been a danger ever since giving birth. Yet another less-than-sexy problem I deal with on the regular.

"I'm glad to see you're not in your bed," she says, sitting down on the arm of my chair and pulling me into a hug.

Nina is a high school counselor and very adept at handling grief, which is a real pain in the ass for someone who's trying to avoid talking about her feelings. "How you doing?" she asks, backing up and looking me over, her gaze lingering a little too long.

If they see that I've managed to pull myself together, they'll insist on birthday shenanigans, and I'm not quite fond of that idea.

I showered, hoping to wash away the remnants of my earlier wallowing, but it was no use. My pale complexion can't hide the stubborn splotches of distress, even with a Sephora's worth of makeup plastered over my face.

"I'm struggling."

A complete exaggeration.

My head lowers, shaking back and forth, playing up the misery card. Based on how her eyes are narrowed in on mine, she knows better. I've managed to fake it till I make it before, but tonight, I'm failing.

"We know better, Ally," Lanie cuts in, walking toward her typical spot on the outdated ottoman, complete with a gaudy floral print. It's a hand-me-down from my mother, which is about the only thing that woman has ever given up to me. "You're trying to avoid a celebration for the big four-oh, and we are not here for it. You and I both know you'll regret it eventually."

Lanie gets comfortable, stretching her long, lean legs out on the couch as Nina takes a seat on the floor at my feet.

"She's right, Alyssa. This happened on your thirtieth and you still to this day whine about not throwing a party."

"We promised we'd never let you do that again. So pull up your big girl panties and embrace your midlife hotness," Lanie says, earning a stern glare from Nina.

Nina springs back up, putting her arm around my shoulder. She pulls me into her embrace again. "Don't listen to her. We all know she's about as comforting as sitting on a cactus."

The most unladylike snort rips through me.

Lanie's mouth opens and then closes like a fish out of water. "I didn't say anything *bad*."

Nina rolls her eyes, turning her focus back on me.

"I know you're struggling, love. We won't push you into going out if that's not what you want," Nina coos, hand running down my untamed hair soothingly.

I look up into Nina's ice-blue eyes, framed by the longest non-manufactured eyelashes I've ever seen, determined to change the subject.

"Have I gained weight?"

She nods and Lanie gasps.

"Nina Joy Dunbar, what the hell's the matter with you?" Lanie's high-pitched squeal is enough to pull a smile from me. I try to smash my lips together to contain my laughter, but it's no use. A fit of preteen giggles escapes me.

Nina's eyes widen as her head bounces back and forth between us. "Huh? What did I say?"

Lanie rolls her eyes this time. "Pay attention. You're not typically the space cadet."

Nina ignores her, gaze settling on me. "I'm sorry, love. I'm . . . distracted."

I want to ask her why, but she forges ahead, beating me to the punch.

"My mother called. She wants to come to town for the holidays."

Nina isn't distracted, she's distressed, and I can't blame her. Samantha Woods is equal parts obnoxious and terrifying.

"Why?" Lanie says, parroting my thoughts.

"I'm sure she needs more money." Nina sighs, picking at her fingernails. "She had a botched cosmetic surgery and is tapped out of funds to fix it."

"Oh, please. The woman is fake from her head to her toes. What more can she need?" Lanie practically spits the words. None of us are fond of Nina's mother, but Lanie in particular despises the woman.

"This time it's true. I heard it myself via an unwanted video call."

My eyes narrow. "You heard it? What, pray tell, does that mean?"

Nina's lip tips up. "She went back to get bigger implants and now her boobs squeak." She waggles her eyebrows, grinning so widely her brilliant white teeth are on full display.

"Squeak?" Lanie asks. "Like a rubber duck?"

Nina's head bobs. "Let's just say that the neighborhood dogs follow her around. And I am not exaggerating."

We all burst into laughter. Of all the people for something like that to happen to, the universe got it right this time.

Lanie wipes under her eyes. "Don't you dare help her fix that. Let her suffer in squeaking until she finds Husband Number Six to pay for it."

I take a good hard look at my friends, recognizing how lucky I truly am, despite the hardships I've endured. Having Lanie and Nina by my side today is something I've rejected, but, man, am I glad they didn't listen.

"I needed this. You two being here," I explain, and Nina offers me a wide smile. "No matter what I said, I'm glad you ignored it."

"If I'd known my stories would make you laugh like this, I would've been here sooner." Nina frowns as she rubs her chest. "I'm sorry I waited so long to barge in, Alyssa."

I wipe under my nose, grunting. "I ate a carton of ice cream and chugged half a bottle of wine. I was fine. Wonderful, even."

"Ally, why didn't you call us?" Lanie's irritated voice draws my attention to the couch. "I would've gladly taken one for the team and drank the other half of that bottle."

"Then you would've tried to force me out of this house. Which was something I was avoiding."

Lanie sighs. "What a shame. I had so many things ready to go."

"And that is precisely why I didn't call."

My hand runs down my face, stopping over my mouth. A cold draft floats through the room and I shiver. It's the one downside to owning an old home. This part of town is the historic district. It's a beautiful area full of charm and ornate buildings, but it's also expensive to maintain.

Neither one of them speaks their thoughts on the matter, allowing me my choices. What's there to say anyway? It's my birthday. My decision. The best thing about our friendship is that we all know when to speak and when to remain quiet.

After several long moments of silence, Lanie changes the subject.

"Ava really wanted to come home."

I wish she were here, but it wouldn't have been good for either of us. I would've made sure to put on a happy face for her, but she would've seen through it. No matter how hard I try, Ava knows how hard forty has hit me, and it likely would've been the last straw. She would insist on pulling out of school and moving home.

"I know, but she's where she needs to be. She doesn't need to be worrying after her middle-aged mother."

Nina nods her head. "You might be right, but Ava isn't like other girls her age, Alyssa. She hates that you're alone. She's struggling. You need each other," she says, giving away that Ava calls her more than I know.

I fake a yawn, done with this conversation. Thinking about Ava only makes matters worse. "I want her to enjoy school. She's living her dream, and that's what I want for her. It's what Garrett wanted."

Lanie smiles sadly. "We all know that girl was made for greatness. She's probably got her nose stuck in a book as we speak."

I smile, picturing Ava curled into her purple bean bag chair, sitting in the corner of her room, nose pressed into the book I bought her last time she was home. "Anything is better than sitting by her phone waiting for my calls."

"What would you like to talk about?" Nina asks, steering the conversation away from Ava. She knows it's a touchy subject. Ava and I have very different ideas of what needs to happen. I want her to focus on her passion, and she wants to move home to babysit me. When I don't speak, Nina presses on. "Want a drink? I brought wine."

Lanie's phone beeps, and she removes it from her overly large bag, frowning at the screen.

"Everything okay?" I ask.

She looks at Nina and then me. "Yeah. All good. I just need to cancel a reservation I made for tonight."

"Oh, shoot. I completely forgot about that," Nina says, fidgeting.

My eyes volley back and forth between my friends.

"Thursday wine night," Lanie explains, avoiding my eyes, while she types a message into her phone.

Thursday wine night is something the three of us held as a standing date for years. Sometimes we'd see a movie. Other times, we'd just do a wine tasting and dinner. The only consistent part? Wine. Since the accident, we haven't kept our weekly date.

I told Lanie over a week ago I wasn't up for a birthday dinner, but it doesn't surprise me she made reservations just in case. Inspecting my friends closely, it's obvious they planned on something.

On a typical night in with the girls, yoga pants and oversize sweatshirts is the preferred dress code. But tonight, Lanie, the brown-haired beauty of our group, has on a pair of black Spanx leggings and a gray off-the-shoulder sweater. Not over the top, but nothing she'd typically wear to hang out here. Nina is still wearing the gray slacks and black V-neck shirt that she likely wore to school.

"Don't cancel," I say, picking at invisible lint. "You two can go."

Nina shakes her head. "We're not going to El Picante without you."

They made reservations at my and Garrett's favorite Mexican restaurant. It's the one place sure to get me out of any slump by simply placing bottomless tortilla chips, queso, and the largest mango margarita possible in front of me.

My lips form a thin line as I war with my yo-yo feelings. One part of me wants to remain in my pajamas, on this chair, sulking. The other part wants to live a little on the wild side, venturing out to do more damage to my waistline via shrimp fajitas—something I haven't indulged in since the accident.

"I'm in." I hardly get the words out before Lanie is popping up from the couch, as though she always knew this would be the outcome. She pulls something from her bag, chucking it at my head. I duck out of instinct.

"About time you come to your senses. You said you didn't want to celebrate, but I brought this for you just in case."

She turns away without another word and saunters through the arched doorway toward my kitchen with a bottle of wine she also pulled from her Mary Poppins bag.

I hold up what I now see is a white T-shirt that reads *Forty-licious* in sparkly fuchsia.

"Forty-licious? She's got to be kidding."

"You are," she bellows from the kitchen.

The woman has catlike reflexes, hawk eyes, and the hearing of a moth—expert-level senses that I didn't possess even in the height of my youth. Heck, I'm not sure anyone possesses such acute senses.

"You might as well put it on. We all know that you'll wear it because you're too nice," Nina whispers, taking a seat on the arm of my chair and peering at the offending shirt with me.

We simultaneously tilt our heads and sigh. Nina speaks the truth.

"I poured the wine," Lanie says, walking in with a stainless-steel tray carrying three wine glasses and the remainder of the bottle I didn't finish earlier.

Lanie's the youngest of our group, and the newest addition. Nina moved to the Midwest her freshman year and ended up attending my high school. I was one year older, but we met and bonded through cheerleading. She was quiet and always seemed a bit sad, mirroring me in ways that hurt my soul.

She was the family I never quite had. Being the only child of two workaholic attorneys, I was always an afterthought. Nina and I saved each other from toxic family dynamics.

After high school, we both went to the East Coast to attend the same college. Lanie joined our group much later, after we'd settled down in the quaint town of Knox Harbor.

She was the barista at our favorite mom-and-pop coffee shop and the yoga instructor at the only exercise facility in our small town. She's the wild child of our little threesome and the one who's always able to test boundaries.

"Drink up, witches. We ride at six." She raises her glass, filled midway with red wine.

"Wait. That's your birthday speech?" Nina glares into the side of Lanie's head, annoyed. "We need a toast worthy of our best friend." She raises her glass into the air. "To you, Alyssa. May your forties be full of health, happiness, laughter, and love. You deserve it."

"Unlike Nina, I've never been good with words," Lanie adds. "But I can't agree with her more. You deserve every ounce of happiness this world possesses. And the largest damn margarita this side of Knox Harbor."

I smile at my dear friends, grateful that they haven't given up on me.

"Happy birthday," they both say in unison.

We clink our glasses together and throw back the wine. Something tells me I'm going to need it to get through this night.

Author photo copyright © Janel Lee Photography

MELISSA HOLTZ is a former publicist and marketing expert in the romance genre. Now in an advisory role to several bestselling authors, she consults on industry marketing trends. *A Charming Touch of Tarot* is her second book.

Visit Melissa Holtz Online

MelissaHoltz.com

AuthorMelissaHoltz